Sarah Ball is getting a little bit older, disproportionately greyer and has now moved to Cambridge with her husband David and two children Ellie and Sam. She is getting through an awful lot of wine and sweets these days but still manages to write for ten minutes every other Thursday.

For more information about Sarah you can visit her website at www.sarahball.co.uk.

*Also by Sarah Ball*

Nine Months
Marry Me

# Written in the Stars

*Sarah Ball*

**PIATKUS**

First published in Great Britain in 2004 by
Piatkus Books Ltd of
5 Windmill Street, London W1T 2JA
email: info@piatkus.co.uk

**The moral right of the author has been asserted**

*A catalogue record for this book is available from the British Library*

ISBN 0 7499 3545 6

Set in Times by
Action Publishing Technology Ltd, Gloucester

Printed and bound in Great Britain by
Mackays of Chatham Ltd, Chatham, Kent

# Acknowledgements

This book could not have been written without the continuing encouragement, support and advice I've received from David, Dad, Simon, Mary and Mike, Mum, Mel, Liz, Dorothy K and many others.

Special thanks and gratitude are also in order for the following ...

Jane, John and David, for buying me some precious time when the deadline was looming by entertaining the children so brilliantly.

Mary and Mel, my top reading guinea pigs, I'm forever in your debt.

Nathan, for taking David off my hands and out to the pub when the deadline had been and gone (and to the lovely Wrench family for loaning him to us).

Teresa Chris, Gillian, Emma and all at Piatkus for being so patient and understanding (and for not mentioning the tractor that Sam tried to draw on the proof pages).

Hugs for Ellie and Sam, my little stars.

And a final huge thank you to anyone who bought a copy of this book – if you felt you were being watched in the aisles by a wide-eyed, excitable woman, it possibly was me and I can only apologise.

*For my lovely friend Mel,*
*who inspired this book.*

# Chapter One

I knew that Adam hadn't planned to say it. It wasn't one of those moments where the man takes his beloved out for a meal and drops a ring in a glass of champagne when she's nipped to the loo. And it wasn't down on bended knee, eyes brimming with tears, either. Instead, it was a rainy Saturday at Alton Towers.

We had driven up for a day out, wanting to go before the kids broke up for the summer and the queues doubled in length. It was years since either of us had been to a theme park and from the moment we arrived its lively atmosphere took over and we regressed to a teenage state of mind. We messed around, teasing and chasing each other, laughing at everything and snacking on junk food.

It drizzled for most of the morning but we didn't mind, our clothes were damp anyway from going on the water rides and the weather had kept away a lot of the crowds.

The sun made an appearance after lunch, warming us up as we made our way to an area of the park where some of the biggest rides were. I had managed to avoid the white knuckle rides until then. I wasn't a fan. I couldn't see the point when they just scared me sick, gave me big hair and distorted my face until I looked like a Wallace and Gromit character. Fortunately Adam didn't seem to mind; there were plenty of other things to do, but the moment he saw Air glinting impressively in the sunshine as steam rose up from its metal railings, he decided that we had to go on it.

It looked like my idea of a nightmare; a ride where you hung in a Superman-style position and shot around the track as if you were really flying, sometimes only a few inches from the ground. Just watching other people on it was making my knees weak.

Adam was relentless in his pleading, convinced that I would love it once I'd tried it. Eventually, after much mental anguish, I gave in. I didn't want him to see me as a cowardly, girlie type and decided that if Adam thought I was a brave, try-anything-once kind of girl he might just find me irresistible.

When the restraints came down and the ride tilted us forwards into a hanging position ready to start, Adam looked over at me.

I could feel my cheeks growing red as the blood began to rush to them and my curly brown hair was hanging all over my face. I was just dangling, petrified, and trying desperately hard to think like Lara Croft. A voice on the tannoy warned 'Prepare for Air', as the floor dropped away and we were bathed in blue light.

Adam was looking at me really strangely. He was smiling, making me wonder if he was going to take the mickey out of my new upside appearance, but he didn't. Instead his face softened and he reached out for my hand. Then, out of the blue, he called out, 'Will you marry me?'

I didn't hear what the voice-over said next. Instead, Adam's words were echoing around inside my head, trying to find a space in my consciousness to lodge into and failing abysmally. My face must have been a picture of shock as my mouth was gaping like the tunnel that lay

2

ahead of us. The couple dangling next to us must have heard as they were leaning forward, looking at me with expectant faces.

The ride was about to start, I had to give him an answer. 'Oh God, Adam . . . Yes!' I said at the same time as the voice-over said 'Now!'

Suddenly we were off, about to be flung down a steel track at speeds of up to seventy kilometres per hour, as Adam had delighted in telling me whilst we were waiting in the queue.

I couldn't keep hold of his hand. My instinct was to clutch the rubber grab-handles until my knuckles went white. I couldn't even look at him as I'd squeezed my eyes shut tight, trying to block out the sight of the ground below me. I couldn't think straight, the gravitational force on my body was too overwhelming and adrenalin was flooding through my veins. I knew I'd heard Adam correctly but it wouldn't sink in. It was so unexpected. Getting him to talk about the future was usually an impossible task. He'd get fidgety and start scratching himself, as if he were having an allergic reaction or something. We weren't even living together yet. Adam rented a tiny, one-bedroom house that was stuffed from floor to ceiling with his things. He needed somewhere bigger but he always put it off. I had a feeling that was because when the time came he'd have to decide if we were buying together or separately and it was easier for him to stay put than answer that question.

A minute into the ride I managed to prise my eyes open and sneak a peek at him. He was laughing, arms stretched out and a look of elation on his face. I closed my eyes again, the image of Adam staying in my mind, and I had that same feeling I get when I take a sip of Baileys on an empty stomach; a deliciously warming sensation, spreading

3

through my body like a velvet drug. It was an amazing feeling knowing Adam wanted to marry me.

When the ride finished the man next to Adam shook his hand, congratulating us. We thanked him then walked jelly-legged away from the crowds, holding hands tightly until we were out of earshot from passers-by.

What if he didn't mean it? I wondered, coming back down to earth. What if he'd been carried away on an adrenalin high and regretted saying it as soon as the words were out.

'Did you mean it?' I asked, preparing myself to laugh blithely and say 'me too' if he said no.

'Of course I meant it.' He laughed, squeezing my hands tightly. 'Did you?'

I nodded.

'It doesn't mean we have to do it straight away though, does it? We can just take our time. Play it by ear.'

Here we go, I thought. I knew it was too good to be true. 'But it's official, right? We can tell people and stuff?'

'Sure! If you want to.' He grinned at me. 'Come here.'

We held each other tightly and I wished I could freeze time, convinced that I'd wake up and find that the whole thing had just been a bizarre dream.

Lying awake I listened to the sound of Adam breathing. It was eight o'clock on Saturday morning, the first day of the bank holiday weekend, and I had been lying awake for almost an hour and a half. Why was it I was never this awake on a workday? Usually it took three hits of the snooze button before I could even lift my head off the pillow and then I would fumble around with glazed eyes, my head in a cloud of early morning fug until I arrived for work. As soon as it was possible for me to lie in until lunchtime then order pizza from the comfort of a king-sized bed, I turned into Brer-bloody-rabbit and woke up all bright-eyed and bushy-tailed.

I looked over at Adam, who was still unstirring from a heavy, dreamless sleep. There was something endearingly masculine about the way he slept. He would lie out on his back and that would be it. No fidgeting, duvet wars or sleep pedalling (Adam's term for my restless feet, which I unconsciously rub together under the covers).

I gently lifted up the duvet, careful not to wake him and peered down his body. As I suspected, the brain was unconscious, but the body, clearly, had its own mind.

Glancing up again I spotted Adam's new suit hanging from the wardrobe door handle and slid out of bed, feeling naughty, to fetch the jacket off its hanger.

It felt cool and silky against my bare skin and I held the lapels, rubbing the fabric between my fingertips. It drowned me of course – Adam's broad shoulders required jackets the width of most doors – but I liked the way it made my own body feel tiny by comparison. The jacket only just skimmed the top of my knees, and it hung heavily on me as I walked over to Adam's side of the bed. I slowly pulled the duvet off him and he moaned, his eyes flickering as he began to wake up.

'Hey,' I whispered, lying down next to him and placing a leg, seductively, over his hips.

'Mmm.' He smiled lazily and reached out for my bottom.

We kissed for a minute then he broke away. 'What time is it?'

'Just gone eight.' I snuggled into his neck, my hand exploring his body.

'I've got to get up.'

'Tell me about it,' I whispered naughtily.

'No Gem, really. The lads will be here at nine and I've

5

not even packed my bag yet.' He started to sit up, rubbing his eyes.

'Oh, you've got ages yet.'

As his eyes began to focus, he looked at me, blinking. 'Are you wearing my jacket?'

I grinned.

'You'll get it all dirty.'

'Promises, promises . . .' I nibbled his ear.

'Oh Gem, not this morning. You wore me out last night, and you know I haven't got time.'

I pouted. 'You might not want me, but your body does.'

'I do want you, you daft moo. Just not right now.' He got out of bed and stretched, scratching his chest.

'But you'll be gone all weekend. Don't you want to make the most of it while we still can?'

Adam feigned boredom. 'Yeah, yeah, been there, done that.'

He went to give me a playful pat on the bum but I pushed him away, tutting. 'Sometimes you can be really . . . mean!' I finished lamely and waltzed out of the room.

'If you're making a coffee I wouldn't say no,' he called after me, laughing as I started down the stairs.

I sighed to myself, disappointed that my plan hadn't worked. And surprised, of course, because a plan to tempt Adam into full sex was usually a challengeless task. I did have dubious motives though. This morning Adam was leaving for a friend's stag weekend in Glasgow with a group of lads from work. I had been hoping that he would leave the house so sexually gratified that he wouldn't be tempted by some big-breasted jezebel sitting on his lap tonight. And there was bound to be one, if not a whole room full.

Richard, Adam's friend who was getting married, is an architect. His office being in the courtyard of buildings where Adam also works, restoring period features for houses. I really liked Richard, and his fiancée Jules, but Richard's choice of best man was not one of his greatest ideas. Grant is a lecherous type and a bit of a sexist. The sort that describes a woman with his hands and tells endless jokes about why they have small feet. I was so used to his crude and lairy behaviour that the only thing to ever shock me about him was that he'd managed to convince Richard he'd make a reliable best man. I only hoped that after this weekend, he wouldn't live to regret it.

'Why do guys always have to go away for the whole weekend when there's a stag do?' I had protested when Adam told me the plan a few weeks back. 'It used to be a night out with the lads then a curry on the way home. Now it's all Dublin, Paris, Edinburgh ... It's not a proper stag occasion unless you've crossed an English border and taken over some unsuspecting old lady's B&B for three nights of debauchery. I just don't get the point of it all.'

Adam just looked amused and wrapped his arms around me. 'Don't you trust me? Is that why you don't want me to go?'

'No, it's not that,' I sighed, although I wasn't sure I meant it. Adam had never given me any reason to doubt him, but with Grant in the organisational hot seat for the weekend, anything could happen. And some of Adam's friends were a worry. They were typical lads: hard-drinking, rugby-playing, commitment phobics who, although they individually came across as pretty nice guys (Grant excluded), collectively they morphed into a pack of animals. They egged each other on constantly and Adam always became louder, cockier and more indifferent when he was with them. And he never, *ever*, called me 'hun' when they were within earshot.

I couldn't put my foot down and stop him from going, and I wouldn't want to. I had my pride. Instead I tried not to appear overly concerned and told him not to get any seedy ideas for his own stag night, whenever that might be.

It'd been three weeks since our trip to Alton Towers. Three weeks and not much has changed, I thought as the kettle flicked off, revealing the sound of Adam having a shower in the bathroom above. There was no ring on my finger and no date under discussion. We joked about it sometimes, and talked about 'when we're married' as if it was a long way off yet. It didn't feel official somehow and I would have felt fraudulent bulk-buying bridal magazines and making a big announcement to my parents. I had, however, told my best friends Nikki and Fay.

Years ago, when we were little, we had promised each other that whenever one of us got married, the other two would be the bridesmaids. We would dress up in my mum's old net curtains and walk up the garden path together, using the bird bath as our altar. None of us wanted to play the groom – where was the fun if you couldn't have a big puffy dress? And so we would use Thomas, the toddler from next door, who didn't seem to mind so long as he got a Penguin biscuit for his efforts.

We were always talking about the future, planning to live next door to each other and have babies at the same time. The future seemed simple then, like in the Disney books. Girl meets boy, girl falls in love with boy, evil family members tries to throw a spanner in the works, boy slays a few animals, defeats the evil family member and whisks girl away to a castle with untold riches, a squashy four-poster bed and some cute little talking pets. Of course as we got older the plan kind of changed somewhat and weddings seemed less and less likely, but the bridesmaid plan stayed our faithful pact.

When I told them about Adam, neither of them could contain their excitement. They wanted details; how it happened, who I'd told, how I felt, had it changed things? It was one of those events that really required a get-together to discuss it at length, and so a girlie reunion was planned for the weekend Adam was in Glasgow.

Adam walked into the kitchen wearing a fresh white T-shirt and a pair of indigo jeans. His skin glowed honey brown and a subtle hint of aftershave followed in his wake, teasing me as he walked past to fetch his boots.

I had dressed quickly whilst Adam was in the shower and felt grubby by comparison. I needed to go home and freshen up before Nikki arrived. 'Are you all packed then?' I said.

He nodded, straightening up from having tied his laces and gestured to the door, where he had left an overnight bag.

'Right, well, I'd better leave you to it.'

'I'll call you.' He glanced at the window as he spoke, looking for a car.

I knew he wouldn't call until he returned and couldn't help feeling deflated. Adam must have noticed and moved towards me for a hug.

'How about we meet up on Monday? If there are any jeweller's shops open for the Bank Holiday we could maybe go and look for a ring. If you want to? Make it official.'

I broke into an involuntary smile. 'Really?'

'Yeah, that'd be great.' He put his arms around my waist and lifted my feet off the ground. 'And of course it helps to ward off the competition, you know, let the other guys know you're a taken woman.'

I smiled flirtatiously. 'I'm not a taken woman, *yet*.'

'You will be,' he said, sitting me on the kitchen table.

A horn beeped outside and Adam looked out of the window. 'Right. That's them. I'd better go. We've got miles to drive.' He kissed me fleetingly and fetched his bag. 'Will you lock up on your way out?'

I pulled a face and hopped down off the table to look outside. There was a blue mini-bus parked across the street with the engine idling and half-a-dozen of his friends crammed in near the window. They reminded me of the monkeys at Bristol Zoo.

'Come on laddy,' one of them yelled and the driver beeped the horn again.

Adam walked down the short path towards them and a couple of his friends called out to him whilst the others moved up to make a space on the back seat.

I waited for Adam to look back at me and wave but he didn't, and as the van pulled away down the road, I thought I spotted a blow-up woman float into view in the back window.

# Chapter Two

After leaving Adam's house I took a detour out to the village where my parents lived. They were away for a few weeks and I had promised them that I would call in and check on the house every couple of days. It seemed like a good idea to get it out of the way then and there so that I wouldn't need to break up my weekend with the girls.

My parents' house is in a village called Langley Green, about five miles south-east of Bath. It's a picturesque village set in a stunning valley, split by both the river Avon and the canal which wind their way out from Bath to Bradford-on-Avon. When I was younger I would cycle into the city down the path that followed the canal, stopping to watch the boats and when I was a bit older, the students, boating or cycling past me. It's a tiny village. When I lived there I found it isolated. I wanted the vibrancy of the city and couldn't wait to move away. Once I had moved away, I found myself being drawn back. There was something in its tranquillity that I found restorative. And then there's the space. No parking problems or narrow, car-lined streets where there wasn't enough space to swing an alley cat, let alone do a three-point turn in a mini-cab. Driving down the country roads was like stretching out after a fitful sleep.

The family home was a little pre-war semi on Midsummer Lane, which had barely changed since I could remember. We moved there when I was six after my brother, John, had moved out. He was fourteen when I was born and at twenty he moved to Australia to become a tour guide. That's where my parents were now, visiting John for the first time in three years. They had offered to pay for me to go with them but I declined, knowing they couldn't afford it now that Dad had retired.

Walking through the front door I was hit by those old familiar smells. The most detectable being beeswax polish, lavender and a faint hint of burnt bread (Dad refused to buy a toaster).

I bent down to pick up the morning's post and carried it into the kitchen, propping it up in front of the kettle, and then I took a jug from the cupboard under the sink, filling it up from the tap to water Mum's plants. I wandered around the house, hearing only the sounds of my footsteps on the wooden flooring in the dining room and the ticking of the clock in the hallway. It was eerie being there without my parents. It was never usually this quiet. Even when Dad had snuck off to the garden or the loft, Mum would be making enough noise for both of them, banging around, annoyed at him, or calling out, reminding him about jobs he hadn't done. I didn't think there were any plants upstairs but went to check anyway, peeping around the doors of the bedrooms. When I got to my old room I couldn't resist going inside. It wasn't quite as I had left it when I moved out, eight years ago. Mum had redecorated with fairly neutral pastel shades and plain walls. The posters had long been taken down but the furniture was still the same and the cupboards were stuffed full of my old things. Dad was always asking when I was going to clear them out, as he was angling to use the room for himself. He'd call it a study but I doubted he would ever get any studying done. Most likely he would put a desk and a big leather chair in it then just sit about reading the daily papers. Basically the same as he did when he excused himself off to the bathroom but without the smell of bleach and the need for cold legs.

Mum wouldn't have it though. 'It's Gemma's room and it always will be,' she would say firmly. 'What if she ever needed a place to go? Or John, what if he came back and needed a room? I want them to feel that they can always return.'

*Not likely*, I thought. I knew John was relieved as I was to get away from their constant bickering, from being torn between feeling sorry for Mum when Dad ignored her and sorry for Dad when she was hassling him. I loved them both but together they were emotionally exhausting and incredibly frustrating. I never argued with her though, because I knew how much Mum missed me and was comforted by having my things lying around. I also suspected that if Dad made himself a den in here Mum would never see him again except for mealtimes and seasonal celebrations.

I sat down on the bed. It seemed tiny now: a child's bed. It faced a wall of fitted cupboards and I got up and walked over to them, opening the doors wide. It was full of things I'd left behind. There were some dog-eared teddy bears that I had never grown sentimental about, some old books, videos and knick-knacks, schoolwork, old letters. Lots of junk really. I wasn't surprised that Dad wanted me to sort it out. I took down a cardboard box from the top shelf. It was full of letters from Fay and Nikki that we used to pass to each other in lessons. I rummaged around inside and my fingers located a pendant I had been given from a boy I'd met in Lyme Regis. I didn't think it was worth much; it looked as though it had fallen out of a cracker, but looking at it now, it had an innocent charm and I smiled to myself before putting it back. I picked out a letter at random and read it.

*Dear Gemstone,*

*Having such a stress, Justine Arnold's been giving me nasty looks all morning. What's her problem? Perhaps her body is so tight it's giving her a wedgy!*

*Think we should meet up at the reccy after school. T said he'd be there. Oh my God!!*

*N xx*

It was from Nikki, written on a screwed-up piece of lined paper that looked as though it had been ripped out of a textbook. I laughed out loud, trying to remember who T was, but there were so many boys at school that Nikki had fancied it would have been impossible to remember them all. I put the box on my bed, deciding to take it back and show the girls. We could have a laugh at the ridiculous things we used to say and get up to and reminisce about old times. With my curiosity sparked, I decided to go through some other bits and pieces and see what else I could find.

An hour later and I felt almost fourteen again. I had been so immersed in old memories that I'd completely lost track of time. I was surrounded by old boxes and my hands felt dry from the dust that covered them. There was a stack of old photos I'd uncovered that I'd forgotten all about until then and a textbook that I had got my classmates to sign on the last day of term. I collected them all together and put them in the box with the old letters, ready to take back with me and then began to pack the things away.

I lifted up a heavy box full of A level notes and tried to push it back onto the high shelf above my head. As I slid it back it stopped, as though something on the shelf was in the way. I pushed it harder but it still wouldn't go so I put it down and fetched a chair, planning to climb up and see what it was.

I still wasn't high enough to see onto the shelf and the lighting was limited. I ran my hand along the shelf, wrinkling up my nose and squinting as the dust was disturbed and went in my eyes. In the far corner of the shelf I touched what felt like a metal box and closed my fingers around it, bringing it down to look at.

Stepping into the bedroom to hold it to the light, I gasped at what I saw. It was an old cash box that Dad had given me years ago. He often gave me old stationery and bits and bobs from his office and I recognised this as one of them. It was matt silver and made from heavy metal, with smooth rounded corners and was about the same size as a child's shoebox. It was locked, with no key attached; I had no idea where that would be now. Over the lock was a blob of molten wax about the size of a fifty pence piece. The seal around the lid had been taped over and over with Sellotape which had now faded to a dirty yellow colour. Scratched onto the lid were the words: DO NOT OPEN TILL 1 JANUARY 2000 ON PAIN OF DEATH.

'Oh my God!' I whispered, smoothing my fingers over the writing. 'This is brilliant.'

I hadn't thought about the box for almost ten years, but as soon as I touched it, I remembered the day we sealed it up as though it had just happened.

It was New Year's Eve, 1989. Fay, Nikki and I had planned our first New Year celebration without parental scrutiny. My parents were going to a function with a visiting colleague from Gloucester. They agreed to let us stay in the house so long as we let the colleague's daughter, Miranda, stay with us. I pulled some faces. From what Dad had said about his colleague he was strongly religious and a bit serious. I imagined that his daughter would be the same and would spoil our party atmosphere.

She was a year older than us, at fifteen, and to say she was a little off-the-wall would be putting it mildly. She arrived eccentrically dressed in a black all-in-one and an old grannie's shawl, which got a raised eyebrow from Nikki. Her long black hair was pushed off her face with a silk scarf that was tied at the back of her neck, making her look like a gypsy. For someone we had never met she was amazingly confident, breaking the ice quickly by producing a pilfered bottle of vodka from under the shawl as soon as our parents had left.

We played *Now That's What I Call Music 15* and danced around the living room until I was dizzy from exertion and first alcoholic experience. We talked at length about the turning of a decade. It was exciting for us all, we were teenagers and our lives were changing drastically. In the 80s we were children, in the 90s we would become adults. The possibilities were endless. The last ten years of the millennium would be the last ten years of our youth, the decisions we made in that time could affect the rest of our lives. We wondered where we would all end up for the next milestone, the year 2000. Then Miranda came up with a suggestion that got us all interested. Why didn't we make some kind of time capsule that we could all open together in ten years' time? She became animated, infecting us all with her enthusiasm. The deal was, she explained, that we would be reaching across time to our future selves, so we should write something down, something that would make us laugh and remind us of the way we were. And we should all make predictions about where we saw ourselves. Would we have husbands? Children? Success? Because it would be funny to see how we saw ourselves when we were young and see how right we were. And so, in the spirit of *Blue Peters* past, it was done. We all wrote our own individual messages, then placed them in a box I found. We each added a personal memento or two and I took a photograph of us all with Dad's Polaroid and placed it on the top. Then it was sealed, hidden and forgotten about, until the moment my fingers closed around it and it all came flooding back.

# Chapter Three

I took the key out of the door and let it swing shut behind me.

'Oh, hi Tim,' I said, spotting my housemate about to head upstairs with a doorstep sandwich and an unopened pint of milk. 'I thought you'd be away this weekend?' I tried to keep the disappointment out of my voice but the words still came out sounding flat. Feeling immediately guilty I smiled at him, by way of an apology. Tim probably wouldn't have noticed that though. He was one of those people who always seemed to have something else on his mind. He was quiet, preferring not to give much of himself away and would let other people talk instead. I was never sure whether he was really listening. And he was always on the phone or looking at his watch, always with something or someone to hurry off to.

'I'm going soon,' he called back, taking the stairs two at a time. I watched him go then went off to find Fay.

The three of us lived in a three-bedroom mid-terrace, just off St James Square and a short walk from Bath city centre. There were four of us if you included Fay's cat Dexter; a temperamental tortoiseshell which she named after the character Cary Grant played in one of her favourite films, *The Philadelphia Story*.

Our house is on Alexandra Terrace, a line of three-storey, narrow Georgian houses that all stand impressively tall and proud, apart from ours. Ours is the only house painted yellow and it's a storey shorter than the others, sandwiched in between them like a younger sibling that the others would rather pretend didn't exist. It's Victorian, so Adam tells me. He raves about its original fireplaces, cornice and sash windows. But the sash windows didn't serve us well last winter when we woke up to find the washing-up frozen solid in its bowl. Fay and I had become experts in building fires and Fay, at one time, had started a nice line in draft excluders made from stripy knee-high socks. I'd sit close to the fire with Dexter curled up on my knee and convince Fay that the socks made all the difference, then Dexter would yawn, his breath contradicting us with a puff of mist, and we'd have to go back to the drawing board.

At first it had just been Fay and me. We moved in together after she returned from a year's travelling. She took various temporary jobs, unsure what to do with her life after her travels had helped reaffirm her suspicions that her degree in art history wasn't going to lead to a job she enjoyed when her real passion was acting. She'd dabbled in many things since then, taken acting courses, scraped a living by working part-time at an alternative gift shop and kept her foot in the acting door by volunteering for the local amateur dramatics society. And so we had settled into a routine: me working at the pre-school at the top of the hill, and Fay 'bumming around' as she called it, sharing the little yellow house until our landlord had dropped a bombshell several weeks ago. He wanted his nephew to move in to the third bedroom.

We were pretty disappointed. Things had been fine as they were. We didn't want a virtual stranger breaking up an easy, comfortable situation. Plus we had been using the spare bedroom as a walk-in wardrobe and didn't relish the idea of having to give that little luxury up. But we weren't in a strong position to object. Our rent was cheap and the house was a perfect location for both of us. Our landlord insisted it was only a temporary situation and he promised not to put our rent up for the foreseeable future so we agreed, making a pact between ourselves to look elsewhere if Tim turned out to be a problem. But there didn't seem to be any reason to complain about him. He hadn't done anything wrong; he was good-looking, and fairly clean in a he's-a-bloke-so-let's-not-expect-miracles kind of way. There was just an air of mystery about him. He was guarded, he kept his room locked at all times, and we were never really sure what he did for a living. He disappeared over the weekends and when he was in, he often ate in his room. Sometimes I thought I could hear him talking quietly into his mobile late at night.

'Has he gone?' a voice said in a stage whisper. A flash of red hair appeared by the kitchen door and my heart skipped a beat.

'God!' I put my hands up to my face. 'You really made me jump!'

'Sorry Gem,' Fay said, then she laughed and touched her hair, realising what I was looking at. 'I forgot about the hair.'

When I left yesterday it had been what Fay described as conker brown. I wasn't quite sure what you'd call the new shade. Berry red? It wasn't bright enough to be fire engine, and it wasn't ginger enough to call it auburn. It suited her though, it was funky, spiked and fluffy and it made her look so cute with her fair skin and freckles.

'I got bored with dying it so I went to the hairdressers,

asked them to put it back as close to its natural colour as they could get it,' she said, a twinkle in her eye. This was a running joke with us as neither of us could really remember what her natural colour was, but this must be as far removed from it as it was possible to be. She walked across the room and made a beeline for the fridge. 'I've been gasping for a drink ever since I got back from the hairdressers and Tim's been in here for ages, making sandwiches out of big chunks of unidentifiable meat.' She took a plate off the top shelf and showed it to me.

'It's very pink,' I said, wrinkling my nose up.

'I know, and can you tell what animal it's from? Because I don't think I'd recognise it if it still had a face attached.' She put it back, eyeing it suspiciously, then took out a can of coke. 'Want one?'

I shook my head. 'You could actually go in the kitchen whilst Tim's there, you know? He doesn't bite.' I leaned against the work surface, watching Fay with amusement as she checked her complexion in the reflection of a metal teapot.

'I'm shy,' she said unconvincingly, then sighed. 'I've got a massive spot. Trust me to get a huge one when Nikki's coming.' She pointed it out to me, her face forlorn (Nikki is a beauty consultant at a country hotel in the Cotswolds and as you would expect, has the complexion of a Ruben's cherub).

'That?' I said, inspecting her closely. 'It's the size of a pinprick!'

'You're blind,' she said, looking into the teapot again.

I laughed, looking at my own face in the metal. 'It's a novelty shaped teapot, Fay. It's distorting your reflection, that's all, making it look swollen up.'

She peered closer. 'Is it?' She picked it up and was about to hold it in front of her chest when I took it off her.

'Come on, you daft thing, never mind that. I've got something to show you and I think you're gonna like it.'

'Ta da!' I cried, holding the box out for Fay to see.

It took her a moment to register what it was, and when she did her eyes grew wide with astonishment. 'Oh my God! I'd forgotten all about that.' She took it off me, holding it as though it was something valuable and precious. 'Do not open till 1 January 2000,' she read out. 'Oh, what a shame we didn't remember that. We weren't even together that New Year's Eve, were we?'

I shook my head. 'You were in Spain, remember? And wasn't Nikki going out with Fabian then? I think he talked her into going to Piccadilly Circus.'

Fay rolled her eyes. 'I can never keep up with when Nikki was going out with Fabian. Those two were on and off more than Jordan's knickers in a nightclub. And what about that girl?' She clicked her fingers, searching for a name.

'Miranda,' I said.

'Yes! Miranda. Whatever happened to her? We never saw her again.'

'I know. I feel a bit bad about that actually. I promised I'd stay in touch and we wrote to each other quite a lot but I got bored of it and stopped writing.'

'She was mad, wasn't she?' Fay said, remembering for a moment, then snapped quickly back to the present. 'So, where's the key? Or is that a silly question after so long.'

'It's a silly question,' I said. 'I think we'll have to smash our way in.'

'Oh, you can't do that.' She held it protectively against her chest. 'You might damage something. God, I can't even remember what I put in it.'

'All I can remember is the photo of my gran. And those

lists we did, but I can't for the life of me remember what I wrote.'

'What shall we do?'

'Let's keep it till tonight. We can surprise Nikki with it later, after dinner. We could open a bottle of wine and make it a ceremonious event.'

'Excellent idea,' Fay said, grinning at me, then she looked down at the box again. 'Wow! It was so long ago. Over thirteen years, *thirteen*! And it feels like yesterday. I don't feel much older than I did then.'

'I know what you mean. It's mad. There's a girl who lives over the road. You know, the one with the long hair and the big chest? She was *born* the year we did this.'

Fay squealed at the thought, putting her hands over her mouth. 'That's weird!' She put the box down on the kitchen surface and grabbed my elbow. 'Let's not think about this now, OK? I'm going to need a few wines before we start going down that road. Let's get ready and get some food in, before Nikki arrives. This could be a really hilarious evening.'

'Another wine, anyone?' I said, plucking a bottle off the table and refilling our glasses.

We were sitting around the dining table having dinner. I had planned a sophisticated three-course meal, something grown up with candles and napkins, but whilst in the supermarket Fay and I had been seduced by the pizzas in the deli and the giant bags of kettle chips and dips. We ended up having a finger feast of junk food and I was only surprised we had managed to eat it at the table.

Ever since she arrived Nikki had been quizzing me about Adam. She had even come laden with a supply of glossy wedding magazines. We sat poring over the pictures, picking out dresses, reading the wedding tips aloud, and cooing over the men in suits. It all seemed a little premature though and Nikki was visibly disappointed to learn that we hadn't even set a date yet.

'It might be next year,' I said, licking the salt off my fingers and reclining in my chair. 'But more likely the year after that.'

Nikki pouted. 'Oh, I can't wait that long. I haven't been to enough good weddings lately. I thought everyone was supposed to be getting married at our age?'

'Not these days,' Fay chipped in. 'At this rate I'll be going through my funeral-a-week phase before I reach the wedding-every-Saturday one.'

'It's Richard and Jules's wedding next Saturday; that's where Adam is tonight, at the stag do,' I told Nikki. 'Theirs is the first wedding I'll have been to since my Aunty Cathleen's two years ago ...' My voice trailed off as I remembered the stag do. I wondered what they were getting up to now. It was still early, only seven o'clock, but they were bound to be out already, probably having a meal, almost certainly drunk. My stomach lurched at the thought of where they would be going later and what they would be getting up to.

Fay noticed my mood change and squeezed my hand. 'Don't you get all melancholy and start missing Adam. It's not allowed. You're meant to be having fun.' She edged my wine glass nearer to my hand.

'I know, you're right.' I smiled and took a sip.

'I think it's time to open Pandora's Box,' she said devilishly, leaping up to fetch the box from the mantelpiece.

'What's this?' Nikki asked, looking up curiously.

'You're not going to believe what I've found,' I said as Fay placed it in front of her.

Nikki looked down and recognised it immediately. 'No way!' she cried.

Fay and I grinned at each other as Nikki picked the box up and rattled it. 'Have you opened it yet?'

'No!' we both cried in unison. 'We were waiting for you,' Fay said. 'We have to do it all together, don't we?'

'But how do we get in it?'

Fay produced a small jemmy from the pocket of her cardigan. 'I found it in the cellar. I think it must be Tim's.'

Nikki laughed. 'Didn't I warn you about that housemate of yours? It wasn't in a bag with a Balaclava and a pair of night-vision goggles, was it?'

It took nearly twenty minutes with a jemmy, one of Nikki's hairgrips and a couple of plastic chopsticks before the lock finally popped.

'Yes!' we cried triumphantly and scrambled to get the lid off.

Lying on top was the photograph I had put in. We all studied it, gasping at the way we looked.

We had hunched up tightly on the sofa to get us all in. I had taken it by holding the camera at arm's length and it had come out surprisingly well, capturing us all in shot.

Nikki sat on the far left. Her hair was huge; a frizzy, backcombed spiral perm which, back then, I had seriously envied. She was wearing a tight body and jeans with a cardigan so big you could almost call it a house-coat. Fay was unrecognisable next to her. Her hair had been dyed jet black and was cropped short and spiky. She had a lot of make-up on but her face was pale and her eyes a stark contrast with thick black eyeliner.

'I look like a ghoul!' Fay cried.

'Well, at least you don't look like a clown,' I said, looking at my own outfit. I suppose I must have been trying to capture the 'Madchester' spirit with my baggy trousers and psychedelic hooded top. I was smiling with my lips pressed tightly together. I always used to smile like that; I was too embarrassed by the slight gap in my two front teeth. I had been teased at school enough to give me a complex about showing them off in public. That was before I had grown used to them and it occurred to me that gappy front teeth obviously hadn't done Madonna any harm.

Miranda was sitting on the other end of the sofa. She was leaning into us all, grinning broadly, her dark eyes wide and staring.

Nikki laughed. 'You know, when we met Miranda I thought her clothes were really bizarre, but looking back, we were just as weird. Don't you think?'

'Perhaps it was Comic Relief day, that's why we were dressed like that,' Fay said, hoping that one of us would agree and redeem us all from the terrible fashion mistakes we had made.

'Absolutely,' I said.

'Yes,' Nikki agreed, putting the photo to one side. 'That's what it must have been.'

We each picked out our mementos. Mine were a packet of Love Heart sweets and a photograph of my gran, who had died at the beginning of 1989. I lingered on it, studying her gentle features.

Nikki shrieked and picked out a miniature bottle of Samsara perfume and a picture of Jason Donovan posing with a guitar. 'What was I thinking of?'

Fay took out her Kohl black eye liner pencil and a picture of Robert Smith from the Cure, which she planted a kiss on. 'Did you miss me?' she said, ignoring Nikki's incredulous expression.

The only things left in the box were our folded papers and a leopard brooch Miranda had included.

Nikki plucked out a random piece of paper and after

26

skim reading it for a second, blew out an indignant breath at what she saw.

Fay and I gathered around her. 'What? What does it say?'

'This is Gemma's. She said I'd have several men on the go, one of them married! What kind of girl did you think I was?'

I bit my lip. 'I'm sorry, I was fourteen, OK? It wasn't me.'

'And I can't believe you were so wrong about everything. "A super fast train service, Kylie disappeared into obscurity, Fay married." Could you *be* more wrong?'

I picked out another paper and read it. It was Nikki's. 'Me? Pregnant at sixteen!' I slapped her playfully on the knee.

'You were always so obsessed with children,' she cried defensively.

'Other people's maybe. Just because I wanted to work with them didn't mean I wanted to have them!'

We read out the rest, laughing at how naïve we'd been. It seemed that at fourteen we'd seen ten years as a life-changing amount of time. By twenty-four we'd expected to be settled, married and possibly even have children. At twenty-*seven* we hadn't even managed that.

After a while I realised Fay was sitting quietly, reading her paper and seemingly lost in thought.

'Which one have you got?' I asked her, leaning across to peer over her shoulder.

Her brow was furrowed and she seemed shell-shocked. 'Miranda's,' she said quietly.

'Let me see,' Nikki said, reaching over and taking the paper out of Fay's hands. She hadn't read much before she gasped, 'Bloody hell, she got me to a tee!'

'What?' What does it say?' I cried, curiosity over-whelming me.

She began to read it out loud. 'I see Nikki wearing white, in a big country mansion. She's dating a man with a foreign accent, destined for fame.' She looked up from the paper at us both. 'Well that's me, isn't it? I wear a white coat when I'm working and I've always worked in country hotels.'

'You're not dating a foreign man though, are you?' I said.

'No, but I was. I was with Fabian in 2000 and he was obsessed with being a famous entrepreneur. He wanted to be the next Richard Branson.'

'Mmm.' I scrunched up my nose. It wasn't the spooki-est coincidence I'd ever heard, but there were definitely similarities.

'Hold on . . .' Nikki flicked her blonde hair back off her face and said seriously, 'you've not heard the best bit yet. She's put, "give up the cigarettes, before they nearly kill you."' She looked at me and I felt my stomach flip over.

Two years ago Nikki had been involved in a serious car accident. She'd been driving back to Bath after work and was intending to drive straight to our house to get ready for a night out. It was teatime, but the route she took was always quiet. At a little country junction she pulled out slowly. There was no one around so she reached over to her handbag on the passenger seat. It was the last thing she could remember: taking her eyes off the road for a second to get a cigarette from the packet that lay on top of her bag.

Several witnesses sitting in a drive-through restaurant on the corner of the junction had said that Nikki couldn't have seen it coming. The driver that jumped the lights had sped over the brow of a hill so fast he lost control. He ploughed into the front of Nikki's car, crushing the driver's wing so badly she had to be cut free. She was in hospital for seven weeks and had been told by several members of the emergency services that she was lucky to be alive. Her leg had been broken in three places and her wrist and a rib were also broken, she had a black eye and a deep gash to her face. Miraculously the guy in the other car managed to walk free from his own vehicle, which had careered into a verge, and to the astonishment of the witnesses, he had staggered across the road and ordered a 'coffee and a fudge sundae to go' from the vendor at the drive-through. He got five years for reckless driving and leaving the scene of an accident.

Nikki maintains that if she hadn't been reaching for a cigarette, she would have crossed the junction faster and wouldn't have been hit. The few times she's reached for a cigarette since, she's stopped, unable to do it without reliving the grinding crunch of metal and the choking sensation of gasping for breath.

'OK,' I said, holding my hands up. 'That's spooky.'

Fay reached for her glass of wine and took a generous swallow without taking her eyes off Nikki. 'What else did she say?'

'Hang on, let's see.' Nikki skim read down the page. 'She didn't put much about you, Fay, just "Fay will take a long while to get settled on what she's going to do, but when she does, everything will come together at once. She'll find there's a good man right under her nose and all her ambitions, hopes and dreams will finally be realised."'

Fay clapped her hands, 'Ooh, that's exciting. Who could that be?'

Nikki looked at her over the paper she was holding. 'Hun, you've probably not met him yet. By the time you settle on anything you'll be in your fifties.'

'True,' Fay said with a smile.

'Hang on. You're not going to believe this,' Nikki read

on. '"Gemma's in a church but she's not married, she's surrounded by children but not her own."' She took a sharp intake of breath. 'Oh my God! This is seriously freaking me out now.'

She wasn't the only one. The hairs on the back of my neck were prickling up and my heart was pounding. I was deputy playgroup leader at Dizzy Heights, so called because of the steep street it was situated on, but it was also because of the high ceilings we hung banners from. The rooms had high ceilings because the building we used was a converted church.

'Did she put anything about Adam?' I asked, leaning so far forward I nearly toppled off my chair.

'Err, yes. She's put "going out with a gentle giant."'

I nodded, there was some truth in that. Adam was certainly big. He was six foot three, muscular and broad. I wasn't sure about the gentle bit. I always described him as my 'bit of rough', and he'd never struck me as a sentimental type, but then he did like puppies and he loved his nephew.

'Oh hang on, get this,' Nikki said, shaking my arm. 'You're not going to like this at all!' She bit her lip and I wondered what it could be, a horrible accident or tragedy perhaps? Miranda was getting so much right. I wasn't sure I wanted to hear something bad. I was surprised to notice my hands were trembling.

'Don't marry the first man that asks you,' Nikki read flatly. 'Your destiny is someone from your childhood. Someone you met when you were at school.'

Nikki put the paper down and she and Fay both looked at me open mouthed.

I took the paper from Nikki and read it for myself. Miranda's handwriting was deliberately decorative, the letters curly and precise. She had decorated her words with a doodled border of hearts and stars.

I couldn't quite believe what I was reading and kept staring at it as Fay looked from me to Nikki, her hands on her cheeks and her brown eyes wide. Every now and again she'd say something like, 'I can't believe this' or 'tell me this is spooky, right? I can't be the only one thinking this is *seriously* spooky.'

Downing my glass of wine I thought about Adam. He was the first guy ever to propose to me. We'd both lived in Somerset all our lives but we hadn't met until I was twenty-three, when he oversaw some alterations at Dizzy Heights. Miranda had been so accurate. It had to be more than just a coincidence. If Nikki had taken Miranda's advice in 2000, for when it was intended, there's a chance she never would have been in that car accident. There was a sickening feeling growing in the pit of my stomach as I realised I was going to have to think seriously about what she'd written.

# Chapter Four

On Sunday morning the three of us, unable to face making our own breakfast, headed off to Barney's as soon as we were dressed.

None of us had got much sleep the previous night. We stayed up late, talking, drinking and going through my old things. I felt shaken by what Miranda had written and kept getting drawn back to it, rereading it over and over. I was full of doubts and questions. After the initial shock, Nikki tried to laugh it off. 'It's just some freaky coincidence,' she said. 'I wouldn't take it too seriously.' But Fay made things worse by saying, 'It's as though fate's trying to tell you something,' in a voice of wonder.

I had hoped that the drink would deaden the whirling thoughts in my head, but it's amazing how sometimes not even a bottle of wine, two Bacardi and cokes and a hefty slice of Banoffee pie can take your mind off things. In the morning I was left feeling as though the previous night had been a bad dream I couldn't shake.

There was nobody behind the counter when we walked into the café so we picked a table by the back door where the air was fresher and the morning sunlight had illuminated a triangular patch of floor. There was an old man sitting in an annexe on the other side of the room, bent over a paper and smoking a cigar, but apart from him the place was empty.

Barney's was my favourite local haunt. It's only a couple of minutes walk from our house, at the end of a row of shops on Park Lane. It doesn't look like much from the outside, with tiny green windows, making it seem dark and intimidating for passers-by, but Fay and I liked it like that. At least we were always sure of a table. Once inside the atmosphere was cosy and relaxed. The floorboards were stained dark to match the little round tables and bent-wood chairs and on each table was a bottle with a red candle in its neck. Years of old molten wax had oozed down the bottles, setting like laced fingers around the wine's label. The dark wood was cheered by the red gingham curtains, dressing the little windows. I always thought it looked like a traditional trattoria and I suppose that's how it was intended. Barney, the owner, was originally from Sicily and had brought with him some flavours of his home country, including the best ice cream I had ever tasted.

Nikki sat down opposite me, where the sun was at its brightest, and curled up in a chair like a cat, basking in warmth, her eyes half closed.

'I see I have my full complement of girls this morning,' Barney's baritone voice boomed out, making Nikki jump. He walked over to our table, welcoming us with a broad smile.

We all laughed. Barney had never made a secret of the fact that he fancied Fay and we all joked openly about it. He was quite good looking too, bearing an uncanny resemblance to Bruce Willis, with his matured good looks and receding hairline. He had a toned upper body and deep olive skin. He also always wore a white T-shirt that, like

Bruce Willis's famous *Die Hard* vest, became gradually dirtier as the day wore on. Fay and I believed we could tell how busy he'd been by the state of his T-shirt. By the looks of him today, he'd obviously had a quiet morning.

'And how are my lovely ladies today?' he asked, plucking a notepad from the top of his apron.

'Desperately in need of your delicious coffee,' Fay said, looking up at him with a sweet, disarming smile. Barney's eyes went all watery and, obviously happy with the idea that Fay had a desperate need only he could fulfil, he took our drinks orders then disappeared behind the counter.

'Hey, maybe Barney's the "good man" right under my nose that Miranda was talking about,' Fay said, as soon as he was out of earshot.

Nikki snapped her eyes open and sat up. 'Oh my goodness, yes, of course he is!' she said, smacking her forehead with the back of her hand. 'In fact, Fay, I've just thought of the spookiest thing ever. If you wore those boots you've got with the ridiculously enormous 70s heels and stood next to Barney, who is a mere five foot four-ish, then he literally would be right under your nose, wouldn't he? Ooh, now is it cold in here or have I just got the chills?'

Fay looked at her in alarm, then looked at Barney and then back to Nikki. 'Really? You think so?' she said.

'No! Oh . . .' Nikki slumped forward onto the table, her head in her hands. 'What am I going to do with you? Gemma, please talk some sense into this girl. There is no meaning to all this; it'd be crazy to start thinking seriously about what she said, right?'

I looked at them both as they each waited for me to back them up. 'I . . .'

Nikki cocked her head and looked at me with suspicion. 'But you *are* taking it seriously, aren't you?'

I screwed my mouth up and stayed silent.

Nikki looked alarmed. 'Gemma! Are you having doubts about Adam?'

'I don't know,' I said weakly. 'I don't know what to do.'

'I'll tell you what you can do. You can forget all this nonsense! You can't mess up what you've got with Adam because of what Miranda wrote. That would be insane. You *love* him. You're going to get married!'

I slid a menu towards me and started picking at its laminated edges. 'Of course I love Adam. That's not going to change overnight. It's just thrown me a bit.'

'Pre-wedding jitters, that's all it is,' Nikki said. 'It's bound to make you edgy. Everyone gets a bit superstitious about weddings.'

Fay spoke up then. 'Gemma, are you positive that Adam was the first man to propose to you? What if, maybe, you've forgotten someone?'

I snorted. 'It's not exactly something that happens every day, is it? Of course I'd remember. No one's ever said that to me before. Not even in jest.'

Nikki shook her head. 'I can't believe you're entertaining this craziness.'

'Look, you can't blame Gemma for taking this seriously. What if Miranda's right? You know how much I like Adam, I think he's great! But you can't start a marriage always wondering if there was something more perfect out there. And what if she really has got a gift for seeing things?'

'And what if she was a loopy, teenage drama queen with a good sense of intuition?' Nikki bit back.

I looked back and forth between them, feeling more confused than ever.

The previous night, when Fay and Nikki had eventually

fallen asleep, I lay awake for what felt like hours, questioning everything far more than is healthy. For the first time I really thought about the kind of person I wanted to spend the rest of my life with. I thought about Adam, and realised that no matter how much I loved him and felt comfortable with him, he wasn't the man I had imagined settling down with. He hadn't swept me off my feet and vowed to never leave my side. Instead he had skirted around the issue of commitment so much he seemed to want to hold on to his single life for as long as possible. It occurred to me for the first time that Adam had waited for his friends to start settling down before he would contemplate it. I wondered if I had accepted his proposal because it was the next step, and it was easier than thinking about the alternative.

'Just try not to analyse it too much,' Nikki warned me. 'Follow your gut instincts, not the words of some mad girl from years ago.'

Barney came back with a tray of hot drinks and I realised that I had been sitting all hunched over, my shoulders drooping and a troubled frown on my face. I sat up, tried a smile and plucked my coffee from the tray. I can't make sense of it now, I thought. The only thing I could do was wait until I met Adam on Monday. Maybe when I saw him it would help clarify a few things.

'Why do you keep staring at me?' Adam asked as he took his eyes off the road for a moment to look at me.

'I'm not!' I protested, looking out of the window quickly and pretending to be fascinated by the view. I saw Adam smiling to himself out of the corner of my eye as he took a left turn at a junction.

Adam had just picked me up. It was the first time I had seen him since he returned from the stag weekend. When we spoke on the phone he asked if I still wanted to go shopping today but he didn't mention a ring. I wondered with a sinking heart if he had forgotten that he'd suggested getting an engagement ring today.

It was a bad start. With Miranda's words on my mind I was looking for any kind of sign that our future wasn't meant to be. It seemed that I wasn't going to have to look hard. He was dismissive when I quizzed him about his weekend, saying about as much as I'd expected him to: 'We drank too much', 'We didn't get much sleep', 'We stripped Grant naked and left him with only a sporran and a giant tartan hat to wear'. No surprises there then. He admitted there was a stripper but swore he found the whole thing 'a bit seedy and embarrassing' and made him appreciate that I 'have the best tits in the world'. I tried really hard not to sound pleased at that point and I think I pulled it off.

Our conversation left me still undecided. It was good to hear his voice though, all sleep deprived and sexy. This morning he looked equally gorgeous when he pulled up outside the house and when I climbed into his old Land Rover he greeted me with such an enthusiastic, knee trembler of a kiss that I was left wondering how I could possibly have doubted that he was right for me.

'Hang on,' I said, doing a double-take at the Town Centre sign as we turned in the opposite direction. 'Adam, where are we going? This is the wrong way.'

'Oh, there's somewhere I need to go first,' he said, not taking his eyes off the road. 'Just a little thing for work. It won't take long, honestly. There's no hurry to get into town, is there?'

I bit my lip and stared out of the window as I was brought back to reality. He has forgotten about the ring, I thought. How could he forget something like that? Miranda was right. What am I doing agreeing to marry someone who does that?

Just a few miles out of Bath and we seemed to be right in the heart of the countryside. I hadn't got a clue where we were heading. We were driving down narrow country lanes I'd never used before, passing through tiny little Cotswold stone hamlets with village greens and duck ponds. I stayed quiet, watching as the idyllic scenes passed me by, wondering all the time how I felt about Adam. I was so disappointed. I had been hoping that when I saw him again all the doubts would vanish and I wouldn't be able to take Miranda's words any further. But that wasn't how I felt and I was bitterly disappointed and confused. *I just need a sign*, I thought to myself. *I need to know what to do . . .*

A minute later we were just driving out of another quaint old village when a shop caught my eye. It was a tiny, crumbling stone building that seemed to be leaning to one side. It looked ancient, like The Old Curiosity Shop. I looked up at the sign that swung from an ornate cast-iron bracket above the door. It read SIGNS FROM THE HERALD ANGEL.

'Oh my God, did you see that?' I blurted, straining to turn around and get a better look.

'What?'

'That shop. Signs From the Herald Angel. Did you see it?'

Adam glanced at me, looking pleasantly surprised. 'You've heard of it? It's really well known but I thought only people in the trade knew about it. They specialise in antique shop signs.' He looked at me again, as if checking I knew what he was talking about.

'Of course, everyone's heard of them,' I lied, turning

back round. That was weird; I asked for a sign and I got a sign, *literally*. A sign, on a sign, for a shop full of signs, in fact. But what did it mean? Was it a good or bad sign?

'Here we are,' Adam said, slowing down and indicating.

We were in a village at the bottom of a valley. Just ahead of us was a humpbacked bridge with a shallow stream running underneath it and on the corner of the lane was a big old pub called The Trouble Inn.

I gasped. 'The Trouble Inn!' I cried, incredulously.

'Don't tell me you've heard of that too,' Adam joked as he pulled into a little car park opposite the pub.

I looked at its sign. There was a picture of two men facing each other over a couple of pints.

'Gemma, what's up? You're acting really odd.'

'Oh, nothing.' *Oh God, oh God . . . this is so weird!*

I tore my eyes away from the pub and struggled to undo my seat belt. I was feeling suddenly claustrophobic.

Adam was looking at me curiously.

'It's just, it's such a weird name for a pub, kind of depressing, don't you think? Who'd want to drink there?'

'Right, I'll scrub that off the lunch list then. I'm sure we can find a Happy Eater nearby – they always sound like jolly places,' Adam said, looking back at me with amusement as he got out of the car.

*It's a blatant sign. It has to be more than coincidence.* I wanted to call Fay straight away and tell her. She'd understand. She might even be able to make sense of it. I started looking for my mobile but Adam walked around the back of the car to my side and opened the door for me, holding out his hand to help me out.

When I got out he wrapped his arms around me, kissing the top of my head. He felt so strong and solid that I relaxed into him, feeling momentarily better, but when I glanced up I could still see The Trouble Inn out of the corner of my eye.

'Why are we here, Adam?' I asked.

'You'll see,' he said and took my hand, leading me out onto the main street.


At the end of a row of shops Adam stopped and turned around to face me. He looked uncharacteristically nervous and took my hands in his, squeezing them tightly. 'Gemma, I just want to say, if you don't like them that's fine. Honestly. We can go back to Bath and have a look there. But I just wanted you to see these first, OK? Because these are kind of special.' Then he pulled me over to a shop window and stood me in front of it, watching my face for a reaction.

Inside the little shop window was a display of jewellery. Silver rings, bracelets and necklaces sparkled between the folds of a royal blue velvet backdrop. Some had stones set in them: diamonds, sapphires, topaz, all cut in very simple shapes, held by platinum bands. They were contemporary, understated and so beautiful. Nothing like the kind of jewellery I'd seen in high street shops.

My heart was racing as I realised why Adam had brought me here. He must have seen the shop before and thought of me. He had been planning this all along. I hadn't even thought of what kind of ring I would like, and he had managed to pick a style that I didn't even know I would love; but I really did. Tears were forming in my eyes as I realised he knew me better than I had ever given him credit for.

'What do you think?' he asked.

'I love them!'

'And ...' he said, squeezing my hands tightly, '... would you like one?'

I hesitated, my mouth suddenly parched. *Did I?* I couldn't unscramble the words in my head; there were too many: Miranda's; the shop sign; The Trouble Inn; Fay and Nikki's contradictory advice; and Adam ... Gorgeous, strong and capable Adam, looking at that moment as though he'd laid out his heart on the pavement and now had a horrible suspicion I might drop kick it back over the hump-backed bridge. I couldn't say no to him now.

'OK,' a voice said. It sounded like mine. It came from me. It must have been me, because after that he wrapped me in his arms and laughed with relief.

# Chapter Five

'Oh my God that is the loveliest ring I've ever seen in my whole entire life,' Fay said in one continuous breath as she took the length of the sofa in a single stride then made a grab for my hand.

'Whoa! Whoa! Let me get my coat off first,' I laughed. 'And whatever happened to the "Hi Gemma, how was your day?"' I shrugged my coat off onto the armchair then duly offered my hand up for inspection.

'Ooh, a sapphire,' Fay said.

'A Ceylon sapphire, actually,' I said, adding with a smile, 'Adam said he thought it matched the colour of my eyes.'

'Ahhh, that's so nice!'

'I know!'

Fay looked up at my face for the first time, 'He's right too. It's exactly the same colour as your eyes. Oh, and it goes with your left cheek,' she said, pointing out a smear of blue paint I must have missed earlier.

'Ugh.' I rubbed at the spot with the back of my sleeve. 'That was James Daytona. It's his birthday tomorrow so he was maxed out on adrenalin all day.' Speaking of my day reminded me how tired my legs were and I sank down into the sofa next to Fay, both of us looking straight back at my ring again.

'So, things went well with Adam yesterday?' Fay asked. I could tell she had been dying to find out.

'Really well. He was so thoughtful and sweet. After we got the ring we went for a walk by the river then had lunch in a gorgeous pub, right out in the middle of nowhere.' I stretched my left hand out to indicate just *how* far out the pub was, watching to see how the ring sparkled when I moved. 'Then we went back to his place in the evening for a film and a bottle of wine. Just really cosy, coupley stuff, you know? And it was so nice to have some quality time with Adam. We go out so much with his friends that having a whole day alone with him in this secluded place was amazing. It was like we were being held in a little bubble.'

'That's great.' Fay smiled. 'So things are back on track with you and Adam then? You're not going to worry about what Miranda wrote anymore?'

'No,' I said, then made a pained expression as I remembered the shop and pub signs. I just had to tell her.

On Friday evening Nikki came over after work. She was staying the night at our house, on the airbed in Fay's room, and so we'd planned to walk into town to meet Fay when she'd finished her shift at the theatre. She was helping backstage for a visiting youth production and was finishing at nine o'clock, so we had arranged to meet her in the Pizza Express next to the theatre when she was done.

Nikki had been held up, so by the time we arrived at the restaurant, Fay was already sitting at the bar, talking to a young girl I didn't recognise. When she saw us walk in she waved and her friend left to join a group of people at another table.

43

'Sorry we're late, my fault I'm afraid,' Nikki said to Fay, greeting her with a kiss.

'That's OK, I took the liberty,' she said, gesturing to an open bottle of chilled white wine and three glasses.

'Excellent!' We took the glasses and found a table in the corner.

'So,' Fay said when we had all sat down, 'that girl I was just talking to. She's a member of the youth theatre who are doing that play, *You're Not My Mother You're a Death-Watch Beetle*.'

'Oh, right ...' I stifled a grin at the name of the play and noticed Nikki could only nod to encourage Fay on.

'Well, she reckons that there are some big auditions happening in Bristol next week at the George Hotel. It's some kind of BBC initiative. They want to find talent from a wider source so they're holding open auditions to anyone off the street, for all kinds of roles. You don't need to have a drama qualification or an equity card or anything, and do you know what the best part is? NO singing and NO dancing!' She beamed at us both then poured out the wine, adding, 'Although I bet you both a bottle of bubbly there's a girl somewhere in the queue singing "The Sun Will Come Out Tomorrow".'

I laughed. I'd lost count of the number of times I'd accompanied Fay to an audition only to find it was like backstage at *Pop Idol*. And no matter how talented an actress she was, Fay's singing and dancing abilities were as limited as *The Clangers*' grasp of the English language.

'That sounds brilliant Fay. It's about time you got your big break. And just think ...' Nikki took a sip of wine and got a faraway look in her eye, '... you might end up on TV. You might get so famous you're invited to the BAFTAs, then you'd meet the gorgeous one with the eyebrows from *Doctors on the Job*. Oh God, if you meet him will you put in a good word for me? You never know, I might end up marrying him and getting my picture in *OK!* magazine.' We stared at her in surprise as she went quiet and thought to herself for a moment. 'I'm really in the wrong job,' she said finally.

Fay burst out laughing. 'OK, where's the real Nikki gone? Who's swapped my straight-talking, sensible friend for a starry-eyed nutter, because that sure isn't my fantasy.'

Nikki rolled her eyes. 'Alright, maybe not *OK!* magazine, but when you see *Doctors on the Job*, you'll understand.'

'If you say so,' Fay said, smiling. 'But to be honest, I'm not so bothered about the fame or the famous boyfriend. I'd settle for a job I'm passionate about, or even an equity card and an income that would cover the minimum payments on my credit card.'

Ten minutes later I reached for a top-up, only the whole bottle of wine had been drained.

'Blimey, we're going to have to slow down if I want to have a clear head for the wedding tomorrow,' I said, disappointed, as I was harbouring a thirst only wine could quench. Nikki got up and went to the bar for another bottle before I could talk myself into getting a diet coke.

'So, what's Adam up to tonight?' Fay asked when Nikki left the table.

'He's with Richard; they went for a pint or two at the hotel bar so they can check on the last-minute wedding arrangements and try to calm Richard down. Apparently he's terrified of standing up there with everyone looking at him. Jules is fine though, taking it all in her stride. She's having a meal with her parents tonight. I talked to her earlier and she sounded like she couldn't wait to get up there and do it. There wasn't a single, detectable, last-minute nerve in her voice. I wish I was that brave.'

Fay was about to say something when Nikki interrupted us by sitting back down, doling out the drinks and saying, 'Actually girls, I have a confession to make. And I think you're going to be disappointed in me.'

We both groaned. It was bound to be something awful then. Last time we'd heard that was when Fay had told us she had given all our hand luggage, complete with passports, to a total stranger as we boarded a bus bound for Corfu airport. The stranger made his getaway on a smoking Vespa and we were left stranded in Corfu Town for three days.

'Don't tell me,' Fay said, 'you're seeing a married man.'

'No! What is it about you two thinking I'd do that?' She looked indignant. 'I'm totally against that sort of thing. You know how I feel about loyalty.'

She was right, that was one thing she had always made a firm stand on. 'It must be because you have high standards and you like older men,' I concluded. 'If he fits your exacting criteria, chances are high that he'll already be taken.'

'Well, Fabian's definitely not married. We kind of got back together yesterday.'

'No way! How?' I was surprised. Last time Nikki had seen Fabian was about a year ago and after the run around he gave her she had sworn off him for life (although admittedly swearing off Fabian had become something of a catchphrase for Nikki).

A devilish smile played on her lips. 'He came to the spa in the morning. He'd booked in under a false name for a full body massage and a Decleor facial. He'd asked specifically for me and I didn't cotton on who it was till he arrived. He'd paid for a full day package which includes a four-course meal and he'd already found out what time I was getting off work so had booked for me to join him.'

'Presumptuous,' I said, at the same time as Fay said 'romantic'.

Nikki looked coy as she trailed her finger around the rim of her glass. 'Actually, I think you're both right. But I just couldn't help myself. He's so gorgeous.'

Suddenly I remembered what Nikki had been saying about *OK!* magazine and I sat up in a flutter of excitement. 'That's a point. Is he the next Branson yet? Did it seem like fame was looming on the horizon?'

'Not that I could gather. I think he's been struggling to keep his business afloat actually. He's still got the flashy car though.'

'Oh.' My excitement subsided as quickly as it started and I sat back feeling weirdly deflated.

Fay, who had been watching me, suddenly gasped. 'You're disappointed! You actually want Miranda to be right, don't you? You want her to have got everything right.'

'No I don't.' I twisted around in my chair and made a show of straightening my already poker straight collar.

Nikki narrowed her eyes. 'She's right, you do! Gemma, what's gotten into you? Does that mean you don't want to marry Adam? Are you hoping Miranda's going to turn out to be some kind of amazing psychic and you just *have* to do what she says? Because that sounds a bit flaky to me. It sounds like you're just looking for a convenient excuse not to be with Adam any more.'

'No!' I was shocked. It sounded so awful when Nikki put it like that. 'No, that's not it at all. Of course I want to marry Adam.' I sighed and looked at my ring. All week it hadn't quite felt part of me. I'd spent a lot of time gazing at it, turning it this way and that. It was so beautiful it actually made me jealous. Ridiculous, of course, because it was mine. But somehow it didn't feel real. For some reason I wasn't allowing myself to *feel* engaged. 'You know what I really want?' I said quietly.

Fay and Nikki leaned in.

I thought for a moment.

'Yes?' Fay said.

'What I really want is . . .'

'Yes?' a middle-aged waitress said, licking the tip of her pencil and standing poised with a notepad.

'Give us a minute,' Nikki whispered to her.

'What I really want is . . . is to feel like we're meant-to-be.' I took a deep breath. 'I want that feeling people talk about, you know, when they say how they just knew they'd found the right one. How it all felt so right. I want to feel like I've met my soul mate and tell people that fate must have brought us together. I just . . . I just want it to be special, and know it's special, and not even have to question it. Do you know what I mean?'

Nikki looked concerned. 'But Gemma, how many people really get that feeling? Everyone has doubts. Surely most of us just keep snogging people in nightclubs till they finally meet someone they don't want to be without. You don't need to feel like you've been brought together by some kind of other-worldly force.'

'No, I think she's right,' said the waitress, squeezing into a spare chair like she was Robert Kilroy Silk. 'I've been married four times. Never felt like any of them were soul mates. I never even believed in soul mates. I loved them at the time, but there wasn't any magic, you know? And it turns out they were all losers anyway, but the last one . . .' she waggled her pencil at me. 'The last one's different. We met at a mate's fortieth in a pub in Devon.

48

Got chatting straight away, and turns out we're both called Brian.' We all looked startled at one another and Fay couldn't help but giggle. 'Well,' the waitress amended quickly, 'I'm called Bryony. But it was a coincidence, right? So that got us sharing our last names. Well, you won't believe this ... Brian Minden was his name. And Bryony Rose, that's me.' She paused, looking around the table at us all, but I didn't get it. 'Neither of us had ever been to that pub before, and do you know what it was called?' We all shook our heads, transfixed. 'The Minden Rose,' she said, sitting back with her arms folded as we gasped in shock.

'No!' Fay's eyes were wide.

'That's amazing!' I said. 'And did you marry him?'

She showed us her wedding band saying, 'Eight years this month and never been happier. I'm telling you, a sign like that, you can't ignore it. We were meant to meet that night.'

Someone behind the bar called Bryony's name and she shot up, fetching her notepad. 'I'll be back for your orders in one tick,' she said with a wink and hurried off.

'Oh my God, that's such an amazing story,' I said after she'd left.

'Hmm.' Nikki wrinkled up her nose. 'Are you sure she was telling the truth though?'

'Nikki!' Fay and I cried, balling up our serviettes and lobbing them at her. She was such a terrible sceptic.

By the time we were nearly home it was past midnight and my head was spinning from the wine I'd drunk. It was a warm and cloudless June night, a promising start for Richard and Jules's wedding day. I looked up at the sky, filled with stars, and nearly fell over. 'All the stars are moving,' I said.

'Ooh, are they shooting stars?' Fay asked, tipping her head back to look.

'More likely she's just pissed and therefore visually impaired.' Nikki took my elbow and guided me through the park gates and out onto the main road. 'You should have stopped drinking when I did. It'll play havoc with your complexion, you know?'

'Hey, Barney's lights are on. We could call in for a special nightcap. He does a lovely coffee with some kind of noxious spirit and cream.' Fay quickened her pace and walked ahead of us.

'I don't know if that's a good ...' Nikki began to say when Fay stopped suddenly in her tracks and held up her hand.

'Hang on. Is that Tim?' she asked, squinting into the dark.

We all looked and sure enough, there was Tim, our housemate, standing at the corner of the road, dressed in a long black coat and peering around the wall. He was looking in the opposite direction to us and wasn't aware we were behind him.

'What's he doing?' Nikki whispered. 'He looks kind of suspicious.'

He appeared tense, as though unable to keep still and was smoking furiously. A few seconds later he flicked his cigarette to the ground and walked around the corner onto the main road, crossed over and walked straight into Barney's.

'Let's peek through the window,' I said, intrigued. We'd never seen Tim outside the house and knew so little about him, this might be an opportunity to discover a bit more about him.

'Perhaps he's meeting a woman,' Nikki said as we crossed the road towards Barney's. Then the lights in the front window went off and the café went dark, all apart from the glow of a light in a back room. As we got closer we saw that the sign said CLOSED.

'Now that,' Fay said, scratching her head, 'is weird.'

# Chapter Six

I could feel Adam's hand creeping past the small of my back and over the fabric of my beaded skirt. There was a wet, guttural noise as an elderly gentleman cleared his throat in the row of chairs behind us and Adam's hand quickly returned around my waist. 'I told you we should have stood at the back,' he whispered.

'Behave,' I warned him, grinning.

'I can't help it, you're just so gorgeous I can't keep my hands off you.' He leaned in closer. 'No one would notice if we snuck out now. I have the key to our hotel room in my pocket.'

'I'm so glad *that's* what it is. Now, if you don't mind, one of your best friends is about to get married and I think we should stick around.' I rolled my eyes in an exaggerated gesture, as though having a man that couldn't keep his hands off me was starting to get tedious, but actually I couldn't help but be pleased. Richard and Jules have some pretty stunning female friends and I had suffered a major inferiority complex when I first arrived at the hotel. I didn't want to stand next to these incredible, delicate women, when inside I was still feeling rough and ravaged from the effects of the night before.

Fortunately I was one of the chosen few blessed with a beauty therapist for a best friend. If Adam had seen me just four hours earlier he may have been tempted to call an ambulance. The wine I'd drunk had left me with puffy, bloodshot eyes and dark circles that made me look as though one of the Dizzy Heights children had painted a pair of giant blue sunglasses on my face whilst I was asleep. Nikki had taken one look at me over the breakfast bar and had gone straight back up to Fay's room for her toolkit. Half an hour later I was sipping green tea with honey (which looked like washing-up water but when your body's as hydrated as chalk dust, anything's a bonus) and was having what Nikki called 'the latest scientific breakthrough in super-oxygenating, hydration serum: emergency, advanced formula' massaged into my vital acupressure points. It worked miracles and by the time Adam had picked me up I no longer resembled a ravaged blueberry muffin. I was peaches and cream. At least outside I was; inside I was still churning and coming to the conclusion that a little hair-of-the-dog was my only remaining option.

The string quartet took their positions and started to serenade the audience with one of Vivaldi's *Four Seasons*. The music was as clear as crystal as it soared elegantly across the banqueting hall. Those guests who weren't already standing now took to their feet and all heads turned to see Jules enter the room.

She hesitated by the door as her father helped her rearrange her dress, which was a gorgeous, almost medieval-looking, cream, silk gown with a wide scoop neck and trumpet sleeves. Her hair was down and natural with a small filigree tiara just showing through. She was grinning; her smile almost rictal on her face, a cross between joy and terror as she started to walk towards Richard.

53

My throat felt suddenly tight and my eyes began to well up as I saw the couple exchange glances. It was so moving I had to look away, worried I'd make a show of myself by crying. Surely only the mother-of-the-bride could get away with that. When I looked back at Jules I saw her little eight-year-old sister following behind, holding Jules's train and looking like the proudest little girl in the room and my throat got even tighter and began to throb.

The ceremony was tortuously long for a civil service, with three songs in all. *Three*! The lump in my throat made it nearly impossible to sing and when I could get words out they sounded wobbly and strangled. I was constantly fighting to keep my emotional state under control but just when I thought I'd recovered myself, the registrar would say something about love, or Richard's mum would blow her nose, or Richard would take three attempts to put Jules's ring on her finger because his hands were shaking so much, and I'd feel myself wavering again.

By the time they had signed the register and led us all outside, my head was pounding and it hurt to swallow.

'Are you OK?' Adam asked as we walked out into the fresh air.

'I'm fine,' I said brightly. 'Just a bit of a sore throat, that's all.' Adam squeezed my waist then reached across to a waiter's tray and helped himself to a couple of glasses of champagne.

I thanked him and drank half of mine in one gulp.

'That'll be us one day,' Adam said, taking me by surprise.

'When?' The word popped out after I'd swallowed my drink, leaving me startled. I'd had no idea I was going to say that until the word had formed. It wasn't even a very friendly or enticing 'when'; instead it was so blunt and challenging I cringed.

Adam looked taken aback. 'Well, we've never really talked about it, have we? But I kind of thought we'd give ourselves a few years. We want to plan it, don't we?' He reached for my hand and squeezed it, smiling. 'And it'd be nice to be living together, so we should sort out a house first. Get settled.'

'Oh. When?' There it was again! What had gotten into me? Had I developed some kind of syndrome? Would I sit through this afternoon's dinner speeches and start blurting out 'get on with it' or 'you're all shaggers'?

He laughed and ruffled my hair like I'd said something that amused him then he looked up and saw Grant heading our way, drink in hand.

Grant looked as though he'd had his hair specially shaved for the occasion. He always did have it closely shaved but with his pale skin it was obvious when it had just been done as he looked paler, his head not having had a chance to be coloured by the sun. It made him look severe, like a bouncer, and he seemed out of place at a wedding.

'All right? Ready for your speech?' Adam said.

He groaned, holding his pint closer to his chest. 'I've been ready since I first got up this morning. I just want to get it over with, then I can relax. Why do they have to have the speeches after the meal anyway? Seems a bit bloody cruel if you ask me. Now I'm going to be bricking myself for hours.'

'You'll be fine,' Adam said. 'At least you've got a prop to hide behind.'

I looked puzzled between the two of them but they just smiled at each other, obviously not willing to give anything away.

The guests started to gather under a large magnolia tree for a group photograph and one of Richard's relatives waved us over.

'C'mon then, let's do it,' Adam said, taking my hand and leading me down the grassy bank to join the others.

I blew my nose for the third time and the tissue disintegrated in my hands. A lady next to me, who I'd earlier learnt was the mother of Jules's best friend, passed me another and I took it gratefully. We laughed at each other as she too had to dab tears from the corners of her eyes.

' . . . and then the doctor came out and said to me, she's OK, she's going to be OK . . .' Jules's father paused for a moment, steadying himself. He took a small sip of water, 'and right then I knew my daughter was a fighter. That she was my special girl and every day with her would bring me joy and make me proud.'

Jules and Richard, who had been holding hands tightly and looking at their plates during most of the speech, looked up at each other and smiled. Jules was obviously touched.

'And then, twenty years later,' her father continued, his voice stronger, 'Julianne told me about Richard. A bright, intelligent young man and a gifted architect. Well, it sounded to me as though he had designs on my daughter, and I have to admit I was a little worried about anyone being good enough for her. So, I gave her the same advice I'd given her throughout her life: don't choose anything unless it fills the fundamental requirements,' Jules jokingly rolled her eyes and shook her head as her dad ticked off a list she'd obviously heard many times with his fingers, 'are they sensible, hard-wearing, waterproof and cheap?' His audience began to laugh. 'Of course this advice mostly applied to the many times we went shopping for shoes, but it was good advice then and shouldn't be dismissed as entirely irrelevant now. When I first met Richard it was on site, where a house he had designed was being built on the grounds of an old orchard in the village next to mine. I'd spoken to him on the phone and he'd invited me to pop over and have a look. When I arrived there was a sudden cloud burst. Rain began sheeting down the moment I got out of the car. I pulled my coat up over my head and ran under the cover of a tree and I stayed there for several minutes, looking out over the site. There were workmen everywhere, running for shelter, splashing through muddy puddles or hurrying to cover up equipment. And that was when I first saw Richard. Of course I'd never met Richard before, but I knew it must have been him. He was standing in the middle of all this organised chaos, ankle deep in mud and not in the slightest bit bothered. He had a long waterproof jacket on, big black steel toe-capped Wellington boots, a yellow hard hat and was holding a giant umbrella over his less-prepared client. As the rain began to ease off I went to join these two men, and after I'd introduced myself to the other gentleman as Richard's prospective father-in-law, he turned to me and said, "Richard's great, he's one of those rare breeds, a bit like a decent accountant, because he's so good at his job I'm sure he's saving me more money than he's costing me." And there I had it. All my basic requirements were fulfilled before Richard had even uttered a word; he was sensible, hard-hat wearing, waterproof and cheap.' He paused and we all laughed heartily. Richard said, 'Err, thank you, I think,' and Jules's dad continued. 'Right then I felt like someone was trying to tell me something, trying to tell me that I had no need to worry about Julianne. That Richard was now the man to take care of her. And I haven't worried since, because I'm reminded of what Julianne said when she wanted to spend her first ever month's wages on a pair of handmade leather boots, "Daddy, something this perfect will last you a lifetime", and this time, *this time*,' he emphasised, making us all laugh again, 'I'm inclined to believe her. And so, I ask you all to raise your glasses to Richard and Julianne, and wish them a lifetime of happiness. To Richard and Julianne . . .'

We toasted the couple and Adam looked at me with affection. 'Have you got tears in your eyes?'

I sniffed loudly and blushed. 'I'm just so happy for them,' I said, then excused myself to the Ladies.

The toilets were empty when I walked in so I sat on a loo with the door open and called Fay from my mobile. She wasn't at home so I tried her mobile number.

'Hey Gemma, how's it going?' she asked when she picked up. I could hear a thumping bass and the sound of cash registers grinding in the background.

'Oh Fay, it's so embarrassing. I keep getting all choked up and emotional. I've had a lump in my throat from the moment Jules walked down the aisle. I haven't wanted to cry this much since that time you forced me to watch *Dawson's Creek*.'

'Ahh, weddings make me do that too. Even on the telly. Weddings, births, emergency service vehicles, they all do it.'

'Pardon?'

'Yeah, you know, when they whiz by with their flashers on and everyone pulls over to let them by, oh, it's like everyone's put all their road rage behind them and can unify for a common good, and dammit, we're going to get that ambulance to the hospital on time even if we all have to mount the pavement to do it . . . It gets me every time,' she said, her voice wavering.

'Really?' Suddenly I didn't feel quite so mad.

'Of course. Don't worry Gem. You're emotional and you're romantic; you're bound to feel like that. Especially with you thinking about your own wedding lately,' she said tentatively.

'I suppose, I'm just being silly. What are you up to anyway? Are you shopping?'

'For Britain. Nikki's in the changing room as we speak. Then we're off to Marks and Spencer's to stock up on nibbles and we're going to have a night of junk food eating, reality TV watching debauchery. You're not really missing much.'

'Sounds like the perfect night in, you'll have to do it all over again tomorrow with me. Oh, I suppose I ought to go. Grant will be doing his speech next, I just had to get a breather.'

Fay was silent for a moment then said, 'Are you sure you're OK? Nothing else worrying you?'

'No, no, it's fine. I just, oh I don't know. I suppose it's got me thinking, that's all. And there was Jules's dad's speech. Even he was talking about getting signs, about knowing when something was right. Everyone's getting signs, they're everywhere. I just wish they were easier to decipher.' I sighed heavily then wiped my nose with the back of my hand and looked up. On the toilet door in front of me a sign said NOW WASH YOUR HANDS and I laughed at myself. 'I'd better go,' I said. 'You have a good evening, and don't wait up.' We said goodbye and I rang off, getting up to go to the sinks and freshen up before I returned to the table.

When I entered the room Grant was standing at the top table looking incredibly nervous for a man who looked like he made his living being as hard-as-nails.

In front of him was a life-size cardboard cut-out of Richard wearing a tartan hat that looked like a giant tea cosy and only a sporran to protect his modesty. Richard's mum was staring at it in disbelief and I couldn't tell whether Jules was smiling or if she had her lips pursed tightly together.

'Then, with the policewoman holding the glitter spray and the balloon Richard was holding starting to deflate . . .' Grant continued. Adam caught my eye and I breathed a sigh of relief, realising that the chances of Grant bringing an emotional tear to my eye were highly unlikely.

My leg was starting to go numb. I wanted to shift positions but I didn't dare in case I jolted Sophie, Jules's little sister, who had perched herself on my lap fifteen minutes ago. She was bent over a table with a paper napkin and her mum's ballpoint pen, making me a 'secret, special surprise', which she shielded with a protective arm.

Adam was standing a few feet away on the patio, chatting with an all-male group of Richard's friends next to where the barbeque was just beginning to crackle and smoke. I couldn't believe anyone would be able to eat another mouthful after the delicious five-course meal we'd finished just a few hours earlier, but the kitchen staff were now trooping out with trays of marinated chicken and bowls of exotic salads which they laid out ready on the buffet tables.

Around me there was a happy hum of conversation as groups of guests stood on the lawns or reclined on the wooden seats, able to relax now that the day's formalities were over. The live band was playing renditions of Elvis classics in the banqueting hall and the last time I looked there were a dozen or so people dancing and more looking on, not daring to join in until the lights were lower and they'd had a bit more to drink.

'You're going to love this,' Sophie said, biting her

bottom lip in concentration. Every now and again she would say something like this, just to remind me what she was doing and whip me up into a frenzy of curiosity. 'I showed Angela Bradbury how to do this last week,' she'd say, or, 'You're not trying to peek, are you?' and I'd have to feign impatience and try to look, or say something like, 'Can I see it yet? You're taking ages.'

I felt a hand on my shoulder and turned around to see Jules beaming at me, eyes sparkling, make-up perfect and such an all-round vision I could understand what people meant when they tried to describe an aura.

'Hey, how's your big day going?' I asked as she pulled up a chair beside me. Everyone seemed to be looking at her and I felt honoured that she was sitting with me. It gave me a strange sense of importance.

'Oh it's just crazy. It's whizzing by so fast and I want to memorise every last detail but I can feel it all slipping away from me already. It's one big blur.' She sounded almost breathless as she spoke. 'And I've been dying to have a good chat with you all day. For weeks in fact. It's been ages since I last saw you, I've been so tied up with the whole wedding palaver everything else has fallen by the wayside. And I won't see you for ages after this either. I'm so sorry.'

I couldn't help but laugh, her expression was so earnest. 'It's fine, of course I understand.' Jules and Richard were about to embark on a six-week honeymoon, visiting all their favourite countries from when they went backpacking several years earlier, only staying in more expensive hotels.

'I've been dying to congratulate you properly on your engagement as well. I hope you won't be having a party whilst we're away.'

'I don't think there's much chance of that,' I said. 'We're still getting used to the idea ourselves right now.'

She shook her head wistfully. 'I can't believe you and Adam are going to get married. How grown up are we? Hey, can I see the ring?'

I held out my hand and she took it, whistling. 'It's gorgeous. So perfect. Did you choose it together?'

I nodded.

'I knew you'd love that shop,' she said. 'It's Sod's Law, isn't it? I spend months looking for the perfect ring, trawling the streets, then a month after I finally get one I see a whole gorgeous shop full of one-off, handmade versions of the sort I love *and* they're no more expensive for it.'

'Oh, so you knew about the shop? Hearts and Arrows?' I could feel my heart sink a little. Adam hadn't seen it and thought of me after all.

'Of course, I told Adam about it when he told Richard you'd got engaged. I figured if I'd missed out on it then the least I could do is spread the word. That shop is seriously back of beyond.'

'Ta da!' Sophie said, spinning round to show me what she'd made. It was an origami fortune teller, just like the ones Fay, Nikki and I used to make when we were at school. 'Right, pick a number and I'll tell you the name of your future husband,' she said, wiggling the paper squares under my nose.

# Chapter Seven

I sipped my coke and watched around me as people got drunker, louder and more uninhibited as time passed. The band had packed away about half an hour ago and now a disco was playing the old school disco songs to a heaving dance floor. I'd managed to join them for two or three songs, but halfway through Vic and Bob's 'Dizzy' I realised how apt the title was and I had to return to my seat with Adam not far behind me. At our table, Jules, Richard, Grant, Mike (a fellow architect and friend of Richard's) and Wendy and Ian (a couple Jules had known since university) were all sitting low in their chairs, a relaxed haze surrounding them. They'd all danced until they were too tired to dance anymore, and no one looked like they had the energy to do anything more strenuous than sit and drink. Jules was barefoot after realising she couldn't dance in four-inch heels, especially ones so pointy they had practically fused her toes together. She had her feet up on Richard, who was stroking them absently, listening to something Mike was saying. On Jules's other side was the life-size cut-out of Richard, which had been bent in the middle so that it could sit down with us. It now had white ribbons hanging around its cardboard shoulders and someone had even bought it a drink.

A blonde-haired girl, who'd obviously had a lot to drink judging by the way her eyes were half-closed, sidled up to the cut-out. 'All right, gorgeous?' she said to it then cracked up laughing. I thought I detected a faint Scottish lilt to her accent.

Jules swatted her playfully. 'Hey, he's taken.'

The blonde drunkard sighed and pulled up a chair next to Grant. 'Story of my life. Anyone here not taken? Everyone's being far too well behaved for my liking. What happened to the wild men of Glasgow?' She looked specifically at Adam and I decided that whoever she was, I didn't like her.

Wendy spoke up. 'Were you at the stag night then?'

Blonde-drunkard nodded, silenced by the cigarette in her mouth which she was trying feverishly hard to light.

'Marcia's my cousin,' Jules explained to Wendy, smiling with sweet innocence. 'She's doing a masters at Glasgow Uni so when I told her Richard's stag weekend was on her stomping ground, well, she just had to call in and say hello.'

'Spy on us more like,' Richard said, narrowing his eyes at her in an expression meant to be accusing but which really came across as affectionate and adoring.

'You have nothing to fear, Richard,' Blonde-drunkard said, inhaling her cigarette smoke so deeply there wasn't a trace of it left when she breathed out. 'You are so oblivious to other women we all decided you have to be secretly gay and your wedding's one big cover-up.'

Jules looked at Richard proudly. 'That's my boy.'

I was feeling increasingly riled by this woman. Not only had I been unaware of there being a woman at the stag do (besides the stripper, unless *she* was the stripper), but I didn't like her saying 'we all decided' as though the collective stags, Adam included, agreed that Richard was weird for not looking at other women. I didn't want Adam agreeing with her on anything, let alone that. I looked at Adam but he didn't seem interested in what she was saying and was humming along to the Frankie Goes to Hollywood song that was playing, his hand tapping a beat on his knee. Perhaps I was being over sensitive, I decided. My thoughts had been running away from me rather a lot lately.

'Did you bring the other photos with you then?' Blonde-drunkard asked Grant.

'Of course,' he said, tapping his jacket to indicate that they were in the inside pocket. She reached in and grabbed them before he could stop her, although he didn't look as though he would have put up much of a fight.

'Those are the edited ones,' Grant said, and I thought I saw him give Adam a wry glance. Something definitely didn't feel right anymore. I felt uncomfortable, as though I was being left out of a private joke. I looked at Jules but she was leaning away from me, laughing at one of the pictures that were now doing the rounds of the table. Adam leant over to me. 'I'm just going to the Gents,' he whispered, then left the table.

A few minutes later I got up too. I walked out into the hotel foyer with the intention of going to the Ladies, but as I felt the fresh air from the open front door hit me, I was drawn outside. I walked out into the car park, breathing in the cold and enjoying the sudden hush around me. It was so quiet outside, the loudest noises were the voices in my head, echoes from the night's conversations, replaying over and over. There was a low wall fronting a little garden ahead of me and I wandered over to it, sitting down on the rough brick and nearly jumped out of my skin when I saw Adam standing a few feet from me, his hands thrust into his pockets.

'I thought you'd gone to the loo?' I said, confused.

'I did. Then I came out for a breath of fresh air. It was starting to get a bit much in there.' He came and sat beside me, putting an arm around my shoulders. 'It's been a long day.'

I nodded an agreement then yawned.

'We could go back to mine now; we don't have to stay any longer. You look tired.'

I looked up at him and he bent down and kissed me. I felt the same fizz of adrenalin I always got when Adam kissed me and I kissed him back for a moment then pulled away. There was a short silence then I said, 'Adam, do you think we'll ever be like that?'

'Like what?'

'Like Jules and Richard. You know, married, and kind of, comfortable.' I was struggling with my words. I didn't know how to verbalise what I saw in them that I wanted for us. 'They really know each other; it's like they've grown-up together or something and they have this amazing understanding and trust. It's really special.'

Adam frowned. 'Don't we have that?'

'Yeah, kind of. Well, no. Not on the same level. I've not even met your parents yet, and we're not living together so we haven't gone through that whole living together thing.' I wished I'd not drunk so much today. I knew I wasn't making much sense and was talking without thinking, but I didn't want to lose the opportunity to discuss things with Adam. We rarely talked about our relationship – we just let it happen and went with it. Now there were things I wanted to say; things that were coming out, brought on by my weeks of analysing and a day of high emotional atmosphere.

'But you often stay over at mine, and you know I can't leave yet: I've got to fulfil the lease. And all those other things will come. You can meet my parents if you want, it isn't that big a deal. You know we're not really close. It's not like I'm keeping them from you, it's just that I don't see them much, so it stands to reason that you wouldn't either.'

I did know Adam didn't have a good relationship with his parents. They'd split up when he was seven and he hadn't spoken to his father much since. I often wondered how he'd felt as a boy, not for any pseudo-psychological reason, but just because it was part of what made him, and I wanted to understand it. Adam never really talked about it and brushed aside the subject whenever it came up. I didn't feel I could push the issue. It was just one more example of how I felt Adam was sometimes holding me at arm's length.

'What are you trying to say, Gem? Aren't you happy with us?' He was facing me now and I didn't dare look at him.

'I am happy.'

'But?'

'But what?'

'There was a but coming then. I am happy ... *but*. What were you going to say next?'

'Nothing!'

'I'm happy with you, Gemma,' he said, holding my hand. 'I think I understand you and I definitely trust you. Don't you feel that with me?'

'Yes,' I said, but not with confidence. It was more of a long-drawn-out 'yes', the sort that always precedes a 'but'. Adam obviously anticipated that was coming again because he dropped my hand and stood up, the tension in his body indicating suppressed anger.

'I'm going back inside,' he said, then turned around and walked away from me, his footsteps crunching loudly on the gravel.

I watched him in stunned silence. How on earth did we get to be mad at each other? Everything had been going so well. I looked around, feeling foolish. I couldn't go back in now, Adam would go back to the table, he'd be laughing and talking with the others and I couldn't bear the awkwardness of it. I rummaged in my bag for my mobile, wanting to call Nikki and Fay. It beeped at me; the battery was low. Someone had left me a voicemail and I listened to it, my heart starting to speed up. It was Fay.

'Gemma, it's me. You have to call us, you're not going to believe what's happened!' That was all she said. I could hear Nikki in the background. She sounded hysterical, like she was shouting at someone. I felt sick. What if something had happened to her? She could have hurt herself. What if they'd been drinking and she'd fallen down the stairs? Or Tim had turned out to be a housemate from hell; a crazed psychopath on a drugs high and had smashed up the house then hung himself in the shower. I tried to call them back but the phone switched itself off.

A taxi had pulled into the drive, dropping someone off by the entrance, and its headlights shone on me for a second as it swung around.

'Hey, stop!' I called out, chasing after it. 'Wait for me.'

I burst through the door and scanned the hallway. All was normal: no bloodstains at the bottom of the stairs, no signs of damage. I opened the living-room door and there were Nikki and Fay, sitting like five year olds, up as close to the television screen as they could be without going cross-eyed, a giant bowl of popcorn between them.

'What's going on? I thought someone had died or something!' I called out, almost indignant at seeing the house in such a state of normality.

Fay and Nikki jumped up when they realised I was home and began talking hysterically at me. They were almost hyper, grabbing my arm, jumping around and I could only decipher snatches of what they were saying. 'Unbelievable! . . . It was him! . . . Live!' Then Fay ended their double prattle by saying, 'Why oh why didn't we get digital TV?' and they both fell silent and stared at me, waiting for my reaction.

'Because Adam said that to put a dish on a period building was almost sacrilegious and you threatened to pull the cable man's arms off because that's basically what they did to trees when they dug up the street. And anyway, what?'

'It's Fabian,' Nikki said. 'He was on TV! It's that new show, *Date Live*. You must have seen the trailers for it.'

'No.' I shook my head and joined them back down on the floor by the television. 'What is it?'

'Basically, it's a new dating show,' Fay explained, her voice animated. 'Six single girlfriends go out onto the streets and have to find a guy to date for the night. They're all wired up and have a camera following them. Then they've got till ten o'clock to make a guy fall for them, so if they're not having any joy with one guy they have to rush off and find another. Then the viewers vote for the girl who's bagged the best guy and the winner gets the choice between a thousand pounds or a week in Thailand to get to know her new date better.'

'Okaaay,' I said, waiting to find out where Fabian fitted into all this.

'So, they were filming in Covent Garden,' Nikki carried

on. 'And who do you think was sitting at a table on the pavement outside some bar?'

I took an educated guess. 'Fabian?'

'Yep. And what do you think he said when the gorgeous contestant with the anatomically impossible Barbie figure went up and asked him if he was single?'

I stared at Nikki in shock. 'You're kidding me!'

'Sadly not. He didn't even bat an eyelid. The camera has hardly left those two all night – they hit it off straight away. Fabian was doing the Mr Smooth-but-a-tiny-bit-vulnerable act we all know so well, and just before the time ran out they were snogging over a table in the Ice Bar. All on live telly.'

I gasped. 'Oh my God, that's awful! Are you all right?'

'I'm OK, I'm not upset. I think I'm still in shock, but I'm also mad as hell. Just the thought of all those viewers thinking, ahh, what a nice guy, what a great couple, and actually voting for them. It's awful! They probably all think he's really genuine and this is the start of a proper romance from the way they were acting. And perhaps it is. But it's so surreal seeing him there, acting just the way he does around me and realising he can turn it on just like that.' She clicked her fingers. 'Ugh, I can't believe how stupid I feel.'

'No, Nikki, you mustn't feel like that,' I said and squeezed her shoulder. 'Let me get you a drink. Is it going to be back on tonight?'

Nikki nodded. 'It's on the digital channel now, they've got a panel of body language and relationship experts assessing the different couples whilst the phone lines are open for the voting, and then it comes back live on Four in about five minutes.' She went quiet for a moment then said, 'I don't know if I can bear to watch though.'

I got up and went to the kitchen to fix us all a drink.

There was deadly silence in the bar as the camera flitted between the impossible Barbie and Fabian. 'I choose ... the holiday,' she said and Fabian threw his arms around her as everyone around them cheered.

'Bastard,' Nikki muttered and flicked the television off with the remote. 'I can't believe he's doing this. Do you realise they'll probably film the holiday too? I can't bear the humiliation!'

I felt the hairs on the back of my arms prickle. 'He's going to be famous, isn't he? Just like Miranda said.'

'I know,' Fay said soberly. 'I thought that as soon as I saw him on the telly. That's one more thing Miranda got right. It's so weird. It's like the kind of thing you hear about on Richard and Judy.'

'We are not going on Richard and Judy,' Nikki said, horrified. 'I don't want anyone thinking we're crackpots. It's hard enough getting a decent boyfriend as it is,' she said gesturing to the television. 'It's just some kind of weird coincidence.'

'I'm not so sure,' Fay said.

We sat in silence for a moment then I said, 'You realise she's got almost everything right now – there's only what she said about Fay, and it's too early to say whether she was right about that, and there's what she said about not marrying the first guy who asks me. That's the only other thing left to come true.'

'That wasn't a prediction though, was it?' Nikki said. 'It was advice. It's not like you have to take it or anything.'

'I know,' I said feebly, staring into my drink. I remembered my earlier argument with Adam and sighed heavily. 'But I keep thinking about what she said. I've got so many

71

questions. Maybe it's silly, but I think if I could just speak to Miranda. Clarify a few things. I'd feel a whole lot better.'

# Chapter Eight

'OK,' I said on Sunday morning. 'So none of us can remember Miranda's name, I haven't got any of her old letters and all we know about her is that she came from Gloucester.'

'Or was it Colchester?' Fay was munching thoughtfully on a piece of toast as Nikki flicked between the television channels, looking for any kind of coverage on the previous evening's TV.

'No. It was definitely Gloucester,' I said. 'I remember it wasn't that far away because she kept saying it wouldn't cost much for her to come down on the train, and that was when I panicked and stopped writing back.' Looking back on that now I felt racked with guilt. She had obviously been a bit short of friends and had looked on our shared night as a bonding of female spirits. Her only real crime was her unique eccentricity and a granny-on-acid dress sense. I hated to think I was once that shallow. 'It's not much to go on though, is it? How on earth do I find her with just that?'

Nikki dropped the remote control with disappointment as the Hollyoaks omnibus started and turned back to face us. 'You could put an ad in the *Fortean Times*,' she said dryly.

'Yes!' Fay agreed, not realising Nikki wasn't being serious. 'Or maybe she already knows we want to find her. Maybe the door will go any minute and it'll be her.' She made a high-pitched squeal and pulled her fleece blanket up over her face.

Nikki tugged it back down and looked her square in the eye. 'You are clearly insane.'

Fay warded her off with her toast. 'You'll be sorry when it happens.'

'What time is it in Australia?' Nikki said. 'You could call your dad and ask him if he can remember what her surname is.'

'Mmm, I thought of that already. I'm going to call him late, before he goes to bed.' Glancing at my watch I wondered what Adam was doing now. Whether he was up yet and when he'd call. I'd been awake since the early hours, half expecting the phone to ring. Why hadn't he phoned me? After last night's disastrous conversation I would have thought he'd be calling me as soon as he could to make sure we were OK; at the very least to check I got home safely. I had thought about calling him myself but I stalled just short of fetching the phone every time. I kept thinking of how since Miranda had got me questioning Adam's suitability as my one-and-only, I had started to realise I wasn't that confident about his feelings towards me. It was always me pinning him down, making arrangements, baring my soul. He never really confided in me, he was always that bit cooler and he never went much deeper than the occasionally hard-to-interpret looks I'd catch him giving me when I was doing something inconsequential like making a cup of tea or clearing up around him in his workshop. When we first met that was his biggest pulling factor, the fact that although he was chatting me up, asking me out and flattering me constantly, he was also deep into his own life, thick with his own friends and had interests independent of my own.

Adam came just a month after my last boyfriend, Luke – a guy so emotionally needy he would have loved me to take him to work and give him a cookie in the quiet corner. He had worn me out with his constant phone calls and 'Do you love me?'s I started to worry that he had that kind of late Sunday night drama about a boyfriend turned desperate stalker who tries to murder his ex and spell out his name with her intestines potential, and the relationship went way over time as I put off the inevitable, worried about how he'd take it. Eventually he gave me just the excuse I needed when, during a drunken night out at a club, I caught him trying to kiss a completely baffled-looking Fay. Two changes of telephone number and three weeks worth of my avoiding the house later and Luke gave up. A poor effort at fighting for your woman, I'd thought. Adam was a breath of fresh air by comparison. He was every inch a man. He was strong and capable, creative but practical, fun, passionate and saw no need for relationship dissection. When he'd said, 'Sorry I didn't call you last weekend, I'd been out with the guys and time just ran away with me. Am I awful?' punctuated by this cheeky, infectious laugh, I don't know whether I swooned or sighed with relief. But could that really last a lifetime? Was he husband material? Deep down I was thinking that now would be a good time for him to show me that he was.

'It's a shame Miranda didn't try to predict her own future as well, isn't it?' Fay was saying. 'Then we'd know exactly what she was up to.'

'Don't you think it's just all a massive coincidence?' Nikki said. 'I mean, weirder things have happened. And it's not like she'd been really detailed, you know, names of husbands or anything like that. And anyway, I remember watching a programme about strange coincidences once. There was a woman whose husband had taken her daughter off for the day, to a friend's party. The woman had remembered that her husband had forgotten something and she dialled his mobile number. Her husband was walking his little girl down the street where the party was; he'd walked past a phone box when the phone had started ringing. Without thinking about it the guy answered the phone and his wife had been on the other end. His wife had tried to dial the mobile but hadn't realised she'd dialled completely the wrong number, different dialling code and everything, but the number she had dialled was the number of the call box he was just walking past. A mad, mad, coincidence. There was another one about a boy who threw a bottle with a note in it into the sea in Barbados and his aunt, who lived in Australia, had picked it up off the beach. All that way and it went to his aunt.'

'Wow,' Fay said, 'that's amazing.'

'Yes, but my point is that someone once said, "every eventuality can and will happen". Sometimes coincidences occur and there's no rhyme or reason for them, they just do, and amazing as they might seem, for the rest of your life, nothing so strange will ever happen and yet things are happening all around you all the time. You only notice the weird things, the different things, because they seem weird and different. But really, they're just as likely to happen as anything else. They aren't trying to tell you anything, it's not some great plan, it's just a matter of chance.'

'So you're saying that what Miranda said was nothing to do with her, they were just random comments and the fact they all came true is pure coincidence?'

Nikki shrugged. 'As far as I can see there are only two possibilities here,' she counted off on her fingers, 'one: it is, as I said, just a coincidence; or two: Miranda is a gifted psychic. I know which one I'm opting to believe.'

'What about three,' Fay said. 'That it is a coincidence engineered by fate and put into Gemma's hands before she marries Adam, to warn her and to make sure she's making the right choice.'

Nikki just stared at her coffee, obviously not willing to credit that with an answer.

I looked between them seeing sense in everything they said. They could both be right. How were we to know? My head kept trying to be sensible, to think like Nikki and give it a practical explanation, but my heart was all over the place. I'd always prided myself on keeping an open mind; I couldn't dismiss something so personal out of hand. I had to think seriously about the consequences. 'I just want to find Miranda,' I said. 'However ridiculous it is I want to rule out possibility number two or I'll be forever wondering. Either that or confirm possibility number two and ask her what the hell I'm supposed to do now.'

Nikki leant across the coffee table and picked up her now tepid cup of coffee. 'It'd be interesting to find out what happened to Miranda. She was certainly different. It might get a bit heavy though. What if she's gone insane or has become a hermit, or a drug addict, or one of those mad women that sells lucky lavender on street corners, and when you say "no thank you" yells at you in some indecipherable language, and all the passers-by think she's putting a hex on you.'

Fay and I looked at Nikki in surprise. 'That's odd,' Fay said, 'they always tell me I'm going to live in the country and have many beautiful children ...'

'And be your own boss?' I finished for her.

'Yep. We've obviously met the same lady.' Fay laughed

as Nikki pretended to look offended. Just then we were silenced as the front door slammed shut. We all froze, our eyes darting to the living-room door.

'Hi,' Tim said, coming in seconds later. He was holding a carrier bag and had a paper tucked under his arm. 'You're in then.'

We all nodded, staring at him.

'Going out later?'

We all shook our heads. 'Not sure yet,' I said.

'Ahh. OK.' Was it my imagination or did he look disappointed?

'Oh my God!' Nikki cried, suddenly leaping off the chair and making a grab for Tim's paper. She unfolded it for us all to see. On the front page, in the bottom right corner was a picture of Fabian and the Impossible Barbie, posing for photographers in what looked like an airport terminal. The tag line read: LOVE AT FIRST FLIGHT? Fabian was unmistakeable with his golden, Mediterranean skin and smoothly shaved head. He looked like a model and was clearly a natural in front of the cameras. Together they made a strikingly attractive couple, the sort that tabloid photographers loved. Something told me this wasn't the last we were going to see of him in the media spotlight.

By the time Nikki left after lunch Adam still hadn't called. I put it down to a late night. Perhaps he'd felt sorry for himself and stayed up drinking. Surely he'd call me when he got up?

I'd spoken to Dad instead, who couldn't remember much about the colleague from New Year's Eve or his daughter, Miranda, but did tell me an immensely long story about an Aboriginal artist called Jennie. Dad was usually full of fascinating facts and throwaway trivia, which was why I found it so odd that he couldn't remember anything about Miranda. How could he forget? Fay looked chilled when I told her; as though Miranda must have been some kind of ghostly apparition, or visitation from the future, sent back to right some terrible mistakes. I put it down to Dad getting older and vowed to confiscate Fay's *X-Files* tapes.

It was odd though, and disappointing, because it drew a blank on my brief search for Miranda. I had really wanted to find her and try to make sense of it all.

'Can I turn this off now? I don't think I can bear any more,' I said to Fay as the repeat of *Date Live* returned from its commercial break, the presenter jumping with excitement as one of the girls was shown to be dirty dancing with a guy who had his shirt unbuttoned to the waist.

Fay got up and flicked the TV off, jumping as Tim came back into the living room.

'I'm off out then. See you tomorrow,' he said then was gone.

'I wonder if he's going back to Barney's,' I said after the front door had banged shut. When I looked at Fay, I noticed she was blushing. 'What's up?'

'Oh, nothing,' she dismissed.

I narrowed my eyes. 'No, come on, something's up. And why are you always so jumpy around Tim anyway?'

'Am I?'

'Yes.'

'Well ...' She tucked her hair back behind her ears and scrunched her nose up.

'You don't,' I said in disbelief.

'What?'

'You think he might be the one Miranda meant. The good man right under your nose.'

'No! No, no, no. Well, you never know, do you,' she said looking at me from under her lashes.

My jaw dropped as I realised she wouldn't be too disappointed if it did turn out to be Tim.

# Chapter Nine

By Monday morning the lack of a phone call from Adam was getting ridiculous. Surely we were solid enough to shake off some minor disagreement. I could barely even remember what it was about now or how it started. Perhaps something bad had happened, I thought, walking to work. That made me feel terrible. What if he'd been lying in his flat, unconscious after slipping on a bath mat or something and all his friends had just assumed he was with me and I had never called and he was cold and unconscious with a huge great lump on the back of his head and ... perhaps I would call him. But then it would be me running to him again. And he'd probably just have been out with his friends and forgotten all about me. Oh, why did it have to be like this? Why couldn't it be simpler?

I'll call at the end of the day, I decided. If I hadn't heard from him by tonight, I'd call him and make like I'd been so busy with Fay and Nikki all weekend that I hadn't had the chance before. Unless he really is unconscious on the bathroom floor, then I'll have to pretend that my phone was broken.

Jill was in the garden setting out the water play and

sandpit when I arrived at Dizzy Heights. The warmth of the morning sun had already dried the dew on the grass, promising a perfect day ahead for the children to play outside.

Jill is the pre-school leader. She's forty-six, although has that kind of affinity with children that makes her ageless when she is with them. The children all love her, even when she has to be firm. They just seem to fall into line, as if they don't want her to be disappointed in them.

Looking at Jill this morning I could see she had pulled another interesting creation out of the wardrobe again. She dressed herself the way I imagine a child would if left to their own devices: all clashing patterns and styles, as though she wanted to wear everything in her wardrobe at once. Today she was wearing one of her many pairs of leggings. This particular pair were a slightly faded floral design that she had put together with Tweety-Pie socks and a green short-sleeved polo shirt. She had tied a silk scarf around her neck that had a completely different pattern of flowers on it. Jill's logic for her outfit would probably be something like, 'Well, I thought it was rather jolly, don't you agree?' to which you would be left with little choice. If someone were ever brave enough to try to educate her on a more flattering or stylish way of dressing, she would most likely agree with everything she was told with boundless enthusiasm, then go and buy an enormous jumper with a cat on the front, saying, 'Yes, but isn't this just so much fun?'

'Hell-ooo,' she sing-songed when I stepped out of the back door to join her. 'How was your weekend?'

'Oh not bad, you know,' I said vaguely. I didn't really feel like talking about it. Jill was one of those perpetually jolly souls that worried about nothing. I knew that if I told her about Adam she'd dismiss it quickly, tell me not to worry and that we would be 'right as rain' tomorrow. 'How was yours?'

'Marvellous.' She beamed. 'Spent all weekend on the narrow boat. Nothing like messing about on the water. You must come with us some time. Bring Adam too, you'd love it!'

'Right. Yes. Err, lovely.' However much I liked Jill and her husband, I wasn't sure about spending a day with them travelling along a canal at a rate of four miles an hour. Especially as she had once told me that they never stop at pubs as 'there's never any need when we have a perfectly good tea urn on the boat'.

'Coffee, Gemma?' Helen, one of the assistants, called through the window.

'Yes please,' I said gratefully. 'Just coming.'

Helen and I drank our coffee whilst setting up the day's activities, chatting as we worked.

Helen must have said 'you're so lucky' in a wistful voice at least half-a-dozen times as she lamented about her lack of a boyfriend. 'I mean, what's so great about Adam,' she persisted, 'is he always seems so sure of himself. Not in an arrogant kind of way, but with a quiet, take-me-as-I-am confidence. The kind of guy that'd look after you and be there for you.'

'You mean like the kind of guy who'd make sure that if, say for example, you were going home after a wedding reception, late at night, on your own, would make sure you'd got home safely?' I said, energetically slicing up some brightly coloured card with a guillotine.

'No,' Helen said, completely missing any significance in what I'd said, 'Adam's more like the kind of guy who'd insist on taking you home and seeing you safely to your door yet without making you feel like you had to shag him afterwards in gratitude. I'm telling you, Gem, you're onto a winner there.'

'Right then, let's do it,' Jill said, interrupting us as she crossed the room to the front door to let the parents in.

I got up and went to join her in the foyer to welcome everyone and soon the room was full of the lively sounds of chaos as the children filed in to take off their shoes and jackets and get changed into their Dap shoes.

'Gemma, Gemma, look what I've got,' Megan said, holding up her toy for me to see.

'Oh yes, isn't he a beautiful unicorn!' I said, inspecting it with exaggerated admiration.

'It's not a unicorn,' Megan said frowning, 'it's a horse with a party hat.'

I bent down to apologise and was about to ask its name when I was suddenly knocked to the floor as a blur of a boy cannoned into me. I lay winded as he sat heavily on my stomach. 'I love you,' he said, holding my hair like a horse's reins.

'Billy, come on, get off. You can't do that, you could have hurt her,' Stewart said, plucking Billy off me with one strong arm and helping me up with the other. 'Sorry about that,' he said to me, 'he can be a bit over-the-top sometimes.'

'Oh, don't worry, he's a lovely boy.' I watched as Billy ran into the playroom to say hello to Helen. We all loved Billy. We tried hard not to have favourites but he had quickly wormed his way into all of our hearts. He was very bright for his age, and confident, always talking to the adults, and he was disarmingly affectionate and cheerful. By themselves they weren't unique characteristics, but when you took into account the fact that his mum had died when he was a baby, it amazed us all how well he was growing up. Stewart, his dad, looked after him whenever he wasn't at Dizzy Heights and he was obviously doing a great job.

'So, Gemma, are you coming to the parents do next week?' he asked, smiling at me.

By 'the parents do' he meant the small party we had every term. It was a chance for parents to meet and mingle without the children, and it was also our way of thanking them for their help, either on the commitee or with fundraising. We supplied a bar with the help of the pub at the bottom of the road and everyone brought food. I enjoyed seeing the parents and getting to know them better, but it was always one of those events that had a family function atmosphere about it. As though everyone was on their best behaviour. Adam came with me once but seemed out of place as most of the other guests were older and more conventional than him. He visibly relaxed when we left and went into town for last orders. He never complained though and had offered to come with me again, but I could tell his heart wasn't in it and said I didn't mind going alone.

'Yes, I'll probably put in an appearance; not sure how long I'll stay though. How about you?'

Stewart had his hands deep in his pockets and rocked onto the back of his heels. 'I was thinking about it, babysitter depending I suppose.'

'Of course, well, I hope you make it. It'd be nice to see you there.' Billy returned then and took my hand, tugging at it impatiently. I smiled at Stewart as Billy led me off.

'Have a good morning, Billy,' he called after us.

At break time, when the children were all sitting down with milk and biscuits, Helen and I stood in the entrance to the kitchen, watching over them.

'Don't you think Billy's dad is attractive?' Helen said quietly.

'You think so?'

'Definitely. It sounds so awful,' she looked guiltily around the room before continuing, 'but it's something about him being a single dad. He's so good at it. Despite everything, Billy's going to have a really secure, loving childhood. There's something so tragic and moving about it all. I don't know, I suppose it makes Stewart seem kind of strong and noble.'

'Do you fancy him?' I asked, taken aback.

'No! Not at all! Well all right, I wouldn't say no.' She giggled. 'But I saw the way he looked at you when you walked off with Billy this morning and I'd say he definitely has feelings for you.' She nodded at me confidently.

'Do you think?'

She carried on nodding. 'I *know*.'

I thought about it for a minute. 'Nah.'

The phone rang and Helen went to get it, leaving me on my own. As soon as she was gone, I realised that I was still thinking about what Helen had said. Of course I didn't think Miranda could have meant Stewart, he wasn't someone from my school days. But Dizzy Heights was technically a pre-school. What if she'd meant that? I felt a flicker of excitement, then quashed it almost immediately with thoughts of Adam. No, it was a ridiculous idea. It didn't even fit well enough with what Miranda had said. I felt suddenly unnerved as I realised I'd been so worried about Miranda's words meaning Adam wasn't right, that I hadn't stopped to think about who was.

When I arrived home from work the house was quiet, unusual as it was Fay's day off and she usually spent those in her pyjamas, watching her favourite old films. I called out a 'hello' as the door simultaneously slammed shut behind me. At the top of the stairs I caught sight of Fay outside Tim's room. She sprang back from the door in one giant leap as though the door handle was attached to a buzzer and she'd just received several hundred volts straight through her fingertips. 'I wasn't doing anything, I wasn't, it's not what you think,' she blurted out, her eyes huge and guilty.

'Wasn't doing what?'

'I wasn't, well, I wasn't sneaking about,' she said and looked down, tugging girlishly at the bottom of her cardigan.

'Right. And here was me thinking you wait for me to go to work then spend the whole day prowling around the house, bobbing down below windows and peering in cupboards,' I said, climbing up the stairs to join her. I looked at Tim's room and the door was slightly ajar.

'He's out,' Fay whispered.

'O-*kaaay*.'

'And he left the door open.'

'I see.'

'Well, he never leaves the door open, does he?'

'Fay, you didn't?' I hissed.

'No! I wouldn't.' Her voice got louder. 'I was just curious. I was just going to peek around the door, that's all.'

'Did you see anything?'

She shook her head. 'You came back just when I was about to.' She sat down at the top of the stairs and I squeezed in next to her. 'I just wanted to get a better picture of what he's like. I mean he's so mysterious, isn't he? What do we know about him?'

'Not much.' I frowned and thought for a moment. 'He works in computing, but we don't know what or where. He does weird hours and is a away a lot, often all night. People only ever call him on his mobile. He eats loads of carbohydrates and still manages to look fit ...' Fay nodded an enthusiastic agreement. '... he doesn't drink much, smokes a bit but not in the house, has a very expensive looking watch, doesn't seem to have a girlfriend and laughs really loud at *EastEnders*, like he gets some kind of hidden joke no one else understands.'

'Dot is pretty funny though,' Fay said, smiling.

There was a brief silence then I looked at her. 'What if he's into something dodgy?'

'You mean like bondage?'

'Mmm, no. More like drugs or stolen goods or something?'

Fay shook her head. 'I don't know. Nikki thinks he's really suspect, and I suppose that's why I wanted to look at his room. I didn't want to go through his private stuff or anything, I just wanted to make sure that it was a normal guy's bedroom, you know, damp towels and small black gadgets, a general trainer whiff about the place.'

'You mean you wanted to make sure he was suitable boyfriend material. A *good man*?' I teased.

Fay mashed her lips together and looked away.

'Perhaps we should take a peek,' I said, curiosity overwhelming me now. 'Just a quick look around the door, just to make sure there isn't anything dodgy in there like a pile of hi-fi equipment still in boxes or some bin liners and a shovel. Just a quick look, for our own sakes.' My words hung in the air between us for a moment as we pondered on them, then, at precisely the same moment, we sprang up and returned to the door.

I leaned against it and it creaked open, Fay bent down under my arm and the two of us peered through the opening, hardly breathing at all. The curtains had been left drawn and so the light was dim, restricting our view, but everything seemed pretty normal: a double bed with a navy bedspread, slightly ruffled; a desk with a laptop but no obvious signs of paperwork; some clothes on a chair, deodorant and aftershave on a set of drawers and a large metal box with a big padlock on it sticking out from the bottom of the bed. I was just about to ask Fay what she thought it was for when the doorbell chimed and the pair of us shot back squealing. We grabbed each other tightly and ducked down behind the banister, out of sight from the front door.

My heart was pounding in my ears. 'Oh God, what if it's Tim? What if he's forgotten his keys and he's seen what we were doing through the window?'

The doorbell rang again and we stared at each other in panic.

'I'd better get it,' I said eventually.

I walked downstairs, weak kneed from adrenalin and guilt making my face burn red. I opened the door, hardly daring to look in case it was Tim, and I felt my breath catch in my mouth when I realised who it was. It was Adam. Adam had come at last. He smiled nervously at me.

'I'm really, really sorry Gem,' he said.

# Chapter Ten

I hadn't meant to be so easily forgiving, and in fact with hindsight I was disappointed with myself for caving in so quickly. A winning smile was all it took to melt my steely determination. When Adam had taken me out for dinner on Monday night I practically evaporated behind my menu.

He always had that effect on me. We never argued. Instead, whenever I felt frustrated with Adam, he was usually so blissfully unaware of it that I wouldn't want to spoil things. I hated seeing couples arguing, I didn't like awkwardness or confrontations, I didn't want to nag him and I didn't want to talk him into any kind of commitment. I wanted those kind of gestures to come to him without pressure. That was the only way they could mean anything to me. And as Adam never seemed to find fault with anything I did, our relationship usually sailed along without fear of stormy weather, just continuing on its fair-weather journey, never really knowing where it was going.

Adam had chosen a Chinese restaurant I'd been wanting to go to for a while. We walked past it sometimes on the way into town and I always admired its decoration with its simple white, red and black colour scheme. There were paper lanterns on every table, rather than candles and a golden dragon was etched onto the big window at the front. Adam had often suggested that we go there but I always said we'd wait for a special occasion, worried about the prices which were quite a bit more than we would usually pay for a meal.

Now, from the smells all around me and the look of the other diners' meals, I could tell that the prices were high for a very good reason.

After we'd been seated we made small talk whilst the waiter poured our wine and took our orders. He was just returning to the kitchen when I saw the couple to one side of us breaking open fortune cookies and I called him back.

'Those fortune cookies,' I said, pointing the couple out.

'Yes madam.'

'Do you give those to all your customers or do you have to order them separately?'

'Oh no madam, we give them to everyone. They are gratis. On the house.' He bowed at me, smiling widely.

'Would you mind if we didn't have them? It's, erm, it's an allergy thing.'

'Ah,' he looked surprised then smiled and bowed again. 'No fortune cookies, thank you madam.' Then he left us alone.

Adam was staring at me strangely. 'What was that about? You love fortune cookies.'

'I just, well, I didn't want to tempt fate, I suppose,' I said hurriedly, ignoring Adam's obvious confusion. 'Look Adam, I think we should talk, you know, about the other night,' I started.

Adam winced and put down his wine glass. 'I know, it was all my fault. I don't know what got into me. It was the drink talking, making me paranoid,' he said, half-heartedly dismissing it with a wave of his hand.

'Well, I'm sorry if it was anything I said or did.'

'No, I'm sorry.' He looked at me seriously. 'You know how important to me you are, don't you?'

I felt that lovely feeling of warmth rush across my chest and nodded.

'I suppose I look at you sometimes and wonder how I ever got so lucky. I keep wondering what I'm going to do to mess this up.'

'What do you mean?'

He hesitated self-consciously as a waitress brushed past our table. When she'd gone he stayed quiet, tapping the table with his finger as though something was bothering him. I watched him, waiting and eventually he spoke.

'You know, when I was little, probably about six or seven, Dad had been gone a few months and I hadn't seen or heard from him that whole time. One day he was there in the house, signs of him, smells of him everywhere, then the next day he was gone. He must have packed up the car when I was in bed one night. But it couldn't have been a spur of the moment thing, because instead of getting in a car and driving away with only the stuff he stood up in, he had taken everything. He must have planned it. Every little trace of him had vanished from the house. He never had a lot of things, but I still noticed as soon as I woke up. I went into the bathroom and it looked completely different to me, like a jigsaw with gaping holes in it or something.' He paused and looked across the restaurant as though seeing in his mind what he was describing, then shook the memory away. 'Anyway, so a few months went by and there was no word from him, no nothing. Mum was carrying on doing all the same things, but seemed to be doing them quicker, you know, tidying the house and cooking and washing, everything busy busy, like if she paused for a minute her act would slip and she would allow enough time to pass for me or my brother to say, "Hang on a minute, where's Dad gone?" So we all carried on, trying hard to act normally and not mention anything about it.'

I nodded, mesmerised by Adam. He'd never spoken about his parents like this before. I had no idea how he felt about them splitting up and no idea of how it had happened, getting only the vaguest sense of bitterness when he spoke about his dad. I couldn't bear the thought of him like this; as a little boy, feeling hurt and confused. My stomach was constricting and I didn't know how I was going to be able to eat anything with those images in my mind.

'So anyway, one day, I was out in the garden. I think I was digging or something. I can remember crawling around under this giant rhododendron bush and feeling something hard under my fingers. I picked it up and held it out into the sunshine and I saw that it was my dad's wedding ring. I knew it was his because it was pretty distinctive. It was a Celtic knot. I'd always liked it and looked at it whenever I'd sat on his lap. I used to trace the pattern with my finger over and over. I couldn't believe it was lying there in the dirt. I put it in my pocket before anyone saw and ran off into the woods. I found a bank of grass, out of sight, and sat there for what felt like hours looking at it, wondering how it had ended up in our garden, whether Dad had lost it or thrown it away intentionally. I had this vision of him throwing it back at Mum because couples were always doing that on TV, throwing rings at each other then storming off. I'm sure Mum would have gone spare if she'd known I had it, and I should have given it back to her, but I wanted to keep it. I worried that if she had it, it would disappear like all of Dad's other things and it'd be like it never existed. So I decided to keep it. But then, as I was sitting there, I started to get angry, and I threw this ring in front of me, down on the ground where I could see it. I glared at it for a while then I went and fetched it and threw it again, saw where it landed, then picked it up and did it again.' He laughed bitterly at himself and shook his head. 'I don't know why I did it; it was a stupid thing to do. I really felt like that ring was special, like it was a connection to my dad, some lost treasure that proved he'd existed in our lives. But I kept throwing it further and further away, like I was testing myself to see if I could find it again. Eventually it landed in a pile of sticks. It bounced right through them and was gone. I searched until it was so dark I couldn't see anymore. I had to go home when I heard people out looking for me, calling my name.

'I never said anything to them about the ring. The next day I went straight back as soon as the sun came up but it wasn't there. I looked for it every day for a long time after that until eventually I had to give up.' He frowned and looked down at the table. 'I still don't know why I did that. I never found it and I never told anyone.'

I reached across the table and put my hand on his arm.

'The point I'm trying to make,' he said, 'although I'm not really going about it in the right way, is that sometimes, for no reason at all, I'm an idiot. I'll do something really stupid, or I'll push away the people I care about, and I don't know why I do it. I never think things through.' He took my hand off his arm and interlaced his fingers with mine. 'I don't want to lose you, Gemma.' He smiled at me, the light from the lantern bringing out the gold flecks in his warm brown eyes. 'And I know I don't say it enough but I do love you.'

My heart leaped and tears came to my eyes. 'I know,' I said, squeezing his fingers.

When I lay in bed with Adam that night, my body spooned into his, both of us warm and pulsing, I felt closer to him than ever before. Finally Adam was opening up to me, slowly peeling off the layers to reveal his vulnerable side. He hadn't said much, he wasn't a heart on his sleeve kind of man, but he'd hinted at much more than was said, and the sensitivity in his eyes and in his voice spoke volumes. He was far deeper than you would first imagine, but he hid it well, and now I was beginning to understand why.

On Friday, Grant was having a house-warming party. He'd recently bought a little end of terrace in Lower Weston and had been threatening 'the mother of all parties' for weeks. I wasn't keen but Adam had begged and pleaded with me to go with him so earnestly that I had been flattered into it. Fay was also invited so we were going to go together and meet Adam there.

I really wasn't in the mood for a big party. I'd had four days of me and Adam. Adam and I. Just the two of us. Me sleeping at his, eating breakfast and sharing a morning shower together, Adam going in to work late and coming home early to be with me, and us leaving the house and getting fully dressed only for work or fetching food supplies. I'd spent all of that time with a delirious smile on my face, bed hair and a shortage of clean clothes, but I didn't care. We were enjoying a happy, coupley state of need and I didn't feel I'd had enough of a fix yet to be trooping off to a party only to sandwich myself between a bunch of strangers who would end up shouting to be heard and accidentally spitting in my ear. Still, Fay was keen to go, desperate to get out of the house after a boring week. I felt guilty abandoning her in the house with a guy I had my suspicions about whilst I indulged in my relationship, and so I returned home after work on Friday, armed with a bottle of wine and a couple of instant face packs, hoping to make it up to her.

We sat opposite each other with our legs up on the sofa, looking like clowns after a pie fight with our faces covered in an apparently edible face mask. An exotic smell of coconut and kiwi filled my senses every time I breathed in and I would have been tempted to stick out my tongue and lick some off my chin if it hadn't looked so convincingly like pureed sprouts.

'So, things are going well with Adam then?' Fay said in ventriloquist's voice as she tried not to use her facial muscles.

'Great. Really good. I feel like things are finally moving on for us now.'

'Really?'

'Yep. Honestly, forget Miranda, forget everything she said. I don't doubt Adam any more. How can I doubt he's right for me when he makes me this happy? Maybe we are meant to be together after all. Maybe we were meant to meet. Just because it wasn't a big crash bang moment, doesn't mean destiny wasn't playing a hand. It was probably just doing it subtly. Who knows how these things work. All I know is we're so good together. I love—' Fay wasn't looking at me anymore; she was looking behind me at the door. I turned around and saw Tim standing in the doorway. 'Looking good, girls,' he said, laughing as he winked at Fay and disappeared out of the hallway and thudded up the stairs. I turned back to Fay who looked mortified. She must have been blushing because her ears had turned pink and a glob of face pack slid down her face, as though her hot cheeks had melted it, and landed with a gloop in her glass of wine.

*

We had been cajoled into joining a group of girls who were sitting in a circle on the floor at the far end of the living room, simultaneously drinking shots of something that in the interests of public safety should surely have a skull and crossbones on the bottle. They were animated and friendly, drawing us into their group like co-conspirators as they laughed with raw humour and glanced continuously in the direction of the men in the house. It was always like that with Grant's friends. The men and women didn't seem to mingle, instead they stayed separate, like the Pink Ladies and the T Birds, fascinated by the opposite sex but seeing them as a whole other species they didn't fully understand. This led to lots of gossiping and 'Is she going out with him?' or 'Does he fancy me?' type conversations as they huddled in like footballers talking tactics. I couldn't get into all that tonight; it seemed a bit pointless when I had my man and I could read his thoughts perfectly well judging by the way he was undressing me with his eyes every time he was in the room. I liked watching Adam from a distance, not as good as up close of course, but I did like to watch him when he didn't know I was looking, thinking, *this is how other people see him*. Several of the girls in the room had already given him the once-over and looked interested. I wasn't surprised: he stood out. Not just because of his tall frame and broad shoulders, but also the softness in his eyes, the huge easy smile that played on his lips and the honey brown skin of a man who leads an outdoors life. He looked approachable, easygoing and strong. He always looked strong. Not in an *I can bench press my own weight and take Phil Mitchell in a fight* kind of way, but more like *an average sized woman can fit in the crook of my arm and feel like nothing and no one can touch her there*, way. That's my man, I thought happily.

97

'Gem-*ma*,' Fay said, leaning in towards me and wafting her hand in front of my face.

'Hmm?'

'You were miles away.'

'Was I?'

'Yes. Bridget was just asking how you met Adam.'

Bridget was grinning at me. 'He seems like a really nice guy,' she said.

'Yes, he is. We met when he helped renovate the church where our pre-school is based.'

'Ooh,' she cooed, 'so he's a handyman too. Lucky you.' She leaned in and whispered. 'You know, between us girls here,' she gestured to her friends sitting nearby, 'we've only got one boyfriend between us!'

Fay's eyes grew wide. 'What, you mean you share him around?'

Bridget burst out laughing. 'No! I mean we're all single. We were even talking about trying to sign up for that new dating programme, you know, *Date Live*? We figured it's worth a try if someone could bag a guy like the one from last week's programme.'

'You mean Fabian?'

'Yeah, did you see it?'

I blinked at her in astonishment. 'Er, yeah. I did. He wasn't really my type though.' Now that is fame, when people you don't know start talking about you at parties, I thought to myself. I was glad Nikki wasn't around to hear that. There can't be much worse than people thinking your lying, cheating ex is some kind of dream date.

Fay, who was starting to show signs of being drunk, had been listening with interest to my conversation with Bridget. She leaned in and said, 'I read about him. He's had Botox injections and a penis enlargement apparently.'

Bridget looked surprised. 'Really?'

'Oh yes.'

I stifled a smile and stood up. Suddenly I was feeling the effects of whatever it was we had been drinking. It seemed to have shrunk the lining of my bladder, compressing its contents like a squeezy bottle. I signalled to Fay that I was off to find the bathroom and pushed my way through the heaving mass of people dancing and talking loudly over the thumping music. I caught a glimpse of Adam in the kitchen; he was pouring his drink into a glass as Grant and a couple of other guys talked over his head. He looked up and smiled at me, waving me over to join them, but I mouthed that I was desperate for the toilet and carried on to the stairs. I hadn't been upstairs in Grant's new house before so I wasn't really sure where I was going. There were four doors leading off from the landing. The one straight ahead was shut, with an empty chair next to it. The others were all slightly ajar. I decided that the shut one must be the bathroom and sat down on the chair, looking around. The landing was dreary. The walls were cream but didn't look like they'd been repainted in the last decade. They had a greyish tinge to them that not even the bright scarlet carpet could cheer up. The curtains must have come with the house as there's no way I could imagine Grant choosing the floral chintz they were patterned with. The whole look had the feel of an old people's home and I felt a wave of sadness as I sat there. My gran's house had a similar feel to it just before she died. She refused to live in a home and stayed in her cottage till she was eventually taken to hospital. It was a gorgeous old Bath stone house with arched windows and big open fireplaces. She'd lived in a village just a few miles from our house in Langley Green, a little bit closer to Bath than we were, and nestled in a lane just above the river. I always loved that house. It made me so sad that she had lost the strength to look after it and it had become neglected, hidden from the path by its overgrown bushes. Dad was working then, and tried his best to keep on top of the jobs for her but the house almost seemed to be giving up; it became dimmer and developed a musty smell. This landing had the same kind of smell. I wondered if someone had died here too.

I nearly jumped out of my skin when sounds of laughter emanated from the room next to the bathroom. I looked up and from the crack in the door I could see that two girls were sitting cross legged on a bed. I recognised the girl facing me straight away. It was Marcia, Jules's cousin. The one from Glasgow that I took an instant dislike to at the wedding. Then I remembered Jules saying that Marcia was staying at her and Richard's place, house-sitting whilst they were on their honeymoon. I looked away, pretending I hadn't seen her.

'Here they are,' I heard her say. 'Grant has hidden them in his bedside cabinet.'

I froze. What were they doing going through Grant's stuff? Did he know they were there? I didn't want to hear any more of what they were saying: it felt wrong, like I was spying on them, but I had no choice now. If I moved they'd spot me and think I had been listening all along, but if I stayed where I was, they only had to look up to spot me outside. I tried to stay as still as possible, barely daring to breathe, and willed whoever it was in the bathroom to hurry up.

'Here we are, here's one of all of us, standing outside the club,' Marcia said and I heard the other girl laugh.

'Oh my God, I love your skirt. It's tiny!'

'I know, I didn't hear the lads complaining though,' she said, the self-satisfaction evident in her voice.

I wrinkled my nose.

'Here's one I took of the lads. Look at Richard: poor guy didn't know what'd hit him. He'd drunk a whole pint of Flying Scotsman cocktail by then. I don't think he had any idea how much whisky goes into one of those.'

My heart quickened as I realised they must be looking at the stag night photos. *Please, please, please hurry up in the bathroom; how long does it take to have a pee?* I strained to concentrate my ears on the bathroom, listening out for a hopeful sound: a zipper, a flushing toilet, a tap being run. Nothing. I felt so self-conscious just a few feet from Marcia and her friend, who thought they were alone.

'Here's Adam. Isn't he gorgeous in this picture?'

*Oh my God, no. Surely they mean a different Adam. It's a common enough name. Zipper and a flush, zipper and a flush, c'mon, c'mon . . .*

'Oh yes, I do recognise him. He's the guy downstairs isn't he? The tall one with the dark grey jumper on?'

*Please stop talking, please stop talking, la la la la la . . .*

'And here he is again.'

'Oh my God, what is he doing to you there? Has he got his hand up your top?'

*What?* All of a sudden I felt ice cold. My knees began to shake and I felt sure that if I stood up now I would pitch forward and fall all the way down the stairs.

'I know, all those drinks definitely loosened him up. Between Adam and Grant, I didn't have a quiet moment all night.'

'So,' her friend said triumphantly, '*Adam*'s the one you went back with after the wedding!'

*No!* I felt a rush of shock hit me like a lightning bolt. *I have got to get out of here now.* Finally I heard a toilet flush.

'Oh, quick, let's put them back,' Marcia said, getting

up and turning her back to the door. The urge to use the toilet had left me and in its place was a choking, dizzying sensation and an overwhelming need to run away. I stood up on unsteady legs and hurried down the stairs.

# Chapter Eleven

I hadn't got a clue how long I'd been sitting on the bath-room floor. It could've been anything from ten minutes to two hours. I was cold leaning against the cast-iron bath, but I ignored my discomfort and stared hard at the colour-ful row of lotions and potions on the shelf above the radiator. Fay always brought L-I-P products home from the shop where she worked; it was an acronym that stood for Life Is Pie, and not, as Nikki often said, 'Look, It's Puke'. I read the pastel labels; HUNPOT, HONEY HAIR SHINE; PAMPLEJUICE, TROPICAL BATH ESSENCE; JAMMY DODGER, STIMULATING STRAWBERRY SCRUB. I concentrated on the words, the happy, positive, indulgent words, and felt my vision swimming before me.

'Come on, Gem, please open the door,' I heard Fay plead from the hallway. I ignored her.

The last bottle in the row was one I hadn't seen before; it looked as though it hadn't been used yet. The label read GIN & TONIC, JUNIPER BERRY FACIAL WASH WITH INVIGORATING BUBBLES.

'Gemma, I think he's gone, please come out, you're worrying me.'

She sounded upset. 'OK, just a minute,' I said and

gingerly stood up. My knees were aching and I stretched, looking into the mirror. You couldn't really tell I'd been crying, but I still felt like I needed to freshen up. I plucked Fay's bottle of Gin & Tonic face wash off the shelf, wondering if any of the label's positivity could wash off on me now.

When I opened the bathroom door Fay hugged me. 'Are you OK?'

'I'm fine,' I said weakly.

'I didn't answer the door to him, I kept the lights off and eventually he gave up and walked off up the road.'

I thanked her then wandered over to my bedroom, Fay following behind.

'Are you going to tell me what happened now?' she asked gently, sitting opposite me on the bed as I switched on the dim bedside light.

'It's over,' I said flatly, looking down at my duvet.

Fay's eyes grew large. 'What? Why?'

'That girl, Marcia, the one I told you about that was at Richard and Jules's wedding . . .'

Fay thought for a moment then frowned. 'Jules's cousin, the one that crashed Richard's stag do?'

I nodded. 'She was at the party tonight; she's house-sitting for Jules whilst they're away. Grant must have kept in touch with Marcia and invited her along.' I told Fay what I'd heard whilst waiting in the hallway and her expression grew gradually more incensed.

'The bitch!' she said. 'What's she playing at?'

'What's Adam playing at more like?'

'Gemma, surely it can't be right. Nothing would have happened with her. Adam wouldn't do that.'

'Wouldn't he?'

'He loves you!'

'Maybe. But is it enough? It's possible to love someone and still cheat on them, you know.'

Fay's mouth was hanging open but no words were coming out.

'The thing is, Fay, it all makes sense now.' Suddenly I wanted to unburden everything I'd been torturing myself with on the bathroom floor. 'It's why he was uncomfortable with her at the wedding reception; he wouldn't look at her and she was looking at him a *lot*. It's why after she turned up he went all edgy and had to go into the car park for a breather. He just wanted to go home with me after that, probably worried one of them would give the game away. It'll be why he didn't come round or phone after I left him at the reception. He was probably holed up at his place shagging her all weekend!' The last words caught in my throat as images I didn't want to allow to form started crowding my mind. 'You know, when we were in the restaurant last week, he said something. I thought it was odd at the time but now I understand. He told me about something he'd done when he was younger, something stupid, that made no sense and how much he regretted it. He said that sometimes, for no reason at all, he's an idiot. He'll do something stupid, push away the people he cares about and he doesn't know why. Then he said he loved me and didn't want to lose me.' I looked at Fay, my eyes welling up again. 'He was trying to tell me then, wasn't he? I thought he was talking about his childhood, opening up to me, but he was really talking about Marcia.' I sniffed loudly and looked away from Fay's sorrowful expression. 'I think I've always known he's got problems with commitment. It was only recently, after reading Miranda's predictions, that I started thinking about it seriously. Now this confirms it, in the worst possible way.'

At one o'clock in the morning Fay and I were sitting on the sofa in the dark with only the flickering light of the television to focus on. We'd left the lights off in case Adam came back, hoping he'd think we were either out or asleep. I didn't want to see him now; I needed time to get my head around it all so that when I did face him I would be able to speak rationally. I didn't want him to see me upset – I already felt like enough of a victim.

Fay checked on me every few minutes or so with little questions: 'Are you OK?', 'Can I get you anything?', 'Do you want a drink?' I didn't feel like conversation, the sadness I felt almost paralysing. My mind was torturing me with images of them together, of Adam pressing Marcia against a wall, his hand fumbling urgently under her top, or of them sharing Adam's bed, naked and clammy, her hands gripping his chest, where I liked to lay my head. It was painful, but it was also deeply humiliating. I wondered who'd known, whether Richard had seen something and told Jules. Perhaps everyone at Grant's party knew too. Grant certainly must have done, he'd taken the photos. He'd probably egged him on, I thought bitterly; he'd never seemed happy about Adam and I getting together. And how could I go to work on Monday and face everyone? The children, Jill chirpily asking me about my weekend, and Helen, who I'm sure believes I've struck gold with Adam, how could I face them all now?

'Perhaps you should go to bed, hun, sleep on it. You're only going to be torturing yourself down here,' Fay said gently.

'I'm OK. I couldn't sleep. You go if you want to though, please don't stay up on my account.'

'Oh no, I'm fine,' she said, fixing her eyes on the television again and stifling a yawn. 'I'm not tired either.'

Ten minutes later we heard a key in the front door. I looked at Fay and she sat up, staring expectantly at the crack in the door. 'It's Tim,' she said under her breath.

Then I heard the sound of voices. He'd brought someone back with him. I silently prayed it wasn't a girl-friend, or a boyfriend for that matter. One broken heart was enough for one night. The voices grew louder then the door opened.

'Gemma? Are you in here?' Tim whispered. 'I bumped into your boyfriend on the way home.'

I saw Adam's unmistakable silhouette appear behind Tim and my heart skipped a beat.

'And what are you doing sitting in the dark anyway?' he continued, squinting at us both.

'Come on, Tim, let's put the kettle on,' Fay said, springing up and steering him in the direction of the kitchen before I had a chance to reply.

'Gem, what's going on?' Adam asked, stepping into the darkened room. 'Has something happened?' He turned the light on, but when I shrunk away, blinking, he turned the brightness down with the dimmer switch. 'Have you been crying?'

So much for my *you can't tell* theory, I thought, looking away from him self-consciously.

He crossed the room and knelt down by my feet, reaching out for my chin to inspect my face. 'You look awful, are you ill?'

'Thanks Adam. No, I'm not ill.'

He looked shocked by the coldness in my voice. 'Gem, what's happened? One minute everything's fine, the next you've gone, without even a word to me. I was worried about you.'

'Adam, I know.'

His face was blank, uncomprehending. He really didn't know what I was talking about, and for a moment I had hope. 'What? You know what?'

'About Marcia,' I said, and my last ray of hope was snuffed out as he registered what I just said.

I hadn't wanted to face Adam until that point, I hadn't wanted to deal with it, but right then I was glad I had been able to tell him to his face. If he had heard it second hand he would have been able to prepare his reaction better, and I would have heard excuses, apologies, maybe even denials, but up close like this, the tiny nuance in his expression spoke volumes. He looked guilty, frightened. His mouth was slightly open and his eyes were hurt and fearful. He knew what was coming. 'Gem,' he started.

'Please don't.'

'It's not what you think.'

'Don't tell me. I really can't bear to hear the details. I've heard enough. I know you were all over Marcia at the stag do and I know she went back with you after Richard's wedding. I . . .'

'Whoa!' Adam held his hands out, trying to stop my diatribe of accusations. 'Hang on a minute. That's not true!'

I stared levelly at him. 'I *know* it's true.'

He screwed his face up. 'OK, technically it's true, but not in the way you think. Nothing happened with Marcia. Yes, she came back to mine but she had nowhere else to go. I felt like I couldn't say no to her.' He looked down at my hands and saw that I was struggling with the ring on my finger. 'Gemma, don't do this. It's ridiculous. We need to talk. You've come to conclusions and you don't know what happened.'

'I know enough,' I said, holding the ring out for him. He wouldn't take it.

'Please take it back,' I said, feeling the tears coming and wanting him out before they started again.

'No!' He stood up. 'I can't believe you're doing this

108

without even discussing it with me first; you've just made up your mind. What happened to trust?'

'I don't know if I ever had trust,' I said quietly. 'And I don't think I can go on without it.'

He looked up at the ceiling, breathing out, as though trying to control himself.

I got up, unable to look at him for fear of giving in and wrapping my arms around him, in the hope it would all go away if I buried my head deep enough into the folds of his top. 'Adam, I can't do this anymore,' I said, as firmly as I could muster. 'I think you should leave.'

'Right. Of course.' He turned around and strode out of the living room, not looking back. I followed nervously behind him. When he stepped outside he looked as though he would head straight up the drive without looking back, but something stopped him and he faltered, turning back again. 'Four years we've been together; how can you never have trusted me?' he said, his face so tense I couldn't work out whether he was angry or upset.

'Adam, please . . .'

'You can't just give up on us, we need to talk about this.' His eyes pleaded with me and he stepped forward, reaching out for my hand. 'Gemma, please. You're so special to me. I really thought we were moving on. Moving forward together. We're meant to be together.'

'That's just it, Adam,' I said, my heart pounding, 'I don't think we are.'

# Chapter Twelve

'Three people have asked me if I'm OK today and it's not even lunchtime yet,' I said to Fay as the shop bell announced my arrival.

Fay looked up from her copy of *The Stage*, which she'd been reading whilst pricing up a box of miniature Buddhas. 'Oh no!' she said sympathetically.

'One woman on the way to the doctors. She was giving away flyers for a religious group; probably thought I was the perfect candidate. Then an old lady in the waiting room told me not to worry as "It'll all come out in the wash", which I thought was ironic considering that's why I was there in the first place,' I nodded to the rainbow of L-I-P products that had just been unpacked and were waiting to be lined up on the shelves, 'and then I saw that guy, Daniel – you know the one from the glass-blowing place opposite Adam's workshop? It was awful, Fay! He must have heard about me and Adam splitting up. He took one look at my face and started speaking in a really quiet voice and touching my arm. He must have thought I'd been sobbing all weekend. I tried to tell him I had an allergy and he just looked at me with this doe-eyed, understanding expression, like I was in denial or something.' I took a deep breath and Fay patted a chair behind the counter for me to sit on. I went to it gratefully, putting down my shopping bag. 'It's bad enough having my heart broken, but for people to think it's written all over my face like this is just plain humiliating. I mean, I may be upset, but I don't want people *thinking* I am, and I definitely don't want people reporting back to Adam, saying they saw me and I looked terrible.'

'Poor you,' Fay said. 'And what did the doctor say? Did she think it was the facial wash?'

'Most likely. Perhaps an allergy to juniper oil. Anyway there isn't much they can do; it should go in a day or so. And the rash has gone down a bit.'

'Mmm, it's much better than yesterday. In fact if you squint your eyes like this,' she made a face and put her head to one side, 'you can't even tell!'

'Thanks.'

'And at least you got to have a day off work to be with me,' she concluded with a bright, reassuring smile.

I smiled back. Fay was right, it was good to have a day off work. I really hadn't wanted to face anyone, and I appreciated having an extra day to get my head around what had happened. Perhaps by Tuesday I might even be able to talk about it without the terrible sinking sensation you get when you realise your life as you know it is being whipped out from under you. 'I think I'll put the kettle on,' I said, spotting a potential customer looking through the window, and ducked into the stockroom before they saw the state of my face.

I was just putting two mugs and a packet of biscuits on a tray when I heard my mobile ringing. I stood rigid. This could be Adam, I thought with a subtle flush of excitement. Perhaps he's going to explain everything. Give me an honest, innocent explanation of what happened with

111

Marcia. Maybe he was mad at me for not trusting him but he could understand now, and wanted to try again. How to play it though? Cool and distant? Happy and over him? Soft and wounded?

Fay plucked the phone from my bag and held it out, waving it in front of me as though trying to break a trance. I took it and answered nervously.

'Gemma? It's your father speaking.'

My shoulders slumped with a mixture of relief and disappointment.

'Hi Dad! How's it going in Australia?'

'It's fine, fine. I think it's all gone to your mother's head a bit. She's started wearing suntan lotion in stripes across her nose like some kind of dreadful war paint and last night she was drinking lager from a tin. I think your brother's finding her a little embarrassing, but anyway, are you at work? Am I taking you away from the children?'

'No, no, it's fine, I'm on a break,' I lied, opting for the easy explanation.

'Good, good. I shan't keep you long. I just wanted to let you know that I remembered your friend's name. The one you wanted to get in touch with? I wasn't sure if it was urgent so I thought I'd better let you know before it went out of my head again. It's a funny story actually . . .' I rolled my eyes and shifted from one foot to another, hoping it wouldn't be a long one. 'We were outside the Sydney Opera House this morning watching the *QE2* leave the docks, and I was telling your mother how I remembered it being launched in the 60s up in Glasgow. As it happens there was a chap standing next to me. He overheard me talking and he joined in the conversation because he comes from Glasgow, you see. He's an artist who paints the tall ships in the harbour. Anyway, he told me

112

his name. It's Ken Patterson, which, strangely enough, was the same as the chap from Gloucester. I remembered as soon as I heard it. They aren't the same person obviously, it's just a coincidence, but isn't that funny? You were only asking me his name the other day, then I bump into someone with exactly the same name.'

'That's ... that's really weird,' I said, catching Fay's eye. She perked up, raising her eyebrows curiously.

When I'd said goodbye to Dad I relayed the conversation to Fay.

'Wow!' she cried, clapping her hands together. 'That's like fate again, isn't it? A sign that you are meant to contact Miranda. That she wants to be found.'

'Oh Fay, don't start,' I said, leaning back against the doorframe. 'I don't think I want to contact Miranda any more. That was when I was confused about Adam, when I wasn't sure if there was a future in it. Now I know there's not. She was right. And as for my soulmate, I don't think I care anymore. If Adam's not for me, I don't think I want to know who is, not yet. Not for a long time.'

'Of course,' Fay said. 'I understand.' She looked pained then, as though trying to quell her growing curiosity. She didn't manage that for long. 'But aren't you just a little bit curious about her? About what she's become? Whether she really has a gift or if she's just like us? Don't you want to tell her she got all those things right and find out how she did it or what she thinks about it?'

I looked down at the tray. It was all getting a bit too much for me. 'Right now, all I care about are those chocolate digestives, and how many I can eat without having to undo the top button of my trousers.'

Early that evening Nikki came over. I hadn't been expecting her, and when I opened the door I noticed straight

113

away that she looked flushed. 'Quick, let me in,' she said and hurried past me into the hallway, where she peeped through the stained-glass window out into the street.

I stood in the doorway, my mouth forming the shape that the word 'Hi' would have come out of, given half a chance.

'Hurry up and shut it,' she hissed at me.

I clamped my jaw shut.

'The door!' she cried, waving her arms erratically to hurry me up.

I pushed it, making it shut with a solid clunk. 'What's going on?'

'Ohhh,' she breathed and looked up at the ceiling. 'Fabian came over after work.'

'Really?' I was surprised. We'd all seen the photographs of Fabian and the Impossible Barbie in the papers. They seemed to have hit it off straight away judging by the half-dressed images of them kissing by the pool or drinking wine on a hotel balcony.

'No way!' Fay cried. She'd just come out of the kitchen and was now standing next to me, her hand half suspended in a bag of Kettle Chips.

'I know! I half expected never to see him again.'

'What did he say?' I asked.

'Basically that he doesn't want to be with this girl, he only went along with it because it was good publicity for his company, and he knows he shouldn't have done it and he's sorry. You know, all the usual crap. He said he wants to keep seeing me but he doesn't want the press to find out about me and drag us both through the mud.'

'Is he still seeing the Barbie?' Fay asked suspiciously.

'He says not – only to promote the programme but it's all superficial.'

'And do you believe that?'

114

'No, of course not! I told him he was an arse and threw him out. He followed me over here in a cab but I think he's gone now. Probably edgy that someone will recognise him and let on to the press, although I think he's got an overinflated idea of how many people actually care. He's hardly a celebrity. I bet most people have forgotten who he is by now. I'm certainly going to.'

'Good for you,' I said and took her elbow, steering her into the kitchen. 'From now on we're putting up with no more arsey behaviour. Unless it's the real thing, we'll be single and proud.'

'Right on, sisters!' Fay cried, stepping into the kitchen, then yelped with surprise when she saw Tim sitting at the kitchen table, looking at her and laughing.

Ten minutes later, after we'd shared a pot of coffee in the kitchen, Fay suggested we go to Barney's for something stronger. She looked around the kitchen as she said it, her eyes wandering over Tim and therefore including him in the proposal. Nikki and I agreed and we all looked at Tim, who was still sipping the coffee Nikki had made him and chewing on an enormous sausage roll. He noticed the silence and looked up, his eyebrows raised.

'You want to come, Tim?' Fay said, in a squeak of a voice that sounded as though someone had sat on her windpipe.

'I'm good, thanks,' he said. 'I've got a few business calls to make later. You girls have a good night though.'

He smiled warmly at us all and Fay headed out first, trying to hide her blushes.

We sat in almost silence, pondering on the day's events; Fay and I had ordered a generous wedge of chocolate cheesecake and two forks to share and we set about devouring it, occasionally making appreciative noises, whilst Nikki sipped her hot lemon and looked anywhere other than our plate. She was humming softly to herself as though trying to block out our happy little noises and pretend she wasn't missing out on anything.

'Oh come on, Nik, surely one little forkful wouldn't hurt?' Fay said, offering her fork over. 'It's one of those tastes that really has to be experienced to be believed.'

Nikki looked longingly at the plate then waved her hand. 'I'd love to, but sadly this skin doesn't come naturally to me,' she said, patting her cheeks with her fingertips. 'All the fat in that little forkful would group together en masse and form one big spot in the middle of my chin. A brief moment's pleasure and I'd end up looking like a toad's gross bits and no one would ask me on a date again, let alone trust my skincare tips.' She put down her cup and sighed. 'Oh, I'm so fed up.'

'Me too,' I agreed, with my mouth half full.

'And me,' Fay said, pushing the plate away. 'Do you know what I think we should do?'

Nikki and I looked at her expectantly.

'I think we should find Miranda.'

'Oh, not that again!' Nikki rolled her eyes.

'Yes but we know her last name now. Gemma's dad called to say he'd remembered. It's Patterson, Miranda Patterson!' She looked at Nikki, as though waiting for her to be excited, but instead Nikki groaned and shook her head.

'The last thing I need is to meet up with some loony psychic, only to be told my relationship's up shit creek and I'm going to end up a lonely, middle-aged woman with calloused feet, sitting in a doctor's waiting room and reading about the exploits of my one-time lover in *Whoopee Look at Me!* magazine. I don't think I want to know any more about what my future holds.'

116

'So you admit Miranda might be able to tell you?' Fay said triumphantly.

Nikki laughed and gave her a jokingly pitying look as she stood up. 'I'm off to powder my nose; hopefully you'll be talking sense by the time I get back.'

The moment she'd gone Fay turned to me. 'Gemma, you understand, don't you? You understand why I think we should see her? I just want answers.'

'I know,' I said quietly.

'The thing with Nikki,' she continued, 'is she's not very open minded about that kind of stuff. She's scientific; only believes things that can be explained with logic. And of course that's fine, and I love Nikki to bits, but I think it's important to look at the bigger picture. Don't some people say we only use ten per cent of our brain's potential? If that's true just think of all the things we could do. I know there are a lot of cranks out there but surely some people must have a real ability. The evidence pretty much speaks for itself in Miranda's case. It can't be a coincidence. And remember what it said in *The Celestine Prophecy*?'

Oh hell, I thought. What did it say? Fay begged me to read it so I skimmed over the first two chapters until I got side-tracked by *The Beach*, which I thought had a much better plot.

'You remember, the First Insight? That every coincidence happens for a reason. Honestly Gem, it made so much sense, and it said that these coincidences will start happening more frequently, and we have to learn to suspend our doubts and acknowledge them, because when we do, humanity can move towards a higher consciousness. A kind of global awareness.'

I looked at her sceptically but then I remembered that my gran always said the same thing, well, perhaps in a simpler form, but she did say that there was no such thing

117

as 'just a coincidence', that everything in life happens for a reason, and I'd always believed her. I nodded, suddenly feeling as though my whole life was mapped out before me and I had no way of controlling it, but I could try and understand it better. Perhaps I was meant to go upstairs, just as Marcia was talking about Adam. Perhaps I was even meant to have loved and lost Adam, to show me the kind of man I can't ever be happy with, so that when I meet the one I *can* be happy with, I'd appreciate him more.

I was lost in thought when I felt Nikki nudge me. When I looked up Fay wasn't there.

'She's gone to the loo,' Nikki explained. She looked around sheepishly then leaned in. 'Gemma, I just wanted to say. Oh, this sounds awful, and I don't mean it in a bad way. You know I love Fay, but I was worried about her encouraging you to see Miranda.'

I felt a weird sense of déjà vu. 'Why? Why were you worried?'

'The thing is, I just don't want you to give up on Adam because of what Miranda said.'

'I'm not, you know why . . .' I started to protest.

'I know, I understand how upset you must be about the way things turned out. But you were so great together, I just think it's such a shame.' Her eyes shone and I was surprised to see she looked tearful. 'When you were together you always had this great attraction between you. It gave me hope. I just don't want you writing it off as not meant-to-be because of some silly coincidence, when before you'd read Miranda's predictions, you might have thought things with Adam were worth fighting for. I can see why Fay thinks the way she does, but it's all a bit, oh—' she looked up to the ceiling, searching for the right words, '—it's just a bit improbable, isn't it? And even though I wouldn't change Fay for the world, she is still the girl that won't turn the radio off mid-sentence because "it's rude" and swears blind she once saw her PE teacher levitate.'

We both laughed and looked up with equal affection as we saw Fay come out of the toilets. As she walked over Nikki said quietly, 'Just promise me that if Adam tries to talk to you, you'll give him a fair chance?'

'OK,' I said, quietly unconvinced that I'd ever have the opportunity to give him another chance when he'd given up on us so quickly.

'Right, this time I've got a suggestion,' I said brightly when Fay had sat back down.

'A sensible one this time I hope,' Nikki said, smiling.

'The most sensible one of the night. I suggest we order that bottle of wine we talked about and flirt with Barney till we feel better.'

'Yes!' they said in unison and we all stood up at once to head for the bar.

# Chapter Thirteen

'I feel sick,' Fay said in a small voice as we turned onto the harbour side path and saw the George Hotel in front of us. She faltered, clutching her stomach, and looked at me with a grimace.

'Don't panic Fay, you'll be fine. You know you always enjoy it once you're inside doing your thing.' I nudged her towards the hotel before she could change her mind.

It was an imposing Georgian building, with recently whitewashed walls and rows of sash windows, dressed in heavy red and gold drapes. Two large white sandwich boards were placed on either side of the hotel's canopied entrance. The familiar BBC logo was clear at the top of each one, and in large type underneath the message read; BBC CAREER DAY, OPEN AUDITIONS AND WORKSHOPS SATURDAY 9am–4pm.

Outside there must have been a hundred people waiting to be let in, they had formed a haphazard line and many were talking amongst themselves, creating a general hum of anticipation. We joined the end of the queue, a few feet from a group of teenage girls, dressed as though they were about to go to a nightclub and singing a Sugababes' song in harmony. They sounded pretty good, and I was just getting into the song when one of them noticed they were attracting attention from the crowd and started to giggle in a half pleased, half self-conscious way. A mime act covered from head to toe in white bandages worked his way down the queue and blew me a kiss as he passed by. I tried not to look at him for fear of being dragged into a mortifying double act, and when I peered over my shoulder to make sure he'd gone I came face to face with a portly middle-aged man dressed like Henry VIII. I turned quickly back round in alarm and shuffled closer to Fay. It was one of the busiest auditions I'd ever accompanied her to, and with half an hour to go before the doors opened it was set to get a lot busier as more people were arriving from every direction. I felt the vibe of the group wash over me. They were all in good spirits and it was catching, making me glad I'd come. I needed to distract myself from a week's worth of thinking about Adam, each day passing confirming that we were over, and that I would have to come to terms with not having him in my life for the first time in four years.

Adam had called me a few times early on in the week but I hadn't spoken to him; he'd also sent me a text asking if we could talk and I'd replied saying it would be pointless. After that there'd been nothing. I shouldn't have expected him to try any harder than that. I knew what he was like by now, but I was disappointed and kept wondering what he would have said if I had spoken to him. It was only the children at work who'd kept me from going insane with my thoughts. It helped to know that life was carrying on as normal, that it hadn't all come to an end and there were other things I could occupy myself with.

Twenty minutes after the doors had opened the queue was edging slowly forward as people registered in the hotel lobby. It was going to be a long wait before Fay could get through the doors so I nipped off to get us both a cup of coffee from a snack van I'd seen parked a little further along the water's edge.

As the man who served me was putting the brown paper cups into a moulded carrying tray I turned around and watched the people gathering for the auditions. I hoped Fay wasn't put off by the number of people. I realised that it was easy to spot Fay in the queue; her deep red hair caught my eye and her dark green vintage, military jacket stood out amongst the high-street fashions. I gave her a wave and was about to collect our coffees from the counter when a man walked in front of me, heading in the opposite direction to the George Hotel. I felt a sudden surge of familiarity, yet something didn't quite add up. I thought I knew him, yet I didn't think I could. Perhaps he's vaguely famous, I thought to myself, dismissing him briefly. Then it occurred to me: he looked just like a guy who'd been in my class at school for a few years, until we got separated when we moved up to the secondary school. I couldn't remember his real name because everyone called him 'Boober' after the character in Fraggle Rock. At that time he had red-brown moppish hair that always covered his eyes and a Roman nose that looked more prominent for not being able to see his forehead. He even used to wear the same kind of hat as Boober. The man who'd just walked past looked different, in a good way; his hair was cut shorter and – I strained to see his profile as he looked across the street – had he had a nose job? That's why I didn't recognise him straight away, but I was sure it was him: he was one of those people that had a distinctive look. Then I realised that he was someone from my schooldays and my curiosity rocketed. Perhaps he's the one Miranda meant? What if we were meant to bump into each other today? I had to get a better look and see if it

122

really was him. I took the tray of coffees and sped off after him. He was alone and walking quickly, weaving easily between the mass of people heading for the hotel. I followed in his trail, holding the coffees up with my left hand, the way waitresses always do on the telly, but without the accompanying skill or grace. I bumped into a teenage boy, jolting him to one side, but I kept my sights on Boober, calling out an apology over my shoulder. People were suddenly coming from everywhere, crowding out my view. I spotted an empty milk crate outside the door of a bakers and I stood up on it to see over the crowds. I saw Boober straight away, rounding a corner towards the main road. As I jumped off I felt some hot coffee slosh out of its cup and onto my wrist, making it tingle with heat. I ignored it and sped up towards the corner. I dodged a couple who were holding hands, taking up the whole path, and stepped out in front of a little girl in a ragged dress, who started the second verse of 'The Sun Will Come Out Tomorrow', making me stop and pivot on one foot, terrified I'd drop my coffee on her. For a moment I lost my balance, my free hand making crazy circles in the air until I regained it again and steadied myself. When I looked up I managed to catch a glimpse of Boober crossing the main road just as a green pedestrian light began to flash. *I have to make the lights or he'll be gone and I'll never know*, I thought, making a final dash towards the road. They changed to red just as I stepped off the path. Out of the corner of my eye I saw a driver shake his head impatiently as he revved his engine, waiting for me to clear the road. I broke into a run as Boober disappeared down an alley. 'Bugger!' I cursed, making a leap over a puddle onto the pavement. Before I could think about what I was doing, I heard myself calling out to him in a desperate bid to see his face before he was gone. I

123

made it as far as 'Boob ...' when I felt my legs knocked away from under me. I splayed my hand out to catch myself, lifting the coffee up higher, for some irrational reason deciding it was better for my face to get it than the drinks, when I felt my body make a rough, undignified contact with the ground.

I lay still, my brain switching to damage assessment mode, totting up which parts of me hurt the most. I had taken the fall on my right side and I could feel my right arm heating up quickly. My right knee was also throbbing. I sat up slowly to see for myself. Fortunately I'd worn my jeans and although the fabric around my knee was scuffed, it hadn't torn and my knee was protected.

'Are you OK?' I heard someone call out and looked up to see a lady approaching me from a group of about half-a-dozen who'd stopped to look at me.

'I'm fine, honestly,' I said, forcing a smile.

'I'm so sorry, I just didn't see you in time,' I heard a man say, and looked across the path to see that I wasn't the only casualty. A man was a few feet away, picking both himself and his bike up off the pavement, and I realised that he must have collided with me and fallen off his bike in the process. He propped the bike up against a lamp post and came over.

'Are you OK? Anything broken?'

'I don't think so,' I said, starting to feel giddy. I closed my eyes and swallowed hard.

'Oh!' His voice suddenly changed and he sounded surprised. 'You're Gemma. It is Gemma, isn't it?'

My eyes flew open and I looked up at the man who was now stooping over me.

'Yes ... do you ...'

'I'm Jamie, you know from Monkton Combe High School?'

'Really?' I looked at him properly for the first time. He was good looking, with kind hazel eyes and short dark hair, fashionably spiked up in the middle. I couldn't remember a Jamie in my year at school. He looked a little bit older; perhaps he was in the year above me. Then I realised. 'Of course! You're Mr Wade, my art teacher?'

He smiled shyly. 'Please, call me Jamie.'

'Right, yes, I do remember. You had glasses then, didn't you? For a minute there I thought you meant you were in my class or something. You don't seem old enough to have been my teacher.' I stopped myself then, realising how that sounded. 'Sorry, I just meant . . .'

He laughed and held up his hands to reassure me. 'It's fine, I know what you mean. I was a student teacher then, not much older than you were. That's why you're easy to remember. You never forget your first class.' He shook his head, looking at me, then seemed to remember that I was still sitting on the pavement. 'Anyway, come on, let me help you up.' He went to put a steadying hand under my elbow but stopped when he saw my arm. 'Ouch! That doesn't look too good. You're bleeding. Hang on.' He took a hanky out of his pocket then knelt back down beside me.

Looking at him I felt a strange sensation of familiarity spread over me. I remembered his art lessons, how funny and inspiring he'd been. He only took our class for one year but he was one of the best teachers I'd had. He was young and on our level, motivating us with humour and encourage-ment. I remembered how much Nikki had regretted choosing textiles over art after she'd seen what our teacher looked like. Funny how quickly I'd forgotten about him once he'd moved to a different class. I felt guilty about that now, as I looked up at him. He was holding my arm gently, concentrating on dabbing away the blood without hurting me. Suddenly I felt an embarrassing urge to cry.

'Does it hurt?' he asked in a soft voice.

I bit my lip and my eyes filled with tears.

'Oh, hey, it's OK,' he said. 'Look, my sister's restaurant is about two blocks around the corner. Why don't we go there and get you cleaned up? We might even get a nice cup of coffee if we're lucky too. Her coffee is out of this world.' He smiled at me and I nodded, blinking back a tear as I saw that the two cups of coffee I had bought were lying upturned on the ground, the coffee long since soaked into the pavement.

'She's fine,' I said, stepping back into the seating area of the little restaurant. 'Apparently there's a workshop for most of the morning that she's signed up for, so there's really no need for me to go back to the hotel. I said I'd meet her at four o'clock.'

I had called Fay from the ladies' toilets, relaying the story of how I had met Jamie. I used a hushed voice, paranoid that someone might hear me. I played down my injury so as not to worry her. I didn't want her thinking about me this afternoon and being distracted at her auditions, but the truth was, I was sporting an enormous and deeply unattractive graze that ran the whole length of my arm. It had only just stopped bleeding and was stinging like crazy. In Jamie's well-turned-out presence I couldn't help but feel self-conscious and clumsy.

I sat back down at our table, angling my right side away from him and smiled shyly. 'You were right about this coffee,' I said, sipping gratefully from the steaming white cup and licking the froth from my lips. 'And your sister's restaurant is lovely. I can tell I'll have to come here again.'

Just as I said that, Cassie walked through the kitchen door and appeared behind the bar.

'How are you now, Gemma? Is it still hurting?'

'Oh, it's fine, really. And you've been so kind, I should get going. You'll want to be opening up soon and I don't want to be in the way.'

Cassie looked horrified. 'Don't you go anywhere! You've had a nasty shock. I don't open till eleven so I have loads of time; stay all you want. Stay for lunch if you like, it's on me.'

I laughed gratefully at her open generosity and thanked her again. She was so kind when we arrived, making me feel welcome straight away. She'd even helped clean me up with tissues and antiseptic from her first aid box and had put a blue plaster on the smaller graze on my hand. 'Catering standard, I'm afraid,' she'd said apologetically, explaining about the brightly coloured plaster. 'That way we know when we've dropped one in the soup.' After that she seemed keen to give Jamie and I some time alone, popping her head around the kitchen door every minute or so to offer us more food and drink.

She took a bottle down from a glass shelf behind her, poured some bronze coloured liquid into two large brandy glasses and brought them over to the table. 'Finest Mandarin brandy, good for shock. Sip it slowly; you don't have anyone to rush off for, do you?' she said, patting her brother on the back.

Jamie rolled his eyes at me and we laughed as Cassie said, 'Enjoy!' and hurried back into the kitchen.

'Sorry about my sister,' Jamie said when she'd gone. 'Although I have to say she's being surprisingly restrained today. Usually she just introduces me to attractive young women by saying "this is my brother he's single and lovely" as breezily as though she were talking about the weather or something. She may not let you out of here till you've given me your contact details.'

I grinned at him and felt my cheeks begin to warm up. 'So, what's this brandy like then?' I said, picking up my glass and swilling the liquid in front of my nose. It was an intoxicating mixture of liquor and oranges, and also strangely medicinal, like molten Tunes with a kick.

'Let's find out.' Jamie held his glass up to mine for a toast. 'To chance meetings,' he said, as our glasses clinked together.

We both took a sip of the brandy and screwed up our faces as the strong liquid hit the back of our throats.

'Wow!'

'Powerful stuff,' I said, smacking my lips together appreciatively.

'Delicious.' Jamie took another sip then sat back, relaxed in his chair. 'Now, Gemma, you have to explain how you came to be leaping in front of my bike with a tray of coffee, shouting "Boob" at the top of your voice. Because I have to say, I'm very curious.'

# Chapter Fourteen

'So, to summarise,' Fay said, as I pulled off the motorway and began to slow down for the roundabout, 'Jamie is lovely . . .'

'He is, he's such a nice guy.'

'And his sister is also lovely.'

'And so welcoming, it was like I'd known her for years.'

'And her restaurant is . . .'

'Oh, really lovely,' I said, then jumped as the driver behind me beeped and I realised I had been staring into space rather than pulling out at the now empty roundabout. I signalled right and joined the A46 that would take us back to Bath.

'And you now have a new favourite Christmas drink.' Fay smiled at me and I realised I was being teased.

'I wouldn't go so far as to say a new Christmas drink. I could never replace Baileys, but Mandarin brandy is . . .'

'Don't tell me,' Fay said, holding up her hand, 'it's lovely.'

'Hey, I didn't have to tell you about my day you know, you insisted!' I waggled a finger at her.

When I finally met up with Fay I'd been dying to know

about her auditions but she'd been more interested in finding out about Jamie and kept steering the conversation back in his direction. The most I'd managed out of her was a nonchalant shrug and a 'Hmm, I'm not holding my breath.'

'Now, c'mon Fay, you have to tell me more about how it all went today,' I tried again. 'Did you at least enjoy it?'

'Oh yeah, it was brilliant fun. It's just, oh you know how it's always been with me.' She looked out of the window and watched the fields flash past the window. 'It's always "we like you but you're too old", or "too young", or "you're not blonde enough" or "you don't have the right kind of image". I've had some brilliant auditions that I thought had gone really well but they rarely amount to anything.' Her face brightened and she looked back at me. 'I did have a nice chat with a woman called Sylvia over a cuppa though; she was nice. She was asking me what had drawn me into acting in the first place, so I told her about seeing *The African Queen* with my mum years ago, and how I'd always kind of idolised Katharine Hepburn ever since. We got chatting about all the old films we liked and we had a lot in common; she took down my number, so I guess I made a friend at least. Oh, and I got a third audition, one I hadn't been expecting to do. It's for a part in a low-budget movie some student's making; we wouldn't get paid or anything, but it sounded kind of cool. He was quite positive, but I'm not getting my hopes up about anything yet; we'll just see how it goes.'

Fay looked back out of the window and I nodded to myself, settling into a comfortable silence. As the road started descending into Bath and the trees thinned out I looked across to the view of the city, with its pale and elegant buildings lit by the late afternoon sun and I felt happy. Not exactly a tap dancing on the bonnet of my car kind of happy, but instead a more comfortable, more hopeful kind of happy. As though I was acknowledging that I hadn't been truly satisfied for a long time, but now that stage in my life was over, and creeping in its place was a mild, tantalising excitement about what could happen to me now.

Fay was the first to break the silence by laughing to herself.

I glanced over at her. 'What's so funny?'

'It's just, I can't believe you could ever think that Boober was the one Miranda meant. I mean, you and Boober . . .' She laughed harder and I started giggling with her.

'I know, I know, I realise it was crazy now. But it was a spur of the moment thing I suppose. I saw someone from school when I was least expecting to, and her words just popped into my head.'

'It's weird though, isn't it? How thinking you'd seen someone from school actually led you straight into someone from school.'

'I know.' I shook my head.

'If you'd never found that box and read what Miranda had put, you wouldn't have chased after Boober, would you?'

'No, I don't think I would.'

'And that's what kind of spooks me out, because we don't even know Miranda and it almost feels like she's affecting our lives. Does that sound crazy?'

'Err, yes,' I said, 'it does, but I know what you mean. In fact put me in the crazy bracket too, but I can't help but feel like I was meant to meet Jamie today. I keep thinking about what you said, you know, about how everything happens for a reason, and I really want to believe that's true.' I sighed and tapped my fingers on the steering wheel, suddenly feeling very aware of the phone number Jamie had given me sitting conspicuously in my jacket pocket.

I drifted in and out of sleep, woken first by the church bells, and again an hour later by the clattering sounds of someone making breakfast. Tim was around this weekend so I assumed it was him, as Fay rarely bothered with breakfast, and I squeezed my eyes closed against the sounds, choosing instead to wallow in thoughts and daydreams. The sun was shining through the fabric of my calico curtains, warming up the bed nicely and making me feel cocooned inside. I hadn't heard any sounds from Fay's room and I wondered if she was doing the same thing as me, letting the day drift blissfully by.

It was eleven o'clock before I was awake enough to sit up properly and contemplate getting up. I swung my legs out of the bed and looked around the room blinking. For some reason I was becoming increasingly aware of Adam's things dotted around the room. There was a mug he'd bought me from a craft shop in town last Christmas; it had an angel with big curly hair handpainted on the side that he said reminded him of me. There was a leaflet on the dressing table advertising an art deco fair he wanted to go to, and the pizza delivery menu next to it was covered in his doodles. And then there was his T-shirt. A plain, pale grey that he'd worn in bed once when he was cold and which was now hanging on the back of my chair. I'd found it last week, crumpled on the floor and spent the following few days sniffing the smell out of it. I couldn't face doing that anymore; I didn't even really want to look at it. Instead of blending in, the way they used to, they jarred, reminding me of our failed relationship.

I reached across to the CD player by the bed, picked the most cheerful album I could find and put it on, then I got a box out from under the bed and began to collect Adam's things together.

Halfway through 'Shake Your Groove Thing' I remembered that the Disco Fever album also belonged to Adam, so I begrudgingly stopped the music and added that to my collection too. The box was nearly full of bits and pieces now, and it hurt more than I'd imagined it would to look at them all. I didn't relish the thought of returning them, but I didn't want them around reminding me of Adam either. I reached across to open the drawer of my bedside table and took out my engagement ring, still sitting in its little velvet box. I faltered for a second, holding it in my hand, tempted to look at it one last time, then I shook my head and rested it on top of Adam's CD. I slid the whole collection under my bed then I reached back into the bedside drawer and took out the papers I'd found. The ones with the predictions we'd written on. I slumped down on the floor, the papers in my hand, and reread Miranda's words, wanting to remind myself that this could still be the best thing for me.

Half an hour later I got dressed and ventured out to find Fay. Her room was empty so I carried on downstairs to see if she was in the kitchen. Tim was standing by the sink, washing up a saucepan.

'Morning,' he said as I walked in. He looked over his shoulder, smiling, and I smiled back, looking around the room for signs of Fay. There was a pile of library books on the kitchen table and I cocked my head to read the spines; *What Are The Chances? real life stories of unexplained coincidence; Hollywood Legends: silver screen icons from a golden age*, and *The Beginner's Guide To Psychics: for when life starts getting predictable*!

Tim must have seen my surprise and said quickly, 'They're Fay's. If you hadn't already guessed. She just got back from the library.'

Fay walked in then and looked guilty when she saw what I'd seen. 'I just thought they might be interesting,' she said. She had her hands hidden unnaturally behind her back.

'Fay, what are you hiding?' I ducked behind her and saw a piece of paper in her hands. 'What's that?'

She handed it over with a please-don't-be-mad expression. 'I photocopied the phone book at the library. The Gloucestershire phone book.'

I looked at the list of names on the paper and saw straight away what she'd done: she'd copied the page of Pattersons. 'But there's loads! I'd never know the address now, and they won't still be living in the same place after all these years, surely?'

She shrugged. 'My parents do, and so do yours.'

'Well, yes, but ...' I stared at the names. 'There must be hundreds here.'

'Eighty two. I counted,' she said. 'But you're forgetting something: we know the dad's first name is Ken. There's only two Ken Pattersons and three K Pattersons. Unless it's under her mum's name, which we don't know, it's going to be a piece of cake.'

'OK, that's the last one. I give up,' I said, putting the phone down and stretching back against the cushions of the sofa.

'Oh, that's so annoying. I really thought that'd work,' Fay said with dismay. She took the list of Pattersons from me and crumpled it into a ball, throwing it against the wall. Dexter shot off the sofa in stealth-like pursuit. 'We've hit a brick wall, haven't we?'

'There must be another way,' I said. 'Perhaps I should look at the stuff in my old room again. There might be one of her old letters still knocking around. Or what if we spelt it wrong? There must be other ways of spelling Patterson.' It was as though with every lack of success today I'd made myself more determined to find Miranda. Now it felt like a challenge. 'What about the Internet?'

'I googled her name when I was at the library; nothing fits with her, and I even looked her up on Friends Reunited and there was nothing.'

'There must be something we've not thought of.'

'Oh I don't think I can do any more today,' Fay groaned. 'My brain feels like it's been populated with the Pattersons of Gloucestershire all day; now all it wants to do is throw them out and have a bit of a clear up. Can't we watch a film instead? Please, please, pleeease?'

'Yeah, you're right,' I said and leaned my head against the arm rest, closing my eyes. Now there was only one more person I wanted to ring. I just didn't dare do it yet.


'I'm sorry, Mrs Hewins, but I'm not mistaken, Freddie definitely has head lice. I just saw one a minute ago, trying to nest in his eyebrow. Yes, well I think under the circumstances you should collect him early,' Jill said, trapping the phone with her chin as she simultaneously packed away a jigsaw and rubbed her temples. I bit my lip to stop from laughing and left her to it, joining Helen to help group the children into a circle. Usually we had an extra pair of hands, as the parents worked out a rota for whoever was available to take a turn helping for one day in every term. Today though the mum in question hadn't

135

turned up because her daughter was ill, and when we finally realised what had happened there was no one around to ask to volunteer. As a result it had been a more hectic morning than normal.

'OK children, gather round, we're going to sing some songs,' I said, clapping my hands together. As the children quietened down I heard the doorbell ring.

'I'll go,' Helen sing-songed and bounded off to the lobby. I laughed. Helen had been like an excitable child since the parents do last week, when it transpired that Stewart, the single dad, had fancied her all along, and not me, as she had thought. They'd been seeing each other ever since.

I shook my head at the irony of it only being a week since Helen had been envying my love life and lamenting about being single, and walked across the room to fetch the last remaining children. They were trying on outfits in the dressing-up corner with Alice, one of our assistants. 'Olivia, Erin, come and be with us,' I said, stooping down to take their hands. When I stood up Helen came back in and signalled me over.

'There's a guy here for you and it's not Adam,' she said. 'He says he's a friend and he can come back when you've finished if you like.'

My eyes shot across to the lobby but I couldn't see the door. 'Who is it?' I whispered.

'Never seen him before. Cute though,' she said with a sly grin.

My knees went weak when I saw Jamie's face appear at the doorway. He looked at me then smiled charmingly at Jill, who went across to have a word with him.

'Oh my God, what's he doing here?' I said through clenched teeth. I felt my cheeks grow fiery hot. 'He's the one I told you about, the one I bumped into on Saturday.'

'Oh, you mean when you hurt your arm?' Helen looked back at Jamie, which only embarrassed me further as it became obvious we were talking about him.

Jill came over then, beaming, with Jamie following behind.

'You didn't tell me you knew Jamie,' she said.

I stared at her flustered, wanting to say '*neither did you!*'

'I'm sorry to disturb,' Jamie said. 'They closed the school today because of a burst water main so I thought I'd call in and see if you were OK. I'll come back later though, when you're not so busy.' He gestured to the children who were now all sat in a circle on the carpet, staring at us with big moon faces.

'Why don't you stay and help out?' Jill said. 'We're a helper short and could use an extra pair of hands.'

'Oh, I'm sure Jamie's got lots of . . .' I started off but Jamie grinned and butted in. 'I'd love to help. I'm free all day now.'

He started taking his jacket off and Jill whispered to me, 'Helen, Alice and I will do the songs. You two can get the art things ready.' She joined the circle then, before I could argue and I flushed with shame, knowing full well that Jill said that on purpose to give us a moment alone. I wished I hadn't told her about Adam and I splitting last week after all: she had a meddling glint in her eye.

I took Jamie over to the far end of the room where the drawers of art materials were, pulled out some of the chairs and sat down at a little table. Jamie sat opposite.

'I'm sorry if I've made you uncomfortable,' he said, looking at me as though testing my mood.

'It's fine, honestly, it's good to see you.' I caught his eye and held it for a moment and he visibly relaxed. 'I'm just surprised, that's all. I wasn't expecting to see you here.'

'Well, it was a whim I suppose. I was driving home with not much more to do other than looking over some course work, then I thought of you, and I was worried about you after your accident. I wanted to make sure you were OK. I tried to call you yesterday actually but your phone was permanently engaged.'

'Oh, really? That must have been my housemate,' I said sheepishly, remembering how long I'd spent ringing strangers called Patterson yesterday. 'And I'm fine.' I showed him my arm which had now scabbed over and then wished I hadn't when he winced.

'I know, attractive huh?' I said, angling myself so he couldn't see it anymore.

'Does it hurt?'

'Oh no, it's fine. I learned this morning that I can't use my salt scrub until it's gone though; that certainly woke me up, but no, it'll be fine.'

He looked at me sympathetically and I changed the subject. 'So, how do you know Jill, anyway?'

'Oh I met her a few years ago. She came to the school to do a talk on working with children and she got the kids so interested she comes back every year now. Jill's great.'

I nodded, remembering that I had known Jill did that. I watched him as he talked some more and then realised, when he faltered, that I had been looking at him with a smile on my face. 'What?' he said, touching his forehead. 'Have I got a sequin on my face or something?'

'I'm sorry,' I said with a laugh, 'you just look so funny on these tiny chairs, it must be weird for you. A bit different from the art classes you take.'

'Oh no, it's great! I love kids this age. It's where it

all starts, isn't it?' He looked over to the children who were singing 'The Wheels on the Bus' and stumbling over the words. 'They're far cuter than my lot. All kids love art at this age, don't they? There's none of this "oh I can't, sir, I'm not good enough"; they just get stuck in. I love that.'

I passed him a pile of coloured paper. 'That's good. You'll enjoy cutting out fish templates then. We're making under-the-sea collages after break.'

The kids loved Jamie, but I wasn't surprised. Watching him over the course of the day took me right back to our classes at school. He still had that same uninhibited enthusiasm, and mucked in with them all, making some beautiful, elaborate fishes for the children to admire that got them all desperate to have a go. He'd also read them all a story in the afternoon as Jill looked on, beaming with pride as though Jamie was her only son. He sorted out a few minor altercations over toys and comforted Megan, who I couldn't help but suspect was pretending to be upset so she could sit on his lap. She was so happy after that she giggled and burped simultaneously until she got the hiccups. All the time I kept checking he was OK, giving him opportunities to say it was time he should go, but he just insisted he was fine.

'I cannot thank you enough,' Jill said as we were putting on our jackets at the end of the day.

'Thank you for having me, Jill, it was a lovely change and very nice to catch up with you again,' he said, causing her to giggle like a schoolgirl and fiddle furiously with the buttons of her blouse.

'See you tomorrow,' I called out, stepping through the doors and out into the fresh air.

'Peace at last, hey?' Jamie said, putting his hands in his

jacket pocket. 'I'm knackered! How do you manage doing that every day?'

'You get used to it. And it can't be stressful like teaching.'

'Ooh, I'm not sure about that.' He looked at me sideways. 'Have you ever thought of being a teacher or is it the really young ones you like?'

'You know, I often thought about being a teacher. I love what I'm doing now but I see these kids go off every year and I wonder how they'll get on with school and I want to see them through that next step.'

'Why don't you be a primary teacher then? I bet you'd be great at that.'

'Oh, I don't know. I feel like I've left it too late. For a long time I've tried not to plan the future too much and now I think it's probably too late to change. I'd have to do a BEd and that's another four years of my life. I'm not sure I could do it.'

'Four years isn't that long for something you really want. You're still young.'

'I know.' I sighed. 'Maybe I will. Or maybe I might end up running my own pre-school, a little one in the countryside, near a stream where we can go hunting for mini-beasts. I don't know, who knows what'll become of me,' I said, forcing a jovial voice and looking around me, half expecting to see a number 32 bus with a THOSE WHO CAN, TEACH poster on it. That was how weird my life was getting at the moment. Instead we approached the corner of Landsdown Road and I slowed down, gazing up the hill. The artisan courtyard where Adam worked was just a ten-minute walk up the road from here. I'd gone to see him many times after work to share a cup of tea if he had a quiet moment. It felt weird not doing it anymore.

We turned around the corner and started down the slope

past a row of shops. A customer bell pinged as someone came out of the florists and when I looked over my shoulder I saw Adam, standing in the open doorway, holding a gorgeous display of red and pink roses wrapped in red cellophane. He was looking from me to Jamie, his expression unreadable, then with a half nod in my direction, he turned away and walked quickly up the hill.

# Chapter Fifteen

I stood on the step with my back to the front door, talking to Jamie. Or should I say Jamie was talking to me. I was trying to avoid speaking, aware that my voice had cranked up an octave as I reverted to my teenage self. Instead I nodded and giggled nervously at what he said, looked at him through my eyelashes and agonised about inviting him in for a cup of coffee. It wasn't that I didn't want to; it seemed only fair after he'd helped out so heroically at Dizzy Heights today, but it'd been a long day, and although I tried to give him one hundred per cent, I felt drained. It didn't help that my mind was also still replaying the memory of Adam, frozen in the doorway with a 'romantic' bunch of flowers.

Jamie must have sensed that as I wasn't letting him in straight away, I must want some time alone, and eventually looked at his watch, saying, 'Crikey, I only meant to check in on you and I've been here all day. I ought to get on before I totally outstay my welcome.'

'No, honestly, it's fine,' I said quickly but he held up his hands. 'I really should go. You must be tired, and I should get back and call the head, find out what's happening with the school tomorrow.' He looked at me seriously.

'It was great to see you though, and I should thank you. I had a good day.'

'Really?' I looked at him sceptically.

'Yes, really. It was a tonic. I'd forgotten how crazy kids that age can be. And I'm sure the constant ringing in my ear will go with time,' he joked. 'And of course it's been great catching up with you. Perhaps we could do it again sometime? A drink at the weekend maybe?'

'I'd like that,' I said, smiling shyly.

'OK, great, I'll call you soon. We can arrange something then.'

There was an awkward moment then, as we had to quickly assess how to leave things. My heart quickened as he leaned in for a kiss and I automatically turned my face at the crucial moment, accepting a kiss on the cheek instead. He smelt different to Adam, I noted. Spicier.

'Have a good week then, and I'll speak to you soon,' he said, starting to back away down the path.

'You too.' I smiled and waited for him to turn around, then practically fell through the front door with relief.

When Fay got home from work I told her all about my day with Jamie, the possible date next weekend and seeing Adam with the flowers, before she had even managed to take her coat off. She stood in the hallway, gaping at me until she eventually held her hand up to her forehead and said, 'Information overload, can't take it all in.'

'Fay, please, what am I going to do?' I said, pacing the floor.

'About what?'

'Well, who do you think the flowers were for?'

'You probably,' she said, shrugging her coat off and hanging it on the bottom of the banister.

'No. I don't think so. I saw him first, and he wasn't

going in the direction of our house, he was going back up the hill.'

Fay thought about that for a minute then said, 'Who do you want them to be for?'

'What does that mean?'

She ignored me and cocked her head to one side. 'Are you going to go for a drink with Jamie?'

'Yes. No. I don't know. Probably.'

'Do you fancy him?'

'I . . . I . . . I . . . Stop looking at me!' I gathered up the post that Tim had propped up on the hall table this morning and took it through to the kitchen, rummaging through it twice before I managed to read the names on the envelopes. 'One for you,' I said, holding it out for Fay. Among the bills and bank statements for me was a postcard from Richard and Jules, who were now in Singapore. They'd addressed it to 'Gem and Adam', making my heart sink. I dropped it on the table.

'Oh my God!' Fay cried, making me jump. She was gripping the letter with both hands, her eyes glued to it.

'It's from that woman. The one I told you about from the BBC auditions, the one I had lunch with. She's a producer! She never said when I was talking to her, but she's a bloody producer! She's asking me over to BBC Bristol for a screen-test next week!'

I gasped. 'Fay, that's amazing, well done! What's it for? Does it say?'

'No.' She looked up from the letter, baffled. 'I've no idea.'

'Oh, but that's so exciting, isn't it? It's something. And just think, this could be it, your big break.'

She grinned at me and I laughed at her as she started jumping manically up and down.

\*

I spent most of Tuesday with my mind flitting sporadically between Adam and Jamie. Thoughts of Adam were messy and complicated, some too painful to entertain. I'd stopped torturing myself with images of Marcia and questions that always seemed to start with 'Why?'. Instead I kept remembering him as he was in the florist's doorway. It was weird; it'd only been a little over a week, but already he looked different. I couldn't put my finger on what was different; it was everything and nothing. Like looking at someone else's reflection in a mirror. You still see the person you always knew, but your perspective has shifted and it takes you by surprise. He'd also been wearing a red T-shirt I hadn't recognised and I found myself feeling ridiculously hurt whenever I thought about it. He had blatantly been shopping, buying things that he looked good in, and I didn't like that at all.

Thoughts of Jamie were a welcome relief by comparison. They were uncomplicated and not marred with bad memories. Every time I had been with Jamie it'd been good. Well, on the two occasions this decade. Even though he hadn't called to arrange our drink at the weekend yet, I didn't doubt that he would, and I liked that. It was flattering, and it made me comfortable.

When it was time for the children to go home, Annette, one of the oldest girls in the group, came to me with a painting. 'I did this for you,' she said, holding it up so that the wet paint began to dribble down the paper and pool on her sticky fingers.

'That's lovely, Annette, is this your mummy?' I said, bending down to look at the two orange faces, sporting spindly arms and legs growing out of their chins.

'No, it's you, getting married,' she said.

'Oh, yes, I can see that now,' I said. 'And who's this here?' I pointed at the other face and wondered if she

145

would say Adam or Jamie. She had met both, but she hadn't seen Adam for a while. *If she says Adam*, I thought, *it's a sign*. I held my breath whilst she pondered the question, tapping her chin.

'It's Dylan, my brother,' she shrugged, turning away and skipping off to find her shoes.

'Of course it is,' I said, laughing at my own foolishness. I looked back at the picture, noticing for the first time that she'd drawn hearts above our heads. All those old feelings about Adam started to return, and slowly it dawned on me that the conflicting emotions I'd felt since I met Jamie wouldn't go away until I finally dealt with Adam. I needed closure before I could start imagining a future again, and if I did it before Jamie called about our date, perhaps it'd help get rid of the uneasy sensation I felt about the whole thing. I'd go around tonight, I decided, hanging Annette's picture up to dry. I'd take Adam's things back and put a full stop on this whole episode once and for all.

I took Adam's box out of the car and walked down the narrow path to his house, my hands shaking. I was pretty sure he'd be in because I'd seen his bike in the passageway when I'd driven past. I'd wanted to check for signs of visitors after torturing myself with the possibility that Marcia might be with him, and he'd come to the door half dressed, with lipstick on his face and the sounds of 'Oh, *Ad-am*' drifting down from the bedroom.

Thinking about that possibility again made me falter and I stopped still on the path, not wanting to go further, yet unable to turn away. Before I could act the door opened and Adam appeared in the doorway. He had his denim jacket half on and was jangling his keys in one hand. He was about to pull the door shut behind him when he saw me and froze, his face a picture of surprise. 'Gemma!'

I felt a tug in my stomach as I had to stop myself from automatically going to hug him. 'Hey,' I said, walking over to join him at the door. We sized each other up for a moment and I sensed he was glad to see me, but wary.

'Can we talk?' I said.

'Of course, come in.' He swung the door open behind him and led the way, clearing a path through the clutter in the hall and out into the narrow kitchen.

I was amazed to see it was a mess. Adam was usually surprisingly organised for a man who had so much stuff in his house, but I had never seen it like this before. The washing-up was piled high in the sink, the curtains were half drawn, and there were all kinds of assorted items vying for surface space, from files and notebooks to boxes of wrought-iron door handles and hinges and piles of reclaimed fireplace tiles waiting to be cleaned up.

'Work's been crazy,' Adam said, by way of explanation. 'I've hardly been here lately.'

'It's good that you're busy,' I said, sliding my own box on to the breakfast bar and knocking over a pile of bank statements in the process. 'Oh God, sorry.' I bent down to pick them up at the same time as Adam did.

Crouched down underneath the table I caught his eye and felt my awkwardness vanish. 'Look Adam,' I started, but he butted in.

'I'm glad you came. I wanted to come and see you so many times but, oh, I don't know,' he shook his head and tutted. 'I suppose I was being cowardly. You've been avoiding my calls and I didn't want to see you when you were angry and give you the opportunity to say things you couldn't take back. I wanted to give you some time, talk to you properly.'

I looked down the papers and concentrated on gathering them neatly together.

'Look Gemma, you know nothing happened with Marcia, don't you? Not in the way you think.'

'I don't know what to think.'

'At the stag do she was all over me, and Grant. I thought it was just the drink. She came back to mine after the wedding because the hotel had double-booked. She slept on the sofa. I don't know what you've heard but that's all there was to it, I swear to you.'

'So what about the photo of you with your hand under Marcia's clothes then?' I said, unable to keep the resentment out of my voice.

Adam winced. 'I can see how that must have seemed, but it wasn't what you think. She'd taken my wallet and dropped it down her top.'

'Right,' I said sarcastically.

'It's true, she'd been doing little things like that all night, acting crazy. It was annoying us all.'

'So when she openly fancied you and was flirting with you, it didn't occur to you that letting her sleep at yours was a bad idea?' I stood up and went to the kitchen window, not looking at him.

'Of course it was a bad idea, I realise that now.' He stood up too.

'And what about the roses?' I asked, fixing my eyes on the courtyard outside. 'Were they for Marcia?'

'Gem, they were for you. I was coming round to see you but I saw you through the door with that guy and I backed off. I wanted to see you alone. Look, why can't you trust me? I trust you. Notice I haven't asked you who that guy was you were with.' There was a hint of sarcasm in his voice and I sensed he was beginning to get angry.

I turned to face him. 'If you're so happy with me then why are you so afraid of commitment? How come we're not living together? How come we never talk about the future?'

'I asked you to marry me,' he said, his stance defensive.

'But it doesn't feel right, does it? You've never been comfortable with it.'

'I'm comfortable with you.'

'But not with commitment, which is what I don't understand, because if you'd really felt it was right, if there was that something special, you'd just know. You wouldn't need to force yourself into anything, you'd do it naturally, impulsively.'

Adam tensed up. 'It's not always as simple as you'd like it to be,' he said.

I sighed. 'Well it should be. Either I'm right for you or I'm not.'

He was about to speak when the box on the table caught his eye. He saw what was inside and his jaw clenched. 'I see. So you really have decided it's over. You're not even giving me a chance?'

'I feel like we've had our chance,' I said sadly, 'and we blew it.'

'Yikes,' Fay said after I told her what had happened. We were sitting in Barneys, drinking wine from glasses the size of cereal bowls. Fay had taken one look at my face as I'd walked into the house and grabbed her jacket from the banister, announcing that a medicinal drink was called for.

'Well, at least we both know where we stand now. It's officially over and we can both move on.'

'I know. It's just such a shame things didn't work out for you,' Fay said.

'Don't let me dwell on it,' I said, knocking back half my wine in one gulp, 'I'll end up all morose again.'

'Of course.' She gave me a cheering smile. 'And anyway, now your path is free for Mr Right.'

As she said that my mobile began to ring. I picked it out of my handbag and answered it. 'Jamie, hi,' I said, my jaw dropping at his timing.

'How many signs can a girl get?' Fay said under her breath and I kicked at her with my foot.

'No, no, it's just Fay, my housemate. She's chatting up the staff,' I said to Jamie, and teasingly gestured for Fay to look over to where Barney was standing, polishing a glass with a cloth behind the bar. He winked at Fay and she turned back quickly, pretending not to have seen. 'On Saturday? No, no, I've got nothing on. Dinner would be lovely.' I glanced at Fay and she raised her eyebrows at me.

# Chapter Sixteen

Early on Thursday morning I was picking my parents up
from the airport. They'd been in Australia for a month and I
wondered if they'd spot a change in me. A lot had happened
since they'd been away. I felt like I'd been driving down the
same road for four years without even realising I'd got
windscreen wipers. Now I'd found them I realised that
everything looked different and I wasn't sure I liked the
view. Gone was the old me, ticking along nicely without
questioning what I was doing or why I was doing it and in
her place was a new me, more aware and in control of my
life yet more terrified and confused about the future than I'd
ever been. I hadn't told my parents about splitting up with
Adam. I'd wanted to wait until I saw them, and what with
Fay talking about signs and fate, and Nikki berating me for
becoming a 'woman who thinks too much', I was looking
forward to some unconditional, parental support from them.

Driving back down the M4 from Heathrow the opportunity finally came up. When Dad was dozing on the back
seat and Mum had finally exhausted herself talking about
their adventures in Australia and filling me in about what
John had been up to, she turned to me and said, 'Anyway,
how are things with you? How's Adam?'

'Actually I've been meaning to talk to you about that.'
I bit my lip and Mum nodded.

'It's OK darling, I know. Anthea told me.'

'Who's Anthea?' I looked at her, surprised.

'Oh, you know Anthea, from the bridge club? She works in the planning office, husband called Maurice. The one Dad calls a Woolly Woofter because he had his high-lights done. Anyway, she's good friends with Julianne's mum. She saw you with a ring at Julianne's wedding but never got round to asking you about it. She called whilst we were away to pass on her congrats. Anyway, we think it's wonderful news, we're so pleased for you. But why all the secrecy? You know how much we love Adam.'

I groaned and resisted the urge to bash my head repeatedly on the car horn. 'Actually Mum, we've split up. We were engaged for a short while but it kind of went wrong. It just didn't seem to be working, going anywhere. Maybe we never told anyone because deep down we both knew it wouldn't work.'

'Poppycock', Mum said and gave me the same no nonsense stare she used when I was twelve and trying to convince her I was too ill to go to school.

'It's true!'

'The trouble with young people these days is they give up too easily. One little hiccup and it's back out to some grotty nightclub for a white wine spritzer and another go.'

'Mum, it's really not like that.'

'Just look at me and your father,' she continued. 'He's not perfect by any means, but we just get on with it. You have to. It's part of having an adult relationship, accepting someone's faults and living with them.'

I wanted to tell her she had a funny way of showing acceptance when she spent her entire married life trying to nag him into submission.

Dad did a kind of double snore in the back then said, 'Has Adam finished French polishing our sideboard yet?'

'Oh go back to sleep, Andrew,' Mum snapped.

'Look,' I said. 'You can't seriously think that I should just marry the first man that asks me. I mean look how many people get divorced these days. Surely everything needs to be perfect to agree to something like that.'

'Darling, that'd be true if someone off the street asked you, but you've been with Adam a long time, and believe me, he's a nice man. A really nice man. If you go out there and find yourself another nice one, somewhere down the road you'll find he's not so perfect either. As my Antipodean friends would say, "Same shit, different view".'

'Mum!' I looked at her, gobsmacked, as she smiled knowledgeably at me. Mum never usually swore: she thought a tosser was a salad chef and still said 'jam and sugar it!' whenever she was stressed.

'Honestly Gemma,' she continued. 'I just don't want you to make a rash decision and regret it further down the line. Why don't you bring him over at the weekend for Sunday lunch? Dad'll talk some sense into him.'

I tutted, saying nothing, then switched on the radio and turned the heat up, hoping that might send her off to sleep.


By Saturday I was beginning to get paranoid that Mum would end up marching over to Adam's workshop and bundling him into the back of Dad's Volvo, holding him as a captive audience as Dad drove around the Avon Valley and Mum lectured him on the sanctity of a decent relationship. She wouldn't accept that we had split up and her attitude was making me feel guilty about my date with Jamie. I hadn't dared tell her about that. Instead I tried to block out what Mum said by convincing myself I was doing the right thing. I had often sat in my bedroom, listening to my parents and promising myself that I wouldn't end up like them, married out of a sense of duty rather than for any romantic reasons, with my husband spending half his life locked in a different room because we shared no common ground. I wanted the kind of love I'd seen in adverts: the waking up smiling, the meaningful looks over a cup of coffee, the laughing together as you found new and original ways to feed each other chocolate. But above all, I wanted to feel that it was special; that something magical had happened. Something magical had happened when I bumped into Jamie that day. It was as though, for some reason, fate had taken me to him. Now I just had to find out why.

Late that afternoon I sat on the floor of my bedroom whilst Nikki did the impossible and straightened my hair with her irons and Fay lay on my bed, a phone clamped under her chin as she went through every variation on the spelling of Patterson she could think of.

She left a message on an answering machine then returned the phone to its cradle. 'OK, I've done all I can. Now I'm spent,' she said dramatically and flopped backwards with her arms splayed out.

'Why don't you get the Yellow Pages out and look under institutions, you might get further that way,' Nikki said and then looked up to see our horrified faces. 'What? She was clearly as mad as a badger; what do you expect?'

'You're awful,' Fay said, swinging her legs off the bed and sitting down with us.

'Yeah well, so are your socks,' Nikki rebuked, pointing her straighteners at Fay's rainbow-coloured knee-highs.

'Hey! Don't get personal; you know I'm having a difficult day.' She looked at us mournfully and we let out a harmonious 'Ahh'. Dexter hadn't been back all night and we had combed the streets for him in the morning without success.

'Perhaps I should cancel tonight. We could go out for another look, knock on some more doors.'

'No, you can't do that. I'd feel awful, and anyway, he's done it before. It's probably just a male cat thing.'

'He'll be sowing his wild oats like you should be,' Nikki said to me. 'We can all have a scout around tomorrow if it makes you feel better. But I won't have you missing a date with the teacher half the girls in our school dreamed about for four years. I mean, if you're lucky enough to get yourself a date like that, you should at least have the courtesy to see it through. I'd kill for a date like that tonight.'

'Me too,' said Fay, resting her hands on her chin. 'I haven't had a date since forever.'

'Now I feel even worse!' I cried, standing up and clutching my stomach.

'Oh come on, relax! We're only joking,' Nikki said. She fetched some hairspray and dosed me with it, making me cough. 'We just want you to make the most of it and have some fun.'

I touched my hair and looked at my reflection in the mirror. It wasn't very often I got to see my hair looking tamed and sleek.

'Does it make my head look small?' I asked Fay and Nikki, inspecting myself from every angle.

Nikki burst out laughing. 'I've never heard that one before.'

Today was officially the first day of summer and the temperature had gone up a notch to mark the occasion. I couldn't believe there was still over a month to go before we broke up for the summer holidays. I was wearing a thin strappy vest top in order to stay cool; the heat of the day had made my cheeks so pink it wiped out the need for blusher and I was starting to worry that I'd get a heat rash on my chest, as I was too pale to go a nice golden colour.

I fiddled nervously with the thin spaghetti straps of my top. 'Perhaps I should wear something else,' I said. 'Something less, I don't know, less smart.'

'Don't you dare!' both Fay and Nikki cried.

'Stop finding things to stress about. You look perfect, it's not like you're really dressed up or anything. You're just used to your casual boil-wash work clothes, that's all,' Nikki teased. 'You look elegant yet understated. Just right for a first date.'

I took a deep breath and fetched my bag, ready to go. I couldn't believe how nervous I was. I'd spent so long with Adam I'd forgotten what it felt like to get ready for a date with someone I hardly knew. I'd forgotten about the butterflies and the anticipation. About being with someone you weren't completely relaxed with. I was beginning to wonder what I'd got myself into.

I arrived at Browns ten minutes early, probably breaking all kinds of dating rules I wasn't aware of. It was half empty inside and the bar was quiet so I got myself a glass of mineral water and found a table that was nicely secluded behind a leafy plant. I sat down and was about to start reading the menu when Jamie stepped in from outside. He saw me and smiled, striding across the room to join me and I realised I had a huge grin on my face.

'Hey,' he said, kissing me on the cheek and taking the chair next to mine. 'It's good to see you. You look great!' The warmth in his voice was evident and I relaxed a little, remembering how easy it was to chat with Jamie. There were never any awkward moments with him.

'Thank you, so do you.' I had no idea whether that was the right thing to say and blushed at the flirtatious way I'd said it.

Jamie laughed, and as he did I noticed he had faint laughter lines around his eyes, reminding me that despite the young way he dressed and spoke, he was still older than me. They made him more attractive though, an indication of his happy, easy-going nature.

A bored-looking waitress approached us and Jamie turned to me. 'Do you want to share a bottle of wine and get some food in a bit?'

Glad I wasn't going to be the only one drinking and still too jittery to think about food yet, I gave an enthusiastic nod and let Jamie order the wine. As he was talking to the waitress I became aware that a group of men had entered the restaurant and I looked around quickly, worried that one of them might be Adam. Of course none of them were and I turned back, cross with myself for letting it bother me. Surely it wouldn't matter anyway? I was a free agent and it was about time I had some fun. I made myself sit back into the leather chair and relax. Tonight, I decided, I wasn't going to think about anything other than making the most of my time with Jamie.

A bottle and a half of wine later and the waitress was getting frustrated. Every time she thought we'd finished our meals one of us would pick up a fork again and she'd have to shrink back towards the other tables. We were taking our time, having a mouthful of food every now and then to punctuate our conversation, which was still going strong, although beginning to make less sense and have more foolish laughter in it.

I started to think I should call it a night when I tried to focus on the wine label and found that the words wouldn't stay still long enough to be read. By that time there were only a couple of other tables still occupied and the restaurant seemed to be winding down.

'Do you fancy some fresh air?' Jamie asked, as though sensing my thoughts. 'I can walk you back if you like? Then I can catch a taxi from St James Square.'

'OK, I'd like that,' I said. 'I can't promise I'll walk in a straight line, but I'll give it my best shot.'

We took the scenic route home, past Pulteney Bridge, stopping to lean over and watch the water cascading over the weir, the reflection of the dim lights giving the surface an orange shimmer, then past the abbey, walking in its shadows in the alleyway below. We ambled along, reminiscing about school life and by the time we walked out into Abbey Square I was helpless with laughter as Jamie reminded me of the time we'd had a sit-in in the drama room.

'I'd forgotten all about that,' I said. 'And I can't for the life of me remember why we did it.'

'I think you were protesting about the teachers' strike earlier in the week; you all decided if we could have a strike there was no reason why you couldn't either,' Jamie said. 'What you didn't know is that just before you'd all decided to take over the drama room, me and Ian Naylor, the pottery teacher, had gone down into the props cupboard for a quick cigarette. You lot sat on the trapdoor and we couldn't get out.'

I gasped. 'No way! What did you do?'

'We had to crawl through that tiny little window, the one the size of a cereal box, and climb down the drainpipe. I broke my glasses and when my afternoon class realised I was half blind without them a couple of the lads took advantage, drew a forest that, let's just say, looked very phallic with the benefit of good vision, and I was so

158

clueless I told them it was brilliant and staple-gunned it to the board.'

'Oh yes! I remember someone telling me about that.'

Jamie cringed. 'I don't think there was anyone in the school who hadn't heard about it, and after my tutor group turned up in the morning and saw the pictures they took the piss for two years.'

'Oh, that's awful.' I bit my lip, trying to keep a straight face. 'And all because we went on strike.'

'I know, I blame you entirely.' He smiled wickedly. 'In fact I'm sure it's not too late for me to give you a detention if you want to come to my class after school.'

'Oh, how weird would *that* be? Going back there with all those memories . . .'

We fell silent and I thought about what Jamie had just said, or rather the way he'd said it. It was the first time I'd been aware that he was flirting with me all night. Or was it flirting? It'd been so long since I'd had to think about it that I didn't trust my ability to read the signs anymore.

'I'm so glad I bumped into you in Bristol,' Jamie said eventually, giving me a sidelong look. 'I don't mean knocking you over and you getting hurt, obviously, but I am glad we met up again, and I got the chance to get to know you better.'

'Me too,' I said shyly. 'It's been good. Weird, but good.'

'Weird? Why?'

'Well, because you were my teacher, I suppose. Usually when I see my old teachers they're wandering around the town looking like my dad: all sensible trousers and crazy hair, and I revert back to the old "them and us" way of thinking, you know? I call them by their last name and stand up straight, and they ask what I'm doing these days, as though making sure I've become a responsible adult. They still, even years on, feel like my teachers. And I don't really get that with you. I have to keep reminding myself that you were one of them, and not one of us.'

Jamie looked down at the path and frowned. 'Yeah, I can see why you'd say that, but you have to remember that I was a student teacher then. I was still learning myself and I definitely felt more like the student than the teacher.'

'But are you one of them now?' I teased.

'Hmm, well, the kids do take the mick out of my crazy hair,' he said, ruffling the top of his head so that it stuck up even more. 'And have you seen how many pockets these trousers have got? That's pretty sensible in my book.' He covered his face with his hands. 'Oh no! I'm one of them!'

We laughed again, but as we reached the top of the road that opened out into the Circus, Jamie's face fell and he sighed heavily. He was looking at a group of lads on the green in the centre of the circle of houses. Two of them were on the floor struggling as another two tried to break it up.

'Hey!' Jamie called out. He turned to me and said under his breath, 'They're in year eleven, and that one,' he pointed to one of the lads who was trying to pull them apart, 'is in my form.' The lads continued their scuffle and Jamie put two fingers in his mouth and whistled loudly. They all froze and looked up.

'Gemma, I'm sorry. I'll just have to have a quick word. I'll only be a minute.'

I shrugged, 'Of course, it's fine.'

As Jamie approached the lads one of them got up off the grass and ran off across the road in the direction of the town, another one following closely behind. The remaining two stayed where they were as Jamie approached them. I watched, half amused, as they adopted a Kevin the Teenager stance, their heads bowed and their shoulders slumped.

I looked around but there was no one else in the street, the windows that looked down on the circle were mainly dark, with no sign of life and the shop and restaurant near the corner of Brock Street were both shut up. A cat crossed the road in front of the shop and paused long enough for me to see it clearly under a street lamp. It was Fay's cat, Dexter. I glanced back at Jamie but he was still busy talking to the boys on the green, so I began to approach the corner of the street, careful to be as quiet as I could so as not to scare Dexter away. He was sniffing at the door of the shop as I crossed the road towards him.

'Puss, puss, puss,' I called out softly, 'Come on Dexter.' His whole body flinched nervously then he suddenly shot off down the narrow alleyway that led to the back of the shop.

'Damn,' I cursed under my breath. 'What are you, a pussy?' I followed him, peering around the corner. The alleyway was dark and I faltered briefly, wondering whether I should go in, then I saw Dexter turn a corner into a half-open gate that led to the shop's back yard. I followed him, my heart thumping as I realised that Jamie was now out of sight and I was feeling increasingly uneasy about being in a dark alley on my own. I was about to walk through the gate when I froze. There was the faint sound of hushed voices coming from the shop's yard. I tiptoed to the other side of the gate, where it was darker and I was less visible and tried to peer through the fence to see if I could see anything. Instead I saw three men. One had his back to me and was dressed all in black. He had a hood up over his face and he was counting money. Opposite him was another man, also dressed in dark, baggy clothes. He was looking down as he too was counting something out. I looked harder and saw that they were small, tightly packaged bags. They were white. Drugs? A wave of adrenalin passed over me as I wondered what they'd do if they caught me watching. The third man was looking around skittishly. 'What was that?' he whispered and the other men looked around too. I held my breath.

'It was just a cat,' one of them said and they carried on with what they were doing. The man who was looking out turned back around and I saw a brief glimpse of his face. I snapped my head away from the fence in shock. I could have sworn it was Tim.

Faintly, off in the distance, I heard Jamie call out 'Gem?' and my heart stopped as the men in the yard scrambled to hide what they were doing. For a minute I thought they were going to come out, but the man who looked like Tim went to the gate and shut it and I heard him warn, 'Stay where you are' to the others.

With the gate shut I saw my opportunity to go and crept past it. When I was a safe enough distance away I broke into a run.

Jamie was further up Brock Street and I caught him up, grabbing his hand and pulling him around the corner at the end of the street.

'What's the matter? Where were you?' Jamie asked as I stopped to get my breath back and check the street behind me. Jamie looked around too. 'What is it? Are you OK?'

I nodded, putting my hands on my hips and sighing with relief. 'I'm fine. I just thought I saw Dexter. You know, Fay's cat? I followed it down an alley and I got a bit spooked. I saw some guys in a yard and it looked like they were dealing drugs so I just ran.'

Jamie looked surprised. 'Really? Are you sure? If they're still there perhaps we should call the police.'

'No, oh, I don't know. I couldn't see too clearly, what if I was wrong? There's not much I could tell them.'

Jamie put his arms around me and held me closely. 'I'm sorry Gemma, I shouldn't have left you on your own.' He kissed the top of my head and rubbed my back. 'Are you sure you're OK?'

'Yeah, it's fine. I'm fine,' I said as we stepped apart. 'Let's just go back. Do you want to come and have some coffee?' I asked as breezily as I could. The prospect of going back to the house alone with Fay in bed and the possibility of Tim returning was making me nervous.

'Sure,' Jamie said, smiling, but still looking at me with concern. 'Let's do that.'

# Chapter Seventeen

When we walked into the house it was dark, except for a chink of light escaping from under the kitchen door. It sounded like someone was in there and I hoped it was Tim, clattering about as he made himself a late-night snack, the way he often did. If he was in the kitchen then there's no way it could've been him in the alley. He couldn't have got back home before us.

I pushed the door open and saw Fay. She was sitting at the kitchen table, rocking backwards on her chair as she thumbed through one of her library books. When she realised she wasn't alone she jumped, causing her chair to tip backwards and bang against the cupboard behind her. She sat up quickly, readjusting her clothes and fingering her hair.

'Hey! Blimey, you scared the life out of me,' she said, laughing with relief. I wondered if she had automatically checked her appearance because she'd thought I could have been Tim. 'How was your ...' she started, then saw Jamie behind me and said 'Mr Wade!' with a mixture of surprise and excitement.

He laughed. 'Jamie. *Please* call me Jamie. I've been trying to convince Gemma all night that I'm not a teacher figure anymore, and so far it's just not working. In fact I've done everything but throw chalk at her.'

Fay looked sympathetic as Jamie picked a chair and joined her at the kitchen table.

'I'm afraid we don't have chalk,' she said with mock sincerity. 'But you could always borrow my book. You could drop it really hard onto the table and tell us to pay attention. That'd be OK. Or you could say "Send me to the bottom of our stairs!" in a Brummie accent like Mr Bamford the maths teacher and it'll be like we'd never left school.'

'Brummie Bamford. I remember him, he took early retirement about five years ago,' Jamie said, and suddenly they were off, reminiscing just like we'd done earlier.

I laughed at them and busied myself making drinks, thankful to have a moment to myself to think. My mind was still replaying what I'd seen in the alley and I was glad that Jamie hadn't mentioned it in front of Fay. The more I thought about it the more I doubted what I thought I'd seen. Perhaps it wasn't Tim at all? It was dark, and I only saw him for a second. Plus I'd been drinking so my vision wasn't exactly reliable. Perhaps it was all perfectly innocent? Somehow I doubted that from the way they'd been acting, but as long as it wasn't Tim. That was the main thing.

I poured the boiling water into a cafetière and was just getting some biscuits out of the cupboard when I heard the front door shut. I turned around and saw Tim walk into the kitchen, smiling broadly. 'Good, I'm glad you're up, I've got something to show you,' he said. I realised he had a jumper bundled up in his arms as though it were hiding something and for one horrifying minute I thought he was going to show us a stash of class A under the misappre-

165

hension that we'd all be thrilled and start whipping out our credit cards and a roll of foil, but then Dexter poked his head out from under the folds of fabric and let out a timid meow.

'Dexter!' Fay cried, leaping up to take him. 'Where did you find him?'

'Oh, he was just skulking around nearby,' he said, waving a dismissive hand.

It must have been him, I thought, watching as he handed over the cat, seemingly the most innocent guy in the world.

Fay checked Dexter over then flung her arms around a pleasantly surprised Tim. 'You're a hero, thank you!' she cried. 'And you're just in time for coffee. Will you have one with us?'

I sat at the kitchen table, holding my mug of coffee near to my lips and sipping from it occasionally as I watched the others through an aromatic wisp of steam. The evening had taken on a slightly unreal atmosphere now, not helped by the fact that I was sobering up; something I usually preferred to do in my sleep. Occasionally Jamie caught my eye and would smile meaningfully, clearly trying to convey some kind of message with his eyes that was too complicated to translate. I imagined that it would have been something to do with us not being alone, and how perhaps we ought to be alone together for a while, to talk, and to gauge where things were going to go from here. But I could have been wrong; I did, after all, only have a wry smile and a slightly peaked pair of eyebrows to go on.

Tim was in good spirits and didn't seem to be as distracted as usual. He wasn't clock watching, his mobile wasn't ringing and he seemed settled in for the night. He was taking an interest in everyone, deflecting attention away from himself in the manner of a verbal tennis player, lobbing all questions straight back at their server.

Fay: 'What were you up to tonight then?'

Tim: 'Not much, a quick drink with some friends. What about you? Did you have a good evening?'

Jamie: 'What is it that you do, Tim?'

Tim (swishing his hand as though holding a virtual racket): 'Nothing very exciting I'm afraid, just IT. I'm a systems analyst. How about you?'

Jamie (ignoring Tim's deflective question): 'Oh, computers, hey? My brother's in IT, makes me green with envy every Christmas when he comes down to see me in his latest two-seater convertible. Makes me wonder sometime why I ever took up teaching. Do you work for a consultancy? You might have heard of his company, Com-it Solutions?'

Tim (after a second's thought): 'It doesn't ring a bell, but there's so many out there. It's a massive business. And we're not all doing quite as well as your brother either, by the sounds of it. I reckon you're better off being a teacher, far more rewarding. What is your subject?' And so on . . .

When Tim managed to deflect yet another personal question by suggesting we all move into the living room where the chairs were comfier, Fay was quick to get up. Jamie stayed put at the table. 'We'll join you in a minute,' he said and waited for them to leave the room before he spoke again. 'Are you OK?' he started. 'Only you've been so quiet since we got back. Are you worried about the people you saw earlier, in the alley?'

'Oh no, not at all. I'm just tired. It's been a long week.' I gave him a bright smile then glanced over to the kitchen wall, thinking about Tim and Fay in the room beyond it. They seemed to be getting closer, and Fay had been worryingly attentive to his every word, her eyes never straying far from his face. I had a sinking feeling that Fay was becoming increasingly convinced Tim was the 'good man' Miranda meant. I wanted to warn her, tell her what I'd seen, but I couldn't see a way to do it. She seemed determined to make the most of his presence, staying as close to him as possible whilst she had the chance.

'You do look tired, Gemma. I should probably go.'

'Oh no, it's OK. You can stay. Do you want another cuppa? Something stronger?'

Jamie looked tempted then seemed to think better of it. 'I'd love to, but I think I'd better get going. We should do this again sometime though? Maybe you could come and see my house. I could get some take-out from that fantastic Thai place in town and pretend I'd cooked it for you.'

I laughed. 'That sounds very tempting, I'd like that.' Jamie had told me about his house when I'd first bumped into him in Bristol. It sounded lovely: a little end-of-terrace cottage in Bradford-on-Avon, backing onto the canal, with a couple of old outbuildings. Just the kind of place I'd dreamed of having myself one day.

Jamie got up and I walked him to the door. Again that feeling of what-to-do returned. I smiled up at him and he responded by putting his hands on the curves of my shoulders. It made me feel small and girlish.

'You take care,' he said, his voice softer, then he bent down and kissed me on the lips. Just one kiss, but slowly, and without moving his face away afterwards. I breathed him in for a moment, enjoying the closeness. We were a hair's breadth apart, and although it may only have been for a second, it felt like minutes. When we moved back to look at each other properly I felt light-headed and buzzy.

'Call me anytime,' he said.

I nodded and made a little noise that sounded embarrassingly swoony and he backed away down the path, still looking at me until he was off down the road and out of sight.

I stayed by the open door, savouring the moment a while longer. I didn't fancy shutting myself back into the house with Tim and the dilemma of whether I should, or how I should, get Fay to think differently about him.

When I went back in I hovered by the living-room door. It was half open but I couldn't hear them inside. I wasn't sure whether I should join them or call Fay out for a chat. Perhaps calling her out would look too obvious, especially if Tim knew I'd seen him. That was a worrying possibility. He would have heard Jamie call out 'Gem?' when I was just a few feet from him in the alley. If he'd heard me run off he could have worked it out. I'd tried to act normally around him when we were all in the kitchen, but I'd been unable to relax in his presence. He could easily have picked up on that, and I had noticed that when we were all talking he barely looked in my direction.

Perhaps I should join them in the living room and then I could wait until Tim went out to get a drink or visit the bathroom. If he was out of the way I could tell Fay I needed to talk to her urgently.

I decided that was my best option and poked my head around the door. Fay and Tim were sitting closely, like mirror images of each other; their legs were curled behind them and their heads resting on the back of the sofa. They were bent in together, talking intimately and were completely unaware that I was there. They reminded me of those pictures of swans that you see, where they are facing each other, perfect imitations of each other, their bodies almost forming a heart shape in the space between them. Then I noticed that Tim had Fay's hand in his, his fingers absently stroking hers, and I moved away, slipping quietly back into the hall. It was too late to do anything now.

I couldn't sleep. It wasn't even worth trying. Instead I sat up, straining to hear the telltale sounds of Fay coming to bed. I'd decided that if she came up alone I'd go and find her for a chat. But hours seemed to pass and still there was no sign of Fay. I lay wide awake, staring at the ceiling and thinking about everything. My mind was getting ahead of itself, second-guessing what was down the line for all of us. I kept worrying about Fay. She'd had several flings but had never really fallen for anyone. What if things got serious between them? What if he hurt her? Or got her into drugs? I wouldn't be doing her justice by saying she was easily led. She was far too individual for that. But gullible? Maybe some would say she was; Nikki certainly would. I preferred to think of her as open-minded, willing to consider most things if people made it sound interesting and harmless enough.

When trying not to worry about Fay I found myself daydreaming about Jamie and wondering what his house would be like. I imagined him having a studio, conjuring up an image of a converted outbuilding, full of paintings leaning against walls and piles of interesting assortments of easels, paints and sketchbooks. It'd have to be light, with a big window overlooking the garden that would be wild and natural with crumbly stone walls. Maybe a low gate at the bottom, leading to the canal, where we could sit and watch the boats go by at dusk with a glass of wine.

I'd always been drawn to creative men, those who could take something uninspiring and turn it into something unique and beautiful to look at. It was a big reason for my attraction to Adam, who would spend hours restoring something like an old fireplace or a stained-glass window, working on it meticulously, bent over with a soldering iron or a chisel, sanding and polishing until the colours, the clean lines, the carvings and the grain and polish of the wood were revived and able to shine again.

Thinking about them both made me realise how similar they were, particularly in their profession. They shared a 'labour of love' mentality, motivated by creating and inspiring, rather than money or career advancement. They were passionate, skilled and imaginative, attributes I found powerfully seductive. But there was also a yawning gap between them. Jamie, being a few years older than Adam, did have that quiet confidence you get with age. He was at peace with himself, which made him easy to be around and he was pretty good at voicing what was on his mind. Adam was more physical, and he was struggling with something, internalising feelings he found hard to let go, making it difficult to know what was really going on in his head. Maybe in five years' time Adam would resolve his issues and become more like Jamie.

I sat with my duvet pulled tightly around me, despite the warmth and stillness of the night, and my thoughts kept returning to the kiss.

It was so different from my first kiss with Adam. With Adam and I, it had been after I'd met him several times when he'd worked at Dizzy Heights, restoring the old vestry. It was a messy, dangerous job so the work had been done over the summer holidays when the children weren't around. Adam had worked mainly with Jill as she was responsible for the organisation of the project, but there were times when I went along to see what was going on or to let the builders in and make them cups of tea. The first stage of Adam's job was to restore the flooring, which was made up of Portland stone flags, laid in a diamond pattern. Several of the flags were damaged or missing and they had been so dirty I hadn't even noticed the pattern of them until Adam had cleaned them up. He was able to source some replacements for the broken stones and the day they arrived Jill called up to ask me to let him in and give him a spare key. I wandered over early in the morning, not expecting to hang around, but Adam got me chatting and we ended up sitting on the stone floor, drinking fresh coffee from a flask he'd brought with him. That was when he asked me to go for a drink with him after work, and I was so pleased I agreed without hesitation. I'd been hoping he would ask from the first day I met him. I think the involuntary way my face broke into a picture of undisguised delirium was all the encouragement he needed to lean over and kiss me at that moment. As soon as his lips joined with mine all the usual dating etiquette disappeared through the vestry window. There were no small kisses, testing the water, leading somewhere. There were no shy glances or Dawson and Joey style crisis talks. Instead we skipped over a few pages in the manual and went straight to the 'deep wet kisses and panting breath' section. We lay on the stone cold floor, his hands in my hair and his warm mouth over mine, stopping only to catch a breath and to laugh at our own surprising behaviour, until a knock on the door echoed around the church and we had to prise ourselves apart.

It was Jill at the door, she had made it after all and was 'dying to have a look and see how it was all coming along'.

Adam told her he was really pleased with how things were progressing and gave me such a meaningful look I thought my knickers might actually catch fire. I couldn't believe Jill was oblivious to an atmosphere so heavy with attraction it could have been visible, hanging in the air around us like a warm, magnetic mist. But she chattered on, keen to see the new flagstones and talk about Adam's ideas for the windows. Whilst they were talking, an inspector from English Heritage arrived and Jill insisted that I didn't need to stay around, hurrying me off into the sunshine like she was doing me a favour.

I walked out into the daylight on wobbly legs, feeling like I sometimes did when leaving the cinema after an emotionally involving film. I wasn't ready to leave those feelings behind and go back to ordinary life. I was confused, unsure what was real and what wasn't. I was starting to think I'd imagined the whole thing when Adam came running out of the door after me.

'I told them you forgot your pen,' he said, holding out an ordinary blue biro and he looked at it, laughing at himself. 'I know, it was lame, but I couldn't think what else to say.'

'Well, thank you. Err, what would I have done without it?' We smiled at each other.

'I wanted to check you were still on for a drink tonight.' He looked worried then, as though in the bright light of the day I had come to my senses.

'Of course. Just say when.'

'How about I meet you at the bandstand in Victoria Park? Say, half-past seven? Then we can see what we feel like doing.'

'Sure.' Looking into his eyes I was back in the cinema again, watching the two leads and cheering them on.

And that was it. The beginning of our relationship. We hit the ground running and for four years that's how we stayed: still passionate, still unquestioning.

Not so with Jamie. His wasn't a passionate kiss: it was a gentle, affectionate, curious kiss. That's not to say that passion was out of the realms of possibility for us, but we were older now, and more experienced. Taking our time

173

and savouring every little moment could be just as exciting. The most important thing Jamie's kiss had over Adam's was a magical feeling, a feeling that every moment in my life had led me up to that point. And if that's what fate had in store for me, I was happy to go with it.

I must have dozed off eventually because when I opened my eyes again the room was filled with daylight and my alarm clock radio was playing quietly in the background. I lay still with my eyes open as I thought back to the events of the previous evening. I remembered Jamie's kiss and I touched my lips, wondering how he felt about me this morning and when I'd see him again. The radio, which was set to a local station, was playing a pop song that was trying to muscle into my thoughts with its incessant rhythm. I reached over to flick it off but paused, my finger hovering over the button, as I realised the song they were playing was 'Painter Man' by Boney M. I turned it up instead and lay back against the pillows, humming the tune and smiling to myself until the DJ faded it out and told me I was 'listening to 104.6 FM at eleven o'clock on a lazy Sunday morning'.

'Bugger,' I muttered to myself, throwing back the duvet and flicking off the radio, which was now playing 'Easy' by the Commodores. I hadn't realised it was so late. I'd told my parents I would go over for Sunday lunch and I still hadn't managed to talk to Fay about Tim. I got up, put on my dressing gown and went in search of Fay.

She wasn't in her room or the bathroom and Tim's door was half open, letting sunlight from his bedroom spill out onto the hall floor. That was unusual for Tim, who usually kept his door locked. His relationship with Fay, if it wasn't too premature to call it a relationship, was getting him to let his guard down, I thought.

174

I found them downstairs. Tim was in a pair of baggy grey pyjama bottoms and a T-shirt; he was leaning against the sink with a bowl of cornflakes in his hands and looked as though he had just woken up. His eyes were still sleepy, his hair was standing up on one side and he was stifling a yawn as he greeted me. Fay was in a similar state. Her red hair was sticking out, the same as it always did, but her eyes were tired and her lower lids were smudged with the previous night's make-up. She was sitting at a kitchen chair, bent forward over the table so she could rest her head on her arms.

'Morning,' I said brightly.

Fay smiled and made a monosyllabic little noise that I took to be a 'hi'.

'Tired?'

They both nodded then Fay mumbled quietly, 'Mmm, not much sleep. Stayed up talking.'

'What, all night?' I said in surprise, and then regretted it when I saw them exchange hesitant glances. Of course they hadn't stayed up all night, not talking anyway.

'Tim's off to London this afternoon,' Fay said, changing the subject abruptly.

'Yep, I won't be back until late. I've got to go and see a client about a server.' He pulled a face that suggested he was going only under duress and it'd all be very dull. For some reason I was reminded of that saying 'I've got to see a man about a dog' and concluded that Tim had just come out with the modern-day equivalent.

'Oh, and Nikki called,' Fay added. 'She wanted to know if we were up for going to her house tonight.'

'Great. I've got nothing on. I'm off to my parents in a minute but I'll be back late afternoon. I'll drive us if you like.'

I'd have to leave my chat with Fay till then, I decided.

It didn't look like I was going to get her on her own before I went out. And there was definitely a morning-after-the-night-before kind of atmosphere in the kitchen. Much as I didn't want to give them time alone together, I got the feeling they needed it right then. I made my excuses and left them to it, heading back up the stairs for a shower.

# Chapter Eighteen

Pulling into Midsummer Lane I was surprised by the number of parked cars there were outside my parents' house. Usually I pulled straight onto their drive and parked bumper to bumper with my dad's car. Today though, there was already a little blue Peugot in my place. I couldn't park on the road outside the house either as all the spaces were taken. This occasionally happened on a Sunday morning, when ramblers arrived in Langley Green en masse to go for walks in the valley. There wasn't a public car park in the village and it drove my dad mad when they all used their little lane instead. I took the last parking spot on the corner and walked up the path to the house feeling increasingly unsure. We'd made the arrangement for lunch when I'd picked them up from the airport on Thursday, but I hadn't called them since and I should have done. They would have both been tired from their journey. They might have forgotten and made other plans with someone else.

I rang the doorbell but no one answered and when I peered into the living room it looked empty. There's something not quite right, I thought, hearing the sounds of laughter in the distance, yet unable to fathom where it was coming from. There was a smell too, as though someone had set fire to Mum's herb bushes.

I wandered around to the gate at the side of the house and found it open. The sounds of voices and laughter and the smell of scorched rosemary grew stronger and I realised they were both coming from the back garden.

'Gemma, at last! Your father said he thought he heard the doorbell.' Mum had appeared around the corner, waving a skewer. She looked as though she'd had her hair done and was it my imagination or had her tan darkened since I'd seen her on Thursday? 'Come along darling, we're just about to put the snags on.'

'The what?'

Mum disappeared again so I followed after her into the garden and was greeted by the sight of a dozen or so people milling around with drinks in their hands. Two of them I recognised: they were my Aunty Cathleen and her husband, Jim, and there were several others that I knew – friends, either from Dad's old work or Mum's bridge class.

Dad was standing over a brick-built barbeque that hadn't been there when I came over to water their plants the week before, prodding what looked like marinated chicken pieces. Mum walked through the patio doors into the dining room then returned with a tray of sausages. 'Come on darling, don't stand there gawping,' she said, then sing-songed to Dad, 'snags are here, Andrew, I hope you've left enough space on the barbie for them.'

'Mum, what's going on? I thought you were doing Sunday lunch?'

'I am! This is lunch.' She looked at me with obvious disappointment. 'It's not compulsory to have a roast *every* Sunday. Don't be so traditional, Gemma, really.'

I was left staring slack jawed at her. It could be the hottest day in history and my mum would still spend three hours roasting on a Sunday morning. Even on self-catering holidays she'd somehow manage to replicate the lunches we had at home, right down to the paper hats she put on the chicken legs.

'Anyway, you haven't said what you think of the new barbeque,' Mum carried on. 'Your father built it on Friday, clever man. Just like that. He said he didn't want to sleep; he was trying to stay awake to combat the jetlag. I got up on Saturday morning and it was all finished. I don't think he's ever finished a job that quick in his life.'

'It's great,' I said, feeling bewildered. Dad had never been anything other than fit and healthy for as long as I could remember, but I didn't like the thought of him forcing himself to stay awake to mix concrete and do some bricklaying. He was nearly seventy after all.

'Adam said your father's brickwork was first rate.'

*Oh God*. 'Adam? Adam was here?'

'He still is. He's in the kitchen sharpening my vegetable knife. Come in and say hello to him, then you can get yourself a drink.' She led me into the house by the elbow and I was too shocked to argue with her. I followed dumbly, the thought of seeing Adam again making me feel increasingly nauseous.

'Mum, I don't know if . . .' I started, but she ushered me into the kitchen then disappeared.

Adam was drying his hands on a towel when I walked in. He looked up straight away and when he saw me he took a very measured intake of breath.

'Hi.'

He didn't say 'hi' back, he just nodded.

'I wasn't expecting you to be here.'

'No, well I didn't expect to still be here. I came about an hour ago to return your dad's sideboard and your mum's been keeping me busy ever since. I had a feeling

179

she was trying to keep me here till you arrived.'

'Ahh. I'm sorry, she can be a bit, er . . .'

'It's OK. She means well.' He smiled briefly. 'I'll get going in a minute though.'

'Oh no, you really don't have to. Why don't you stay and have something to eat?'

'I don't think that's a good idea.'

'No, perhaps you're right. Mum has been acting more Australian than the real thing since she got back. She'll be serving up kangaroo meat and calling Dad a dingbat any time soon. But stay for a drink at least.' I cocked my head to one side and looked at him, waiting for a smile, but he stayed serious. 'Look, Adam, we are OK, aren't we? I mean we can still . . .'

'Don't tell me we can still be friends. I don't want to hear that.' He folded his arms across his chest and looked at me properly. I felt almost like he was staring me down, confronting me. It took me by surprise. Adam was usually so easy-going.

I swallowed hard. 'Are you OK?'

'I'm fine. How about you? How did your date go?'

'My date?'

'Yeah, you remember. The one you had last night, or do you have a lot these days?'

I stared at him, speechless.

'Daniel told me. He was drinking at the bar in Browns and he saw you cosy with some guy. Sounds like the same one I saw you with outside the flower shop?' He raised his eyebrows, waiting for a reply, and my lack of an answer seemed to confirm his suspicions. 'Dan met up with me later on. He didn't want to tell me at first but I think eventually he felt sorry for me. I'd been talking about you a lot, so perhaps he thought I should know what was going on.'

180

'Nothing's going on,' I said in a timid voice.

Adam held up a hand. 'It's OK, you don't need to explain to me. You can do what you like now. I just find it hard to deal with, you know? You finish what we had for something that didn't even happen, you talk about trust and honesty and as soon as we split up you're starting a new relationship. Looking back it seems to me you were just waiting for an excuse, a way out.'

'That's not true!' I didn't trust myself to say any more than that in case the tears I could feel lurking close to the surface spilled over.

Adam breathed out and rubbed his face with his hand. He looked tired. 'I'm sorry, I shouldn't be talking like this. Not here. It just still hurts, and it's going to take a while, OK?'

'Ooh, if it isn't love's young dream,' Aunty Cathleen cooed, stumbling into the kitchen. She made a bee-line for the bottle of sherry that was standing on the kitchen table, tucking it securely under her arm. 'Are you going to come out in the garden now? Join us for a little drinky?' She moved closer to Adam and looked up at him through fluttering eyelashes.

Adam cleared his throat. 'I'm afraid I can't hang around. I've got to catch up on work this afternoon.'

'Noo. Not on a Sunday.'

'I'm afraid so. Another time.' He gave her a momentary winning smile then picked his keys up from the kitchen table and after one last glance at me, walked out.

I sat on the floor in the corner of my old bedroom, mopping my face and nose dry with half-a-dozen sheets of a toilet roll I'd pinched from the bathroom. I'd been able to keep the tears at bay until I'd got to my room. Then, safe behind closed doors, they'd spilled relentlessly, speckling my top with wet dots and turning the tissue paper into mush.

What's happening to me? I kept thinking. How did everything suddenly get so confusing? Adam had made me feel terrible, and if what he said was true he had every right to. Perhaps I did give up too easily, but I was doing what I thought was right at the time, wasn't I? If I couldn't trust Adam then surely we couldn't have had a very meaningful relationship? Thinking about Marcia and how upset I'd been I couldn't see what else I could have done, but now, seeing Adam so hurt, I felt terrible, confused, and even guilty. What if I was wrong? What if Miranda was wrong?

I heard the sounds of laughter coming from the garden and frowned. I couldn't go back out there now. They would all be wondering what had happened to Adam and I got the feeling Mum hadn't told Aunty Cathleen or Jim that we had split up.

There was a soft tapping at the door. 'Gemma, are you in there?' It was my dad.

I quickly got up, stuffed my soggy tissues down the back of the radiator where he wouldn't see them then leaned against the window sill, as though taking in the view.

'Yes, come in.'

'I brought you a cup of coffee. I thought you could use one.'

'Thanks Dad.'

He came over and put the mug on the sill next to me.

'Are you OK, love?'

'Uh huh.' My eyes were beginning to fill up again at the sound of Dad's voice, all concerned and yet slightly awkward, as though willing me not to say 'no' and start sobbing on his shoulder.

He stood beside me, looking down at the valley and the

hills beyond, lit dramatically by the sun. The river a pale silver ribbon between the trees.

'Did I ever tell you about the time I was offered a job in London?' he said.

'No, when was that?' I looked at him but he kept his eyes on the view from the window.

'A long time ago now. We weren't living in this house but we were still in Langley Green, in that tiny cottage next to the old mill. Your mother was pregnant with John and we were struggling for money. There was talk of redundancies and we were very worried at the time. I called an old college friend of mine and he had a word with some people and a few days later the phone rang. It was the director of Plastics Injection International in London. He offered me a job as a design manager, right then. More money, more responsibility, and a subsidised flat whilst we found somewhere to live. Your mum was keen so we took the train to London to meet with them. They were good sorts, the job was ideal, the company was still quite small but clearly going places and London, well, it was on the outer edges, in an industrial park. Not a bad part of town, you know, tree-lined avenues, rows of Victorian houses in red brick, which was quite exciting for us then, having lived in Bath all our lives, surrounded by Georgian stone. It all seemed very nice. I was meant to call them back after I got home, let them know one way or the other, but I kept putting it off, finding something else to do. I went to see your gran and we talked about it and she said something to me that rang very true for me at the time. She said, "If it doesn't feel right, wait until it does, and if it's too late by then, it was never meant to be." So, I called them back, told them thanks but no thanks. Carried on in my job and did all right. There were redundancies but I was one of the fortunate ones.'

183

'So you never regretted it?'

He shook his head. 'Your mum wasn't best pleased at the time. Sometimes I still think she's disappointed that we didn't go for it. When John first told us he was moving to Australia it was one of the first things she'd said. "If we'd gone to London there would have been enough going on to keep John happy." And then there was the money. PII were one of the first companies to win a contract making mobile phone covers in the 80s, they floated on the stock market and every member of their staff made a small fortune; we would have done too, but no, I still don't regret it. It never would have been the right time for me, and a view like this, well, you don't get this in London. You can't put a price on ...'

'Andrew, you must come down soon,' Mum called from the bottom of the stairs. 'I can't find where you've hidden the photos – you'll have to get them for me, and I'm having a nightmare with the lamingtons.'

Dad looked at me and rolled his eyes comically. 'Will you come down and see everyone soon?'

'I'll be down in a minute. Thanks Dad.'

When he had gone I sighed and turned away from the window. I felt sorry for Dad; his story had shed some light on why Mum was always frustrated with him. Maybe she blamed him for denying them a better life. But he had still helped. I wasn't sure whether he had told me that story to give me some subtle advice or whether he just wanted to take my mind off what was troubling me, but I guessed that he was trying to make me feel better. That he was trying to say, in his usual, roundabout sort of way, that if I had felt things weren't right with Adam, then I probably did the right thing. And that was exactly what I needed to hear.

I felt in my pocket for a tissue to blow my nose but couldn't find one, then I remembered I'd hidden it behind the radiator. I went to get it back, sliding my hand along, but I couldn't feel it. I bent at an angle so I could see behind and saw that it had fallen down too far. I was going to leave it when I noticed there was something else down there, covered in cobwebs and dust. It looked like a letter. It was too far to reach so I got up, walking across the hall to find something I could reach it with. I found a long plastic ruler in Dad's desk drawer.

'Perfect,' I said and ran back to my bedroom with it.

It was still hard to get the angle right and I tried it from several directions until finally the tip of the ruler caught on the paper and nudged it. I hit it several times until it was low enough to reach from underneath and then I reached up with my hand and pulled it out. It was filthy and dried up from years of dust and central heating. I opened the paper. It was just as I thought. As soon as I'd seen it I'd known it would be one of Miranda's missing letters. It had to be.

It didn't say much, and there was no address on it. It was dated 13 October 1991. I sat down on the carpet and read it.

*Exams are crap*

　*I hate my family*

　*It's raining . . .*

　*I'm sorry, I'm fed up, and here it is, the reason for my pessimism . . . my parents are moving to Devon! Of course if my parents are moving to Devon, that also means I am moving to Devon.*

　*Apparently Dad has a can't-say-no kind of job offer and Mum has relatives there. They've been talking about me leaving school for a while – predicted grades are 'disappointing' and apparently I am 'in with a bad crowd'. What do they know?! Nothing, that's what.*

*And so for now the rain clouds gather and I have to weather the unbeatable storm. But worry not, I'm sure there is sunshine just around the corner.*

*I have no new address for you as yet but will send it when I do.*

*Sorry this letter's so crap. Must do better!! I will do better ... soon. For now though, tell me all your news, I want to hear some Nikki and Fay adventures that'll make me smile and remember our mad night of dreaming.*

*I will stop this nonsense. I'm tired, I'm wishing impossible things ...*

*Love always,*
*Miranda*

*Let's stay here forever and block out the light,*
*then sleep till it's bedtime and dream through the night ...*

The last bit she had written at the bottom of the page in curly silver writing, decorated with vines that she had drawn to look as though they were growing up the page.

She really was strange, I thought, skim reading it again. This letter brought it all back. I'd forgotten about the poetry she would often add at the end; little things she'd written herself or song lyrics she liked. She always sounded down but never went into much detail about why. I suppose she was waiting for me to ask her but I never did. I'd also forgotten about her move to Devon. She had written again after she'd moved and sent on the new address but I don't think I ever wrote back and I felt terrible about that now. Still, this might be enough to find her, I thought. I folded the paper over and put it in my back pocket.

\*

I showed Fay as soon as I got home.

'This is great!' she cried. 'Now all I need to do is photocopy the Patterson section of the right phone book and we can find her.'

'*Might* find her,' I corrected.

'No, we will, I know we will. I've got a good feeling about this,' she said confidently. 'I'll call in the library on the way home tomorrow then we can ring around tomorrow night.'

'Oh God, not again!' I groaned, leaning my head onto the living-room wall.

# Chapter Nineteen

It didn't take long for Fay to start talking about Tim, and once she started she barely paused for breath. In fact we were half way across town to Nikki's house before I could get a word in edgeways.

'So, you feel like you're getting to know him a lot better now?' I asked her as we inched forward in the queuing traffic. 'He's not being such an enigma?'

'Mmm, yeah. I do feel like I understand him, or at least I'm starting to get to know what makes him tick but I get the feeling he's a bit shy, well, not shy exactly, but take this whole thing with his job, for example. He's ever so dismissive. It's like he's embarrassed or something, and I can understand why. Not that it's a crap job at all: it's a very good job, but it just doesn't suit him. I can't picture him being very happy doing it for long, I mean, he's not your typical IT guy, is he? He's more of an outdoor pursuits man, I reckon. I think his job bores him, and he doesn't like talking about it because it doesn't give people the measure of who he is.'

'Really?'

'Oh yeah, and he's so interested in other people. I never realised how much until we started talking properly. He remembers things I said ages ago when I never really thought he was listening. He asks a lot of questions and he really does take in what I say. He actually thinks about it. I think that's why he's so intuitive.' She said this with a little smile.

I wrestled internally with the many inadvisable things I wanted to say and instead stared daggers at a man in a souped-up Fiesta, trying to jump the queue.

I tried to tactfully broach the subject as we stopped at the next traffic lights, but just as I opened my mouth Fay spoke again. 'Hey, you know what his favourite film is? You'll never believe it when I tell you.'

I shook my head, completely at a loss, and waited for her to enlighten me.

'*Twelve Angry Men*,' she said, unable to keep from grinning with pride at his choice.

'Is that the one about the jury?'

She nodded. 'Of course, as soon as he said that it made sense, because he's so thoughtful, he studies people and pays attention to detail, and I can't think of many films that do that as well as *Twelve Angry Men*. It's an amazing film. And you know the best bit?'

'Nooo.'

'Henry Fonda is in it,' she said with satisfaction. 'I love Henry Fonda. And he played opposite Katharine Hepburn in *On Golden Pond*.'

'Ahh.' I knew how much Fay loved Katharine Hepburn. She would no doubt have taken the fact that they both loved films with leads who famously played opposite each other as a sign of their suitability for each other.

'It's a sign,' Fay said, gazing happily out of the window.

Nikki wasn't nearly so careful to hide what she thought

189

when Fay told her about her developing relationship with Tim.

'Oh God, Fay, just because he lives right under your nose doesn't mean you *have* to end up dating him,' she said, rubbing her temples in despair.

'I really like him though. We click.'

'He's weird.'

'He is not! He's just a bit quiet that's all; shy. Once you get to know him all that disappears.'

'He's always sneaking off with his mobile phone.'

'That's a shy thing.'

'A shady thing more like. And he's always going away without any explanation.'

'That's 'cos there's not much to tell.'

'Unless he's leading a double life. He could have a wife and children for all you know.'

Fay faltered as she thought about that. It could explain a few things.

'That's true,' I said, seeing Fay's momentary crisis of conviction as an opportunity to add my own suspicions. 'Or he could be a drug dealer.'

Nikki and Fay both stopped and looked at me as though I had just said something completely random and obscure. 'Right.' Nikki said. 'And that would explain his trips away because ...'

'Well, I don't know. He could be getting more stuff. Setting up deals. Meeting with his, erm, his top people ...' I trailed off lamely. I wanted to tell Fay about what I'd seen but the timing had been lost. Now it'd sound like I was on the defensive, dreaming up situations to make myself sound more plausible.

'OK, let's not go that far,' Nikki said. 'But there is still something that doesn't add up about him, you have to admit. He's not telling the whole story and of course I could be wrong, it could all be very innocent, but my instinct is still to be wary.'

We both looked at Fay but she was no longer listening, her attention instead taken by a newspaper left open on the coffee table. Her head was inclined towards it as she surreptitiously tried to read her horoscope.

I hadn't seen Fay when I left for work on Monday morning, but she'd phoned me at lunchtime sounding breathless and excited.

'I've got it,' she whispered.

'You've got what?'

'The phone book. Or rather, the Patterson page of the Exeter and East Devon phone book.'

'Ahh.' I had suspected as much.

'And you'll never believe it.'

'What?'

'There's only one K Patterson in it. I think we've found them.'

I thought about it for a moment. What were the chances? 'There were K Pattersons in the other phone book, though none of them turned out to be him. And there are loads of names beginning with K. It could be a Keith, or a Katherine, Kate, Kevin . . .'

'Oh come on, Gem, of course it's them. We know they're in Devon. It has to be them. There's no such thing as coincidence, remember? It's got their address on it too. It's in a place called Abbotstone.'

'Have you called the number yet?'

'I thought we should do it together.'

'OK, I'll come straight over to the shop when I've finished here,' I said, feeling a flicker of anxiety. What on earth were we going to say without sounding ridiculous?

*

191

When I got to the shop, Fay was leaning against the counter looking bored. She was wearing her favourite top, a canary yellow 'Brownies' T-shirt she'd found in a second-hand shop. With her angular elbows and awkward teenager stance, it made her look far younger that she actually was.

'Is it just me, or does pan pipe music make everyone tense?' she said.

'That's just you, Fay. My God, look at this place.' It was immaculate. The floor was reflecting the spotlights in the ceiling, the glass shelves sparkled, and every single item on them was arranged facing the front, all at perpendicular angles. There was even a perfect pyramid of L-I-P face creams arranged on the circular table in the centre of the room. For a shop that had always had the same haphazard feel as the aftermath of a church jumble sale, this was a surprising sight.

'I've had four customers all day,' Fay said, by way of an explanation. 'And I found that tidying up calmed me down.'

'Wow, you must have been spectacularly tense to have done all this,' I said, taking it all in.

'Everything has its place,' Fay said. 'And I wanted everything to be just right.'

I shrugged my coat off and went to hang it up in the store room. When I came out Fay had 'tidied up' my bag by putting it on a shelf under the counter, sandwiched neatly between two boxes of price labels.

'Ahh.' Suddenly I realised what was going on. 'This is like before you go to an audition, isn't it? The way you always have to tidy the house before you leave?'

'Things just go better for me when everything's just right. It's not like I'm an obsessive compulsive or anything.' She looked at me as though daring me to contradict her.

'Of course. It's an acting thing – you're a superstitious lot.'

'It's not superstition, it's positive energy and good placement,' she said, her eyes following a woman outside who was window-shopping as if worried that she might come in and mess up her 'placement'. When the woman wandered away Fay's shoulders relaxed.

'What's up with you today?'

'Oh, I don't know.' She sighed. 'I suppose it's finding Miranda. Well, I know we haven't yet, but we might find out where she is today. We might get her phone number and even speak to her and I suppose I'm just a bit worried about it.'

'Why worried?'

'Well . . . maybe because I want her to tell me what I'm doing's OK and it'll all work out. I know it's silly, but I feel like she's the only one who can tell me that at the moment. What's happening with Tim—' she smiled '—it's so exciting, and the screen-test on Friday. This is a big week for me; everything's happening at once, just like she said it would. That bit about all my ambitions, hopes and dreams coming true could be right now. Nothing in my life has been this promising for a very long time and I so badly want it all to come true. I want her to tell me that I'm hoping for the right thing. That Tim and the job are the things she meant to work out.'

'She might not be able to tell you anything at all.'

She scrunched up her face. 'I know, and that would be awful too, wouldn't it? If she's a real sceptic and can't see anything amazing about what she'd written I know I'll be disappointed.'

'Look, let's just call the number, then we can think about everything else later,' I said, taking the phone from its cradle before we could procrastinate any longer. Fay had written the number on a pad by the phone and dialled it slowly, taking a deep breath. 'It's ringing,' I whispered.

Fay covered her face with her hands and leaned onto the counter.

It rang half-a-dozen times then stopped. A man answered with a clear and quiet 'hello'.

'Oh hello, is that Ken Patterson?' I said.

'It is.'

Fay looked at me, trying to ascertain his reply, and I gave her a thumbs-up signal. 'Miranda's father, is that right?'

There was a long pause. 'Who is this?'

I was surprised by the change in his tone. 'Well, my name's Gemma. I'm an old friend of ...'

'Miranda's no longer here,' he said, just before he hung up.

I stared at the phone, and then at Fay, with total surprise. 'He hung up on me!'

Fay straightened up. 'Why? What did you say to him?'

'Fay, you heard me. I barely said anything to him. He said "Miranda's no longer here" and hung up, just like that. He sounded pretty pissed off actually.'

'Miranda's no longer here?' She tapped her chin, thinking. 'So we definitely got the right number then.' Suddenly she gasped in horror. 'Oh my God, what if she's dead? That would explain it, don't you think? He'd be upset about getting a call for her if she'd died. And you saying you're an old friend, he might think you're a pretty rubbish friend to not know something like that. Oh no. Oh God, I hope it's not that.'

'No, it can't be.' I held the phone away from me, staring at it in confusion, half expecting Mr Patterson to call back to explain. 'What shall I do?'

'Phone them again and apologise,' Fay said.

'D'you think?' I didn't want to. What if Fay was right? I wasn't sure I'd want to know something like that. I would regret ever having found that box, ever having wondered what had happened to her. It was the one possibility I had never entertained.

'I think you should. Then we'll know one way or the other. You'll always be wondering now.'

She was right, I would. I pressed redial, nervous energy making my fingers shake. The phone rang for a long time then finally it was picked up. This time a woman spoke. She also only said 'hello' but this time I was struck by the amount of emotion it was possible to get into just two syllables. She sounded surprised, curious, guarded and even fearful. I tried to sound as reassuring as I could.

'Mrs Patterson?'

'Yes?' The same emotion was there.

'Mrs Patterson, I'm so sorry, I called a minute ago and spoke to your husband and I think I may have upset him. I'm an old friend of Miranda's. I've been wanting to get back in touch with her. I found this number and, well, I hadn't realised ...' I was struggling for words and getting no encourgement from Miranda's mum, who was staying unnervingly silent. 'If something's happened to her ...'

'Has something happened to her?' she asked, her voice even more loaded with emotion than it had been before.

'Oh no, well, er, no. It's just your husband sounded upset when I mentioned her. I worried that maybe something had happened that I wasn't aware of.'

'Miranda moved out a long time ago,' she said stiffly. 'I'm sorry, I can't help you.' The phone went silent.

'She's hung up on me too!' I said with disbelief, returning the phone to its cradle. There was no way I was calling them a third time.

'Did she say anything? Any clue?'

195

'I don't think she's dead, she just said that Miranda had moved out a long time ago. They must have had some kind of huge fall out. I don't think they were ever that close.'

'So now what do we do?' Fay asked, looked deflated.

I shrugged. 'I don't know. We've tried everything else.'

Fay went to the bookshelf in the corner of the shop and scanned the spines, eventually pulling out a tall hardback book. She put it on the counter and slid it towards me.

*Geomancy in the UK: A comprehensive guide to the Ley lines and mystical history of Great Britain*, the cover read. I looked from the cover to Fay in confusion.

'It's the only map of Britain we have in the shop,' Fay said with a shrug. 'Let's find out where Abbotstone is. Perhaps we could pay it a visit at the weekend. Take some flowers to the Pattersons and charm them into giving us a contact address or number. Even an old one would do. Or, if it's a small village, perhaps someone else knew her and can give us some information to go on.'

'I'm not sure. I don't think they'll take kindly to us pestering them.'

Fay flipped the book open and started to look in the index for Abbotstone. 'Well, they can only say no, then at least we'll have tried. Anyway, a day out in Devon will be fun. And if all else fails we can cheer ourselves up with a cream tea. You get scones the size of top hats in Devon, you know?' She looked at me, eyes pleading.

'Go on then, you've twisted my arm,' I said, squeezing in next to her to look at the map.

We spoke to Nikki that evening. She was all for joining us on our trip to Devon, although not, as she pointed out, because she could see any sense in tracking down Miranda, but more to get away from the whole situation with Fabian. He had been publicly dumped by Impossible

Barbie, who was photographed kissing a bit-part actor from Eastenders in a Knightsbridge pub. The papers had painted Fabian as a wounded hero, a hopeless romantic looking for love. There was even an article about him in one of the Sunday tabloids, complete with a photo of him posing in a bath with a rose between his teeth. He still kept calling Nikki for a date and she was fuming about the whole thing, saying he'd made her feel like a mug.

We agreed on Sunday, when the traffic would be quieter, and then Fay and I planned our route to Abbotstone. It wasn't as far away as I'd expected it to be, and it wasn't by the sea, which was disappointing. It ruled out my plans to stand at the water's edge and stare majestically out to sea, the way people in films do when they have a lot to think about. When I told Fay about that she was very understanding and offered to drive so that I could do the next best thing and drink cider till I went blind. I took her up on that, just in case.

# Chapter Twenty

When the phone rang on Tuesday night I knew it would be Jamie. I'd been wondering about him all day. We hadn't spoken since Saturday night and I was beginning to wonder if I had put him off calling me altogether. Our date had lost its momentum after I'd seen Tim in the alley and I knew I'd been distant afterwards, mulling over what to do. But I had really enjoyed being with him and I wanted to see him again, despite a new-found guilt, brought on by seeing Adam at my parents' house. How had he managed to make me feel as though I was the guilty party, like I was the one that had brought about our break-up? He was confusing and frustrating me, but after hearing Jamie's easy-going voice on the phone I made a mental pact with myself not to let Adam knock me off my current course. When Jamie invited me to a meal at his house the following Saturday I accepted without a second thought, and when he said he was looking forward to seeing me again, I knew I felt the same.

By Saturday I was high with excitement, although I wasn't sure whether that was entirely to do with my impending date with Jamie or more to do with spending the morning with Fay. Fay had been buzzing since she came back from her screen-test on Friday. A day which had turned out to be an audition for a job fronting a BBC Four documentary on female movie icons. Fay had spent the day at BBC Bristol, meeting with writers, commissioners and controllers for factual programming and was blown away by the positive feedback she'd got. They'd apparently been having BBC talent auditions countrywide to find people who had the knowledge and the passion to make programmes on a number of subjects, but they hadn't found anyone suitable for the movie icon series until Fay had had the good fortune to have lunch with the producer. It sounded as though Fay was exactly what they were looking for and although they still wanted to run through the tapes and talk amongst themselves before giving her an answer, they had been so encouraging that even Fay was confident.

'This has to be the single most exciting week of my life so far,' Fay said as we left the deli and walked out onto Milsom Street.

I looked at her with amusement. She had been in a daydream for most of the morning, smiling amiably at passers-by, buying a copy of the *Big Issue* from anyone that asked her and telling me everything I tried on in the changing rooms was 'perfect', despite one of them contorting all my fat bits until I looked like I'd got six breasts. I'd given up trying to get any kind of balanced opinion out of her and gone for a see-through linen shirt to wear over a vest top with my favourite jeans and sandals. Picking an outfit for a date was becoming something of an art form, something I hadn't spent much energy thinking about when I was with Adam. Suddenly I was finding myself questioning whether I was over-dressed or under-dressed, too obvious or not obvious enough.

We had just started back towards the house when I heard my mobile ringing from one of the carrier bags.

'Hang on, hang on, whoa,' I said to Fay, who was still striding along, bags swinging. 'Where is it?' I put mine on the floor and searched through its contents, copies of the *Big Issue* spilling everywhere. 'God Fay, how many of these did you buy?'

She just smiled placidly and handed me my phone from her handbag. 'I think it's Jamie's number,' she said.

I felt a flutter of anxiety when I saw she was right. 'Hi Jamie, how's it going?'

'Terrible,' he replied.

'Why? What's happened?'

'Gemma, I owe you an apology. I'd completely forgotten that I'd already made arrangements for tonight.'

I felt my mood deflate. I was being stood up. 'That's OK.'

'Oh, it's not. It's not OK. I'm so sorry. It was an arrangement I made weeks ago. I invited Cassie over for dinner with her new boyfriend. She's been dying for me to meet him and it's the first Saturday she's managed to have away from the restaurant in so long, I don't think I can put them off.'

'It's fine, I understand, we can do it another time.'

He went quiet for a moment. 'Gemma, I still want you to come. You will still come won't you? I wasn't phoning to put you off, I was phoning to apologise for the unexpected guests.'

'Oh, oh I see, right well, so long as you're sure. It'd be nice to meet Cassie again.'

'Great, phew, now I just need to revise the dinner plans. I hadn't been kidding about the Thai from over the road, you know. Unfortunately I don't think I can do that with Cassie, well, not again anyway,' he said sheepishly then groaned, 'and with Cassie being a chef and her boyfriend being a vegetarian, I, ahh . . .'

'Jamie, are you sure you don't need some help?'

'Can you come now?' he said in a small voice.

I laughed. 'I'll leave in ten minutes. I'll just have to get back home and drop my bags off first.'

'You're an angel,' he said, with undisguised relief.

Of course when 'get back home and drop my bags off' was translated it actually meant 'bolt back home, shower, put on the contents of my bags, untangle hair, redo make-up and paint toenails'. I left the house forty minutes later and got to Jamie's house at three o'clock in the afternoon.

His house was even more idyllic than I'd imagined, set on a quiet, sheltered lane of identical cottages. They all had arched windows above the front doors that had the house numbers etched into the glass. Their tiny front gardens were well stocked with tall hollyhocks and foxgloves that were blooming already and stooping with the weight of their flowers. Jamie's garden had a slightly more masculine feel in that it was mainly gravelled, but flowers still lined the low wall at the front and there was a potted bay tree next to the front step. It looked like a home rather than a bachelor pad and I wondered if that was partly due to his age. He was more settled than a lot of men my own age and home comforts were clearly a higher priority. I liked that, I thought, and tapped on the door with a wrought-iron door handle, similar to the ones I'd seen in Adam's workshop.

'Hey,' Jamie said with a smile that softened his face with tiny creases. He kissed me quickly on the cheek then hurried me through the hall and into the kitchen at the back of the house.

It was an open-plan house, with a big kitchen diner that must have previously been two separate rooms and an archway from the dining area led to a living room. All the walls were painted in muted creams which gave it all a fresh, airy feel. There were French windows looking out onto the garden and a big dining table already set with a tablecloth and candles. The kitchen area was in disarray though, with piles of open cookbooks, vegetables and saucepans cluttering the work surfaces.

'Wow. Where to start?' I said, putting my bottle of wine down on the last available bit of space.

'Ooh, why don't we start by having a small glass of wine in the garden?' Jamie said, rubbing his hands together. 'There's only an hour of sun left before the trees block it out and I think we should enjoy that before I have to cook.' He took a couple of wine glasses and a bottle from the side and beckoned me to follow him into the sunshine.

It was exactly as I'd imagined: a long narrow garden with a pathway leading to a table and some chairs on a patio that looked out onto the canal. I sat down on a metal chair that had been warmed up by the sun and looked around at the view of the hill that rose up from the other side of the canal and then looked back at the cottage. I was amazed by just how similar it was to the way I'd imagined it. It was almost like déjà vu. There was an ancient looking outbuilding attached to the back of the house and I asked Jamie if that was his studio.

'No, it's totally empty at the moment. I paint in the spare room. The window's got a lovely view out across the nature reserve.' He pointed up to the window above the kitchen. 'I must show you around when we go back in.'

I was disappointed. If the outbuildings had been a studio my image of Jamie's house would have been spookily complete.

'It's funny you should say that though,' he carried on, looking at the outbuildings thoughtfully, 'because I did get a friend to draw up some plans when I first bought the house. I've been planning to convert it into a studio all along, but I wanted to finish doing up the rest of the house first. I'm hoping to make a start next year. It is perfect for a studio in there.'

'I can imagine,' I said, sipping my wine. Perhaps it wasn't déjà vu, I thought excitedly, perhaps it was a premonition?

By half past six we had an hour until Cassie and her new boyfriend were due to arrive and I was beginning to understand why Jamie wasn't a natural in the kitchen. We had opted, eventually, to make a vegetable chilli as Jamie had bought an excessive amount of vegetables from the market and he claimed to be fantastic at doing rice (he had a rice cooker). We had been preparing vegetables for what felt like forever as Jamie sliced each one carefully, trying hard to make them all equal sizes. I'd begun to tease him until eventually I lost patience. I took him by the shoulders and shook him jokingly. 'OK, now it's time to make like Jamie Oliver and start boshing things in and mushing stuff up. There's no harm in boshing you know – his food always looks great.'

'He's had years of practice getting it perfect,' he said, taking a Jamie Oliver cookbook and flipping it open randomly. 'You see? Look at that pasta salad, it's perfect, and all the vegetables are the same size. That's how I want the chilli to look.'

'Why don't we try for an artistic interpretation instead?' I suggested with a smile.

I was enjoying cooking with Jamie, it felt comfortable, and I liked seeing more of his vulnerable side. He really wanted to impress and make it special. Cooking was something he seemed to think he should be good at, being a practical, creative person. The fact that this skill was eluding him made him seem all the more attractive.

He topped up my wine.

'It's a good job I got a taxi over here, we seem to be getting through this pretty fast.'

'We're making a good team, I think,' he said, holding out his own glass for a toast.

'We are. A great team.' I clinked glasses with him, noticing that the alcohol was already making me feel slightly heady, then picked up a handful of wrinkled red chillies and held them out. 'So, how hot do you think we should make it tonight?' I said, grinning.

'Oh my God, Jamie, my mouth is actually on fire,' Cassie said as he took her plate away and went to put it with the others by the drainer. 'I can no longer feel my lips.'

We all laughed and Patrick leant over to kiss her.

'You see?' She rubbed her lips together, pouting comically. 'Nothing. Didn't feel it. I think they've died.'

'Don't worry, Jamie, I thought it was really tasty, thank you,' Patrick said. 'Cassie's just a lightweight, but we have to forgive her, the girl can't help it.'

The chilli had been hot, probably something to do with the fact that Jamie and I had drunk a whole bottle of wine between us before the guests arrived. Our taste buds must have been dulled by the alcohol as when we tested it we agreed it tasted bland and had sprinkled Tabasco Sauce liberally into the pot. It looked good though, and the first thing Cassie had done when she saw it was comment on its evenly sliced vegetables. She'd winked at me when she said it, as though Jamie's perfectionism in the kitchen was a long-running joke.

Cassie and I had got on well. She reminded me of Nikki in the way she was able to say what she thought, no matter how blunt, and still get away with it without offending anyone.

I liked Patrick too. He was an impressively tall and strikingly good-looking Jamaican. He had soft brown eyes like warm chocolate and when he laughed it sounded like it was echoing from deep within his voluminous chest. They were a very tactile couple, which seemed to be rubbing off on Jamie and me, helping us to relax our inhibitions and be more affectionate too.

'We've got a choice of dessert,' Jamie called out from the other side of the kitchen. 'It's either apple strudel or Bailey's ice cream. Any preferences or would you like both?'

'Ice cream,' we all called out in unison, sticking our tongues out to indicate that something cold and numbing would be a welcome relief.

'Yes, all right, very funny. I get the hint.' He started to gather glass bowls together and Patrick got up to help him. When he was out of earshot Cassie beckoned me to sit next to her.

'So, how are things going with Jamie?' she asked in the manner of a playground gossip.

I had been expecting this kind of questioning from Cassie at some point over the evening and laughed at the inevitability of it. 'Fine, yes, he's a really great guy.'

'He really is. He's going to make someone a cracking husband one day.'

'I'm surprised he hasn't already,' I countered.

Cassie watched Jamie for a moment as though making sure he wasn't about to return to the table. 'He nearly did, you know. He was engaged last year; broke it off after a few months.'

I looked at her, surprised. He had mentioned an ex but I hadn't realised they'd been engaged.

'He didn't want it to finish and he was pretty upset at the time, but he knew it was the right thing. He never felt like he could trust her; she used to flirt with his friends and sneak around a bit. He gave up trying in the end – didn't seem to be getting the right kind of commitment from her. I'm glad he's not with her anymore but I do feel sorry for him. He's got a lot to give.'

We both looked over at Jamie again and I felt a tug of empathy for him. I knew exactly how he must have felt.

Cassie and Patrick stayed until the early hours of the morning. It had been a good night and I knew I was drunk. I was slurring my words and walking unsteadily, giggling at myself and the lack of control I had over my faculties. After we'd seen them off at the doorstep Jamie suggested making a pot of tea and I accepted gratefully, flopping down on the sofa whilst he made it.

'I'll help you clear up in a minute, Jamie. I just need to sit for one, no, two minutes,' I said holding up three fingers and sniggering again.

'Don't you worry about that. I want you to put your feet up. The washing-up can keep till tomorrow.'

I patted the sofa next to me, wanting him to sit down too. His pottering around was making me feel guilty.

He brought a tray of mugs and tea things and put them on the table in front of us then sat down next to me.

'Thanks so much for coming early and bailing me out,' he said.

'I hardly bailed you out. You were doing fine on your own. It was a great evening and a lovely dinner. I've really enjoyed myself.'

'Me too. You've been the perfect date.'

'Have I?' I smiled at him, flattered.

He moved towards me and suddenly we were kissing. Not cautiously, like last time, but with a heart-racing, uninhibited passion. I was genuinely surprised at how it just happened. I hadn't been aware of any obvious sexual tension between us when we'd been cooking earlier but now it felt as though it had been there all along, humming under the surface, building up for hours and hours until we finally found our moment.

He lay back on the sofa, pulling me with him and I moved onto his chest, our mouths not breaking apart. It felt so good to be kissed like that. It had been a while, and after weeks of feeling uncertain and insecure, questioning everything, it was a massive release to let that all go and sink myself completely into the moment. His hands were in my hair, cupping my face, following the curves of my body and lightly trailing inside the low waist of my jeans, touching my bare skin until it made me shiver.

My kisses trailed from his mouth to the nape of his neck where I breathed in his spicy, intoxicatingly masculine aftershave, then back to his mouth again, kissing harder, neither of us caring about technique; we were all clashing teeth and bumping noses, our wet lips covering each other's faces, licking and exploring.

When we stopped briefly, panting to catch a breath, Jamie pressed the curls of my hair off my hot cheeks and looked at me. I propped my head up on his chest and looked back at him. My body was pulsing and it felt as though all the nerve endings were bristling, standing up like the hairs on the back of my neck, anticipating being touched again.

'You never did show me your bedroom.' I was trying to sound seductive but with the slur in my voice I sounded more like I'd had root canal treatment.

'Mmmm, it's comfy up there,' Jamie murmured, nuzzling into my neck. 'And the view's so good.'

'Yeah? Can I see it?' I started tugging him up.

'Really? In the dark?'

'We could look at the moon,' I said and we both started laughing childishly at the double meaning and at our own sudden urge to scramble off the sofa and head upstairs.

# Chapter Twenty-One

I opened my eyes tentatively, certain that a sudden surge of sunlight would have the same devastating effect on my head as a bolt of lightning.

It was bright in the room, hazy light shining in from the window behind the bed. Jamie and I had never got around to closing the curtains, I seemed to recall. We had fallen on top of the bed, entwined in each other and had, oh God, oh no . . .

I looked over at Jamie who was now under a thin sheet, lying on his back with his face turned towards me. His breathing was heavy and regular and his eyelids flickered. He was fast asleep. I pulled the sheet self-consciously higher, despite still being half-dressed in the clothes I'd worn the night before. My bra was still on and so were my jeans. My top was hanging off the bedside table. Jamie was probably in a similar state, I thought, not wanting to check and find out. We'd been so drunk, we must have fallen asleep before we'd got much further than kissing and groping. *How classy am I?* I thought, cringing. I looked up at the ceiling; what was I going to do? I couldn't sneak off before he woke up, could I?

As I glanced upwards I spotted a tiny pebble come in

through the open window. It arced over my head, bounced off Jamie's midriff and dropped onto the floor. His body tensed and his eyes flickered open. 'Mmm?' He looked around then winced, touching his temples as though the light was hurting him too. 'What the . . .?' Another pebble bounced off the middle pane of glass, making a clattering sound.

I got up and I looked out of the window just as a third came up and bounced off my forehead. 'Hey!' It was Fay and Nikki, standing in the street next to Fay's old blue mini.

'At last!' Nikki cried. 'Do you know what time it is? We were supposed to set off at eight.'

'Oh God, I'd forgotten.'

'Duh! We didn't get any answer on your mobile and we've been knocking on the door for ages.'

'What's going on?' Jamie said, appearing at the window. He was also bare-chested and still in his jeans, I noted.

'It's Fay and Nikki. I'm sorry, I'd completely forgotten we were supposed to be going to Devon today.' I looked at him, mortified. We'd not even had a chance to talk about the night before.

'It's OK, I'll go and let them in,' he said, the expression on his face unreadable. He quickly grabbed a T-shirt off a chair and pulled it over his head. I gratefully followed his lead, putting on the vest top I'd worn the night before then slipping my shirt over it, not bothering to do up the buttons.

Jamie pulled back the curtains in the kitchen to reveal the remains of the night before. There were piles of dirty dishes and glasses on the work surfaces and I noticed that the tray of tea things Jamie had made before we went

210

upstairs was still on the coffee table, untouched except for the sugar bowl which was turned over on the floor, sugar grains everywhere. I had a mental flashback of Jamie and I trying to get up from the sofa, still kissing, and knocking the bowl over in our haste. To me it told a story and I looked at Fay and Nikki, certain that it would say the same things to them too.

'We can always come back later,' Nikki was saying, standing in the doorway with Fay. 'It's fine. There's no reason why we need to race off to Devon, is there?' Fay agreed with a nod. 'Or we could go to a café in the town. You can meet us there when you're ready.'

I liked the thought of meeting them in a café. It would give me a chance to clear the air with Jamie. I wanted us back in our normal, comfortable state, not this hunched shoulders, hands in pockets, stumbling for the right words nonsense.

'Oh no, don't be daft, it's fine, isn't it Gemma?' Jamie said, all smiles again.

I nodded, my head reverberating painfully, and asked for a glass of water.

We chatted over a cup of tea and then I left them to it so that I could freshen up in the bathroom and collect my things together. I could hear their easy banter as I came down the stairs but when I walked in the room it seemed to fizzle away and go quiet. Jamie looked at me, my bag in my hand, ready to go, and I looked from him to Nikki and Fay, not sure how to handle it.

'We'll go and wait in the car,' Fay said, getting up and nudging Nikki to do the same.

I smiled gratefully. 'I'll be out in a minute,' I told them.

'Nice to meet you, Jamie,' Nikki said, lingering at the door before Fay pulled her out.

Jamie laughed and got up. He leaned on the edge of the

table near me and squeezed my hand. 'Are you OK?'

'I'm fine.'

'Sore head?'

'A bit.'

'Me too.' He laughed. 'We had so much wine last night, didn't we? I hope it didn't show too much.'

'I think we got away with it,' I said, unconvincingly.

'It was fun though, wasn't it? I haven't done that in ages. Get drunk like that, I mean,' he amended quickly, looking at me with faint embarrassment.

I laughed. 'It's OK, I know what you mean.'

He laughed too, but quickly became serious again. 'Gemma, I just wanted to say I'm sorry if . . .'

'It's OK, you don't have to.'

'No, I should. I don't want you to think that I was going to, you know—' he sighed heavily and pulled a face like he was finding the whole conversation awkward, '—to think that I was trying to take advantage of the situation or anything.'

'No, please, it's cool, I'm fine about everything.'

'I'm usually such a nice guy though,' he said, looking at me with an apologetic smile.

'You *are* a nice guy,' I said and touched him briefly. 'Don't worry, I had a lovely time. Perhaps I'll call you when I get back? We're only going for the day.'

'Yes, do that. Call me any time. Let me know how your day went.'

We both glanced at the front door, then back at each other again, conscious of Fay and Nikki outside and the fact that I was going to have to rush off before things were properly resolved. Neither of us spoke. It'll have to keep, I thought, and walked reluctantly to the door, more confused than ever.

\*

'I can't believe you,' Nikki said as we pulled out of Jamie's road.

'Hmm?' I opened one eye, squinted at her, then closed them both again.

'You stand up your friends because you're out all night getting your leg over, then when we finally manage to spirit you away from *lover* boy you've got the cheek to fall asleep in the backseat without even filling us in on the gossip first!'

'My head hurts,' I moaned, leaning it against the cold glass of the back window.

'Ooh, you're gonna love us then,' Fay chipped in. 'There's a cool bag on the back seat with some cans of coke and some bottled water.'

'Ahh, you're angels.' I opened the bag and could have wept at the almost seductive sight of a can of coke, misted over with condensation.

Nikki peered around from the passenger seat with what she clearly hoped was an angelic expression. 'See? We're very thoughtful friends, so you should feel able to confide in us.'

I groaned. 'I don't want to talk about it.'

'Really?' Fay looked at me in the rear-view mirror. 'With you two peeping out of his bedroom window half-dressed this morning I assumed things must have gone pretty well.'

'They did, it was a good night. We just got a bit too drunk, I suppose.'

'Oh no, he wasn't ... don't tell me he couldn't ...' Nikki looked at me with pity in her eyes.

'Erm, I don't think he had a problem in that department, but I didn't really get to put it to use. We both fell asleep once we made it to his bedroom.'

'Ahh, really? I think that's sweet,' Fay said.

213

'Hmm.' I frowned. It'd be sweet it we'd woken up in the morning and carried on where we left off. Now I wasn't sure what was going on or how he really felt about me. I didn't feel like talking about it right then. I was tired, confused, embarrassed, and had a hangover not helped by the fact that Fay's mini felt like a go-kart and sounded like a lawnmower. I popped the ring pull on my drink and sighed when a spray of sticky, saccharine fizz exploded from the can. I'd forgotten how that always happened in Fay's car.

It took us an hour longer to get there than we had bargained for. This was partly because we had ended up following the M5 all the way to Exeter. We hadn't needed to go that far but Fay had chickened out of exiting at the two previous junctions because according to her, she needed an uphill exit lane or her mini wouldn't be able to stop in time. Nikki and I weren't exactly cheered by the fact that she had so little faith in her brakes. She'd also refused to go more than sixty miles an hour because apparently the last time she did that, her car used up a whole pint of oil between Bath and Bristol.

By the time we had negotiated our way out of Exeter and found ourselves lost in the Devon countryside, Nikki and Fay were barely even speaking to each other.

I looked again at the Ordnance Survey map. 'It's definitely round here somewhere,' I said.

Nikki groaned. 'That's what you've been saying for the past half an hour. Let's face it, we're lost.'

'Yeah, well, there are so many turns and crossroads, it's confusing. I swear there are a lot of roads that aren't marked on the map.' I squinted at it again, looking for the name of the village we'd just driven through. The trouble was my hangover seemed to be playing havoc with my

214

brain. I was struggling to make sense of anything. 'I think it must be straight on,' I guessed, trying to sound confident.

Fay pulled the car out onto the narrow lane and Nikki tutted with exaggerated annoyance as Fay's row of cuddly toys were once again jerked off the dashboard onto her lap.

'You don't have to come back with us, you know.' Fay snapped. 'I can drop you off at a train station.'

'Actually we passed a "ponies for hire" sign a mile back. How about you leave me there? I'll bet you a fiver that I still get home before you.'

Fay pursed her lips and stared daggers at the lane ahead. Once again a silence descended on the car and I looked out of the window at the scenery; the rolling green farmland was dotted with thatched cottages and the occasional stone spire of a church. It was very picturesque, very rural England, but not the kind of place I could imagine a teenaged Miranda being happy. I'd grown up in a village myself and I knew how claustrophobic it could be, even with the city of Bath a bike ride away. Abbotstone was miles away from anywhere; there wouldn't have been much to keep a teenager occupied, especially a quirky teenager like Miranda. I felt another wave of guilt. She would have been conspicuous around here, maybe even an oddity. She must have been lonely.

'Pheasant!' Fay cried, snapping me back from my thoughts. The car jerked sharply to the right to avoid the bird that was standing dumbly in the middle of the road and I lurched across the back seat.

'Watch out!' Nikki cried, covering her eyes as a tractor came into view. Fay swung the mini back onto her side of the lane, bumping along the grass verge as we passed the tractor. The wheels lost their grip in a patch of mud

215

outside a farm gate and the car slid into an old, muddied up signpost which clanged on impact then bent over at an oblique angle.

We sat in silence for a few seconds, assessing the situation. We were all fine. We hadn't hit the post very hard. Everything was OK. Then Fay seemed to snap back to life again saying, 'Oh no, oh no, my little car!' She opened her door in a hurry and clambered out. Nikki and I followed after her.

She went to the front of the car and looked at the damage: a slight dent in the front bumper, nothing more. She sniffed, rubbing the bottom of her nose with the back of her hand and I realised she was crying. 'I'm really sorry,' she said. 'Nikki was right, I should have let her drive. I'm such an idiot!'

'Hey, don't worry.' I put a comforting arm around her shoulder. 'It was an accident, no big deal. And it's a small dent, isn't it? It can easily be fixed.'

'But it's my little car,' she said in a small voice, touching the bonnet as if it were the coffin lid of a dear departed friend.

'Oh come on,' Nikki said, 'it'll be fine. Let's all cheer up, shall we?' She nudged her teasingly, then said with a voice of mock mystical awe, 'Hey Fay, look, it's a *sign*!' She gestured to the dipped signpost with all the flourish of a magician's assistant.

'It's not funny,' Fay said. She looked as though she was about to have a go at Nikki for laughing at her but then she stopped, the corners of her mouth turning up slightly. 'Hang on, it really is a sign.' She walked past Nikki to the top of the post and rubbed at the mud with her hands to reveal the writing beneath. It read, ABBOTSTONE ½ MILE. 'See? A sign! Looks like we're not that lost after all.'

*

'It's like going back in time,' I said, staring out of the window at the little row of thatched shops on the high street. There was a post office that was shut, with toys for sale in the window, stacked three rows high in their boxes. The coloured plastic had faded in the sun, as though they had sat in the same spot for years. There was a butcher's shop that looked empty and clinical, with only a steel counter on show and a plastic pig's head above the door. It was adjoined to a farm shop that at least appeared to have some life about it, with bright vegetables on display racks and rows of local jams in the window. There was nobody around. The coloured flags on the bunting that criss-crossed the road flickered in the breeze, reminding me of tumbleweed in a ghost town, the only movement in a village that could otherwise have been frozen in time.

'Where is everyone?' Nikki said.

Fay shrugged. 'There's a weird atmosphere, don't you think? Like the whole place has been evacuated and we're the only ones that don't know.'

'Well, Miranda did say they were moving somewhere quiet,' I said. 'Looks like she wasn't kidding.' I looked at the printout we'd done of the street map of Abbotstone. 'Well, according to this we're almost there. It's left at the end of High Street then Dean's Lane is the first on the right.'

Fay signalled as we approached the junction and I felt a flutter of butterflies in my stomach when I realised we were actually going to face these people who had been so hostile on the phone. What were we thinking?

Nikki knocked on the door again as Fay and I shuffled closer together. It was a large, imposing house with gabled roofs and a sweeping gravel drive that crunched conspicuously underfoot. There was an executive-style car in the drive. I noticed a silver ichthus badge next to the rear number plate: a Christian symbol that was an extra reassurance to me that we'd got the right house. Unfortunately, despite the car in the drive, there didn't appear to be anyone home.

'I don't believe it. All this way and there's no one in.' Nikki kicked at the gravel in annoyance. 'What are we going to do now?'

The sound of church bells broke the silence, taking us all by surprise. It was the first sign of life in the village. 'Perhaps they've been to a church service?' I said. 'We could go and find a pub, get a bite to eat then come back afterwards, see if they've returned.' My stomach rumbled and I realised I hadn't eaten anything all day. I hadn't been able to face it till then. I looked at them hopefully.

'Good plan,' Nikki said, swinging her bag over her shoulder and striding ahead. I followed after her, hoping this wasn't going to be a wasted trip.

The only pub in the village was shut.

'I don't sodding well believe this! What's wrong with this place? It's Sunday lunchtime, surely they have to open for lunch? Where the bugger are they all?' Nikki was getting more and more agitated.

I peered in at the window but the place really was deserted, the lights were off and there were towels hanging over the brass beer pumps. Then I realised there was a poster in the window of the pub; it had today's date on it.

*Abbotstone Summer festival June 28th–29th*
  *Come and join us celebrate the festival weekend!*
    *Saturday – Summer Carnival and Hog Roast all day till late.*

*Sunday – Patronal service at St Peters Church
11am till 1pm.*

*1pm onwards – afternoon tea at the vicarage.*

*Fun and celebration with stalls, live jazz, local
crafts, a vibrant quilting display, an inflatable vicar
plus so much more.*

*Come ye, come one and all!*

I looked at my watch: it was ten past one. 'Of course!
That's were everyone is, and that's why the bells were
ringing, because the service has just finished.' I looked
around the village then spotted a spire behind a cottage on
the other side of the road. 'Follow that church,' I said,
tugging Fay and Nikki away from the pub door.

The closer we got the more signs of life we noticed;
cars lining the surrounding lanes by the church, the distant
chatter of groups of people, the hum of a generator, a
band beginning to tune up. We reached the entrance and
saw that there were some remaining stragglers leaving the
church, dressed in their Sunday best, catching up with a
vicar who was following the path around to the gardens
behind.

'If Miranda's parents are here how do you think we'll
recognise them? I certainly wouldn't remember them after
fourteen years,' Nikki said.

She was right: it was all very well knocking on the door
of their house; picking them out of a crowd was another
thing altogether. 'I suppose we'll just have to ask around.
Someone is bound to know of them.'

The entire population of the village must have been
there, plus several of the surrounding villages as well. It
was buzzing with people, all in good spirits as they either
milled around the different stalls or sat on the white plastic
garden chairs, eating scones and drinking tea from a

makeshift café run by two industrious old ladies.

I scanned the crowd but unsurprisingly no one looked familiar, Miranda's parents could have been any of them.

'I've never been to a vicar's tea party before,' Fay said, looking around in fascination. She was attracting a few curious stares herself with her bottled red hair and typically unique outfit that included a pleated mini-skirt and biker boots.

'Come on, let's get this over with. Where do we start?' Nikki said.

'Why don't we split up, talk to a few people on the stalls and see what we can come up with. I think it's best to hunt them out subtly rather than draw too much attention to ourselves before we have to.'

They both nodded. 'I'll start over there then.' Nikki pointed out a beauty products stall at the far end of the field.

'Ooh, where to go.' Fay bit her bottom lip as though trying to pick a pudding from a dessert trolley. 'It's all just so funny and English and quirky, I can't decide.'

We both looked at her with strained patience.

'Oh go on then, I'll do the tombola first, then work my way around the white elephant stalls over there.'

She bounded off enthusiastically across the field before I could remind her that we had come here to find Miranda's parents and not have a lovely day out at a village fête. Nikki followed behind.

'Well,' I said to myself smiling, 'I suppose that leaves me with the tea and scones table.'

Getting around to a leading subject was so easy it was almost laughable. All it took was a polite smile and the ladies were getting me to sample their scones, fussing over me like a couple of mad aunts.

'So, you're not a local girl then?' the older of the two ladies started off.

'No, I'm just here for the day, looking for an old friend. You might know her, Miranda Patterson?'

The ladies exchanged quizzical looks. 'Miranda? There's no one called Miranda round here.'

'No, no one with that name,' the younger, but still very old lady agreed.

'Ah, well it has been a long time. She moved here about ten years ago. She was a teenager then.'

'Ooh, a teenager. We know a teenager, don't we, Betty?' The older lady looked excited and was tugging on Betty's cardigan.

'We do, Doris. We do know a teenager.' She put her bony finger to her chin and looked up at the sky as though deep in thought for what felt like a very long time. 'In fact, I think I know two.'

'They're terribly exciting, aren't they, Betty?' Doris piped up.

'Oh yes. Terribly. And they have such hair.' Betty held her hands over her head to indicate that their hair was very big and managed to drop the spoon she was using for the cream behind her back.

'Here, let me help you.' I hurried behind the table to get the spoon for her. This wasn't going to be as easy as I'd first thought.

Twenty minutes later I spotted Nikki at the quilt display. She was waving me over.

'I'm sorry ladies, but I'm going to have to leave you now,' I said, untying my apron and handing it to Betty. They both looked disappointed. 'I know, it's been great meeting you. I'll come back later for a cup of tea, introduce you to my friends.'

They brightened at that. 'Ooh yes, do.'

221

'You must,' Doris agreed, 'then we can have some of our gooseberry wine. I've got some under the table.' She showed me an unmarked cardboard box which she'd hidden from view by draping a cardigan over it. Suddenly she put her hand on my arm and gripped it tightly, leaning in towards me. 'You need something to take your mind off that fella you left behind this morning. It'll do you no good at all dwelling on that now.' I looked at her, amazed. After almost half an hour of listening to her nonsense chatter, this sudden moment of clarity had taken me by surprise. How did she know? I hadn't even told her about Jamie. I touched my face, wondering if there was something about my appearance that gave away what I'd been up to the night before; perhaps I really did have sexual frustration and confusion written all over my face? Perhaps as well as a shag-happy expression, there was also a shag-nearly expression I hadn't been aware of? I sighed and looked over at Nikki, who was hopping about and pulling faces at me as though rapidly losing patience. I said a hasty goodbye and made my way over to her.

'At last!' she said impatiently when I appeared before her. 'I was beginning to think you'd found yourself some employment over there.'

'Sorry. I had to help them out. The queue was getting mutinous. Any joy?'

'As a matter of fact, yes. The lady running this stall pointed them out to me a minute ago.' She searched the crowd with her eyes. 'There. See the lady on the cake stall with the pale blue blouse and the brown wavy hair?'

I saw the one she meant and nodded.

'That's Miranda's mum. Her dad's talking to the vicar over by the raffle stall.'

I vaguely recognised the dad, although not enough to

have picked him out of a crowd without help. He patted the vicar on the back then took his position on a makeshift stage and picked up a microphone.

'Ladies and gentleman, can I have your attention please?'

The crowd quietened down and all eyes focused on him.

'I would now like to begin the raffle draw. If you can all get your tickets ready whilst I say a few words of thanks for the organisers of this event . . .'

Nikki nudged me. 'Which one are we going to approach then, the mum or the dad?'

'The mum,' I said, remembering the tone of voice Ken Patterson had used with me on the phone. The mum had been softer, more nervous and therefore, I felt, easier to persuade. 'Have you let Fay know you've found them?'

Nikki pulled a face. 'I haven't seen her in a while. She was mingling so well with the crowd I reckon she'll change her hair to a light shade of blue before the day is out.'

'Well, I don't think we should wait for Fay to come back; the mum might have gone by then,' I said.

'You're right. Let's wait until the raffle is over and the crowd are mingling again, then we can get her, and hopefully she'll be on her own.'

'It's orange and it's one hundred and eighty-three,' Mr Patterson announced, holding up an unfolded ticket for the audience to see.

'That's me that's me that's me that's me,' I heard an excitable voice calling. Everyone looked around to see Fay holding a ticket in the air and beaming as though she had just won the lottery, hurrying to the front of the crowd.

'Oh no,' I heard Nikki groan under her breath as Fay, not concentrating on where she was going, tripped on a cable and flew straight into the eight-foot-high inflatable vicar. It tipped backwards under her and they both slumped to the ground.

Many of the women nearby averted their eyes at the sight of Fay lying horizontally on top of the vicar, scrambling to get up in an undignified manner.

Nikki and I came to her rescue and the raffle resumed with her prize put to one side.

'I want to go home now,' Fay said in a small voice, her face as deeply red as her hair.

'Oh no you don't, lady,' Nikki said. 'You brought us here for one purpose only. Now we're going to see this through if it kills me.'

Approaching Miranda's mum was never going to be easy after a public spectacle like that but we had little choice. When the raffle was over and the people had scattered around the stalls once more, we warily made our way over to her stall.

'Mrs Patterson,' I started.

'Yes,' she said brightly, turning to face us. Her smile faded slightly when she recognised Fay from before.

'I called you the other day about your daughter Miranda.'

Her smile vanished completely and she looked around as though fearful someone was listening to our conversation.

'Mrs Patterson, I'm sorry to bother you again but I was really hoping you could help us. We met Miranda a long time ago now. You came to my parents' house in Langley Green one New Year's Eve. You went out to a party with them and Miranda stayed with us. Do you remember?'

There was recognition in her eyes. 'Yes, yes I think I do. Andrew's daughter. Was it Andrew?' For a moment we had something in common and the suspicion was gone. Although her memory must have been vague, she asked politely after my parents and I told her a bit about what they were up to. Eventually, when the social niceties were out of the way, she said, 'So, you stayed in touch with Miranda? How long for?'

'It was with letters really, up until you moved here. I'm not sure if she ever wrote after you'd moved.'

She didn't look surprised. 'No, well it was a difficult time for her. A lot happened.' There was an awkward pause. Obviously she didn't want to elaborate and I didn't want to push her. I tried to brighten up the conversation instead. 'We all got on well with Miranda. She's one of those people you meet in life that really leaves an impression.'

She smiled at that.

'We've often thought of her over the years. It would be so nice to catch up. Is there any chance you could give us an address? A contact number or anything? Or if you'd rather not I can leave my phone number for you to pass on, let her know we were asking after her?'

Again she looked around anxiously until her eyes fell on her husband. She seemed satisfied that he was far enough away and obscured by people. 'OK, but please understand,' she said to us in a lowered voice, 'my husband and Miranda have had a terrible fallout. It was only a little over a year ago. He's still so angry, he won't have her name spoken in front of him. Please, don't tell him why you're here.' She looked down at her hands, embarrassed. 'He never really approved of her. She always seemed to want to be different for the sake of it, like she enjoyed being something that Ken didn't want her to be, just to disappoint him. When we met up with her the last time she confirmed what I'd suspected for a long time. Ken couldn't take it, said we'd brought her up with good Christian values and for her to directly flaunt her, her beliefs and, uh,' she took a deep breath, clearly struggling, 'and to be practising her beliefs so openly. Well, it goes against everything Ken brought her up to believe. He's very rigid and won't accept it.'

I looked up and saw that Ken had seen us. He looked curious and was beginning to move in our direction until someone stopped him for a chat. His wife noticed this too and grew increasingly anxious. She took her handbag off her shoulder and took out a pen and paper. She scribbled something on it then hesitated. 'If I give you this now, will you go? I don't want Ken being upset. He's got a bad heart and . . .' she shook her head and passed it to me. 'Here, it's the last address I have for her. She should still be living there. I speak to her from time to time. It's not easy, but I do want to keep in touch with her.' She shrugged and laughed, as though at her own foolishness. 'Well, of course I do, she's my daughter.' Her happiness is more important than anything else. I'm glad she's finally at peace with herself. If you see her, will you do one thing for me? Will you tell her I love her? She knows, but tell her anyway.'

I nodded, taking the paper off her and checking that Ken hadn't seen. 'I will. Thank you.' I glanced down at the paper and when I looked up she was talking to someone, her back to us. Our conversation was over.

# Chapter Twenty-Two

It was an address, no phone number, for a flat in Brighton. Fay hadn't been at all surprised when I'd read it out to them on the way back to the car.

'Of course she's in Brighton!' she'd said, slapping her forehead as though she couldn't believe it hadn't occurred to her before. 'It makes perfect sense.'

'Do you know something we don't?' Nikki had asked, not looking so convinced.

'Oh come on, this is Miranda we're talking about. Not happy in a small town, she'd want to live in a city, but it couldn't be just any city; she was so out-there and different it would have to be a cosmopolitan, modern place with modern ideas, to be able to accept her, but not too fashionable, not London. It'd have to be a bit hippyish, a bit bohemian too. Brighton's perfect. I can see her now, reading palms for the tourists.'

'Yeah, or selling lavender on the beach, dressed like a bag lady and doing the sun salutation every morning on the pier,' Nikki added, nodding. 'Now you mention it I can totally imagine that.'

'She could be an ordinary person with an office job for all we know,' I said.

'Never.' Fay shook her head. 'There's something very weird going on with her. And she has to be practising, using her gift for telling the future. That must have been what her mum meant about "practising so openly" and it being against her dad's religious beliefs.'

'Fay, I don't want you getting your hopes up about this,' I said cautiously. 'She could have meant a lot of different things. Obviously something pretty heavy has gone on with her and her family; it could be anything.' Meeting her mum had left me with an uneasy feeling and I was getting worried about what we were getting ourselves into, and just what kind of person we were going to find in Brighton.

Nikki offered to drive us there the following weekend, suggesting that we stay in a hotel by the sea and make a weekend break out of it. We were happy to take her up on that.

Finally I was going to get my chance to stand by the edge of the sea and try for a fresh perspective on life. Whatever had happened to Miranda, whatever she had become, I still had the same unexplainable feeling I'd had since we first found the predictions: that no matter what she'd become and what she thought about what had happened, seeing her again would help me make sense of everything, one way or another.

I spoke to Jamie on the phone every night for most of the following week. Every time I thought about our night together I felt curiously like a nervous teenager. Memories of how it felt to lie on top of him and feel how much he wanted me would flash into my head at odd moments in the day, catching me by surprise and making me flush with a powerful cocktail of excitement and embarrassment. I couldn't bring myself to mention it to Jamie and I got the feeling he didn't dare bring it up either, which was so strange when in every other way we were so comfortable with each other. He's been hurt before, and so have I, I concluded. We've both been in long-term relationships; starting all over again with someone else is bound to be hard. But still, we were both grown adults, so I found it strange how night after night we wanted to talk to each other but did not want to talk about us.

My lack of finesse at handling a potential new relationship was made all the more apparent to me by the fact that I was living in the middle of the hormonal whirlpool which used to be my housemates. For my benefit they tried hard to act normally and keep their relationship discreet, but it was impossible not to notice the atmosphere of attraction in the house. I couldn't help thinking it was like living with Geena Davis in *Thelma and Louise* when she fell for the cowboy, failing to spot that he was actually an armed robber. I was watching Tim more closely than ever for signs of suspicious behaviour but since the night I saw him in the alley he seemed to be making more of an effort to keep his business 'activities' private.

On Thursday night it was Hitchcock night on BBC Two. Fay talked me into staying up late to watch a film with her whilst Tim was out, supposedly having a drink with a client. We watched the film in the dark, sharing a bottle of wine between us. Fay sat forward, so absorbed in the story she hardly touched her glass; I topped mine up regularly, staring bewildered at the screen as I tried to keep up with the plot and decipher the significance of a huge pair of eyeballs and some pointy scissors. As it appeared to be nearing its conclusion, Tim returned. He snuck into the room quietly, looking at the television to see what had captured Fay's attention. '*Spellbound*!' he cried and hurried onto the sofa next to Fay. 'I love this film.'

Fay shushed him but smiled to herself, pleased he shared her enthusiasm for Hitchcock and they settled into silence again.

I sipped my wine, wondering if Tim was really into these sorts of films or whether it was his way of disarming Fay and winning her trust. After all, the TV Guide was lying open on the coffee table and Fay had put a ring around the Hitchcock programmes. He could easily have swotted up in advance. I looked over at him as he put a hand on Fay's thigh. As though sensing my eyes on him, he leaned back and looked right at me. I narrowed my eyes at him and he cocked his head to one side, tapping his ear then pointing at me. I couldn't hide my surprise. *I've been listening to you*, he was saying. My skin prickled as I wondered if he'd heard me on the phone to Nikki earlier in the week, finally confiding to her what I'd seen in the alley. I thought he'd been out but what if he hadn't? With the wine making me feel bold I made a quick decision not to be intimidated and tapped the corner of my eye then pointed straight back at him. *I'm watching you*, I was saying. He looked alarmed and I smiled to myself.

'Gemma, your phone, it's ringing,' he said, his voice loud so I could hear it over the television. Reluctantly I looked away and saw that my mobile on the table was flashing. That's what he meant. I leant forward, trying to hide my mortification, and picked it up.

'Right, I'll er, take this upstairs,' I said, trying to ignore the fact that Tim was now looking at me as though I'd taken leave of my senses, and hurried out of the room.

I answered the phone as soon as I was out of the living room, my hands shaking with humiliation but also with anticipation. Nobody ever called me at half past one in the morning and all sorts of emergency situations were

230

playing in my head, the last of which being Adam, suicidal without me, trying one last time to talk me into a reconciliation.

It was almost disappointing to hear a woman's voice on the other end of the line, especially a relatively cheerful one. 'Gemma, I'm so sorry, I assumed your mobile would be switched off. I was going to leave you a message.'

'Jules? Where are you?'

'We're in Bangkok, but only for a few more hours; we're flying out to Saudi this morning to stay with one of Richard's uncles for a week.'

'Are you OK? Are you having an amazing time?' I felt a wave of sentimentally at the sound of her voice and I realised how much I had missed her. So much had happened that I would have liked to have talked to her about. I had a sudden realisation that now Adam and I were no longer together the balance in our friendship would change. We had always been two couples.

'Oh, it's been amazing. I can't believe the six weeks is nearly up.' She sounded breathless. 'Listen, Gemma, I've got to hurry because we're packing, but I had to call you straight away. I've just been speaking to Marcia.'

'Oh.' I went into my bedroom, flopping onto the bed without bothering to turn the light on.

'She told me about you and Adam. I'm so sorry, I had no idea.'

'Had Richard not heard from Adam then?'

'No, not a peep. We couldn't believe it. I have to say Gem, I feel kind of responsible, what with Marcia being my cousin. I should have realised something had gone on; she's always been a terrible flirt. She feels awful about it, you know. Says it was all her, that she made a mistake and it didn't mean anything. From what she said I honestly don't think anything happened.'

I should have felt comforted by that but I felt empty. 'It's OK, things weren't going well anyway. I guess it just wasn't meant to be.'

'Really? Are you sure? I don't know, this whole situation is weird. I just can't believe you're not together anymore.' There was a pause and a sigh. 'I just wish we'd been there. I know it sounds silly, but maybe Richard could have talked to him, or I could have spoken to Marcia. At the very least I could have been there for you.'

'It's OK, it's fine. I'm fine.'

'Well, not long now till we get back then we can have a good chat,' she said softly, 'but in the meantime, I wanted to tell you that we fly into the UK on Thursday, in a week's time. I've been so desperate to catch up with you all I arranged for us to have a party at our house on the following Saturday, for our friends really, and the people who we couldn't invite to the wedding because the seats were taken up with Richard's over-populated family. I wanted to invite you, and Nikki and Fay, of course. Richard has already texted Adam to invite him. I'm really sorry, we started organising it all before we knew. Now I'm not so sure it's a good idea.'

'Don't be silly, it's a great idea. Don't feel bad because of us, we'll be fine.'

'Well, if you're sure,' she said, still sounding concerned. 'If it helps, Marcia will be going straight back up to Glasgow so she won't be there, and there will be loads of us, plenty for you to hide behind if facing Adam is difficult. Are you sure it's OK? You'll come, won't you? I couldn't bear it if you didn't. Please say you'll come.'

'Course I will,' I said. For a fleeting moment I remembered Jamie and wondered if I should ask if I could bring him along too, but I quickly dismissed the idea as ridiculous before I put it into words. 'I'll be there. It'll be good to see you; all of you,' I said instead, smiling in the darkness in an attempt to convince myself that it was as grown-up and as uncomplicated as I made out.

'There's no going back now,' Nikki said as she sped down the slip road ready to merge in with the traffic on the motorway.

'I've got butterflies,' I heard Fay say quietly from behind me.

'Hey, if it all goes tits up at least we're by the sea, the sun is shining, and the three of us will be together in a city surrounded by bars and beach cafés. It'll be fun.' I didn't feel as anxious as Fay seemed, probably because I didn't really expect to find Miranda. Perhaps because Miranda was feeling less and less like a real person and more like an enigma. Maybe she wasn't meant to be found. Or, more logically it was because I knew that travelling hundreds of miles to an unconfirmed address in the hope that she was a) still living there, and b) not away for the weekend, was always going to be a gamble.

I leaned forwards, taking the piece of paper her mum had given me out of my handbag, and read it again. FLAT 16A, PRESTON BUILDINGS, OLD FACTORY LANE, BRIGHTON. 'I hope it's nice,' I said, smoothing the paper out on my lap as though if it was well presented on paper it was more likely to be a decent place in reality. 'I want her to be happy with her life.'

Earlier in the week I had tried to get a phone number for her address but had drawn a blank. Not that I would have dared call it; somehow seeing her in the flesh was less daunting. I wondered about looking up her address on the Internet, to see if I could find any clues about her lifestyle, but I decided it was best not to, it could have

233

been misleading and I wanted to go without expectations.

'Well, we may as well just relax,' Nikki said, aiming the sentiment mainly at Fay, who was still sitting forward on the seat with her bag on her lap. 'We're going now. We'll know in a few hours. There's no point going over the "what ifs" again.'

Fay nodded and sat back, resigned. I smiled at her but she didn't notice as she was hunting through her bag for something. Eventually she found what she was looking for and took it out, visibly relaxing with whatever was retrieved. I looked down to see what it could be and recognised it immediately as Miranda's leopard brooch. She was holding it tightly, rubbing it with her thumb as though it were a lucky talisman, her thoughts miles away.

The day was getting hotter. We'd driven the final leg of our journey with the windows down, tolerating the noise and buffeting winds for the sake of some cool, fresh air. When we finally arrived in Brighton we slowed down from our relentless pace to join the traffic heading for the south side of the city. The moment we slowed down the noise and the wind ceased, my skin warmed up again and my senses were filled with the atmosphere of a seaside resort: the light, the seagulls, the rows of pastel coloured guest-houses. It was busy; the weather had brought people outside and they were everywhere, most of them loaded up with beach bags and heading for the distant glimpse of silver sea that shone between the tall white Regency buildings.

'I'm assuming we're going to park and see the sea before we go looking for Miranda, right?' Nikki said.

Fay and I readily agreed; after a long journey with only one stop we needed a walk. It was also hard to imagine getting this close to the sea without heading straight for it, no matter how pressing the intinerary. We managed to find one of the few remaining places in a car park just a short walk from the seafront and piled out the moment we parked, stretching and taking deep breaths of the salty air.

'Come on,' I said, linking arms with Nikki. 'Fay and I will buy you an iced coffee. You deserve one after driving all that way.'

We wanted to sit outside and take in the sea view but it was lunchtime and there were queues outside most of the cafés that spilled their tables onto the promenade between the two piers. When we came level with the Palace Pier Fay spotted a snack van with THE VAN OF LIFE artistically, but not particularly neatly, scribed on the side. She got so excited about it that we caved in and went to join the queue.

'Sun in a bun,' Fay said reverently, peering into the paper bag at her lunch.

Nikki sat down on the wall between us and passed out our drinks. 'Fay, it's a fried egg sandwich.'

'It's an amazing fried egg sandwich. Did you hear the guy in the van? He said the double yoke represented the sun sinking into its reflection as it sets over the sea.'

'The guy in the van had a pointy bolt screwed into the top of his pale, bald head.'

'Well, you can't deny the man can cook,' I said, licking salsa from my lips.

Nikki inspected her filled pitta bread then bit into it, conceding with a nod.

We sat and ate in silence whilst we took in our surroundings. The sea was breaking on the pebbles in front of us, the waves barely audible above the noise of the people shouting and laughing, music from the shops, cars passing behind us, and the occasional thump as one of the crowd playing volleyball a few yards from us hit the ball over the net.

Nikki ate her food quickly then took a map out of her bag. 'Right, I can't stay here much longer. I've got no sun lotion and I'm starting to burn. I think the time has finally come.'

Fay looked nervously at me. 'Nikki's right,' I said. 'We've come all this way; we have to see it through. Let's just go straight there and knock on the door, then if she's not there we can relax a bit, see the sights.'

According to the map it was about a mile and a half out from the centre on the north-east side of town. We decided to drive: Nikki was worried about the sun and we knew we could drive and park at the guesthouse we were staying in afterwards. We collected our things and headed back to the car.

We seemed to be driving through a more industrial area of the town. The buildings were darker, more sombre and plainer than the elegant townhouses we'd seen on the way through the town. We drove past a cemetery and my mood deflated further still. I was worried about Miranda. It sounded like she'd had a hard time and I still had this nagging feeling that I'd wronged her. That I'd let her down when she needed a friend.

'Old Factory Lane should be just on the right coming up,' Fay said.

'Yep, this is it.' Nikki signalled right and turned onto the road.

'So, we're looking for Preston Buildings,' Fay said, putting the map away.

I looked out of the window and saw it straight away. It was the only habitable building on the road. 'Crikey.'

'That is a monster of a building,' Nikki said, slowing down to look at it properly.

'Brutal,' Fay agreed.

Nikki pulled into a space on the street outside and switched the engine off.

We all looked at each other as though waiting for one of us to make the first move.

I took a deep breath. 'Come on then, let's do this,' I said and stepped out onto the pavement.

# Chapter Twenty-Three

Old Factory Lane lived up to its name: it was dominated by an enormous building that must have once, unsurprisingly, been a factory. It ran the length of the narrow road, casting a pervasive shadow onto the playing fields opposite. At the far end of the building there were a group of shops and a corner café, clustered together like barnacles on the prow of a merchant ship. There were three storeys of arched windows looking out onto the street, with a fourth storey in the centre where the building rose in a turret. Confused, I stood back, trying to work out where the door was and spotted an archway in the middle of the building where a cobbled path led through to the other side.

I led the way, with Nikki and Fay following behind, all of us trying to figure out just what kind of place it was. We walked through the archway and came out into a large, sunny courtyard that backed onto a wide lawn. The lawned area was neat, surrounded by a stone path and sloped down into a small orchard. There were several people sitting on the grass, reading a book or lying on the slope, sunbathing. None of them looked up to see who had wandered in.

From the front it may have looked like a dark, satanic mill, a desolate throwback to a Victorian era, but from the back it was much smarter. It seemed that it had recently been restored and converted into flats. There were two huge entrance doors, one on either side of the arch. Both doors had chrome plaques on the wall; one said PRESTON BUILDING A, the other PRESTON BUILDING B.

'This must be it,' I said as Nikki went closer and looked at the plaque by the door. There were buzzers for each flat. None of them had names next to them. She found number sixteen and pressed it.

Fay gasped. 'What did you do *that* for?'

Nikki looked at her in surprise. 'Well, I thought you would have wanted me to. You know, what with us driving all this way to see her and all.'

'I wasn't ready yet,' she said under her breath.

There was an agonising pause and Nikki was about to press it again when the intercom crackled into life and a woman's voice said 'hello'.

'Hi. Is that Miranda?' I asked, stepping towards the speaker. 'Miranda Patterson?'

There was another long pause. 'Who's this?'

'It's Gemma Thompson. I'm here with a couple of friends to see Miranda, if she still lives here.'

There was silence. Nikki started looking around again and Fay was just staring at the intercom, chewing furiously on her bottom lip. I began to wonder if the woman had gone off and forgotten all about us when the voice suddenly said, 'Come up. It's the top floor, last door at the end of the corridor.' The door buzzed, swinging open, and we walked inside.

The stairwell was huge, lit with squares of light from an equally large leaded window. It had a high, vaulted ceiling that made our voices echo and so we whispered to each

239

other as if we were in a church.

'Do you think that was her?' Fay asked.

'Surely it must have been,' I said.

'She sounded normal enough,' Nikki added. 'And I'm liking her pad. Either she's done very well for herself or she's got a seriously loaded boyfriend.'

By the time we'd climbed the stairs and located flat sixteen we were all panting for breath. We didn't need to knock. The door flew open as soon as we reached the end of the corridor.

Standing in the doorway was a tall, elegant woman dressed as though she was ready to go out for the evening, wearing a smart pair of black trousers and a thin red chiffon top, her hair pinned up loosely.

It was definitely Miranda. I knew it the moment I saw her dark eyes and the intensity of her expression. I was momentarily stunned. In my mind I had worked her into this Helena Bonham-Carter figure, a kind of anti-fashion art student meets bag lady, but before me was a sophisticated, stylish woman. The only hint of Miranda's old style was the chunky crucifix around her neck and the fact that she was dressed in black and dark red on one of the hottest days of the year.

She was looking at me just as curiously. 'Gemma Thompson. This is so funny, I never would have thought I'd recognise you but I really do. And it was Fay and Nikki, wasn't it?' she asked, turning to them.

They both nodded and there was an awkward moment when we weren't sure if she was ever going to let us in.

'I'm sorry, have we come at a bad time?' I asked. 'you look like you're on your way out.'

'Oh God no, well actually I am, I'm going to a party, but not for a couple of hours. You must come in.' She opened the door wide and beckoned us through into the flat.

It was impossible not to walk in and gaze around at Miranda's flat, which looked like the kind of place you would see featured on a design programme. It had hints to its industrial past everywhere with exposed brickwork on the external walls, an ancient-looking wooden floor, worn smooth to a glass-like finish, and cast-iron columns that broke up the open-plan rooms. Hanging on the vast walls were canvases painted with abstract images of women. At least I thought they were women; they could have been vases, or chairs with holes in the seats.

'Wow,' Nikki said, walking to the huge arched window. 'You can just see the sea. This place is gorgeous.'

'Thank you.' She crossed the room to the kitchen where she started filling up a kettle. 'It used to be Preston's, the old sweet factory. It made sweets and candyfloss for the North Pier in its heyday. I'm not lucky enough to actually own it. Chris, my partner, queued up for a flat when they first came up for sale a year and a half ago. I moved in six months later. I still can't believe how lucky I am to live here. Compared to the place I used to live in, this is some upgrade, I can tell you.' She looked awkward for a fleeting moment and then changed the subject. 'Can I get anyone a drink? I'm making one.'

'I'd love some coffee, if you don't mind?' Nikki said and Fay and I agreed.

'Great. I'll make a pot of filtered,' she said, starting to get things out of drawers. 'So, it's been a long time. How did you know where I lived now? I've moved around a lot and I haven't used my old name, Miranda Patterson, for a long time.'

241

I started to feel uncomfortable; I didn't want to admit the trouble we'd taken to find her. 'Well, we've been wanting to find you for a while. We knew you moved to Devon so we looked up your parents.'

Miranda shut the drawer with a bang and looked up. 'You spoke to Mum?'

'Yes. Well, we saw her actually. We were in the area so we called into the village on the off chance,' I lied. 'We saw your mum at a local fête and she passed on your address.'

'Really? I'm surprised she remembered it,' Miranda muttered then waved it off. 'Mum and I, we're not that close. We try, but Dad has his issues. It can make life awkward. Plus they do like to imagine they live in a bygone age where everyone resides in a community of God-fearing folk who bake their own bread and marry the first potent local that asks them.' She took four mugs from a shelf and lined them up noisily on the work surface. 'So, you went to Abbotstone. What did you make of it?'

'I thought it was lovely. Very picturesque and olde worlde.'

'It is. I can see why my parents love it so much. It drove me mad. Sugar?'

We all shook our heads.

'And you went to the summer fête.' She smiled for the first time since talking about the village. 'That was about as exciting as it got. Every year my mum's aunt would run the tea and scones stall and get drunk on homemade wine.'

I looked up at her in surprise. 'Yes! I think I met her. Is she called Doris? Or Betty? There were two of them.'

Miranda laughed. 'That's right! She's Doris. Betty is

242

her friend. Ha! I can't believe you met my Great-aunt Doris!'

'That's weird. I can't believe I was talking to her and I didn't know you were related.' A memory popped back into my conscious. Something Doris had said. She'd seemed to know I was dwelling on what happened with Jamie and it'd surprised me at the time. If Miranda really does have a sixth sense, I thought to myself, perhaps she inherited it from Doris? 'They were excellent,' I said, 'real characters. I had to help them out at one point; they were struggling with the queue. Kept talking to everyone. The funny thing is I asked if she knew someone called Miranda and she said no. Started talking about teenagers with big hair.'

Miranda laughed. 'That sounds like Doris. She's not been functioning on this planet for a long time. And she never really called me Miranda. Her and Betty used to call me Mimi for some reason. They have done since I was a baby.'

We fell silent whilst Miranda got the coffee machine working. There was a slightly awkward atmosphere, as though the underlying question about why, after so long, we had looked her up, was in all our minds but none of us wanted to be the first to mention it.

Once Miranda was satisfied that the coffee machine had started she asked us all to join her in the living area saying, 'So, come and tell me what you've been up to. What are you all doing now?'

We took turns filling her in on the basics of our lives. Fay spoke slowly, looking at Miranda as if she was telling her something she already knew and was waiting for her to click and remember. Miranda seemed to have picked up on the fact that Fay was acting strangely and watched her with interest.

As Miranda poured out three cups of coffee, I told her a bit about Dizzy Heights but then I broke off. Something she'd said earlier was still niggling at me and I had to ask. 'Look, I hope you don't mind me asking but earlier you said you don't go by your old name anymore and I couldn't help wondering why. Are you married?' That was my first theory, my second being that she was, as Fay had decided, practising in some kind of spiritual arts and had changed her name by deed poll to something more suitable, like Mystic Miranda. My second theory was looking less likely now though as Miranda was turning out to be surprisingly normal.

'No,' Miranda said with a surprised laugh. 'Definitely not married. That's not me at all. No, I changed my name by deed poll a long time ago now.'

*Ah ha, maybe she is a Mystic Miranda after all.* 'So what is your name now?'

'It's Miranda French. French is an old family name.'

'Why did you change it?' Fay asked.

'Well,' she said, sighing, as though it was a question she knew was coming but didn't know how best to answer. 'I was twenty-one at the time. I'd just come through a very difficult patch in my life and I was starting again. I was filling in an application form for a degree course in psychology and when I went to write my name I stopped. I just couldn't write it. It was as though, sitting there, I was reminded of every bad time I'd ever had and every mistake I'd made. I didn't want to be that person anymore. I wrote Miranda French on the form then had to change my real name pretty quickly after that. Of course it took me a degree in psychology to realise that wasn't the answer, but I kept the name. I've been Miranda French ever since.'

'And are you a psychologist now? Is that what you do?' Nikki asked.

'No. I did the degree, but then I went on to do an MSc in substance misuse. I'm a student counsellor for the University of Sussex. I specialise in drug and alcohol addiction. I'm also a part-time advisor for the Brighton Outreach Project.'

'Wow,' Nikki said, impressed. She snuck a brief glance at Fay and me as though trying to gauge our reaction. 'That must be a fulfilling job. It makes mine seem kind of lame.'

'Oh no, you can't see it like that. We're all doing things in our own way. Besides, I only specialised in that particular field because I'd seen it from the other side. I took quite a few wrong paths before I found a right one.'

'Really?'

'Oh yeah,' she sipped her coffee, holding the mug with both hands as she looked at us all. She hesitated, screwing up her face as though wrestling with a temptation to say something, then decided to go ahead and say it. 'I may as well tell you, and in fact you coming here also gives me a chance to apologise, because that night, when I met you all on New Year's Eve, I was high.'

'You mean on drugs?' Fay said, shocked.

Miranda nodded. 'LSD. I'd taken a tab in the car on the way over.'

'In the same car as your parents?' I cringed at my voice which had come out an octave higher than normal and made me sound like a prudish schoolgirl. Perhaps it was normal behaviour? Perhaps everyone took acid tabs in front of their parents and I had led a sheltered life?

She nodded again. 'I know, I was an idiot, I didn't think about the risks. I was anxious about going, needed a confidence booster. I wasn't good at relating to people from my peer group. I was an outsider really, very low self-esteem.' She took a deep breath. 'It wasn't the first time I'd done it; I'd been smoking pot for a year, getting if off some guy I'd met at a concert. He gave me an acid tab one night and I just had this unforgettable experience. For a few hours I was transformed and I honestly felt like I understood everything and everyone. Like the world around me was suddenly crystal clear. It's a hard sensation to describe, but for me it was a turning point. Technically it's not an addictive drug but, right after that moment, I was psychologically hooked. I was forever chasing that high, that spiritual awareness I was convinced I'd had.'

I sat forward, listening to her in silence as my cup of coffee went cold on the table beside me. At first she had shocked me, but slowly it started to make sense. The way that she had been that night made perfect sense.

'Of course I shouldn't have done it, and I hope I didn't freak you out too much. You must have thought I was insane.'

None of us said anything and she laughed to herself, looking at her hands. 'Well anyway, I went on like that for quite some time. I tried taking it every day but you quickly become tolerant doing that so I learned to cut back, only taking it occasionally. I managed to get through my A levels somehow but I knew I'd done badly and I hadn't the confidence to try for university. I was taking speed as well by that time. I started stealing from my family, my dad kicked me out a couple of weeks after the exams and I hitched a ride to London to find an old friend who'd supplied me dope from time to time.

'The next few years are a bit of a blur. I lived in a squat and was going out all weekend on speed benders and stealing from tourists. I was arrested twice. I tried heroin three times but luckily stopped short of mainline injections, and then, one Christmas, I had a bad trip on an LSD tab. I was hallucinating badly and felt this moment of absolute terror. I snuck on a train. No idea where it was going. I thought I was going out of my mind. I tried to force the doors open so I could jump and this man wrestled me to the ground and sat on me. I was arrested at the next station.'

'God, that's awful.' I couldn't believe all this had happened to her and yet she was talking about it so openly and so calmly.

She shrugged. 'I think it had to happen. It's good that it happened. I got help after that. Joined an outpatient rehabilitation programme in Brighton. Had therapy and counselling and gradually sorted myself out. I got talking to Chris at a group therapy meet and we just clicked. Finally I got myself excited about the future. I've been clean for seven years. I no longer have flash-backs and I love my life in Brighton.' She looked at us and smiled. 'And now I have completely freaked you out with my horror story when you probably only wanted to know what I did for a living and whether or not I've had babies yet. I'm sorry.'

'I just can't believe you went through all that,' I said, trying to take it all in. 'I wish I'd known at the time, when you were still writing to me.'

She waved her hand dismissively. 'Don't think like that. Of course you weren't to know. I don't think even *I* knew. I had perfected the art of self-denial.'

'But you weren't happy, I knew that. I should have been more help.'

'Oh God, after reading my ridiculous poetry I'm surprised you wrote back at all. And it's easy to think like that with hindsight, but at the time you had your own life, your own stuff going on. You could never have known how it would turn out and I don't think for a minute you could have changed anything. I was already past the friendly ear stage when I met you. Anyway, it's had a positive outcome for me, that's what you should remember. The rest is history. There's no use dwelling on what we can't change.'

'I suppose.' She was right, but I still felt guilty, and there was something else bothering me: a sense that she was still holding out on us. It was fair enough, we were virtual strangers after all. Why should she feel obliged to tell us any more than she already had? I watched her laugh with surprise as Fay produced her old leopard brooch and I wondered who she really was.

# Chapter Twenty-Four

It was Miranda who finally broached the subject of why we'd come. She asked casually if there was a reason, as though she wanted us to think it didn't matter either way. We didn't need a reason to call in and catch up. But I could tell she was curious and suspected something.

Nikki looked uncomfortable and checked the time. 'Listen, Miranda, we've probably outstayed our welcome already. Didn't you say you were going to a party?'

'Well, yes, I said I'd be there at six to help set up.' She checked her own watch. 'There's still plenty of time. It doesn't actually start till eight. It's at an art gallery in town; Chris is launching an exhibition of new work. I was going to have a wander around the shops before they shut to kill some time beforehand, that's all. Nothing important.'

'Did Chris do these?' Nikki asked, pointing out the paintings on the wall.

'Mmm hmm.' She smiled proudly.

'He's really good. Great colours. I wish I had a skill like that.'

Miranda suddenly looked up, an expression of understanding forming on her face. 'You just changed the subject, didn't you?'

Nikki tried to look innocent. 'No.'

'OK, what's going on?'

Nikki looked at me for help and I understood why she was hesitant. Miranda wasn't the person we thought she'd be. She was actually very rational and with a degree in psychology she might find our reasons for tracking her down ridiculous. But then I remembered what had brought us here, and how her words seemed to have woken me up and started me on a train of thought that had changed everything. I had to know what she thought about it all. There was still a chance she could have answers.

'OK,' I said, reaching for my bag to take out Miranda's predictions. 'You'll think we're crazy, but we wanted you to see this.' I held up the paper and handed it to her.

She took it, looking at it closely, then, recognising what it was, laughed with astonishment. 'Wow! I can't believe you still have this. Did you open it on New Year's Eve 2000, like we said we would?'

'We forgot all about it. I found it about five weeks ago.' I watched her as she skim read it, then I took a deep breath and blurted out, 'The thing is, Miranda, the reason we wanted you to see it, is because you got everything right.'

She looked at us all, bewildered. 'You mean the predictons?'

Fay nodded. 'You got us all right. It was uncanny.'

'Really?' She looked again at the paper and started to read it properly. 'Nikki's wearing white, in a big country mansion,' she read out. 'Dating a man with a foreign accent destined for fame.' She looked at Nikki questioningly.

Nikki nodded. 'I wear a white coat for work, and I work in a country health spa, a big old mansion. I was going out with Fabian then. He was on a dating programme recently and in the papers and stuff. Then there's the bit about smoking. That was strange.'

Miranda read the bit she meant and Nikki explained what had happened to her.

'God, that must have been awful,' Miranda said.

'Read what you put for me,' Fay said, unable to wait any longer. 'It was a bit vague admittedly, but so true.'

Miranda read it. 'Did you find a good man under your nose, then?'

'Well, a week or two ago I kind of got together with Tim, our housemate. He'd been living with us for a few months already so he really was right under my nose. He's great.' She couldn't help but smile when she mentioned him. 'And the thing is, it has been like you said. I did take a while to settle; I'm only just starting now. I travelled, I changed my ambitions, I couldn't find anything I was happy doing, and just recently I've had opportunities and . . .'

'Hang on,' Miranda said, holding up the paper. 'Did you say you got together with Tim after you read this?' Fay nodded and Miranda tapped the paper then looked at it again. 'Are the bits about Gemma right?'

'Yes. Well, I am surrounded with kids all day who aren't mine. I work in an old church, Adam was gentle, well, as in he'd never physically hurt anyone, and he's big: six foot three and muscular. And that last thing you said, about not marrying the first man that asks you, about destiny being someone from my childhood. I don't know, obviously I don't know what to make of that. I was engaged to Adam, he was the first man to propose to me and he wasn't from my childhood. I had been having doubts. Reading that made me realise them, made me wonder whether I was settling for second best just because it was easy. Anyway, in the end the decision was made for me. I heard things; I suspected he'd cheated on me so I finished it.' I sighed and leaned forwards, rubbing my eyes, 'Oh, I don't know anymore. I felt like I was getting signs, everything was telling me Adam wasn't right, not just what you said, and then I met someone else. I ran into a guy on his bike who turned out to have been a student teacher when I was at school. Just like you said, he was someone from my childhood, who I met in my schooldays, and the way it happened, it felt like it was all set up somehow, like I had to meet him for a reason. We've had a few dates now and I like him so much, but I'm struggling. I don't know what I'm supposed to do.'

I looked at Miranda and suddenly felt self-conscious. She was frowning, staring at the paper.

'Do you think you broke up with Adam because of what I wrote in this?' she asked eventually.

'I don't know anymore; this past few weeks I thought I was taking control of my life, but now I feel like I'm losing it.'

'Oh God, I'm so sorry.' She sank back into her chair, resting the paper on her lap. 'Did you think I might be able to give you answers?'

'Well, I ...' I looked to Fay and Nikki, hoping they would back me up, but they both seemed to be avoiding making eye contact with me. 'Look, surely you must think it's a bit strange? Those things you said, you were right about everything. You know we wrote predictions too, but I don't think any of us got a single thing right. You can see why we wondered, why it made us stop and think. Can't you?'

There were three pairs of expectant eyes on Miranda, who was leaning forwards, her elbows on her knees, thinking hard. She shook her head. 'It could just be a coincidence. There have been much stranger coincidences than that happen.'

'I said that,' Nikki agreed.

'And, let's be honest, I wasn't exactly of sound mind when I wrote this. It can't mean anything.'

'And I said tha . . .' Nikki started, then slapped her hand over her mouth, looking embarrassed.

Miranda laughed. 'It's OK, you were bound to think that.'

She stroked the back of her neck as she thought. I couldn't help noticing how calm she was, from her soft voice, so perfect for the radio, to her composed demeanour. It was easy to see why she would make a good counsellor.

'OK, thinking about it logically, it's possible that the acid I'd taken played a part. You see, there's a chemical in psychedelic drugs that amplifies your sense of perception and awareness. That's why I started taking it. I didn't just want to use drugs as a means of escape; I was also convinced that LSD helped me see things and understand things better. That night I was high. Everything would have been exaggerated. I was wired and alert, probably watching you like a hawk, picking up on every little thing and analysing it, fascinated by everything. If you add to that the extra confidence I got on a high, I would have been cocky enough to take an educated guess. That must have been it. I mean, let's look at what I said.' She picked the paper up again and scanned over it. 'Nikki wearing white in a country mansion was probably me imagining you getting married. I think you said a few negative things about the church after you'd heard me complaining about my parents so perhaps I thought you'd have a non-traditional wedding. A foreign accent, destined for fame, well, out of the three, Nikki was the one who had the most crushes on famous people, especially Australian soap stars if I remember rightly?'

'Well, yeah, but it *was* the 80s.' She cringed, making us laugh.

'The smoking thing probably said more about me than Nikki. I was surprisingly anti-smoking at that time, considering my blossoming drug habit. It was one of those crap things I would say to justify myself, you know. "Oh but smoking and alcohol kill far more people than weed and acid, and they're more anti-social. I just get mellow and expand my mind."' She said this in a voice that mocked her supposed naivety.

'But Nikki was anti-smoking too,' Fay argued. 'She always swore she wouldn't touch it. We were really surprised when she took it up. How could you have known she would?'

'Hmm. Well, maybe I picked up on you biting your nails or something?'

Nikki looked shocked. 'I've never done that!'

I looked up at Nikki. 'I thought you did. It's something you've always done, isn't it?'

'That's not my nails,' she said rolling her eyes, embarrassed. 'If you must know, I bite the skin on the side of my nails. That way I don't damage the polish. And anyway, what's that got to do with smoking?'

'Not a lot,' Miranda said. 'But it might suggest that you get tense and hide it well, the nail-biting is a kind of emotional leakage, and it's habitual. Smokers often have those characteristics.'

'It wasn't my nails,' Nikki insisted again, raising her hand to her mouth then freezing as we all continued to look at her. 'I was just going to scratch my chin, all right?'

'OK, sorry Nikki,' Miranda said, returning to the paper. 'So, next there was the Fay thing, which was the easiest assumption of them all seeing as you talked constantly about travel and how many countries you wanted to see.' She smiled at Fay. 'It stands to reason that if you travel around a lot it'll take you a while to settle down, get a regular job and all the rest. And then there's the stuff about Gemma. "In a church", well, we all do that from time to time when someone gets married. "Surrounded by children" was an assumption I probably made after finding out more about you. Your parents had you when they were quite old, didn't they? And you have an older brother. You spent a lot of time with people older than you and so, understandably, when you were the oldest one for a change, you loved having that different role. I remember you talking about the boy next door who you used to babysit. You seemed to have really bonded with him. The gentle giant thing, well, you were a gentle person and you had a romantic streak. Romantics tend to like feeling as thought they're safe, taken care of, but not dominated, so a gentle giant would be an attractive possibility. And the "Don't marry the first person that asks you" line might be because of the romantic thing again, because you were also a daydreamer and perhaps, in my hugely opinionated state, I thought you might fall in love too quickly.'

'And the "someone from your childhood" bit?' I asked.

Miranda sighed. 'Oh, probably me topping it off by being a bit pretentious and mystical?' She looked at us apologetically. 'It's funny, you know, lots of people say that they've had some kind of mystical experience on acid. If you'd come to me with this when I was still using I would have thought I'd managed to tap into a kind of spiritual intuition and really had seen the future. Now though, I suppose it must have been an educated guess, helped along by an altered state of mind.' She held up her hands. 'It's only my theory, but I can't see what else it could be.'

As I listened to her I felt a curious feeling of loneliness

surround me. Slowly Miranda had managed to strip away the magic from her words, the feeling that perhaps there was more to life than circumstance and coincidence. She couldn't help me. There were no answers. I was on my own with decisions to make and nobody could make them for me.

When Miranda found out we were staying overnight she invited us to join her at the art exhibition party later and meet Chris. I was hesitant, in case she was inviting us to be polite, but she did seem to genuinely want us there. I got the feeling that there were things still to be said, things she had run out of time for in the afternoon. As we got up to leave she found us a business card for the gallery where the party was and we agreed to call in later for a drink. We left her to it after that and headed off, planning to find our guesthouse and check in before dinner.

'How weird was that,' Fay said, the moment we were all sitting in the privacy of Nikki's car.

'I know, it was weird,' I said, staring back at the dominating building.

'But it all made so much sense, don't you think?' Nikki was clearly happy with how it had gone, as though Miranda's explanation had helped her to rationalise everything in her own mind, and she was comfortable knowing that her view of the world hadn't been challenged. 'Like her being on drugs. It'd never even occurred to me, but now it really explains the way she'd acted that night.'

'I suppose it explains why she said "wow!" so much,' Fay said thoughtfully.

'And the way she explained the predictions. It clarified everything, don't you think?'

'Yes and no,' I said. 'Something still doesn't add up.'

'Yeah,' Fay agreed. 'I thought that. I mean what about

her parents disapproving of her? She said herself she's been free of drugs for years. And now she's helping other people through it. If I was her mum I'd be really proud.'

'And she was acting strange. She kept looking uncomfortable. And she was far nicer to us that she had to be, like she felt guilty or something.'

Nikki rolled her eyes and started the car. 'You two have got to learn to let go.'

We ate in town, in a little Italian restaurant that reminded me of Barney's. Nikki and I ate our pasta appreciatively, dabbing up the remaining sauce with complimentary hunks of bread, but Fay was quiet, twisting the ribbons of tagliatelle around and around on her fork. She'd had a text message from Tim when we'd first sat down at the table but not even that had snapped her out of her mood.

'I just feel like I'm teetering on the brink of complete and total happiness, and it's too good. Something's going to go wrong, I just know it.'

'What could go wrong, Fay?' I asked gently.

'I won't get this job with the BBC and I'll be unemployable, then Tim will move back to London and I'll never see him again.'

'You've got to stop worrying and just go with it,' Nikki said. 'You just wanted Miranda to tell you everything was going to be all right and she couldn't. But that means nothing; there's every chance things will work out for you. You don't need Miranda to tell you anything. *I'm* telling you, it'll be fine.' She put a hand on Fay's arm and dipped her head so that she could look up at her through her eyelashes. 'And you know, whatever happens, we'll always have Brighton,' she said with a cheeky smile.

Fay laughed at Nikki's reference to *Casablanca*, then she took out her purse and put her share of the bill on the

257

table. 'Come on then, let's make an appearance at this gallery. I want to see if there really is something else going on with Miranda, and if not, there's always the free champagne I heard her mention.'

# Chapter Twenty-Five

We walked through the higgledy-piggledy lanes to the gallery, pausing frequently to look in the windows of shops that caught our interest. There was an abundance of interesting shops selling everything from kitsch knick-knacks to ethnic souvenirs, retro clothing to designer labels and vintage memorabilia to modern art. The major-ity of the shops had shut but the cafés were doing good trade in the warm, summer night and there were plenty of people ambling through the little streets and alleyways.

The art gallery where Miranda's boyfriend's exhibition was being held was nestled right in the centre of the bohemian area of town. It was smaller than I had imag-ined, with the front of the building being so close to the narrow path that you almost had to step back out onto the road to be able to see properly what the place was like. Through the large windows we could see it was well lit up inside and busy with people. The three of us hesitated by the door, exchanging looks as though checking we were all still happy to go in there.

'Come on then,' I said, walking up the shallow stone steps to the door.

Inside the gallery was starkly lit with white light that

dazzled us after the subdued, last hour of sunshine we had been enjoying outside. The only sounds were the constant verbal patter from the guests who stood around with wine glasses in their hands. It was a small room, with dimensions similar to an average shop, and all that was in it, apart from the people, was a sculpture of a woman. It was a caricature really, almost comical, of a buxom woman in her fifties or sixties with a big round face and 50s-style glasses. She was wearing a dress with socks and slippers and was kneeling on the floor, a look of mindless serenity on her face. It was unexpected. I had imaged the exhibits to be more like the pieces we'd seen in Miranda's flat, minimalist and comtemporary, but this was surprisingly down to earth. I couldn't decide whether I found it endearing or a bit spooky.

The sculpture sat in the middle of the room, level with an opening that led into a much bigger area, with high ceilings and no windows. This was where the paintings were hung; all of them huge, brightly coloured canvases, depicting the same round-faced, slippered woman doing all kinds of things: washing-up, feeding a cat, flying above a church steeple with little wings poking out from her cardigan.

'Mad,' I said, under my breath.

'I think they're fantastic,' Fay said, smiling at them. 'So funny and quirky.'

Nikki didn't look so sure. 'I liked his modern stuff better, the stuff in their flat. Where do you think he is anyway? And where's Miranda?'

It was a busy room, but I knew it would be easy to pick Miranda out of a crowd with her red top and strikingly dark hair. I scanned the room for a glimpse of red and saw her standing by a table of drinks in the far corner of the room. She was listening intently to a slim, bald man who reminded me of the lead singer from REM.

'There she is.' I pointed them out. 'And that must be Chris. Let's go and say hello.'

Miranda saw us coming and her face brightened. 'Hey! I'm so glad you could come.' She turned back to her companion and introduced us to him.

'And you must be Chris,' Nikki said, holding out her hand.

Miranda laughed and her companion looked awkward. 'I'll err, I'll catch up with you a bit later on,' he said, inching back into the crowd.

Miranda waited till he'd gone then said, 'Sorry about that. He's a journalist from a local magazine.' She passed us all a drink then took one for herself.

I watched her, thinking how much more relaxed she seemed. Perhaps because, now that she was with her own crowd, she didn't feel our presence so strongly. She must have felt outnumbered earlier, with the three of us turning up at once, wanting answers.

'I'll introduce you to some people in a minute, but first of all, I should point out my other half.' She rocked onto her tiptoes and looked over our heads. 'That one's Chris, over there. The one with the red hair.'

We all looked around. The only person I could see with red hair was a stunning looking woman in a tight, plain white T-shirt and vintage jeans. I turned back to Miranda, who was waiting calmly for a reaction of some sort. *Of course it was a woman*. My mind started working overtime as little snippets of conversations fitted into place. She had never referred to Chris as a he, we had. We'd assumed and she'd let us. It's what her mum meant about practising her beliefs, and why her father had such a hard time accepting her. It might also explain her problems growing up, why she had felt misunderstood, like an outsider, or took LSD in a desperate attempt to understand herself better.

'I don't see him,' Fay said, still scanning the crowd. Nikki helped her out and after a moment of realisation she turned back to Miranda, her jaw hanging open. 'She's gorgeous!'

Miranda laughed. 'I like to think so.'

'I'm sorry,' Nikki said, cringing. 'I had no idea. I just assumed and started rabbiting on. Why didn't you set me straight?'

'It happens a lot,' Miranda said with a shrug. 'It's fine. I gave up putting people straight a long time ago. It's easier to let people assume. If they need to know, they'll find out soon enough.'

'So is that why your dad's upset?' Fay asked.

She nodded. 'He only found out a year ago. I'd never lied about it, they just never asked and I thought it was easier to leave it unsaid rather than have a big showdown about it. I knew how he'd react, but that's OK. I don't expect him to understand. His life is so different to mine. Maybe one day he'll realise that this isn't some kind of teenage rebellion I never grew out of, and that my sole purpose in life isn't to piss him off. But I won't hold my breath.' She smiled brightly at us. 'Anyway, why don't you come and meet Chris? I told her you were coming and she's looking forward to hearing all about how weird I used to be.'

Nikki had vanished, presumably to visit the ladies' room, and Fay was talking to a first-year fashion student in the front room who had taken an interest in her customised T-shirt. I left her to it and went to have another look at Chris's paintings.

'It's the first time I've done anything like this,' I heard

262

someone say behind me. I turned around and saw Chris standing behind me, looking up at her pictures too. 'I was petrified about the critics seeing them tonight. I've only exhibited contemporary abstracts before.'

'I'm sure you've got no reason to worry, they're great,' I said. 'They've got loads of character.'

Chris smiled. She really was attractive in a natural, luminous skin and vulnerable blue eyes kind of way. It struck me that when stood next to Miranda they would make a traffic-stopping couple.

'Are you staying in Brighton for long?' Chris asked.

'No. We're going back in the morning. I think we'll go back to the guesthouse soon too. It's been a long day.' I looked back at the painting, which showed the slippered woman this time standing on a doorstep, holding a pint of milk and looking up at a night sky. 'It's funny, I'd expected Miranda to be different, but after seeing her again, I'm not surprised at all. Everything is starting to make sense.'

I looked back at Chris again but she seemed puzzled. Suddenly Miranda appeared behind her. 'Anyone for another drink?' she said brightly.

'I'll get them,' Chris said. 'There's a critic over by the drinks who I think I need to try and charm.' She left me alone with Miranda and we smiled awkwardly at each other.

'I think we'll be heading off soon,' I said.

Miranda nodded. 'Look, Gemma, before you go,' she started to look uncomfortable then seemed to pull herself together, 'there's a few things I wanted to talk to you about.'

'Sure.' I turned to face her properly.

'Firstly, I wanted to apologise. I'm afraid I was too dismissive of your reasons for coming here today. Those predictions I made. You saw something in them and I probably didn't take you seriously enough.'

'Oh no, you can't apologise for that. We didn't take it that seriously ourselves. It just sparked our curiosity, that's all.' I could feel myself getting more embarrassed.

'Well, OK, but there was something about what you said that has been bothering me, or rather the way you said it. The stuff about Adam.'

I knew what she was thinking. 'We would have split up anyway,' I said. 'I'm sure of it. I was giving up on us. It wasn't going the way I'd hoped it would and it didn't feel right.'

'I'm just worried you might be taking what I said too seriously. I don't want you to think that Adam wasn't right because you didn't know him when you were at school, or because he asked you to marry him first, or anything like that. I'd feel awful knowing I'd given you these doubts.'

'Maybe you were right though, I mean Jamie . . .'

'That night,' she butted in. 'I was really on a high. I don't know if you've done anything like that, but if you haven't, well, I can't describe how exaggerated everything gets. When it's good, every single feeling in your body is amplified and every thought becomes this incredible life-altering realisation. That's how it was for me on New Year's Eve. I'd had months of agonising. I was changing and I couldn't get to grips with it.' She laughed self-consciously at herself. 'When I saw you it was like those moments in films when a girl walks out of the mist, glowing, and there's this angelic singing and everything suddenly fits into place.'

I was staring at her, unsure what she was trying to say.

'It was the first time I knew.'

'Knew what?'

'That I was gay,' she said, looking at me like I hadn't

been listening to her properly.

My face coloured up and my first reaction was to look for Chris, checking that she was still talking to someone over by the drinks and hadn't heard. Because surely everyone had heard that. It was certainly still ringing in my ears.

'I'm sorry Gemma. The last thing I want to do is embarras you and I can assure you that I have moved on since then; obviously I have. But I had to tell you. What I put in those predictions, I was trying to put an element of doubt in your head, in case when you read them you were with someone. And the bit about your childhood, someone you met at school. I was talking about me. That I wanted you to be with me.'

'You and me?' My mouth had been hanging open for so long my tongue was starting to dry up.

'Please, don't look so worried. It was a long time ago and I was on drugs. Oh,' she looked horrified for a fleeting moment, 'not that I'd have needed to be: you're very attractive, of course you are, just, oh, tell me you understand what I'm trying to say. I'm obviously making more and more of a mess of it as I go along.'

'No. I understand.' I understood perfectly. She'd left me with nothing. There was no magic in what she'd said. There was just me, looking for signs and only seeing the ones I wanted to see.

'I'm sorry,' she said seriously.

'Me too. I should have made more of an effort to find out what was going on with you. I let you down.'

'No,' she said firmly. 'I only have myself to blame for that. I'm not surprised you backed off. I must have scared you.'

'Yeah, but maybe I scare too easily,' I said. That chasm of loneliness was returning.

*

Fay and I found Nikki outside, standing on the pavement. She must have gone outside to take a phone call because when we joined her she was staring at her phone with indignation. 'The bloody cheek of him,' she was saying under her breath.

'Do you mean Fabian?' I asked, shrugging my jacket on as I walked over to join her.

'You won't believe this. He's actually been nominated for a bachelor of the year competition! They must have been desperate for someone to make up the numbers, but all the same, *him*! And what makes it even more ridiculous is there's a party in this big London nightclub on Saturday and the press will be there. Obviously he can't take a date but he wants to see me before. He asked if he could come up to the spa and see me on the Friday and get a wax and a session in the tan shower whilst he's there.'

'The cheeky sod!' I cried. 'I hope you told him where to get off.'

She put her phone back in her bag, trying to hide her expression behind a curtain of blonde hair.

'You did say no, didn't you?' Fay said, narrowing her eyes at her.

'He's arriving after lunch on Friday,' she said, as coolly as she could, still shuffling in her bag, most likely for something imaginary.

The sudden silence in the street made Nikki finally give in and look at our gawping faces. 'What? It's not what you think. I've been over him for a long time now.'

'Then why are you even bothering with him? Why are you seeing him again?'

'Because I just want it finished with. For good. And I know it won't be until I at least let him know that he hurt me, and that he's got no chance now. I've got to get it off my chest. Men like him think they can do what they like

266

and get away with it and I don't want to pick up a magazine one day and see his face and know that I let him walk
all over me.'

'Right,' Fay said doubtfully, 'but are you going to shag
him first?'

'No! I'm going to set him straight then send him
packing, then I'll be free for good.'

'If you say so.'

'I do. Now, how about a nice bracing walk on the beach
before we go to the guesthouse?'

'Great,' I said. She'd read my mind.

'I'll just say bye to Miranda then we can go.'

The air had turned cold and fresh, whipping my hair across
my face as we walked along the wooden boards. We had
planned on walking along the pebble beach but it looked
dark and cold by the water's edge and the pier had seemed
far more inviting, all lit up and magical, with its lights
reflected in the undulating waters beneath. Walking past the
fast food stalls and arcades I was surrounded by lights, noise
and people and yet I barely noticed. I was more drawn to the
silence and the darkness beyond the pier. I stopped at the
railings, looking back at the shoreline, surprised at how far
we'd come and how small the town seemed now.

Fay breathed in the air then sighed out loud. 'I'm so
glad we came here. There's definitely something about
being by the sea, Gem, you were right.'

When I didn't answer Nikki looked at me. 'Are you
OK? You've been quiet ever since we saw Miranda.'

'I'm fine,' I said. 'I suppose it's just got me thinking
about everything.'

'About Adam?'

I nodded. 'A bit. And Jamie. I've been thinking a lot
about Jamie.'

'And ...?' Fay and Nikki said in unison.

'And I want to see Jamie,' I said, 'as soon as we get back.'

When we walked back down the pier it was quieter. Some of the stalls had closed their shutters and the people had thinned out. I was walking in the middle, trying to set a quick pace, wanting to get back into the town where we would be more sheltered from the wind, when Fay suddenly stopped and pulled me by my elbow.

'Look!' she cried, pointing to an ancient slot machine. It was standing in a dark corner of the pier, next to a candyfloss stall that had shut up for the night. 'It's one of those old fortune-teller machines. They're really rare. I tried to bid for one of them on eBay once.'

'Oh my God, you're kidding,' Nikki said, covering her face with her hands and letting out an exasperated cry.

I walked over to it for a better look. It was an old penny slot machine. Sitting inside was a cast metal solar system, surrounded by decorative rings that were painted elaborately in muted colours and gilt that must have faded a long time ago. Above the window were the words THE MYSTICAL WORLDS OF FORTUNE, in a style of writing that reminded me of the type I'd seen before on the Victoriana in Adam's workshop.

'I have to have a go. I came here for answers after all and I never got them from Miranda.'

'But it says one penny,' I said, 'and forgive me but I left all my Victorian change at home.'

'Don't be silly, it's been converted to take pound coins.' She took one out of her purse and put it in. 'See?' There was a clanking of machinery and the whole thing suddenly lit up. The rings around the solar system began to spin and a strange, strangled noise that might have once sounded like eerie music began to play. When the sounds came to an abrupt end a card dropped out into a dish below and the lights went off again. Fay picked up the card and turned it over. 'Now is the time for you to make great changes in your life. Seize the day,' she read out. 'Ooh. Interesting. That's me, isn't it?'

'It could be anybody really,' Nikki said with a shrug.

Fay read the card again then pocketed it, walking around the back of the machine and crouching down.

'What are you doing?' I asked.

'Just checking to see if it's plugged in. Remember *Big*, the film with Tom Hanks? The machine that granted him a wish when it wasn't even plugged in? I thought I'd better just check, just in case,' she said, looking back with a twinkle in her eye.

'And is it?'

'Err. Yeah.' She sounded disappointed then brightened up. 'Hey, why don't you have a go, Gem?'

'Oh no.' I backed off. 'Not again. From now on I'm going to be a suck-it-and-see kind of girl, thank you very much.'

'Finally we start singing from the same hymn book,' Nikki said, laughing as we started walking back towards the lights of Brighton again.

# Chapter Twenty-Six

I sat at a picnic table outside the riverside pub, nursing a cup of coffee. It was a grey day, much colder than it had been in Brighton the day before, and I wrapped my cardigan tighter around my chest to protect myself against the blustery wind.

It was now three o'clock. I'd arranged to meet Jamie here at three and had come early, the thought of sitting in a country pub garden being far more inviting than staying at home on my own.

We had arrived back from Brighton at lunchtime and Nikki had carried straight on to her house to get ready for a meal with her parents. Fay hadn't had much sleep at the guesthouse and after realising that Tim was out, went up to bed to catch up on sleep. I'd called Jamie the moment I was alone. He sounded relieved to hear from me, agreeing that we needed to talk. I hadn't said much to him then, just that it'd be nice to meet up somewhere picturesque, suggesting the local pub in Martin Under-Wood, the village where my gran used to live.

It was a traditional old pub: smoky, dark wood, busy carpets and lots of nooks and crannies. I liked the character of it, but its real charm for me was the large garden that was perfectly placed beside the River Avon. We used to come here as a family when I was little. My parents would sit with my gran whilst I paddled in the river, or when it was shallow, hopped across the stones to the meadow on the other side, to run and hide from them in the long grass.

When I saw Jamie walk through the back door of the pub I looked over to the meadow, half tempted to do it again for old time's sake, but my legs were neither willing nor able. He grinned over at me, calling out to see if I wanted anything. I asked for another coffee and he ducked back into the pub for a few minutes, returning with a tray of drinks.

'Hey. Good to see you,' he said, passing me my cup of coffee and kissing me on the cheek. 'This is a great pub, isn't it? I haven't been here in years but I swear it's still just the same.'

'It's true,' I said. 'The only thing that ever changes is the carpet, once every February after the river floods. I like that though, the familiarity of it. It's cosy.'

'I know what you mean.' He sat down opposite me and we looked at each other, both smiling; the conversation was suddenly forgotten. There were more important things on our minds.

'So . . .' we both started at the same time then laughed.

'You go,' Jamie said.

'No, no, you.'

'Well. I was going to ask how it went in Brighton. Did you catch up with your old friend?'

'Mmm, yeah, it was good, thanks. Weird, but good. You know when you're expecting one thing and it turns out to be something completely different, but then you realise that actually the reality makes more sense than what you'd been expecting in the first place?'

Jamie made a face of exaggerated concentration as he tried to work out what I meant then clicked his fingers together. 'OK, like one time when I came home from school to find some sandwiches on the table and I thought "Hey, Mum's left me a chocolate spread sandwich", bit into it, realised it was Marmite and nearly choked in horror. Then, after I'd spat it in the sink, I remembered that Mum had never bought chocolate spread in her life but was pregnant with Cassie and craving Marmite only the night before.'

'Right, well, I suppose it is like that. Only with less spitting.' Suddenly we were connecting with each other again, laughing and relaxing.

'So, did you get on? You and ... what was her name again?' he asked, pouring himself some tea from the little white teapot.

'Miranda. Yeah, I think we did. She took it surprisingly well, us just turning up unannounced. Didn't seem worried that we might be a trio of single white females or anything. She welcomed us right in like she'd been expecting us or something.' The smile on my face froze as I said that. It *had* felt like she was expecting us. There was an inevitability in her reaction. I shook the thought away. No. She couldn't have, it would be impossible. And anyway, I'd made a pact with myself to stop overanalysing what things meant and start taking them at face value. It was a ridiculous thought, I decided, picking up my hot coffee cup. Definitely not one to share with Fay.

'Are you OK?' Jamie was looking at me strangely. 'You have a far-off look in your eyes.'

'Oh sorry, no, I'm fine.' We both fell silent. Now was the time, I sensed. 'Jamie, about the other night.'

He put his cup down and looked at me. 'Yes, actually I've been wanting to talk to you about it as well.'

For a moment I hoped he was going to take my cue and address the situation first, but he sat calmly, letting me speak.

'Erm, I suppose I want you to know that I had a great time on Friday, I really did. But the thing, the stuff that came later . . .' *Oh God, this was so difficult! Why had I lost the ability to construct a proper sentence?* 'Well, I don't know how you feel but I kind of felt like, oh, that . . .'

Jamie was searching me with his eyes. He was taking me seriously, being so grown up about it that I fought the urge to giggle nervously.

'Do you think,' I continued, 'that it was nice? I mean, oh . . .' I covered my face with my hands. This was awful.

'You know what I think?' Jamie said, chivalrously coming to my aid. I urged him on gratefully and his expression softened. 'I think you're not entirely over Adam, are you? And it's all still pretty fresh in your mind.'

Just when I thought I couldn't embarrass myself any further, tears started to gather conspicuously in my eyes. I nodded.

'It's OK.' He reached across the table and squeezed my hand. 'On Friday I think we were both feeling pretty lonely. It was nice to get close to someone like that again, but don't feel bad, because I don't want this to spoil any friendship we've built up with one night of drunken behaviour. You're excellent, and I'd like to keep seeing you.'

I got the feeling there was a silent 'but'; one he wasn't quite brave enough to say to a woman with tears in her eyes. 'But it was a moment of madness?' I finished for him with a laugh and a sniff.

'Well, hey, I wouldn't go that far,' he joked, pretending his pride was hurt. 'Perhaps we should put it down to the drink and a need for comfort. But, well I suppose you felt a bit like my sister.' He saw that this time I looked surprised and added, 'In a good way,' then cringed. 'Not that I ever kiss my sister like that. Oh God, this is not coming out well at all, is it? Can we just scrub out this entire conversation and start back at the Marmite bit?'

'You thought *that* was your conversational highlight?' I teased and we both started laughing again.

I didn't want to leave Jamie but I had to go. I was tired from our hectic weekend and the travelling. I only just had enough energy to make it back home. I had been sipping my drink slowly, wanting to stay that bit longer. What worried me was that it felt like the end of the road for us. He was right about our friendship. I didn't want to lose touch with him now that we had grown close, but there was always this possibility that once we were home and returning to normality, we'd lose touch. That one of us wouldn't return a phone call and it would peter out. I didn't want that to happen. After we walked back to the car park, preparing to go our separate ways, we hugged.

'I will see you again, won't I?' I asked, looking up at him.

'Of course! In fact, you've just reminded me. I brought something for you.' He reached into the inside pocket of his denim jacket and took out an envelope, handing it to me.

'What's this?'

'It's an invite. My little sister's turning thirty in August and we both want you to come to the party.'

I peeked into the envelope and there was indeed an invitation with my name written at the top. 'Are you sure?'

'Of course I'm sure. Look, fate didn't just drop you under the wheel of my bicycle for nothing, you know. We're supposed to keep in touch.'

'Do you really think so?'

'I know so,' he said, kissing me affectionately on the top of my head. 'Now, off you go. Get some sleep. I'll call you soon.'

I turned back to my car. He's going to make someone a terrific husband one day, I thought, smiling sadly to myself.

On Thursday morning Fay called me at Dizzy Heights. I could hardly hear her above the noise of children, who were banging on the drums we had made, marching like soldiers around the hall.

'You're going to have to speak up,' I said, putting a finger in one ear and poking my head into the kitchen.

'I got it, I got it, I got the job!'

I let out a cry of surprise and excitement. 'Oh my God! That's fantastic. How? When? Did they call you? What happened?'

'Sylvia called me. They all loved my screen test; apparently they said I had a "quirky charm" that their viewers would appreciate. I've got to have a meeting and debrief at the end of next week, then I'm in every day for research and the best bit is, our first subject is Katharine Hepburn. They're even flying me out to Connecticut next month so we can film around where she lived.'

'Ahh!' I shrieked. 'Fay, I don't believe it.'

'I know! It's like a dream come true. I don't think I deserve to be this happy.'

'Of course you do. If anyone deserves it it's you.'

'But what if I mess up? What if they hate me? I've never done anything like this before.'

'We all have to start somewhere, you'll be fine. I can't think of a job better suited to you. Listen, I've got to go, but why don't I come and meet you out of work? We can go for a drink, get Nikki to come along when she's finished, and Tim. We could all go for dinner and celebrate properly.'

'Great! I called Tim already. He won't be back until about midnight, but I'll call Nikki next. I bet she'd come.'

'Excellent. I'll see you at the shop later then.' I put the phone down, doing a silent scream and a jump for joy then heard some of the children giggling and laughing at me.

'All right soldiers, at the double,' I said, grinning back at them.

This was the best news I'd had in ages. After years of Fay doing fill-in jobs that weren't making her happy, her dreams had seemed to be ebbing away from her. Now everything was coming together. It was more than I'd ever imagined possible.

Then, somewhere in a shady corner of my conscious, another thought occurred to me. Now that Fay was being elevated to the position of TV presenter/documentary maker, with all the distractions and the glamorous film locations that would entail, perhaps her relationship with Tim would just peter out naturally? There wouldn't be any reason for her to find out what he was really like, she'd be saved from heartbreak and there would be loads of opportunities for Fay to meet new men now. This day just gets better and better, I thought, going back into the hall to march with the children.

'To your success,' I said, raising my glass of wine.

Fay clinked her glass with mine and we both sipped, melting back into the big leather armchairs. Nikki was meeting us at the restaurant in half an hour and so we were having drinks in the little lobby by the window before she arrived.

'Tim was so excited for me,' Fay said, unable to

disguise her happiness. 'He says he'll be taking a sabbatical from work soon. The contract he's working on is nearly over and he'll need a break. He kind of jokingly hinted at coming with me to America. I think he really wanted to but passed it off as a bit of a joke in case it's too soon. Do you know what I mean?'

'What do you think? Would you want him to come?'

'I dunno. Yes and no. Yes for obvious reasons. It'd be a fantastic way to really get to know him, sharing something big like that with him, but then I'll be nervous about the job. I'll need to concentrate on that. I suppose it depends how relaxed I feel about it all and that depends on how well it goes before I leave. But it's a possibility.'

'Wow. So it's really getting serious with you two then.'

'Oh, I don't know,' she said, trying to look cool and failing miserably. 'It's still early days. We're just having fun. He's putting off a lot till this job he's doing is over. He's always saying "when this job's over we'll do this that and the other" so I hope it's true. I hope we will get some time together before some other contract takes him away or I have to fly off somewhere.' She said the last part with a starry glint in her eye, as though she couldn't believe she was saying it, then seemed to return to reality as she picked up her glass again and looked pensive. 'I hope he was serious about the America thing. What do you think?'

'I'm sure he was,' I said, not wanting her to start worrying and put a dampener on her big day. I hoped he was too, and if they were flying out together I also hoped Fay packed her own suitcase. Oh God. And then there was this contract he was working on. Wasn't drug dealing a bit like gambling? Weren't they always waiting for the one big deal or wager to come in that would set them up for life and set them free from the hole they had dug themselves? That's what Tim was doing, I realised. That's why he moved here only temporarily, why he was working longer and longer hours. It was building up to something.

When Nikki arrived we got a table and ordered straight away. The service was quick because it was still early evening, too early for civilised dining but that was good for us.

After Fay had answered Nikki's questions about the new job, repeating what she had told me about Tim, Nikki turned her attention to me.

'So,' she said. 'You told me what happened with Jamie. Have you heard from him since?'

'The occasional text. I feel good about it though. I know we'll stay in touch.'

'Do you think anything will happen down the line?'

I was reminded by what my dad had said, about how if it doesn't feel right, wait until it does. It didn't fit with Jamie though. 'I really don't think so. There was no real spark. Only friendship.'

'But there must have been a spark the night you stayed at his.'

I still cringed when I thought of that. 'Maybe a super-ficial spark, fuelled by alcohol and a weird notion that perhaps we were meant to. But no. Obviously we both thought about it. It's the Harry met Sally thing, isn't it? You start a friendship with an attractive man and you have to wonder if there's anything more. When it comes down to it though, we just don't fancy each other. It's that simple.'

'So what are you going to do now?'

'About what?'

'About Adam?'

'What about Adam?'

Fay and Nikki looked at each other as though I was

clearly in denial and they were going to have to break the news to me gently.

'Well, aren't things different now?' Fay asked, speaking slowly.

Nikki agreed. 'Yeah, now that you know Jamie isn't for you and Miranda has explained the stuff in the predictions. Doesn't that make you feel differently about Adam?'

I sighed, thinking about it as our food arrived and was passed out by the waitress. 'I never stopped loving Adam,' I said, after the waitress had gone. 'Loving someone and knowing you can live with them for the rest of your life are two very different things. You can love someone and not trust them. You can love someone and feel unsure how much they love you back. You can love someone and feel that there's a possibility you could love someone else more. The thing with Miranda made me realise I'd clung to her words and half wanted to believe them because if it was true, the future I'd had planned could still happen. I'd been ticking along with Adam, trying not to think about the things that weren't right in the hope that they'd get better. Miranda's words made me realise how I felt. Not unhappy, but not truly happy. I started seeing signs everywhere, signs that I had to get out. I think I was seeing them because I was looking for them. It couldn't go on like that.'

'So, you still love Adam,' Fay said.

I put my fork down with a clatter. 'Oh I've made such a mess of things, haven't I? I still love Adam. I never thought it'd hurt this much to be without him. It's made me realise I wasn't trying hard enough. Maybe it was me that was scared of commitment, worried we'd turn into my parents and end up bickering and frustrated.' I realised I'd started to cry and dabbed under my eyes with my napkin. 'I'm sorry Fay, it's your special night and I'm spoiling it.'

'Forget that,' she said, leaning forwards, her food sitting ignored on her plate. 'Do you want Adam back?'

I sniffed hard, nodding. 'If Miranda appeared at our table right now in a puff of smoke and told us she was a white witch all along and Adam and I were doomed, it wouldn't make a jot of difference. I just want him back. Even if it's just the same and I worry and he's vague, it's better than the alternative. I know now that he was meant for me. No one else can tell me any different.'

'Then you have to get him back,' Nikki said resolutely.

'It's too late. I've blown it.'

'No,' Nikki said, spearing a slice of grapefruit from her salad bowl. 'I won't have that kind of talk. You're meant to be with Adam. It's never too late for you two.'

Fay looked up in surprise. 'Nikki! You don't believe in all that stuff about people being meant for each other.'

'Maybe, but with Adam and Gemma it's different,' she said simply. 'They give me hope. Always have. I'm not letting go of that until the fat lady sings. And by the way,' she leaned forwards and waggled her fork at the pair of us, 'if they start playing a woman singing an aria from Madam Butterfly, or something, in a minute that is because this is an Italian restaurant, OK? No other reason than that.'

# Chapter Twenty-Seven

Having finished our meals we made a sensible decision to round off the evening with a sobering coffee rather than something stronger. Whilst we were waiting for them to arrive I got up and went to visit the ladies' room. It was down a steep flight of stairs that weren't very well lit and on the last step I stumbled, toppling backwards until I ended up sitting on a step. 'Whoopsie, clumsy me,' I said to myself then heard someone laughing in the shadows at the bottom of the stairs.

'This is like déjà vu,' the voice said. 'You were drunk and unsteady on your feet the last time I saw you, funnily enough.'

I looked up in surprise, the hair on my arms bristling. 'Who's that?'

'Don't you recognise me?' He stepped forward into the light and held out his hand to pull me up.

As soon as I saw his face I realised who it was. Oh no, this could be awkward, I thought, but said, 'Of course I do. How are you?'

'All the better for seeing you.'

I could tell he was drunk. 'OK, well I'm just err,' I pointed to the door of the Ladies, wanting to escape.

He leaned against the wall, blocking my exit.

'So, who are you here with?'

'Fay and Nikki.'

'Ahh, the terrible twosome.' He laughed. 'I missed them,' he said, suddenly serious. 'I missed you.'

'Don't.'

'I'm sorry. I know I shouldn't say things like that. You've got a boyfriend now, haven't you? Alex, wasn't it?'

'Adam.' I wasn't going to tell him we'd split up.

'I met someone too: Kathy, she works in my office,' he said, gesturing up the stairs to where she must have been waiting for him. 'I found it hard after you, though, you cut me deep.'

He was slurring. Looking at him now I couldn't believe I ever found him attractive. 'Luke, you were the one that went after Fay in the nightclub that night. I didn't do anything.'

He let out a bitter half-laugh. 'That's the bit you like to remember, isn't it? You conveniently forget that I proposed to you, and all you could do was laugh. Can you imagine how that felt?'

'What?'

'I wanted you for once just to take me seriously. Take our relationship seriously.'

'You didn't. You never proposed to me.'

'I did, Gemma. OK, so it wasn't romantic or staged, it was just me, telling you what I wanted. Asking if you wanted it too. It was from the heart.'

'But how . . .? What? Why didn't you ever mention it afterwards?'

'Because I felt ridiculous. You've never heard of foolish male pride?'

I thought about it. No. He couldn't have. 'I was drunk.

282

Really drunk. That whole night is a patchy memory. Surely you can't have been serious.' I could picture the club in my head, us dancing, me looking around for the others, not wanting to be alone with Luke. I'd hinted at things not going well for us a few times but he'd refused to understand that I was trying to gently finish with him. I knew at the time that I couldn't be with him any longer, but I wanted to talk to him when we were alone. An image flashed into my mind of him pulling me off the dance floor, of him suddenly getting serious and me feeling uncomfortable and awkward, laughing and trying to jolly him out of his mood. I'd had no idea. The music had been loud and I hadn't even tried to hear him. I wanted to carry on dancing, I didn't want to get into a serious discussion. I'd been telling him not to be silly.

'I'm sorry Luke, I honestly had no idea. I couldn't have heard you.'

I could tell from his expression that he was beginning to believe me now. He nodded and looked regretfully at his feet. 'Would it have made any difference if you had?

'I wouldn't have laughed,' I said, sincerely. 'But things worked out for the best, don't you think?'

'I don't know. I think we could have been happy,' he said. 'Don't you?'

It struck me that he was still the kind of person who would try and snog your best friend when he thinks he's been hurt, and who would attempt to rekindle a relationship with an ex whilst his girlfriend was sitting upstairs at their table for two. 'No, I don't think we would,' I said quietly and once more Luke stalked away from me, his face pinched.

Nikki and Fay looked horrified when I told them what had happened. I'd bolted back up the stairs, scared of bumping into him again, but on my way up the stairwell was empty, and to my relief I couldn't see him in the restaurant either.

'I always knew that guy was creepy,' Nikki said. 'Don't you listen to him, he's seriously not right in the head. He wants you to feel sorry for him.'

'I kind of did though.'

'You have to remember what he was like, how intense he was, how he manipulated your feelings until you were run ragged.'

She was right. He did do those things.

'Don't let him do it again.'

Fay sat through our conversation grinning and fidgeting like a child waiting for her parents to wake up on Christmas morning.

'What?' I said eventually.

'Don't you see?'

'You're talking about someone asking me to marry them before Adam did, aren't you?'

'Well yeah.' She said this in a drawn-out, are-you-being-deliberately-dumb kind of voice. 'Don't you think that's spooky?'

'I did, for about thirty seconds. Now though, I'm not so sure, because the point is, it doesn't make any difference to me any more. I can't keep thinking on those lines, it only confuses me, and anyway, I can't want Adam any more than I already do.'

Late on Friday night I was alone in the house. It was the night that Fabian was seeing Nikki, and Tim had taken Fay out for a celebration dinner. I found it curious that Tim hadn't wanted to go anywhere local and instead had insisted on driving her out to a restaurant in Laycock, ten miles away. He was an hour late by the time he got back from work. Fay had been starting to look worried when

284

time ticked by and he still hadn't returned. When he did turn up he looked flustered and hassled, rushing to get Fay out the door to the restaurant. Fay had looked puzzled by his behaviour and I hoped they were able to salvage the night and still have a good time.

I changed into my pyjamas after they'd gone and had just made myself comfortable on the sofa with a tub of ice cream and a packet of chocolate digestives, when the phone rang.

'I'm *ba*-ack,' said a sing-song voice.

'Jules! About time too,' I said, curling my feet up under me on the sofa. 'I missed you.'

'Me too, buddy. How's it been going?'

'Oh, you know. Weird, a bit crazy, but that's just me. How about you? How was your honeymoon?'

'The best,' she said, and began filling me in on some of her adventures.

It was good to hear what they'd been up to. They were so normal. A regular, happy couple. Listening to her talking about Richard made me understand what Nikki meant about other couples giving you hope. Richard and Jules gave me hope. 'Anyway,' Jules concluded, 'I've promised Rich that I won't become a holiday bore. I'm not even allowed to get the photos developed till after the party, so I won't go on about it. Ooh, you are coming to the party, aren't you? Did you tell Nikki and Fay?'

'Yes I did. We'll all be there tomorrow, so long as you're sure you're still up for it.'

'Definitely. I can't wait to see you all.' Her voice dropped ever so slightly when she said that, as though she was reminded of something that bothered her.

'Are you sure? Did I just detect a hint of woe?'

'No, no. All's fine.'

Instinct told me this was about Adam. 'Have you spoken

to him? Has he said something about me?'

There was a long pause. 'No, I've not spoken to him. Have you?'

'Not for a while. Is he going to be there tomorrow?' I wasn't sure what answer I wanted to hear to that question.

'Oh Gem, I don't know. Richard tried to get in touch as soon as we got back and it's all gone quiet. He went round to the workshop yesterday and it was shut. No sign of life.'

'Really? It was Thursday yesterday. He never shuts on a Thursday. Did he try Adam's mobile?'

'He tried a few times and left a message then he walked over to the house.'

'And?'

'And ...' She drew the word out, buying time.

'What? You can tell me.' My heart was pounding now. Was he there with a woman? Was the house empty with a TO LET sign on the door?

'Well, I'm sure it doesn't mean anything, but there was no one home. No one *had* been home. The milk was stacked up by the doorstep and the curtains were still drawn. He's probably just gone to stay with someone for a few days.'

'He never shuts up shop to go and stay with anybody,' I said.

'Maybe he needed some time to think: he was pretty upset about how things turned out with you.'

'Do you think he was really that bothered?'

'Gemma. He hides it well, but not that well. He loved you. I'm sure he still does.'

I wanted Jules's words to be comforting. If he was affected enough to shut up shop and go off somewhere to lick his wounds then he really must have loved me, but I just wasn't buying it. I knew Adam. He was a plough-it-all-into-your-work kind of guy, not the type to up and leave when things went badly. Whenever he'd had anything on his mind, it was the first place I'd go looking for him; to the workshop, where he'd always be, pouring his concentration into a project to the point where everything else was forgotten. He probably won't be at the party then, I thought, my disappointment making me realise how much I had wanted to see him there. I dropped my spoon back into the tub of ice-cream, my appetite gone, and wondered where he could be.

Richard and Jules's house was a ten-minute walk from Alexandra Terrace, high up on the northern slopes of Bath. Richard, who took his work home with him in the best possible sense, had completely redesigned it, changing a fairly modest cottage into a work of art, extended with a timber and glass front and modified inside with very high-quality materials. The few times I'd been there I had walked around almost drooling at the loveliness of it. With the front of the house being glass it was always bright and sunny and there was a priceless view of Bath below. The only downside was that to walk to it from town you had to have calves like Jonny Wilkinson.

'You can see my house from here,' Nikki said, turning around to have a look when we reached the right road.

I sat on the road sign, getting my breath back. 'Ours too.' I scanned the horizon until my eyes stopped at the pub on the corner of Adam's road and wondered again if he would come tonight. On the way to the shops this morning I had plucked up the courage to take a detour past his house and it was just as Jules had said: curtains drawn, milk still out. I would have given up and stayed at home feeling sorry for myself tonight if it hadn't been so long since I had last seen Richard and Jules.

'Come on Gemma, party time,' Nikki said, waggling her bottle at me, and Fay came and took my elbow, hauling me up. They were both in the mood to celebrate tonight: Fay was still on a high after her job offer and a romantic dinner with Tim (all was apparently forgiven after his late arrival) and Nikki had the air of a free woman after her evening with Fabian. She wouldn't tell us what happened, only that she was now feeling better about everything and had washed her hands of him for good. I was hoping that after a few drinks I would manage to get the truth out of her.

'I'm coming, I'm coming,' I said, getting up and following them towards the house.

Richard and Jules were making a complete fuss of me, and part of me liked it, but my paranoid streak was getting a little suspicious of their reasons. When they weren't talking to me they kept checking to see if I was all right or if I'd got enough to drink, punctuating their questions with small affectionate gestures: an arm around my shoulder, a hand on my sleeve, as though they were worried I was cracking up and putting on a brave face. In an attempt to allay their fears I began overcompensating, turning up the volume and the facial expressions as I talked to people I'd only ever met when I was with Adam. It was unsettling seeing these people again without him. I wanted to ask if they knew how he was doing or where he was, but I didn't dare. Then I saw Grant walking out of the kitchen, pint in hand, and couldn't stop myself any longer. I marched over and appeared before him.

'Hi.'

He looked surprised to see me.

'How've you been?'

'So-so,' he said, looking around as though he was fraternising with the enemy and didn't want to get caught. 'Yourself?'

'I've been better,' I said, my mask slipping. 'Have you seen Adam? How's he doing?'

He cleared his throat and avoided looking at me. 'You should ask him that yourself.'

'Well, I would if I knew where he was. I've not seen him for a while and Richard says he's shut up shop. Do you know why? Have you spoken to him?'

Finally he looked at me. I begged him with my eyes. 'Grant please, I'm worried about him.'

He shook his head. 'I honestly don't know. Truth is, whatever's going on, he's not told me. The only person I know he's spoken to is Daniel, the guy who has the glass-blowing shop opposite.'

I nodded. I knew Daniel. He was the one who saw me having a meal with Jamie and told Adam about it so I had a feeling if he knew anything, he wouldn't feel obliged to tell me.

'He's over there, why don't you ask him?' Grant said, pointing across the room.

I saw Daniel standing at the foot of a staircase, talking to a group of people I didn't know. 'Thanks, I will,' I said and started across the room towards him.

I was snaking through the guests, my eyes trained on Daniel when someone walked in front of me, blocking my path. I tried to go around him but felt two big hands on my shoulders and I stopped. I looked up and saw Jamie, beaming down at me in surprise. 'What are you doing here?'

My jaw dropped. 'Well, I was invited. Richard and Jules

289

are friends of mine. What are *you* doing here?' I couldn't believe this. Fate just kept lobbing him back at me.

'Richard's a mate of mine,' Jamie said. 'I met him at college years ago. I told you about him, didn't I? He was the one that did some drawings for me, to turn my outbuildings into a studio.'

'Oh, right! I didn't realise you meant Richard. How funny.'

'It is. Well, it's good to see you again.' He chucked me affectionately under the chin.

Suddenly I remembered Daniel and panicked. If he recognised Jamie it would get back to Adam and make things even more complicated. I looked over at him but he'd turned away and was now deep in conversation, unaware that I was there. Thank God for that, I thought, turning back. That was when I spotted Adam. He was standing in the doorway behind Jamie.

I froze. He could almost be an apparition, standing motionless, looking at me with sad, tired eyes. I was surprised by his appearance. He looked as though he'd got ready in a hurry, not bothering to wash or shave first. In fact he looked as though he hadn't eaten or slept in a few days either. His skin was paler and there were shadows under his eyes.

Jamie looked around to see who I was staring at then looked back at me, puzzled. 'Are you OK? Is that ...?'

I nodded. 'That's Adam,' I said, still not taking my eyes off him.

Adam turned around to go out the way he'd come in.

'I'm sorry Jamie, I've got to ... Can we catch up later?'

I bolted after Adam, not waiting for a reply and found him in the hallway, reaching for the front door. 'Don't go,' I pleaded, hanging onto the sleeve of his shirt. He stopped and faced me. 'Why?'

'Because I want to talk to you. You look terrible; what's going on?'

'It's nothing. I'm OK. I've just been busy. Don't let me take you away from your new boyfriend.' He made to go again and once more I took his arm and tugged him back.

'He's not my boyfriend, he's just a friend. An old teacher from school. Look, please, don't walk off. I want to talk to you about us.'

'I thought we'd had our chance.'

'I was wrong. Upset, talking crap. This past month has made me see a lot of things differently. I realise now it was all my fault. All of it. I should have talked to you, asked you what was going on; that's my trouble, you see? I was too scared to ask. Like with Miranda. I knew there was something but I didn't dare find out. I just made like everything was fine because that was easier than dealing with difficult stuff. I wanted everything to be perfect so I tiptoed around the bad signs. It's like that Bjork song, you know, "It's Oh So Quiet"? Because that's what I was like, singing the quiet bits, not wanting the "Wow bang!" bits. I had enough of that at home with my parents; those bits made me nervous, so when it all went wrong I started looking for perfection again, looking for the good signs, wanting the quiet bits again and ...' I stalled, seeing Adam's face. I'd gone too far with the Bjork bit, I realised, wishing Fay hadn't talked me into downing that glass of punch with her. It had been suspiciously syrupy. Half the liquid had evaporated straight up my nostrils.

'You're drunk,' he said, looking at me with disappointment.

'Mmm, maybe a bit,' I said. 'But that's OK, we can still talk.' I stepped closer to him but he reeled away.

'Adam?' I didn't understand. Did he really hate me?

'I'm sorry, not now. Not like this,' he said and he went for the front door, walking out before I could say any more.

# Chapter Twenty-Eight

I couldn't stay there any longer. I had to get out.

Racing into the kitchen I snatched my bag off the kitchen work surface then headed straight back out the front door.

On the street outside I couldn't spot Adam anywhere so I carried on to the hill that Fay, Nikki and I had climbed earlier. It led back to our house, town and Adam's house, so he was bound to have gone that way.

There were only a few other people walking on the hill but none of them looked like Adam. My hope started to drain away until I saw someone disappear around the corner at the bottom. It was him. I ran as quickly as I could down the slope and rounded the corner, just in time to see him get into a taxi cab and be driven off into the night.

'Bugger, bollocks!' I cried, ignoring the sudden interest that got me from passers-by. Where the hell had he gone? Why would he need a taxi? I slumped down on an empty bench, fighting tears of despair. My feet, which at the time had seemed to cope fine with running down the steep hill in the heels I'd squeezed them into, were now pulsing and sore. I took my shoes off, scooping them up into my hand, then got up, trudging barefoot across the road onto Park Lane.

I was just rounding the corner of Alexandra Terrace when I heard footsteps and turned around. Tim was walking towards Barney's on the other side of the road, his head bent low and his hands in the pockets of a black jacket. I ducked around the corner out of sight and peered back around. He hadn't seen me. I felt sick. He had told Fay he was working tonight. Since leaving this morning he hadn't returned and we'd all assumed he'd gone away again. This is seriously dodgy, I thought, my heartbeat ringing in my ears. I had another look and saw that once again he was going into Barney's, despite it being shut up and dark. I waited until the door closed behind him then hurried across the street. I had to find out what was going on, I decided, before things went any further. Fay had a right to know.

There was an alleyway that led down the side of Barney's and out into the backyard, just the same as the shop where I had seen Tim before. *Sneaking around in alleyways is becoming a favoured pastime of mine,* I thought, tiptoeing down the narrow path to the yard. There were lights on in the back rooms of the restaurant but the curtains were drawn shut. The back door, however, was open, enabling me to hear the muffled sounds of men talking. I hesitated. What if they saw me sneaking around? I remembered last time and decided that if he saw me I'd play dumb and pretend to be looking for Dexter. There was what I took to be an outside toilet in the yard, built separately from the main building and situated opposite the back door. I snuck into the yard and quickly hid behind the wall of the toilet. There was the sound of a door banging and every nerve in my body must had gone into a temporary spasm. The seriousness of the situation was starting to dawn on me. Who did I think I was? The ballsy one from *Cagney and Lacey*? I was stuck now. I couldn't leave without risking being caught.

Two voices grew louder and I realised in horror that they were coming outside. Their feet scuffed on the ground as they stopped on the patio and I heard the sound of a match lighting. I crouched lower still. Maybe they would find me and torture me, lighting matches and dropping them on my head until I talked. *Was this what a panic attack felt like?*

'No,' I heard one of the men say, lowering his voice, 'if you ask me he's getting edgy. I want him gone. This is seriously good shit. Best we've had. I'd rather piss it up a tree than let that spineless wonder touch it.'

'What do you think we can get?' I wondered if this was Tim.

'No less than a grand a pop. Cash up front.'

He laughed then whistled quietly.

My feet were freezing and I'd developed a tremble that was spreading quickly from my legs up my body. The men fell silent and I had to hold my hand over my mouth, convinced that they were the other side of the wall, listening for signs of someone breathing. Of course they weren't and eventually I heard one of them grind out the cigarette on the concrete with their foot and say, 'C'mon.'

I stayed still, not daring to move, wanting to be certain no one was there before I made a run for it. I hadn't the bottle to stay any longer. There was a scuffling noise in the alleyway and a slight scratching sound on the fence.

If that's a bloody rat and it comes anywhere near me I might not be able to stop myself from screaming, even if there is a murdering drug lord plotting just a few feet from me. I poked my head around the wall of the toilet, as far as I dared, then snapped it back. It was Tim. He was finishing his cigarette, scratching the back of his neck. I leaned my head against the wall. I was going to be stuck here forever.

Suddenly, the night was filled with the tinny sounds of the theme tune for *Rhubarb and Custard*. To my horror I realised that my mobile phone was ringing. I scrambled for my bag, my hands trembling and pulled out the phone, juggling with it in my haste to turn if off. I saw a glimpse of the name, Fay, on the display before it went dark again and silence descended on the yard. A big pair of shoes appeared on the grass in front of me and I looked up to see Tim staring at me, his face angry.

'Go go go!' a voice in the alleyway cried and suddenly I was caught up in a whirlwind of chaos. There were police everywhere, storming the garden, kitted out with riot gear. In the house I could hear crashing and shouts as a major scuffle broke out, and the throbbing noise I'd put down to a tension headache grew louder as a helicopter hovered overhead. Its searchlight cut through the darkness as it swept across the sky. I felt myself pushed to the ground, my hands secured behind my back as a policeman reminded me of my rights.

The street was filled with riot vans and police cars and I noticed that a small crowd had gathered at the end of the street. There were many pairs of eyes on me as I was led by my elbow to a police car and I cringed, hoping that none of them were parents from Dizzy Heights.

I'd tried talking to the officers in the yard, explaining that I wasn't a criminal, but they were having none of it. They kept saying 'save it for the station, love' until I was forced to give up and stop struggling.

I watched Tim being bundled into the police car in front of me and then felt a hand on my own head, pushing me down onto the back seat. Another officer sat beside me and as the car pulled away I looked out at the scene in fascination. It'd be quite exciting, I thought, as another car screeched to a halt outside the restaurant, if it wasn't so scary. Then I spotted Fay running across the street. She must have seen Tim in the car in front because she was calling him, her face aghast. As his car sped up she stood in the road, watching it go. I banged on the window, calling her name and she turned just in time to see me pass by.

It was three o'clock in the morning by the time I made it home. The moment the front door clicked shut behind me the kitchen door flew open and Fay pounced on me.

'Gemma, thank God, we've been so worried. What happened? What's going on? Where's Tim?'

I trudged into the kitchen, dropping my bag on the table and flopped down into a chair.

Nikki was already sitting at the table, her eyes focused on me. 'Are you OK?' she asked.

'I'm really sorry,' I said to Fay. 'It seems that Tim isn't who you thought he was.'

She sat down hard on the chair next to me. 'Tell me everything.'

There wasn't much to tell. I started by telling her about the time I'd seen him in the alleyway, just before he turned up with Dexter. 'I know I should have told you but I wanted to be sure. You were really into him and I didn't want to cause trouble unnecessarily. I was hoping I was wrong, or that your relationship wouldn't get serious, but when I saw him going into Barney's tonight I knew for sure.' I told them how I'd followed him and what I'd seen and heard before I was taken away. 'It was a big drugs raid. One of the biggest they've had in Bath, apparently.

They kept telling me how serious it all was, like that might make me tell them more. But that's all they said really. I was kept in a room on my own at the station. They kept asking me questions then they'd go off and someone else would come in and ask me more or less the same questions. They asked a lot about how well I knew Barney. I told them I always thought he seemed like a nice guy; friendly, you know, very loyal to his family, always talking about them and about how beautiful Sicily is. I can't believe he's involved in something like this.'

'I know,' Nikki said. 'I have to say I thought he was a decent guy, but then some people would have said Don Corleone was a nice bloke who loved his family. It just goes to show, you never can tell, can you?'

'Tell me about it,' Fay said, looking miserable. 'I'm turning out to be a terrible judge of character. I really thought I was starting to understand Tim. Did they ask much about him? What did you tell them?'

'Just what I'd seen last night really, and the conversation I overhead. I didn't tell them about the time I saw him in the alley. I didn't see how that would make any difference. They'd have enough on him anyway, after last night.' Fay looked even more troubled and I stopped, apologising.

'It's OK. It's not your fault he's a liar and a scumbag. Carry on.'

'Well, that was it really. They had left me for ages and I was really starting to panic, then one of the officers came in and said I could go. Just like that. No explanation. Just thanked me for my co-operation and told me I'd get a call if they needed a formal statement.'

'So that's it? You don't know anything else?' Nikki asked.

I shook my head. 'When the taxi dropped me off there

were still police cars there though. I reckon they're searching Barney's with a fine toothcomb.'

'Oh God,' Fay cried. 'They will want to search our house too, won't they? Tim left his room locked. There's bound to be stuff in there. I can't bear it.' Tears started to roll down her cheeks.

I put my arm around her.

Nikki got up. 'Come on. There's no rule that says we have to stay in tomorrow and wait for the police to turn up. I say we get some sleep now, we're all knackered, then in the morning we can go out for the day. Leave it all to happen without us.'

'She's right,' I said to Fay. 'We'll stick together and it'll all work itself out eventually. We'll be OK.'

I managed to sleep for about two hours before waking up with a start, confused and disorientated. My first thought was Adam, looking so tired and hassled, walking away from me in disappointment. It was a crushing memory and I curled up into a ball, groaning. My next thought was the weird and vivid dream I'd had about Tim and some drugs squad officers. I pondered uneasily on that until my memories shuffled themselves back into order and I realised what had actually happened. After untangling myself from the duvet I hurried over to the window, opening it wide so that I could see right down the street. There was no sign of what had happened at Barney's. No police officers, no squad cars, no people milling around and muttering 'who'd uv thought it' to an equally scandalised neighbour. I went out into the hall. Tim's door was shut. I went over and tried the handle and found it still locked. Fay's door flew open and she poked her head out into the corridor.

'Only me,' I said, holding my hands up.

She sighed.

'Did you get any sleep?'

'I don't even think I managed to blink. I've been driving myself crazy in there.'

'You fancy some coffee?'

'Go on then. But can we make it a take-out? I can't bear to hang around here any longer.'


My feet and the bottom of my jeans were soaked in dew. I dangled them off the rock, laughing to myself as Fay and Nikki sat down beside me.

'What?' Nikki said.

'Well, it's just funny, isn't it? When you think that almost twenty years ago, *twenty*, we were doing this. Climbing up this same old rock with a blanket and a flask to lob stones into the river and talk about boys. Now here we are again, doing just that. Nothing's changed.'

'Apart from the fact that we've progressed to double espresso. It used to be Vimto,' Nikki said, taking the flask out of the rucksack, along with a packet of biscuits that she'd bought from the village shop.

I looked across the river to Langley Green. You could just see my parents' house through a gap in the trees.

Fay threw a stone, which glanced off a fallen branch and landed in a clump of grass. 'My shot still hasn't improved,' she said.

'Do you think we'll still be coming here in another twenty years?' I said.

'Oh God, can you imagine? We probably won't be able to climb this bloody rock by then. It was hard enough today.' Fay pointed out a snag in her fishnet tights.

'If we've still got men problems by then it'll be gin in my flask,' Nikki said. She took out a newspaper from her bag and started thumbing through it. A few pages in she stopped and squealed, laughing and clutching the paper to her chest.

'What? What is it?' I cried, trying to take the paper off her.

'This is excellent,' she said. 'I never thought it'd actually get in the paper.'

'Show us!' Fay begged.

She put the paper down, spreading it on the rock for us all to see. It was a photograph of Fabian, surrounded by people. At least I assumed it was Fabian. It was hard to tell as the picture was taken from behind whilst he'd been stripping off his T-shirt. He looked like he was at a fashion show. The newspaper had added a ring around Fabian's back, as though trying to point out something specific to the reader.

Fay and I bent in closer for a better look then we saw what it was. His back was tanned and brown but parts of it were paler, they were letters, and they spelt out the word GIT. We both looked at Nikki in astonishment. She had perfected a look of feigned innocence, biting her lip to stop from laughing. 'It was an honest mistake,' she said. 'I gave him a massage before the tan shower. He fell asleep so, for a bit of fun, I kind of doodled on his back with some barrier cream. I never realised the tan shower didn't work where the cream had been. It must have appeared over time when the tan developed. Oh, isn't it terrible?'

Fay cracked up laughing as I read the text. 'It says here that a photographer took it during the rehearsals for the Eligible Bachelor night. No one knows who did it, but Fabian was forced to pull out of the show, almost certainly because contestants were scheduled to have a topless parade down the catwalk.' I started to laugh. 'You're a wicked woman,' I said, patting Nikki's back, 'but you're also a genius.'

After we'd worked our way through the packet of biscuits

the mood was starting to deflate again. The change of scenery and the story in the paper could only divert us for so long.

'Oh, what are we going to do?' I said, mournfully. 'Everything's gone wrong. Adam hates me ...'

'My boyfriend's soon to be convicted drug dealer,' Fay chipped in.

'And I'm still single,' Nikki added, then she looked at me sheepishly. 'Actually Gemma, can I be honest with you?'

'About what?'

'Well, last night, I got talking to Jamie.' She paused.

'And?'

'And I really like him.'

I looked at her in surprise. 'Do you fancy him?'

She nodded. 'I'm sorry, I can't help it. He's just so nice and such an attractive guy. I promise I won't do anything about it though. I just had to tell you. Are you mad with me?'

'Are you kidding? That's brilliant news. Of course you have to do something about it.' I smiled at her. At least something was going right. 'I knew there was a reason I was meant to bump into him,' I said, just as my phone started beeping. I took it out of the rucksack and flicked through, reading the new message. 'It's from Jules,' I said. 'She's asking if I'm OK.'

'You know what I think you should do?' Nikki said suddenly. 'I think you should give Daniel a ring. I bet you could convince him to tell you what's going on.'

'I'm not sure Adam wants me to know.'

She shrugged. 'So what? You need to find out. You two have got to clear the air. It won't be sorted till you do.'

Thinking about it, she was right. I was good at giving up. It was about time I stopped burying my head in the sand whenever something tough came along. 'Right, I will then,' I said, picking my phone back up again. 'It has to be worth a try.'

Daniel had sounded surprisingly pleased to hear from me.

'You're right,' he'd said when I was only a few sentences into my plea.

'Am I?'

'He needs to speak to you right now. He's just too pig-headed to admit it.'

'He does?'

'I can't tell you what's been going on. That's for Adam to do, if he wants to. But I can tell you where he's staying. He's at his dad's house.'


I'd never been to Adam's dad's house before. Not surprising as I'd never met his dad before either. I wasn't even sure where he lived until Daniel told me. I'd only known that it was near the racecourse, a few miles out of town.

Nikki had driven me straight there, planning to drop me off and carry on to Bristol with Fay, hoping to distract her from Tim with some retail therapy, but when we pulled up outside the address she looked worried.

It was a ramshackle-looking house; a tiny end-of-terrace cottage with an overgrown garden, rotten fencing and a boarded up window. Adam's Land Rover was sitting in the drive so I knew we had the right house and my heart sank. This place was depressing.

'We can stay,' Nikki said.

'No. It's OK. I've got my phone. I can always call you if I need you.'

Nikki looked at the house again. 'Are you sure?'

'Yeah, it's fine. I'm here now.' I picked up my bag and

climbed out of the car. 'Don't worry. I'll catch up with you later.'

'Good luck,' Fay called after me and I waved at them then took a deep breath before walking down the drive.

When Adam saw me he leaned his shoulder against the doorframe and briefly closed his eyes.

'You can run but you cannot hide,' I said in a feeble attempt to jolly a smile out of him.

He let the door swing open behind him. 'You'd better come in.'

'So, is this your dad's place?' I stepped into the kitchen, trying to keep my face blank and trying to disguise the fact that I was reeling with shock. If it was possible for someone to beat the living daylights out of a house, this was what the end result would look like: two of the kitchen chairs were broken, there was a hole kicked into the pantry door, a window was smashed, the back door was leaning against a wall, no longer attached to its hinges and there were two cardboard boxes sitting on the Formica table, full of broken crockery that Adam must have tidied up. There was a workbench set up in the garden, surrounded by wood shavings that were being scattered across the lawn by the wind.

'So, now would probably be a good time for me to explain a few things,' Adam said, rubbing his face with his hands. He looked exhausted.

'You don't have to.'

'I know, but I want to. It's about time I did.'

I sat down on one of the two remaining chairs that weren't lame and waited patiently whilst he cleared an area of the table and then leaned against it, working up to what he was about to say.

'I hadn't seen much of Dad in a long time. Up until

recently I only saw him the bare minimum: Christmas, his birthday, that sort of thing. We weren't close. We haven't been since he walked out on Mum. I knew he had problems. He blamed her for the split, saying she'd turned cold on him. That she'd treated him with contempt for years. I don't know what's true really, I don't want to know. All I knew was that he scared me.' He looked self-conscious and I felt an overwhelming sadness. How could big, strong, independent Adam be scared of anyone? 'He was unpredictable, you see. Still holding on to a lot of bitterness. He was alone, and he's not a guy that handles his own company very well. I knew he drank a lot, and had dark times when he wallowed in self-pity. I didn't like it but I thought I could understand it, you know? He'd lost a lot. I think I did a good job of convincing myself that he was just one of those people: he'd had a hard life, he was on his own, he wasn't a happy guy. I didn't think he could need me. He'd walked out on me, he hadn't contacted me for years, why would *he* need *me*? I didn't want you to meet him because I thought you'd see what I pretended not to see. A sad, old, nasty drunk who was slowly self-destructing.'

I wanted to tell him that I was sure I wouldn't have thought those things, that I would have seen his qualities, but what did I know? I had never met him.

'I hadn't seen him in months. Last time I came here he'd pretty much ignored me. He said some stuff, not good stuff, and I got angry and shouted back. Remember the night I was meant to come over to yours and didn't turn up? You came looking for me and found me in the workshop in the middle of the night.'

I nodded.

'That was the same day.'

'Why didn't you tell me what was going on? I asked if you were OK and you never said a thing.'

'It's just not something I ever talked about before. I didn't want anyone to know and I thought I could handle it.' He stood up away from the table and paced around the kitchen. 'So, anyway, I have to admit I didn't think about him much over the following weeks, until I got a call from Len. He's Dad's neighbour on that side,' he pointed to the neat fence that lined one side of the garden. 'He's an old guy, in his seventies, and a really good bloke. He knew where my workshop was and got the number out of the phone book. It was last Tuesday, late in the afternoon and I was just shutting up the shop. He asked me to come straight away. Said that there'd been noises, he thought Dad might have been drinking and was in a rage. I came straight over and found him out there.' He nodded to the area outside the back door. It was like an old makeshift conservatory in a bad state of repair. The flat roof was made out of corrugated plastic laid on top of wooden supports. Some of the wood had come away and one of the plastic panels was missing. 'He had climbed up onto the roof and fallen through. Daft sod.' He tutted, looking down at his boots. 'He was unconscious when I found him. Poor old Len was in a right state. Really upset. He'd tried to get in the house and talk to Dad but he's an old man; there wasn't much he could do. I called an ambulance, they came pretty quick, and I rode with him to the hospital. That's where he is now.'

'How is he?'

'He's OK. They weren't sure for a while. There was some internal bleeding, but they managed to find it quickly and it's been sorted out. They're going to let him out in a couple of days if his tests are all clear. They should be. I've been staying here sorting his house out. You think it looks bad now, this is nothing compared to when I found it.'

'What will happen to him though? He needs help, surely? For his drink problem.'

'Yeah, I know. Even he admits that now. The first night he was in hospital he cried; apologised for everything. He asked for help. Said he couldn't do it on his own, that he was in a rut and he didn't know how to get out. I had a word with the doctor and he's referred him to this residential home, a recovery house for alcoholics. They go for a six-week stay and then keep up treatments with various drop-in programmes. Dad wants to give it a go and I believe he'll try his best. He was a broken man when he went in there. He hasn't had a drink in four days so he's not the best to be around right now, but he's got guts, I'll give him that.'

'I wish I'd known all this before,' I said. I remembered the way Adam had looked the previous night at the party. He had needed me then and he'd found me with Jamie, and then I realised why he'd found it so hard to deal with me being drunk. Tears were welling up in my eyes. I'd let everyone down, I was a crap friend and a crap girlfriend. Why couldn't I have done more? 'I'm sorry,' I said, my voice high and strained as the tears came and fell.

Adam pulled up a chair and sat opposite me. 'No, I'm sorry. I should have asked for help but I was stubborn and proud. I ignored what was happening with Dad and didn't let you get close enough to find out. I shut you out.'

I wiped my face with my sleeve, trying to stop myself from sobbing and looked at him. I wished we could just forget everything and start again.

He leaned forwards and took my hands in his.

'Gemma, I need to tell you about Marcia.'

Everything stopped. He was looking at me strangely. I felt sick.

'You were right. I did kiss her. The night she stayed at mine. It's why I didn't fight harder for you. I hated myself. I knew you were right not to trust me.'

I pulled my hands away, horrified.

'It was only a kiss. That probably doesn't make it any better. I didn't initiate anything, I wasn't attracted to her, I never thought about her or anyone like that. You were the only one. She came to me late in the night. I'd fallen asleep on the sofa and she woke me up with a kiss. I was tired, drunk and feeling sorry for myself. We'd had that silly fight. I felt like you didn't trust me, that I was holding back and I knew it was true, I was. I was scared of commitment, I'd seen my parents' relationship torn apart and my dad ruined and I wasn't going to put myself up for that, but I was never unsure about us and I had a feeling you were. I could have made it right. I could have tried to let you understand me better, but, I'm an idiot. I didn't think straight.' His voice was shaking and he took a deep breath, trying to control it. 'None of this is an excuse; it's not even a good reason. All I can say is she kissed me and I kissed her back. Not for long. It was nothing to me. I stopped it going any further and it made me sick, physically sick, the thought of you and how it'd hurt you to know. The only positive thing about it, if that's possible, is that it made me absolutely sure about you. It was too late then though. I couldn't face you. It hurts like hell to know I can't change what I did, I can only apologise and it doesn't feel like enough.' He sat back in his chair, visibly less tense for finally getting it out in the open. 'You know everything now. I wouldn't blame you if you hated me, but I want you to know I will always, always love you.'

I looked down at my hands as he said that. It had hurt to hear his confession and for a moment I was scared that it was worse than I'd feared, but I wasn't surprised. 'I knew it,' I said, my voice small and quiet. 'I knew that'd happened. I could just tell. I know what you mean though. I kissed Jamie, the guy you saw me with at the party.'

Adam's face tensed up and a muscle in his jaw flexed.

'It was weeks after we'd split up. We were both drunk. I haven't been that drunk in years, but I felt just like you said. It wasn't you. I felt sick too, like I'd let you down even though we weren't together anymore. It helped me realise a lot of things.' I leaned forwards and put my head in my hands. 'What a mess. I wish I could take it all back. Everything, and make it right.'

Adam stood up and took my hand, pulling me up too. 'Come here,' he said, wrapping his arms around me. I put my arms around his waist. It felt good, despite everything, it still felt natural.

We stayed like that for a long time then he kissed the top of my head. 'We've got a lot of work to do, haven't we?' he said.

I looked up at him. 'I'll help you. I can clean it up whilst you fix the doors and the windows. We can have it really nice for when he gets back.'

Adam smiled at me, taking a curl of hair from out of my eyes and tucking it behind my ear. 'You're so sweet. I meant with us. We need to work on us. If you still want to.'

'I do.'

He leaned his forehead on my shoulder, sighing with

309

relief then looked up again. 'Thank God. I've been lost without you. You're like my soulmate. I'd decided this morning that if I couldn't work things out with you I was going to be a bachelor for life. I'd already planned on having a dog to stop me getting lonely and I was going to call it Bailey, to remind me of you.'

I laughed. 'You can still get a dog, you know. A man with a dog is an attractive combination.'

'That'll be my job for tomorrow then,' he joked with a glint in his eye. 'Want to come with me?'

# Chapter Twenty-Nine

I spent the rest of the day working on the house with Adam. We were taking things slowly, not wanting to rush back into our relationship too soon. Both of us had a lot to work out, but it felt good. As we worked side by side I knew that Adam and I were closer than ever and I was positive about us. I knew we could make it.

When I'd done all I could and it was getting dark outside Adam asked if I wanted to go back to his house for a takeaway and a bottle of wine. No pressure. I said yes, but wanted to go home and see Fay beforehand, explaining how things had gone with Tim. He understood and offered to drop me off at home, then I said I'd walk over to his a bit later on.

Sitting in his car outside the house we both smiled shyly at each other after we'd said our goodbyes, both of us aware of the pressure to kiss and confirm that our relationship was back on course.

'Go on then, off you go,' Adam said, waving me off with a grin.

I laughed, getting out of the car. I didn't kiss him. I didn't need to. We had the rest of the night to think about it, to get comfortable with each other again, and I was going to relish every moment.

Before then, there was Fay to deal with.

She was in the living room, watching *An Affair to Remember* with Nikki, but she wasn't crying.

When I came in she flicked the television off and sat up. 'How did it go? What happened?'

'I think we can work things out,' I said, happiness bubbling up and spilling over in a wide smile.

Fay and Nikki both sprang up and hugged me. 'That's fantastic!' Fay cried. 'I'm so happy for you both.'

'And what about you? Has there been any news about Tim today?'

'Nothing,' Nikki answered for her. 'It doesn't look like anyone's been here all day. Your mum called, and Jules, but there's been no other messages.'

Fay slumped back onto the sofa and I sat down next to her.

'How do you feel?'

She scrunched up her face. 'I dunno. Confused. I really felt like this was it and now—' she threw up her hands, '—I have no idea what to think.'

'You're not upset?'

'Of course I am, I'm gutted, I'm worried and I'm heart broken. I've tried to be angry with him but I just can't manage it. Not yet. Most of all, I'm confused. It hasn't sunk in yet.'

Poor Fay. She looked so lost. I squeezed her hand and was about to go and make us all a drink when the front door slammed shut. I looked at Fay and Nikki. They'd frozen, their eyes wide as they stared at the living-room door in anticipation. I stood defensively in front of Fay, my legs starting to tremble as I remembered the night at Barney's. The door creaked open and Tim walked in. He went and stood in the middle of the room, looking at the

312

floor with his hands on his hips. 'There are some things I need to say to all of you,' he said, glancing up and catching Fay's eyes.

I backed away, still nervous.

He cleared his throat. He looked nervous too. 'I'm not who you think I am.' He paused, gauging our reaction to his news. We were silent, staring at him with indignation. That was hardly new information. We wanted to know the rest. He nodded, realising we weren't going to make it easy for him. 'I'm a Detective Constable for the Serious Crimes Squad. I've been working undercover for Operation Trojan, co-ordinated by the Met in London. We've been trying to crack a drugs ring that we knew had links with Barney DiBenedetto.'

'Barney from the café?' Nikki said.

'Yes. We had informants that suggested there were large amounts of cocaine coming into the country and being split and spread out by various catering facilities in the region. It was my job to infiltrate the group, find out how it all worked and gather enough evidence to convict. It turns out that Mr DiBenedetto and his gang were receiving cosignments of drugs inside bags of rice that were dropped overboard in the English Channel. They were picked up by fishing boats and smuggled across the country in delivery vans that took food to the restaurants. We'd managed to work out the source of the drugs, the routes they took, the people involved and the dealers they were selling it on to. We'd planned a massive swoop for Thursday night.'

'I don't understand,' I said, unable to comprehend what he was saying. 'You were arrested. I saw you.'

'That's right, because they didn't know who I was. The Met works separately from the regional headquarters. They knew nothing about me until I got to the station.

313

They raided Barney's last night after a tip-off from some hotline the paper was running.'

'Dob-a-druggie,' Fay said and I turned to her in surprise. 'I saw it in the paper. It made me laugh at the time.'

'Right, yes,' Tim said, looking at her almost fondly then continuing, 'so I've been sorting this mess out all day. Barney's has now been searched and we've got what we needed. We've made six arrests so far and seized what we believe could be the biggest drugs haul in the region ever. It's gone to the Home Office lab to be tested.' He looked at Fay again. 'I've got to go back to London tomorrow.'

She showed no reaction.

'I want to say I'm sorry if this has put any of you in a difficult position. I've tried to keep this operation from affecting you in any way but it has, and I can only apologise. Gemma, I owe you an apology for what happened last night. I was about to warn you when the squad came in. It, err, it must have been a very frightening experience for you.'

'It's OK,' I said, my cheeks glowing.

He turned to Fay. 'And Fay, I want you to know that despite there being aspects of my life that you had no idea about, everything else was real. I couldn't tell you the truth. I would have jeopardised the case and put you in danger. I hope you understand and I also hope that we can talk some more,' he glanced at Nikki and me, 'in private if we can, before I go.' He stopped, looking at her anxiously then tutted, momentarily distracted. 'I'm sorry, you'll have to excuse me.' He took his ringing phone out of his pocket and stepped out into the hall.

The three of us sat staring at the door in shock. 'I can't believe this,' I said. 'This is too much.'

'I know,' Nikki said. 'It's crazy.'

Fay looked at us, a smile growing on her lips. 'Oh my God,' she said slowly. 'It *is* true.'

'What?' Nikki and I said in unison.

'Everything Miranda said! I don't care what you think anymore, or about her explanation. I always knew there was something amazing about what she said: she got every last thing right and you just have to accept it.'

Nikki looked puzzled. 'But she never said that Tim was going to be a policeman, did she?'

'A good guy,' Fay cried, her face animated with excitement. 'Miranda described him as a good guy, and that's exactly what he is. He's one of the good guys!'

I wasn't aware that there was anything noticeably different about me but on Monday Jill and Helen could tell almost immediately that something had happened.

Jill took one look and said cryptically, 'I didn't realise that face was catching.'

'What face?' I said, smiling innocently.

'The one Helen's been wearing recently, you know, the one with the doe-eyes, radiant cheeks, contented smile.'

'How do you know I haven't had porridge for breakfast,' I joked coyly.

Jill looked at me dubiously then Helen walked in with a smile on her face that suggested she was daydreaming about something.

Jill raised an eyebrow at me knowingly as Helen swung her coat and bag up on a peg. She glanced at me with a quick 'hello' then did a double-take.

'What's going on with you? You look different. Sort of, happy.'

'I'm always happy!'

'Smug then.'

'Charming.' I carried on setting out the chairs, pretending to be busy.

She scrutinised my face. 'Have you been seeing some more of Jamie?'

'No!' I was momentarily horrified by the thought then that smile started to work its way back again.

She clicked her fingers. 'You're back with Adam.' My grin got wider. 'I knew it! That's fantastic. I love Adam.'

'Who's Adam?' Stewart said, pretending to look jealous as Billy ran up and wrapped himself around Helen's legs.

'Adam's your boyfriend,' Billie sing-songed, pointing at me, and I was pleased that he had remembered, even though he punctuated it with an 'Eurghhh!'

As I stood by the door, letting out the morning children who were going home for lunch, I saw Adam walking up the path, an envelope in his hands. He was smiling at me and I felt that familiar surge of attraction I always got when I saw Adam. He was looking especially good today as well, in the T-shirt I'd picked out for him when he'd been in the shower.

'I couldn't keep away,' he said, kissing me briefly on the lips. 'How's your morning been?'

'Good,' I said. 'How about you?'

'Mmm, it started fantastically well,' he said, his voice lowered as he looked at me flirtatiously. 'And I wanted to talk to you about what I've been doing for the rest of the morning. Is there any chance I could steal you for a chat? How busy are you?'

I looked behind me. All the children in the cloakroom had now gone. 'Hang on, I'll just have a word with Jill.'

Jill let me nip out for half an hour so Adam and I walked to the baker's on the corner of the street and sat outside on the metal chairs.

'Is everything OK? What's this about?' I could tell there was something and suddenly I was nervous, worried that perhaps he had changed his mind about last night. That things were going too fast after all.

'Well,' Adam started, tapping his fingers on the metal table. 'I want to say first of all that I'm so glad we worked things out last night.' There was a definite glint in his eyes and I felt myself melt into them.

'Me too.'

'And I want you to understand that if you want to take things slowly that's fine. I'll totally understand and won't put any pressure on you. But—' he put the envelope that he'd been carrying onto the table '—I just had to talk to you about this.' He slid a piece of paper out of the envelope and handed it over to me.

It was a printout of some house details from a local estate agent. It was for a picturesque, if slightly neglected cottage for sale in Martin Over-Wood, the village that joined Martin Under-Wood, where my gran had lived.

'It's lovely, isn't it?' I said, skimming through the details.

'It came today,' Adam said, leaning forwards and looking at it again. 'A guy I know at the agents dropped it in this morning. He knew I fancied a renovation project. I'm always asking him if there's any good ones coming up that I might be interested in, so when this came along he thought I might like to see it first. Ones like this come on the market a fair bit, it's quite small, but, I don't know, it's got something a bit special about it. I really like the look of it. I had a drive by earlier and it's perfect: in this great spot, close enough to town to cycle in, nice and private, fantastic views, good local walks and pubs. And there's an option to buy some of the land at the back from the parish church, so it's got bags of potential. I was hoping you'd come and see it with me after work.'

'Yes, of course. I'd like that.'

'Actually, Gemma ...' He said looking nervously at me, the way he had outside the ring shop, and my heartbeat sped up. 'I know this might be a bit soon, but I was thinking, if it's as good as I think it could be, and you like it as much as I do, I thought that maybe we could move in together?'

I looked up at him in surprise. 'Pardon?'

'The thing is, this time apart, and everything that's happened to us lately has just made me absolutely sure about us. I don't need time. We've had lots of time. Now I want to show you that I'm serious about us. I was thinking about it this morning, on the way in to work, about how important it was this time for me to get things right and to show you that I'm committed to you. When I opened up the workshop this was lying on the doormat. When I saw it I just knew. This cottage is meant for me. You're meant for me. It all adds up. Obviously you'd have to like the house too though.'

'I'm sure I would,' I said, staring at the photo of it. It was gorgeous. Just the sort of house I'd always dreamed of sharing with Adam.

'But seriously, there's no pressure,' he said. 'I just wanted you to know how I felt about you and how sure I am about this, but if you're not, that's fine. I can always try for this house on my own and we can see how things go with us. Just come and see it with me and see how you feel. Please?'

# Chapter Thirty

I jumped down from the van with the final box of things and walked up the path to the cottage. It was late in the afternoon and I was hot and sweating from exertion. August was possibly not the most ideal time of year to be trooping all your wordly goods from one house to another, but I didn't care. The sun was streaming through the windows of the cottage, bathing everything in warm light and putting us all in a good mood. I stepped through the open door and took the box to the bottom of the stairs, adding it to the rest of the boxes that were waiting to be carried to the bedrooms. I left it there, not wanting to do another thing until I'd had a cold drink. I wiped my forehead with the back of my hand and went to the dining room, looking for Adam and Richard. They were moving a heavy cabinet into the corner of the room.

'Stop, stop, stop,' Richard called and they rested it down, standing back to look at it.

'Perfect,' Adam said then turned to me. 'Is that everything out of the van now? All our worldly goods?'

'Yep, all done.'

'Then it's time we had a drink, I think, and a toast.' He bent down to the cool box and took out three bottles of lager, passing them around.

I took one gratefully, enjoying the feel of the cold glass bottle chilling my hand and clinked it with theirs.

'To our first ever house,' Adam said, putting his arm around me and squeezing me to him.

We'd been so lucky. I was still unable to believe that it was all ours. It was just seven weeks since Adam had taken me to see the cottage after work. We'd been the first people to see it and had fallen so in love with it that Adam had offered the asking price the following morning. I hadn't needed to think about moving in with Adam at all. It was everything I had always wanted and I knew it felt right. We had walked to the cottage several times over the past few weeks whilst we waited for the paperwork to go through. We'd stood by the SOLD sign and looked at it, hand in hand, and every time we did, Adam or I would say again how perfect it was and how it was meant to be.

Adam wrapped his arms around my waist and kissed my neck. 'Can you imagine what this will be like? When we've got rid of the wallpaper and the floorboards are done and the old range is restored?'

'And when the mushrooms on the window frame have all gone,' I said, jokingly wistful.

'It's going to be a great house,' Richard said. 'You wait till Jules comes later, she'll be jealous as hell. She's decorated every room in our house twice and now she's getting itchy fingers. She'd love a project like this.'

I turned around and hugged Adam properly. 'We are so lucky, aren't we.'

'Absolutely,' he said, kissing the top of my nose.

'All right you two, save it for later,' Richard said, holding his hands up.

'That's a point, perhaps we should make the bed up now whilst I still have an ounce of energy left in me. We don't

320

want to knacker ourselves out later only to find that we've still got to build the bed before we can have a rest.'

Adam looked at me affectionately. 'You are brilliant, aren't you? Not only are you very, very thoughtful, but you also share my opinion that the bed is the most important piece of furniture in the house.' He raised an eyebrow at me and I patted his chest.

'Yeah, yeah, well how about I go and get the bedding all ready? You can bring your toolbox up and bolt it all together in a minute.'

'OK, give me a bit of time because I'll have to find it first,' he said, nodding towards the enormous piles of boxes and bags that surrounded us.

I took my drink and headed up to the bedroom, taking the stairs two at a time. I was so excited about seeing all the rooms again. They were so interesting, full of little cupboards and hidden corners. The main bedroom had a beamed ceiling that I loved and the window looked onto a meadow at the back. I climbed over a pile of boxes to get to the window and looked down onto the garden. It was wild and overgrown, with a couple of big apple trees dominating the lawn. Bailey was sniffing around under one of them, exploring with frenzied curiosity, his tail wagging. I tapped on the window and laughed when his ears pricked up and he bounded across the patchy grass, trying to figure out where the noise had come from. I stayed by the window, daydreaming about the parties we could have in the garden next summer. I was already planning a house-warming party for the following month, a good excuse to invite Jamie as he'd been asking when he might see Nikki again and vice-versa. I had high hopes for those two.

I had also invited Miranda and Chris to the party and was looking forward to seeing them again. A couple of weeks ago I'd called them for a chat. Miranda had answered the phone and after she'd realised it was me, said, 'Gemma, that's so funny, I was just thinking about you!' I'd teased her about her sixth sense still working and we'd laughed about it. It was becoming something of a joke between us, but I still had moments when I'd suspend my rationale and let myself wonder. One thing we had agreed on was that we should stay in touch. We led very different, very separate lives, but I knew we'd make time to catch up every now and again. Somehow it felt like the right thing to do.

My mobile phone started to ring and I took it out of my pocket, expecting it to be Nikki or Jules calling to arrange what time they were coming around for a house-warming drink.

'Gemma, it's me!' the voice said when I answered it.

'Fay, hi, how are you? How was the flight? What's it like?' Fay had flown out to Connecticut with Tim the day before. She was filming for her movie icon series and Tim was enjoying a month's break from the Met. They were going to tour as much as they could when Fay wasn't working.

'It's amazing, the whole place is fantastic. Everyone's been so nice and the hotel, oh my God, you wouldn't believe how posh it is. We've got three rooms all to ourselves and they're all so gorgeous. We're going to Long Island Sound tomorrow and in two weeks we're off to Hollywood, ha ha!'

I laughed, I could tell she was jumping up and down in excitement. 'Wow. You really are my most glamorous friend.'

'How did the move go anyway? I'm sorry I couldn't be there to help.'

'Don't you worry, it all went fine. No problems. We

322

haven't even had any breakages.' I leaned on top of a pile of boxes but they were lighter than I'd thought. The top one shifted forwards, knocking into one that was balanced behind it. It crashed to the ground, spilling its contents on the floor. 'Famous last words,' I said. 'I've just knocked a box over.' I peered over at it, wincing when I saw that it was one of Adam's.

'Well, listen Gemma, I'll leave you to it. You must have tons to do and I'm going to have to get some sleep. Shall I call you in a few days?'

'You *have* to. I want to hear all about it,' I said, walking over to the mess I'd made on the floor.

'OK, well you take care of yourselves. Don't work too hard on the house. Have some fun too.'

'We will,' I said. 'Sleep well.'

I put the phone on the window ledge and crouched down, starting to gather up the contents of the box. They were mainly dusty old books and pictures, things he couldn't have looked at in years. I packed them neatly back in the box then picked up an old red, leather-bound album. I sat down with it, wondering if it was old photos and opened it up.

They were photos and memorabilia, faded behind the cellophane. I turned the pages, smiling at the pictures of Adam as a boy, dressed in his school uniform. There was a photograph of him with his dad and I felt a stab of sadness. I'd never seen a picture of what he used to look like before and was shocked at how different he was to the way he looked now. I'd met him a few times since I'd been to his house. In this photo he was a solid man, tall and strong like Adam but slightly less toned. He looked like he was a man who enjoyed his beer. Now he was shrunken with hollow eyes and skin that hung from his bones. He'd improved in recent weeks. So far his therapy had been working, he'd stopped drinking and as a result his colour had improved and he'd put on some weight, but he wasn't the strong, healthy man in the photo. I turned the pages, fascinated by the stills of Adam's life, then decided that he might like to see it too. I snapped it shut, wanting to save it until Adam came upstairs. I had a feeling he hadn't seen it in a while. As I shifted onto my knees, reaching up to put it back in the box, something slipped out, fluttering to the carpet in front of me. I picked it up and turned it over. It was an old newspaper clipping of mine that I hadn't seen in years. I looked at it, confused. How come Adam had got an old clipping of mine in his box? I looked at it again. It was different to mine. It was torn at the edges where I was sure mine wasn't. Mine was neatly cut out. My mum had always carefully cut out and saved any newspaper clippings that had been about John or me. I stood up, shocked, my legs starting to tremble. It couldn't be, could it? I looked closely at the photograph then snatched Adam's old album, opening it onto a page of his old school pictures. It was. The picture was of me at the Royal Theatre when I was only seven years old. I had gone to see a pantomine with my mum and had been called out onto the stage for a song they wanted some of the children to join in singing. It was only a vague memory now: standing under the stage lights, squinting out into the dark audience, searching for my mum. They had chosen me and two others to sing 'We Wish You a Merry Christmas' with the cast. We all held hands and as we sang, a photographer from the paper took our picture. In the photograph I was standing in the middle, holding hands with a girl on my right and a boy on my left. I don't think I'd ever bothered to look and see the names of the other children before but now I held the paper tightly and peered at the text.

'Hey, what're you doing?' Adam said, making me jump. He'd appeared behind me and was looking over my shoulder. 'Oh God, don't look at that,' he said when he saw what I was looking at, 'it's a picture of me singing at some panto. It's a really embarrassing photo. I didn't realise I'd actually kept it. Where did you find it? Oh and look at that!' He put down his toolbox and stooped beside me to pick up the photo album. 'I've not seen these in ages.'

I turned to him. My mouth had gone suddenly dry.

He looked at me again. 'What's up?'

'It's me,' I said.

'Hey?'

'The girl in the photo. The one you were holding hands with. It's me.'

He looked at it again. 'It can't be. She's got straight hair.'

'Mine didn't go curly until I was a few years older than that.' My voice was starting to tremble. *Miranda had been right all along. I had met Adam in my childhood.* 'If you don't believe me read the names,' I said.

He held it to the light and read them out loud. 'Adam Burnell, aged nine, Gemma Thompson, aged seven and Miranda Patterson, aged eight. Oh my God, it is you! Isn't that mad?' He looked at me in amazement then his expression turned to concern. 'Gem, are you OK?' he said. 'You've gone really pale.'

# Other Books By
## Sarah Ball:

**NINE MONTHS**

It isn't until her boyfriend Tom heads off for a year abroad that Holly realises just how much she is going to miss him. But Tom's left her with rather more than just a passionate memory of their last night together. Holly's clothes are getting tighter, she has clevage for the first time in her life, and the sickness she thought was down to the morning-after-the-night-before is lasting all day. Holly Piper is pregnant!

A year is a long time for Tom to be away. But for Holly, the first nine months are going to be the hardest...

**MARRY ME**

Like most girls, Abby has always dreamed of her wedding day. And while her image of the perfect frock may have changed over the years, Nathan Priestly has always remained in her fantasy as the perfect groom.

Only now Nathan's about to get married to one of Abby's best friends and Abby is trying to be happy for them both. She's even volunteered to be their DJ at reception. (Although her secret-play list consists of: 'Don't Marry Her', 'Temptation' and the complete works of Alanis Morrisette.) But is Abby destined to be always the DJ never the bride...?

# A SELECTION OF NOVELS AVAILABLE FROM PIATKUS BOOKS

| | | | |
|---|---|---|---|
| 0 7499 3287 2 | Nine Months | Sarah Ball | £5.99 |
| 0 7499 3379 8 | Marry Me | Sarah Ball | £5.99 |
| 0 7499 3384 4 | Just Married | Zoe Barnes | £5.99 |
| 0 7499 3492 1 | Guilty Feet | Erica Munro | £5.99 |
| 0 7499 3478 6 | Keeping Mum | Stephanie Zia | £5.99 |
| 0 7499 3450 6 | The Chocolate Run | Dorothy Koomson | £6.99 |